# NO WARNING

A thick bolt of energy streaked upward to impact the damaged fighter.

"Warner," Graves gasped over the radio. "Get clear! It's a flak trap down there! Get back and warn!"

Warner rolled hard out of his turn, winding through a series of evasive maneuvers to throw off his enemy's aim. Another PPC discharge lashed out at him, missing the wildly jinking fighter by less than a meter.

*A DropShip,* Warner thought, *they have to be protecting a DropShip.* A DropShip meant 'Mechs. And 'Mechs meant an invasion. He thumbed the comlink switch on his control column, opening the broadband communication channel to warn the base what was coming.

Before he could utter a sound, a corkscrewing volley of missiles clawed his fighter from the sky.

The invasion had begun. . . .

# About the Author

Thomas S. Gressman lives with his wife, Brenda, in the foothills of Western Pennsylvania.

When not writing science fiction, he divides his time between leathercrafting, Civil War and Medieval historical reenactment, Irish folk music, and a worship-music ministry.

*The Dying Time* is his sixth book. His previous works include the *Operation Serpent* books of FASA's *Twilight of the Clans* series, and *Dagger Point,* in the BattleTech Line.

His fifth novel, *Operation Sierra-75,* set in the Vor: The Maelstrom line, has been made available as an e-book through Time Warner's i-publish.

# MECHWARRIOR®

# THE DYING TIME

## Thomas S. Gressman

A ROC BOOK

ROC
Published by New American Library, a division of
Penguin Putnam Inc., 375 Hudson Street,
New York, New York 10014, U.S.A.
Penguin Books Ltd, 80 Strand,
London WC2R 0RL, England
Penguin Books Australia Ltd, Ringwood,
Victoria, Australia
Penguin Books Canada Ltd, 10 Alcorn Avenue,
Toronto, Ontario, Canada M4V 3B2
Penguin Books (N.Z.) Ltd, 182–190 Wairau Road,
Auckland 10, New Zealand

Penguin Books Ltd, Registered Offices:
Harmondsworth, Middlesex, England

First published by Roc, an imprint of New American Library,
a division of Penguin Putnam Inc.

First Printing, January 2002
10  9  8  7  6  5  4  3  2  1

Series Editor: Donna Ippolito
Cover art: Fred Gambino
Mechanical Drawings: FASA Art Department

ROC  REGISTERED TRADEMARK—MARCA REGISTRADA

MECHWARRIOR, FASA, and the distictive MECHWARRIOR and FASA
logos are trademarks of the FASA Corporation, 1100 W. Cermack, Suite
B305, Chicago, IL 60608.

Printed in the United States of America

PUBLISHER'S NOTE
This is a work of fiction. Names, characters, places, and incidents either are
the product of the author's imagination or are used fictitiously, and any
resemblance to actual persons, living or dead, business establishments,
events, or locales is entirely coincidental.

BOOKS ARE AVAILABLE AT QUANTITY DISCOUNTS WHEN USED TO PROMOTE
PRODUCTS OR SERVICES. FOR INFORMATION PLEASE WRITE TO PREMIUM
MARKETING DIVISION, PENGUIN PUTNAM INC., 375 HUDSON STREET, NEW YORK, NEW
YORK 10014.

This book is gratefully dedicated to Donna Ippolito.

Donna, you've done an awful lot of work behind the scenes, to make this book, and many others better than I could have done myself. Through your prompting, questions, and suggestions, you've helped make me a better writer.

Thank you for your efforts, your dedication, and your friendship.

## ACKNOWLEDGMENTS

Thanks once again to all those who have contributed their time, encouragement and expertise to the creation of this story. Particular thanks to Donna Ippolito, for her support, guidance and useful suggestions. Thanks and a tip of the hat to Chris Hartford, whose background information on the Gray Death Legion was so useful in the creation of this story. Any errors in these pages are mine, alone.

A special acknowledgment to the *real* founder of the Gray Death Legion, Bill Keith. Had you not created them, I couldn't have had the fun of writing about them.

Once again, thanks to Brenda, for putting up with me as I labored over this book.

And as always, my thanks to You, Lord, for the abilities you've given me and the opportunity to exercise them once again.

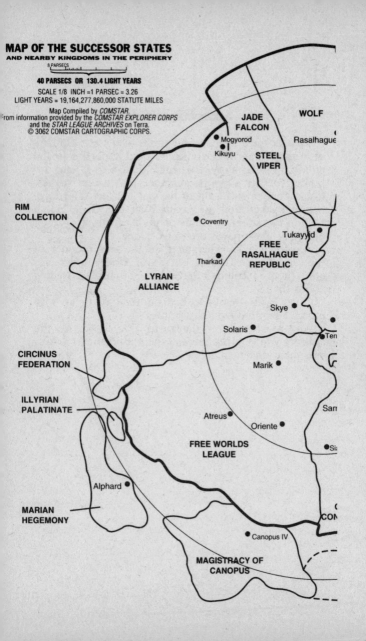

# MAP OF THE SUCCESSOR STATES
### AND NEARBY KINGDOMS IN THE PERIPHERY

8 PARSECS

**40 PARSECS OR 130.4 LIGHT YEARS**

SCALE 1/8 INCH =1 PARSEC = 3.26
LIGHT YEARS = 19,164,277,860,000 STATUTE MILES

Map Compiled by *COMSTAR*.
from information provided by the *COMSTAR EXPLORER CORPS*
and the *STAR LEAGUE ARCHIVES* on Terra.
© 3062 COMSTAR CARTOGRAPHIC CORPS.

JADE FALCON

WOLF

Mogyorod

Kikuyu

Rasalhague

STEEL VIPER

RIM COLLECTION

Coventry

Tukayyid

FREE RASALHAGUE REPUBLIC

Tharkad

LYRAN ALLIANCE

Skye

Solaris

Ter

CIRCINUS FEDERATION

Marik

ILLYRIAN PALATINATE

Atreus

San

Oriente

Si

FREE WORLDS LEAGUE

MARIAN HEGEMONY

Alphard

CON

Canopus IV

MAGISTRACY OF CANOPUS

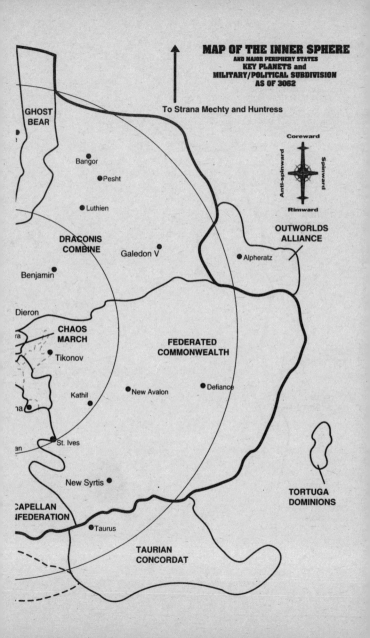

MAP OF THE INNER SPHERE
AND MAJOR PERIPHERY STATES
KEY PLANETS and
MILITARY/POLITICAL SUBDIVISION
AS OF 3062

To Strana Mechty and Huntress

Coreward

Spinward

Anti-spinward

Rimward

GHOST BEAR

• Bangor

• Pesht

• Luthien

DRACONIS COMBINE

• Galedon V

OUTWORLDS ALLIANCE

• Alpheratz

Benjamin •

Dieron

CHAOS MARCH

• Tikonov

FEDERATED COMMONWEALTH

• Kathil

• New Avalon

• Defiance

• St. Ives

New Syrtis •

TORTUGA DOMINIONS

CAPELLAN CONFEDERATION

• Taurus

TAURIAN CONCORDAT

# Prologue

*Royal Palace*
*Avalon City, New Avalon*
*Crucis March*
*Federated Suns*
*16 April 3065*

General of the Armies of the Lyran Alliance, Nondi Steiner watched her niece as the younger woman keyed a few notes into the noteputer sitting atop her desk.

Katrina's movements had an odd, jerky quality, the effects of the "real-time" HPG link the women were using to communicate.

Behind the desk, virtually ignored by the blonde-haired, blue-eyed woman seated there, a broad window gave an excellent and inspiring view of Avalon City, capital of the planet and of the Federated Suns. There, in the northern climes of New Avalon, winter's grip was slackening at last. Much of the snow had melted from the rooftops, and patches of grass could be seen on the palace lawns.

Katrina Steiner-Davion, ruler of the Lyran Alliance and the Federated Commonwealth as a whole, was the most recent occupant of the office, lifted her eyes from the data-storage unit, turning her ice-blue gaze on her aunt, holding Nondi's unremarkable brown eyes for a moment before she spoke again.

"Now then, General," Katrina said in a most formal tone, "what of the Skye Province?"

This was the portion of the daily briefing Nondi had been dreading. Of late, Katrina's moods had been subject to strange, violent swings. As likely as not, the rapid changes in temper were due to the ups and downs of the civil war against Katrina's brother, Victor. Still, as a member of the Archon's cabinet, and as General of the Armies, Nondi owed Katrina the truth.

It was the increasing unrest in the historically fractious Skye Province that had prompted Katrina to make the long trip home from New Avalon. Ever conscious of public opinion, she thought it was time for a personal appearance on Tharkad. In the face of a growing wave of rebellion in the Skye region, she thought her presence on the Lyran throne-world would assure her people of the Archon's concern for the totality of her realm, not just the portion comprising the Federated Suns.

"The Isle of Skye is, as it has always been, a powder keg with a lit fuse," Nondi said, reading from her own note-puter. "Most of the nobles in Skye are aware of your reasons for moving troops into Skye. Most feel it is acceptable, if not particularly prudent, given that your brother is seemingly poised for an attack from Thorin."

"Most?" Katrina asked incisively.

"Yes, Archon, most." Nondi wondered if the sharply spoken question was the first dark cloud of a coming storm. "There are those who feel the measures you have taken to ensure the security of your realm as a whole were little more than an attempt to extend your control over the province as a whole."

Katrina didn't respond immediately. She leaned back against the leather-covered padding of the big chair, her fingers steepled in front of her. Nondi could have recited by heart the steps Katrina had ordered to make sure the Skye Province remained in her hands. She had moved a number of military units, both LAAF and mercenary, into the region. She had also ordered several worlds closed to all interstellar traffic in order to preserve the secrecy of the Alliance's war preparations.

Most of the big interstellar JumpShips servicing the area had been called into military service under a little-used clause in the Lyran Constitution. As a result, military traffic into and within the Skye Province had increased, while civilian shipping had been severely disrupted. Though steps had been taken to ensure that food, medicines, and the like still got where they needed to go, smaller, less important worlds were beginning to experience shortages of essential goods.

That, in turn, had resulted in protests and demonstrations and a rekindled flame of Skye separatism. The smoldering fires of rebellion had caused Katrina to dispatch agents of Lohengrin and the Molehunters, the Lyran anti-terrorist and internal security agencies, to the region. There were even dark rumors that Loki, the shadowy Lyran terrorist organization, had been sent to Skye to eliminate those who opposed Katrina.

"I suppose we know who has been the most vocal critic of my policies?" Katrina said at last.

"There are several who have been quite outspoken regarding their dissatisfaction, Archon." Nondi kept her tone as neutral as possible. A sharp glance from Katrina told her she could equivocate no longer, so she spoke quickly and to the point. "Yes, Archon, there is one whose voice has been raised above all others."

"Robert," Katrina said in a quiet, even voice.

"Yes, Archon, Duke Robert Kelswa-Steiner. He has long been an advocate for independence for the so-called Isle of Skye. It seems Duke Robert has seized upon the military buildup in the province and its attendant increase in security measures as more fodder for his speeches. He has been quite outspoken in opposing nearly every measure you've taken, stopping just short of calling for open rebellion. Not that his 'restraint' is making any difference. Already there have been a dozen relatively minor incidents between our forces and the citizens of the Skye Province. The movement grows with every speech he makes."

Katrina banged her fist down against the desktop. "Will no one rid me of this troublesome Duke?" she fairly howled.

"Archon—" Nondi began.

"No, General, this meeting is over. Leave me." Katrina's voice had risen another notch in pitch.

"As you wish, Archon," Nondi replied, as the Archon severed the connection. Slipping from the communications center as quietly as possible, she was met by Colonel Chris Wyndham, her aide.

"Anything new today, General?" Wyndham asked.

"No, Colonel," Nondi answered. She walked on in silence for a few paces, then changed her mind. "No, wait, there is something new. I want you to contact General Alicia Savinson immediately. Tell her I have an arrest order for her."

"Yes, General," Wyndham said, and Nondi was sure he'd have contacted the head of the Lyran Intelligence corps even before she reached her office. "Can I tell her who the warrant is for?"

"Yes, tell her to arrest Duke Robert Kelswa-Steiner, on charges of sedition and fomenting rebellion against Katrina Steiner-Davion, his liege lord and lawful ruler of the Isle of Skye. He is a filthy traitor who has forfeited his rights as a lord of the realm."

# 1

**Dunkeld, Glengarry**
**Skye Province**
**Lyran Alliance**
**22 May 3065**

**"K**eep on him! Make him fight!" Grayson Death Carlyle bellowed over the ear-torturing whine of the armed hover jeep's lift fans. The driver nodded his understanding and whipped the small ground-effect vehicle into a skidding right turn. A grimy brick wall rushed at the jeep's side as the driver fought to bring it back under control. Grayson flinched, feeling the jeep lurch beneath him. The driver wrestled the vehicle back into the middle of the alleyway and floored the accelerator. A puddle flashed into a dirty gray mist under the wash of the screaming fans. At the next intersection, the driver careened through a left turn, this one better controlled than the last.

A burst of heavy machine-gun fire echoed along the empty streets, followed by the sharp crack of a laser firing. Under all the racket, Gray could hear the rapid thud of a BattleMech's running feet.

A few blocks along, he signaled his driver, and the man at the jeep's controls hauled the vehicle into a tight left turn. This time, the hovercraft ricocheted off a parked ground car, leaving a streak of drab brown-green paint on the blue body-work of the civilian vehicle. When the jeep darted back onto the main street they had left only a few seconds earlier, Grayson saw their quarry. Tall, hunched over, looking like a predatory yet flightless bird, the twenty-ton *Locust* stood in the middle of the street, menacing another hover weapons-carrier. A stroke of manmade lightning reached out to batter the scout 'Mech's armor.

A light 'Mech not intended to stand up to that sort of punishment, the *Locust* staggered. Over the din of battle, Grayson could hear the shriek of overstressed gyros laboring to keep the 'Mech on its spindly legs. In the heat of battle, the enemy MechWarrior had either missed the jeep's skidding arrival or had opted to first deal with the more dangerous opponent, the hover vehicle carrying the deadly particle projection cannon. Either way, it was a mistake that would cost him.

Hunkering down behind the jeep's thirteen-millimeter machine gun, Gray settled the weapon's crude iron sights over the *Locust*'s back and mashed his thumbs down on the butterfly-shaped trigger. The massive gun spoke in a thuddering roar, spitting fire at the enemy. Forty-three-gram armor-piercing bullets ripped into the 'Mech's relatively thin rear armor, shattering the reinforced steel and blasting the *Locust*'s whip antenna from its mounting.

Grayson was sure it had to be getting hellishly hot in that cockpit. BattleMechs, the ten-meter-tall masters of the thirty-first-century battlefield, boasted more armor and firepower than a battalion of twentieth-century tanks. But they also had an enemy they carried around in their hip-pockets: the waste heat produced by their weapons and the fusion plant that drove them. Temperatures in the cockpit of an embattled 'Mech could reach as much as 49 degrees Celsius, enough to cook off ammunition or kill the pilot through heat exhaustion. The *Locust* had been pushing hard all during the running fight and surely must be close to overheat-triggered shutdown.

Reacting to the rear attack, the 'Mech backed into the mouth of an alleyway. That would let it keep both enemies in its front quarter, with its laser and heavy machine guns. Gray's driver slid the jeep forward even without being told, maintaining contact with the retreating 'Mech. The hover PPC-carriers got there first, but a long, chattering burst of machine-gun fire sent them skittering for cover, leaving two soldiers dead in the street behind them. Grayson's jeep lurched to a halt as the driver, reluctant to brave the killing zone of the alley mouth, threw the drive fans into reverse.

Grayson jumped from the vehicle and edged his way toward the intersection. Risking a peek around the corner, he saw that the *Locust* had backed itself into a cul de sac. The air shimmered around the scout 'Mech's stubby body as its heat sinks struggled to bring its internal temperature under control.

"Have you got an Inferno launcher?" Gray asked a hatchet-faced infantry sergeant.

"Sure. Shoulder-fired job. Back in the carrier," the noncom growled.

"Get it."

The sergeant dashed back to the jeep, returning with a heavy, twin-tubed, short-range missile launcher. The tips of stubby missiles jutting from the launcher's business end bore the telltale red markings of Inferno rounds. Unlike armor-piercing missiles, which detonated on impact with a 'Mech's hide, Inferno rounds were triggered by a proximity fuse. They showered a target with a volatile mixture of napthalene palmitate and white phosphorus, which clung to the target with nightmarish tenacity. Though Inferno rounds did little physical damage to the 'Mech, they increased the machine's internal temperature past survivable limits. When hit with Inferno rounds, pilots had been known to eject from otherwise serviceable 'Mechs rather than be roasted alive.

Taking advantage of a burst of covering fire, Grayson darted into the alleyway.

"Hold it right there, warrior!" he bellowed. "One twitch of those weapons and you're cooked! Scan me to see if I'm bluffing!"

For a long moment, the armored Goliath seemed to glare angrily down at the missile-armed David before it.

"You might kill me, but you'll fry," Gray called again. "One round of Willie-Pete is a nasty way to go."

"All right," came the pilot's reply, made gravelly by the dry heat of the cockpit and the *Locust*'s external loudspeakers. "I'm coming out."

A sharp *hiss-pop* sounded from the 'Mech's belly as the pilot broke the cockpit's hatch seal. A length of chain ladder spilled out, jiggling to a stop a half-meter from the ground. As the MechWarrior clambered down the steel rungs, it was immediately apparent that the *Locust*'s pilot was a woman.

A sharp, flat click jolted Grayson awake. Sitting at his side was that same female MechWarrior, the woman who had shared his life for the past forty-one years.

"You're awake," she said, smiling down at him.

"Where . . . ?" he croaked, his voice ragged, as though he'd caught a lungful of smoke.

Lori Kalmar-Carlyle laid gentle fingers across his lips.

"You're in the sickbay," she said with the faintest hint of a quaver in her voice.

"Yeah, sickbay," Grayson answered, his voice becoming stronger, but containing an uneven note that was the mirror of her own. The room came into focus. The pastel green walls hung with cheerful prints of flowers and sunsets belonged to the critical-care section of the Gray Death Legion's base hospital on Glengarry. A rack of machines hummed and beeped and whirred through their normal monitoring routines.

"I was dreaming," he said.

Lori smiled slightly. "Of Trellwan. I know. You were muttering in your sleep. You were dreaming of the day we met."

Grayson didn't reply. Though his initial meeting with Lori had been over the sights of an Inferno launcher, he had come first to respect her, then to love her deeply. That love had grown into a relationship that had lasted a lifetime and had produced a son.

"Yeah," he repeated.

"Hello, Dad," came a voice from just outside his field of view. It took a concentrated effort to turn his head far enough to see the face that was a handsome combination of Lori's and his own.

"Hello, Alex," Gray murmured. "Typical Carlyle luck. You made it just in time."

"Nonsense," Alex said with a smile. "I got leave and decided to come and see my folks. There was no luck involved."

"Alex, I've been a warrior for far too long to kid myself," Grayson told his son flatly. "I know what the docs are saying. I haven't got much time left, and you wanted to see your old man one more time before he dies."

A shadow fell across Alexander Carlyle's thin face at hearing his father speak the truth in so plain a fashion.

"Don't worry too much, son," Gray said. "It's been a good life. I've had everything that any man could ask for. I've got no right to complain."

Even as he spoke, Gray felt an odd, writhing pain deep in his abdomen, one even the morphine-analog being fed into his left arm could not completely mask. Forty-odd years of a warrior's life and all the privations that went along with it had taken their toll on his body. And now that toll was catching up with him. Despite all the advances of modern medicine, nothing could be done to halt the attack of what was still one of mankind's greatest foes. The medics figured that Gray had, in a way, been responsible for his own illness. Exposure to radiation from damaged reactors, PPC discharges, and the like had probably contributed to the rapid, silent killer that was eating his body alive.

Over Alex's shoulder, Grayson could see the room's wide window. Ostensibly, the sunlight was good for a patient's morale, but, in this case, there was no sunlight. A cold front had settled over the city of Dunkeld, bringing with it thick gray clouds and driving rain. Sitting next to that window, dressed in the gray fatigues of the Legion, was another of the outfit's old warriors.

"Davis, how's the Legion?" Grayson asked.

"Dinna worry aboot that right now, lad," Davis McCall's New Caledonian burr came out, as it always did in times of stress. "You let us worry aboot th' Legion, and you worry about getting' some rest."

"I'll have plenty of time to rest soon, Davis," Grayson said in a level tone, despite the feeling of heavy weariness in his breast. "How are they?"

"They're doin' as well as can be expected, considerin' that their chief is lyin' in a hospital bed," McCall said matter-of-factly. "Aye, half o' them are standin' outside in that rain, waitin' t' hear how *you're* doin'."

Grayson and Lori had built the Gray Death Legion, one of the Inner Sphere's elite mercenary warrior regiments, from nothing. Though operational command of the Gray

Death had long since passed to Lori and it had been nearly a decade since Grayson had piloted a 'Mech, he was still the Legion's "Old Man." His men counted standing in a cold, driving rain a small price to pay as they waited to learn the fate of the founder, heart, and soul of the Gray Death Legion.

"Get them out of the rain," Grayson said. "I don't want any of—" He broke off as a fit of coughing wracked his body. When it passed, he continued, "I don't want any of them getting pneumonia on my account."

Lori brushed the sandy blond hair, now thickly streaked with white, from his forehead. "They'll be all right, Gray. You just rest."

Grayson looked up at her with a momentary flash of irritation. Before he could speak, the door latch clicked as someone entered the room.

Another of those bloody-damn doctors coming to poke and prod him again, he guessed, and his sickbed irritation with Lori turned to a hot flare of anger with the medical staff, whose solicitous efforts had become a major nuisance. Well, not this time, not while his family was here.

Grayson tried to push himself up on his elbows, the better to confront the intruder. But the strength to do so just wasn't to be found. He felt the anger well up inside him as the man he guessed to be a doctor or medtech stepped quietly around the bed to stand opposite where Lori sat on one edge.

The indignation drained away when Grayson saw the gray fatigues of a Legion MechWarrior instead of the uniform of the med staff. Looking down on him was the craggy, ruddy face of Charles Bear, another of the Legion's veterans. Bear, a Delaware Indian and the Legion's only Terran native, had, like McCall, been one of the outfit's first members. Unlike McCall, Bear had elected to retire from the Gray Death Legion back in 3055. A year later, he came out of retirement to aid the Legion in its fight against the Fourth Skye Guards during the Second Skye Rebellion. In the years since, Grayson had seen the old warrior only twice. Once when the Legion celebrated Alexander's graduation from the Nagelring academy, and again a few months ago at the military funeral for Hassan Ali Khalid.

"It is good to see you, old friend," Bear said, laying his hand on Grayson's shoulder.

"Is it time?" Gray asked, smiling up into Bear's dark, solemn eyes. Bear had told him he would see Grayson once more in this lifetime.

"Not yet, *Sachem*, but soon," Bear said quietly.

Lori slid off the bed and crossed to the window. Resting her hands on the narrow sill, she stared out at the dull gray sky.

"It's okay, love," Gray said softly. "It comes to all of us."

"I know." Her voice was thick and husky. Grayson knew she was fighting to hold back the flood of emotion that threatened to sweep her away. "I just never thought it would come so soon."

Again, Gray tried to sit up. He longed to take her in his arms just one more time, and in that embrace both find and give comfort. But the disease had robbed him of the strength to perform so simple, yet so important a task.

Alex stepped behind his mother and laid a gentle hand on her shoulder. She turned to face him, her face stained with tears, and melted into her son's arms. Gray nodded to himself, and closed his eyes.

All of a sudden, he was so very tired. Perhaps, he told himself, now he would rest for a little while.

Not long after that, the monitors that had been so dutifully beeping out the rhythms of Grayson Carlyle's life stopped.

For a long moment, no one in the room moved or spoke. Charles Bear broke the spell. He nodded solemnly, rose from his chair, and left the room without speaking to anyone.

As though that was the signal, McCall set his hands on Lori and Alex's shoulders, leaving them there briefly as though he could impart his strength to them through touch alone. Then, he turned also, and with a stride that bespoke iron Highland courage in the face of great sorrow, he went to inform the rest of the Gray Death Legion that its founder and chief had passed away. The door closed softly behind him, leaving Alexander and Lori alone with their grief.

# 2

**Dunkeld, Glengarry**
**Skye Province**
**Lyran Alliance**
**25 May 3065**

"**C**olonel?" Lori looked up sharply at the young man who stood in the doorway to her office in the Legion's Dunkeld compound. He wore the unit's gray uniform as though he were still getting used to the idea he was in the military, let alone part of one of the most famous mercenary units in the Inner Sphere. In his hands, he clutched a thick wedge of black plastic, which Lori recognized as an electronic message pad. The odd-shaped star disc on the pad's housing told Lori it had come from Glengarry's hyperpulse generator station. Operated by ComStar, the age-old communications bureau, HPG units used roughly the same hyperspace technology as starship jump drives to transmit messages between the stars.

"Bring it here, Private," Lori said softly. In days past, the youngster's nervousness might have brought a smile to her lips and earned him a few encouraging words. But, with Grayson's death only two days in the past, Lori hadn't much encouragement to offer. Only the daily routines of running the Legion kept her from sinking into a brooding depression. Even the comforting presence of her son had been taken from her. Alex had suddenly been recalled to

Tharkad, the duty station where he served with House Steiner's Second Royal Guards.

Grayson had always been more than a little suspicious of that assignment. Even though he was Baron Glengarry and most nobles of the Lyran Alliance would have killed to have their only child assigned to such a distinguished post, Gray had expressed an old distrust of cushy, prestigious assignments. The Legion had once fought against elements of House Steiner's military machine back in 3057. Though Archon Katrina had accepted the Legion's subsequent oath of allegiance, Gray often wondered in private if Katrina actually subscribed to the age-old proverb that advised one to hold your friends close, and your enemies closer. His casual paranoia on this point had infected Lori to the point where she had been surprised when Alexander's commander, Leutnant-General Richard Regis II, had allowed him a few days' leave to visit his dying father.

Alex's recall order had arrived on just such a message pad as the young private now held out to her.

"Colonel McCall signed for it, but he says it's encrypted," the youth said, passing her the device. For a moment, he hovered uncertainly on the far side of Lori's formica-topped, green steel desk. She looked up, forced a thin smile, and dismissed him.

The message pad resembled the standard noteputer used by a wide range of people, from university students to military personnel and government planners. This had one additional feature that most noteputers did not, a small numeric key-pad in the upper left-hand corner. Until Lori punched in a specific string of numbers, the pad would remain "locked." Some messages were encrypted in such a way that entering the wrong access code for the second or third time would delete the message from the pad's memory. Lori had even heard about specially "doctored" message pads that would completely reformat the unit's hard drive or explode.

For a moment, Lori frowned at the device, knowing it probably held a set of operational orders for the Gray Death Legion. At least they could have given her a few days, she thought as she set the electronic pad on the desk. Using the tip of her left forefinger, she carefully tapped in the Legion's access code. Up until now, that string of seven digits had been known only to Grayson and herself. She supposed she'd have to give the code to Davis McCall, in case anything happened to her.

When Lori hit the Enter key, the unit flared to life. The dull yellow-gray screen flickered, then resolved into the image of the pentagon-backed, mailed-fist insignia of the Lyran Alliance Armed Forces.

Lori scrolled down through the obligatory formal greetings from Hauptmann-General Rainer Poulin, the Skye theater commanding officer, and Hauptmann-General Almida Zec, the Alliance's Mercenary Troops Liaison officer. Much to her credit, Zec, a former member of the Eridani Light Horse, included a personal message of sympathy to Lori and the Legion on Grayson's death.

Lori merely skimmed the formal and personal messages, having read enough of those over the past few days. She gave her close attention to the rest of the document. Couched in the language of the military bureaucracy was the simple order:

"Given the mounting tensions in the Isle of Skye, and the civil war between those units loyal to the Archon and those following her disaffected brother Victor, the Gray Death Legion is to upgrade its readiness status. The Legion will take ship no later than 30 May and execute a hyperspace jump into the Hesperus system. There, the Legion will occupy the military base at Maria's Elegy on Hesperus II, from which base they will aid in the active defense of the planet, most especially of the Defiance Industries factory complex in the Myoo Highlands."

The document went on at length, including quite a bit of boilerplate setting the amount the Alliance was willing to pay the mercenary unit for its deployment, outlining salvage rights, transportation allowances, and so forth. It simply meant that the Gray Death Legion was going into combat.

Appended to the contract was a rundown of the units with which the Legion would be working. There were two main-line Regimental Combat Teams on planet, the Fifteenth and Thirty-sixth Lyran Guards. Lori didn't know much about either unit in recent years, except that both were firmly in the camp of Katrina Steiner-Davion. Had the loyalty of either unit been questionable, the Archon would surely have rotated them off Hesperus long before now. Had either declared for Victor, effectively placing Hesperus and the critical Defiance Industries complex in his hands, the Legion, and indeed the Alliance as a whole, would be facing a completely different situation. Knowing good intelligence was as useful as a full company of assault 'Mechs, Lori made a mental note to pull down whatever new data she could get on the Fifteenth and the Thirty-sixth Guards.

She took her personal noteputer from a desk drawer. Uncoiling a set of cables, she connected the message pad to the 'puter and downloaded the deployment order. Then, with a few more taps on the pad's console, she erased the message.

Putting the now-blank message pad aside, she punched a control built into her desk's flat formica top.

"Yes, Colonel?" her orderly answered from his office just outside her own.

"Mick, please call all the battalion commanders for a meeting. I'd like to see them in the conference room in one hour."

"Right away, ma'am."

Shutting off the comm unit, she sat back in her chair and stared at the off-white acoustic tile ceiling of her office. She had taken the Legion into battle before, even leading them through full-scale operational exercises in conjunction with the regular Lyran Alliance Armed Forces. But there had always been Grayson's comforting, guiding presence at her back. Now, with his passing, she had nothing to fall back on. Lori knew the feeling was an illusion, a fantasy born of loss and grief. Davis McCall was still there, as was Julio Vargas, commander of the Death Eagles, the Legion's fighter wing, and Tom Leone, the hulking infantry major who was the core of the Legion's Armored Infantry contingent. Each was an expert in his own field, and each would give Lori the benefit of wise counsel, but none of them would ever be Grayson Carlyle.

"Lieutenant-Colonel McCall, what is our current status?" Lori asked, yielding the floor to her executive officer. Like all good commanders, she knew the Gray Death Legion TO&E down to the platoon level. But, like all good commanders, she allowed her subordinates to do their jobs.

"Well Colonel, as y'know, we've got two full battalions of BattleMechs, havin' fleshed out th' Assassins."

Lori shifted a bit uncomfortably at Second Battalion's nickname. Known as "Hassan's Assassins" after Hassan Ali Khalid, the unit's long-time commander, the battalion had been the first to experience the death of a veteran commander when Khalid died back in late December. The battalion voted to keep the name in honor of the man who had led them for so long.

If McCall noticed her discomfort, he gave no sign of it, but continued his briefing.

"All of our 'Mechs are either new models or have been retrofitted with 'foundtech' gear. The same goes for the aerospace wing." McCall used the Legion slang for the new technological devices that had been developed over the past thirty or so years, thanks in great part to the Legion's discovery of an ancient Star League memory core during its early days. "Foundtech" was the Gray Death's tongue-in-cheek answer to the term "lostech," the more common term for such rediscovered technology.

"Major Leone's infantry battalion is now fully equipped with power armor. He's been pushing them through their paces pretty hard lately. He says 'they'll do'. An' for Tommy Leone, that's high praise indeed."

"What about the armored battalion?" Lori asked, glancing toward a slim, dark-haired woman slouched against the briefing room's back wall.

"The Cats are ready to go, if that's what you mean, Colonel," Major Megan Powers said, maintaining her slouch. "I've got one full company of armored scouts who know their jobs well enough for me. I could use two more. We've finally got Second Company converted over to all hover tanks. Third is still a hodgepodge of wheels and tracks. But we'll be ready when the balloon goes up."

Megan pulled herself into a straighter stance. "It *is* about to go, isn't it? That's why you called this meeting, right?"

Lori smiled for the first time in days. If there was one thing that would never change, it was the irascible Megan Powers.

"That's right, Meg. The orders just came down from theater command. We've been assigned to Hesperus II."

A low murmur ran through the small knot of Legion officers. Everyone in the room understood the significance of the orders. As the civil war ran its course through what had once been a united Federated Commonwealth, any facility capable of producing BattleMechs and their various vital components had become a primary target. War, they all knew, was as much a matter of logistics as it was a matter of strategy and tactics.

The Lyran Alliance had two major 'Mech production facilities. One of those, Coventry Metal Works on the planet of the same name, had already fallen to Victor Davion. The other was the sprawling, city-sized Defiance Industries factory complex on Hesperus II, and the smaller, though no less important, Doering Electronics manufacturing installation also on that world. Though Victor had yet to threaten Hesperus directly, everyone knew the Alliance's remaining major war producer was at risk.

Hesperus II lay within the borders of the politically unstable region of the Lyran Alliance known as the Isle of Skye. With the Alliance's attention focused elsewhere, the Skye Separatist faction had used the opportunity to initiate yet another rebellious bid for independence. Given the importance of Hesperus II to both the Alliance and the Skye rebels, the Archon was reinforcing the planet's defenses by reassigning the Gray Death Legion.

"We're going to have to get the Legion together in one tearing hurry," Lori continued as the low rumble of commentary subsided. "We're to ship out in five days, and we'll make all haste for Hesperus. When we get there, we'll move into the base at Maria's Elegy and aid in the defense of the planet."

Lori waited until the note-taking officers caught up with her before she continued.

"Dan, I'll be calling pretty heavily on you once we arrive. You've got a more intimate knowledge of the area around the capitol and the Defiance plant than any of us. Consider yourself part of the strategic planning staff on this one."

The man to whom Lori addressed her remarks was one of the younger officers to wear the Legion gray. In his late thirties, Daniel Brewer was slim, ebon-skinned, and affected the somewhat archaic twin braids of a Lyran MechWarrior framing his face. He also wore the captain's bars pinned to his collar with an air of quiet self-assurance.

None of that was surprising, as Brewer was not just another Legionnaire. He was also the Duke of Hesperus, and a nephew by marriage to General of the Armies Nondi Steiner. Brewer had once been the nominal Chief Executive Officer of Defiance-Hesperus. That was before the Gray Death's last visit to Hesperus, back in 3057. Then, Brewer and the Defiance Self-Protection Force had fought the Legion, with Brewer almost single-handedly breaching their defenses. Following that operation, Brewer had been "enlisted" in the Gray Death Legion by Archon Katrina.

"I'll give you what help I can, Colonel," Brewer said in his characteristically low tone.

"Colonel," McCall put in, "have we got anything resemblin' an intelligence report? Any idea what the *sassanach* might be throwin' at us?"

"Not yet, Davis." Lori smiled at McCall's use of the Gaelic term "sassanach." Originally a corruption of the word Saxon, the ancient Scots of Terra had applied it to the English during their wars for independence, and later to any outsider, especially an enemy. "We've got to figure that they'll hit us pretty hard, though. Defiance-Hesperus is pretty important to the Alliance, and to the Skye Separatists, *and* to Prince Victor. So we have to expect that they'll hit the planet with at least three regiments, maybe more."

Lori paused again, putting her thoughts in order for what she had to say next.

"I want you to understand, people, that there is more to the mission than a simple military deployment. Remember, the Gray Death Legion has been on Hesperus before. That time, we were the invaders. Two of the units we fought are still on planet—the Fifteenth Lyran Guards and the Defiance Self-Protection Force. We are going to have to assume there will be at least some bad blood over our last visit to the place. Therefore, I will expect all Legion personnel to conduct themselves with the utmost professionalism and tact. I know diplomacy isn't a skill much required for piloting a BattleMech, but it is one we'd better pick up on the fly."

Again, Lori waited until her thoughts caught up with her.
"The worst part of this mission isn't going to be the fighting or our relations with the regular Lyran forces on planet. The worst part will be that aspect of internal Lyran politics that made this deployment necessary—the Skye Separatist Movement.

"We can't forget the nightmare the Eridani Light Horse faced on Milos, when they tried to liberate a people who did not want to be liberated. With the Isle of Skye in open rebellion against the Alliance, I'm doubly unsure of the reception the Legion is going to get. And that leads us to a broader question. What if the general population of Hesperus decided they'd rather be free from the Alliance? What does the Legion do then?"

"Colonel, the way I see it, we are under contract to the Lyran Alliance, to the Archon," Julio Vargas said quietly. "I would have to say that we fulfill our contract within the limits of the guidelines set forth by the Mercenary Bonding Commission and the Ares Conventions. So long as our defending Hesperus against any invasion force does not violate those laws, we must do our utmost to keep the Alliance from losing that world."

"I agree, Julio," Lori said. "I guess it falls to me to make the decision, doesn't it? So, here's how we play it. The Skye Separatists have abandoned the political process in favor of armed rebellion against a lawful ruler. Therefore, as mercenaries contracted by the Lyran state, we are bound to do everything in our power to make sure Hesperus remains in the hands of the Lyran Alliance, short of violating either the bonding commission codes or the Ares Conventions.

"All right. Anything else?" Lori asked the question only because Grayson had drilled into her head the idea that there was always one more thing to cover. When no one spoke, she nodded. "Very well, go brief your people. We've got a lot to do and not a lot of time to do it in if we're going to be ready to ship out in five days."

# 3

Lori gripped the back of the Captain's acceleration couch hard as an odd feeling of vertigo drained away and the swirling colored lights faded from her vision. The illusory phosphorescence was a direct result of the effects of hyperspace jump travel on the human body. Some people were more susceptible to Transit Disorientation Syndrome, or jump-sickness, as it was more commonly called. Those unfortunate folks often found themselves experiencing blinding headaches, severe nausea, and other unpleasant physical side effects caused by the eldritch forces necessary to instantly transport a massive JumpShip and its attendant DropShips across thirty light-years of space. She was glad of the magnetic boots commonly worn by spacers. Despite all of mankind's advances in space travel, artificial gravity was still in the realm of science fiction.

Beside her, Davis McCall seemed to be even less affected than she was.

"Right on time, right on target," the DropShip's pilot said in a calm, almost bored, tone. "Those Steiner navy boys really know their jobs. I'll give them that."

The *Durant*, a *Union*-class DropShip named for Grayson's father, along with two more of the Legion's nine DropShips, was mated to the *Invader*-class JumpShip *Invidious*. Not far off, two more *Invaders*, carrying the balance of the Legion's DropShips, floated against the velvet blackness of space.

Following the man's gaze, Lori looked toward the ship's main viewscreen, where the other Legion starships were rendered in a wire-frame schematic. But they were not alone. Standing off at only a few hundred kilometers was the broad, twin-hulled bulk of a WarShip. Nearly a kilometer long, the massive WarShip dwarfed the *Invidious* by comparison. Her forward structure bristled with weapon ports of every type and description.

"That's the *Simon Davion*," Lori said in mild surprise. "I had no idea she was anywhere in the area."

McCall pulled himself across the small bridge to hang in the air before the display. Unlike his chief, he disliked the magnetic boots, preferring to move through the free-fall environment of a ship in space unhindered by the clumsy footgear. He pulled himself along hand-over-hand, using stanchions welded to the ship's overhead and bulkheads for that precise purpose. Some younger, less experienced, personnel moved about the ship by kicking off any convenient surface and "flying." Usually that mode of travel only lasted until the "airborne" crewman or passenger collided violently with someone traveling by one of the more "conventional" means.

"It makes sense, though," McCall said, peering at the hand-long image of the cruiser. "Hesperus is awful important to th' Alliance. If the rebels are really headin' this way—an' we've got no good reason to suspect otherwise— it makes sense that th' Archon would want one of her best WarShips here to meet 'em when they come."

Gazing at the bulk of the huge battle cruiser drove home to Lori the enormity of the situation in which the Legion found itself. Though technically still a mercenary unit, the Legion was also somewhat beholden to the Lyran Alliance. Not only did Archon Katrina still hold their contract but she had made Grayson Baron Glengarry, a noble of the Alliance. That meant the Legion, Baron Glengarry's personal troops, were also part of the Alliance Armed Forces. It was a delicate line to walk for all concerned.

The civil war that had torn apart the Federated Commonwealth added a new layer to the complications. Archon Katrina, Prince Victor's younger sister, was far more politically astute than her brother. A long and unpleasant series of accusations, innuendo, and political maneuvers had served to first estrange, then divide the two oldest children of the late Hanse Davion and Melissa Steiner. When Melissa died, the victim of an assassin's bomb, Katrina allowed a series of rumors to leak out suggesting that Victor was responsible for his mother's murder. She then walked off with the Lyran half of the Federated Commonwealth without so much as firing a shot.

A few years later, Victor went off to war against the Smoke Jaguars, leaving his younger sister Yvonne as Regent of the Federated Commonwealth. Some said the move was a calculated insult to Katrina. Others believed that Victor feared for the welfare of his realm under Katrina's hand. Whatever his intent, by the time he returned from his victory in Clan space, Katrina had seized upon the opportunity to claim the throne of the Federated Suns, ousting Yvonne as Regent in the process.

Unwilling to sit by and watch the domain his parents fought to establish and preserve torn apart, Victor tried to pressure Katrina through political means to relinquish the throne. It was only after the assassination of his brother Arthur three years back that Victor donned the uniform of the Federated Suns and led his troops into Katrina's territory in a bid to oust his sister and reunite the sundered realms.

In the twenty years since the formation of the Federated Commonwealth, many units from both the Federated Suns and the Lyran Commonwealth had been assigned to new duty stations. Numerous Davion troops had been posted to Steiner worlds, and vice versa, in an effort to more fully integrate the formerly separate militaries. As tensions mounted, Katrina issued a "come home" order to the loyal Steiner troops. Many obeyed; some did not. Meanwhile, Davion troops stationed within the Alliance remained in place.

When the mounting tensions erupted into open hostilities, the result was a chaotic situation where there were no front lines, no rear areas, and units that had occupied the same worlds in peace suddenly found themselves pitted against one another in battle. Victor, ever the soldier to Katrina's politician, fought a series of battles down through the Alliance, eventually seizing Coventry, one of the realm's primary sources of BattleMechs. At the same time, Katrina had made a substantial strategic and political gain by destroying the First Davion Guards on New Avalon, when those troops tried to challenge her power on the capital world of the Federated Suns. Thus far, Victor had not moved directly against Hesperus. As events fell out, he didn't have to.

Robert Kelswa-Steiner, a cousin by marriage to the Archon and the leader of the troublesome Skye separatist movement, had chosen that moment to launch another bid for independence for the Isle of Skye. Like all armies, the Skye rebels needed arms. That placed Hesperus directly in the path of the Separatists, exponentially increasing the risk to the planet, the Isle of Skye, and the Lyran Commonwealth as a whole.

As it happened, the sudden flare-up of rebellion in Skye served to aid Prince Victor. Katrina must pull troops away from the struggle with her brother in order to suppress the rebellion. If not, the risk that the Star League might step in with peacekeepers was real. Lori remembered well what had happened in the St. Ives Compact, when Sun-Tzu Liao, acting under the auspices of his position as First Lord of the Star League, used peacekeepers to regain lost worlds in that tiny state.

The huge WarShip hanging motionless in space only a few thousand kilometers away was a graphic reminder of the dire situation into which the Gray Death Legion had been thrust.

"Colonel, Captain Murad is on the line," Lori heard the DropShip captain say, bringing her back to the here and now.

"She says we'll be free to uncouple and start our burn insystem as soon as she finishes orienting the *Invidious*. She estimates she'll be ready to cut us loose in about an hour."

Lori turned to face the spacer. "Very well, George," she said. "Please convey my compliments to Captain Murad. Thank her for the ride."

\* \* \*

Though Captain Hester Murad's estimate had proved correct, it was still more than a week before the *Durant* touched down on the tarmac at Maria's Elegy. The vagaries of space travel in the thirty-first century were such that transport JumpShips devoted the bulk of their structure to the gigantic Kearny-Fuchida jump drives and to cargo space. Little room was given to fuel or reaction mass for maneuvering drives. At most, the average JumpShip had enough fuel to operate station-keeping thrusters as it hung above the system's sun, recharging its engines by means of a massive solar energy collector commonly called a jump sail. WarShips like the *Simon Davion* did boast huge maneuvering drives and vast reserves of fuel to power them, but even they had to rely on DropShips for anyone wanting to make the trip from space to a planet's surface. It took just over two hundred hours for the Legion to make the long trip from the jump point to the spaceport at Maria's Elegy.

Lori stood on the lower level of the *Durant*'s cavernous 'Mech bay. In the dim light provided by the bay's fluorescent strips, she could see the mottled gray bulk of the modified VTR-9K *Victor* BattleMech that had until recently been Grayson's. With its enhanced command, control, and communications gear, it was the Legion's command 'Mech. Now it was hers. Beside it stood McCall's boxy *Highlander*, its barrel chest sporting the image of an ancient Scots warrior wielding a pike, with the legend "Bannockburn" painted beneath. Beyond those two were more 'Mechs, and the rest were housed in the bays of the Legion's other DropShips.

As the thundering roar of the *Durant*'s engines died, Lori thumbed a large green button set into one of the bay's outer bulkheads. A high, shrill whine hissed through the bay as a small, man-sized hatch slid upward on well-oiled runners. Light flooded into the bay, momentarily forcing Lori to screw her eyes shut. As her eyes adjusted, she got her first look at Maria's Elegy in almost ten years.

Little about the spaceport had changed. Some of the systems had been upgraded, making communications masts and radar domes smaller or unnecessary. The main terminal building had been remodeled and enlarged, but that seemed to be the extent of the changes. At the edge of the *Durant*'s assigned landing bay sat a pair of hover jeeps.

A small knot of men clad in dark gray-green uniforms stood next to the jeeps, looking up at the DropShip. Lori and McCall strode down the ramp and approached the welcoming committee. As they drew near the group, Lori saw that two of them, one man and one woman, sported the T-shaped triple-diamond insignia of a Lyran Alliance Leutnant-General.

"You must be Colonel Kalmar-Carlyle. Welcome to Hesperus II," a woman with gray-shot black hair said, raising her hand in a salute, then extending it to Lori. "Leutnant-General Gina Ciampa, Fifteenth Lyran Guards." Lori noted that Ciampa pronounced her rank with the hard, guttural Teutonic accent of one raised in the upper circles of Lyran society.

Her research into her Lyran counterparts suggested that Ciampa was a competent, professional soldier. Because psychological profiles on Lyran officers were highly classified, Lori was unable, for security reasons, to get a complete dossier. She just had to hope that Ciampa's loyalty to the Alliance would outweigh any personal animosity she might feel toward the Gray Death Legion and its past history on Hesperus II.

Ciampa gestured to the man at her side.

"This is Leutnant-General Peter Zambos," she said. "He's got the Thirty-sixth Guards."

The bearded blond Lyran officer gave Lori a rather cold once-over before fixing her with a blank, level stare. For a moment, Lori struggled to find a reason for Zambos' seeming hostility. Then it came to her. According to the briefings she'd received concerning this mission, Zambos was something of a martinet, who held strictly to the letter of the regulations. The glare he was bending on Lori and her staff made it clear that *he* was a *Leutnant-General*, while *Lori* was a mere *Colonel*, and a mercenary officer at that. According to the regulations, *she* owed *him* the first salute.

Not wishing to start an argument her first day on planet, Lori touched the backs of her fingers to her forehead in the palm-outward salute used by the Star League Defense Force and by the Gray Death Legion, which had adopted many of the SLDF's traditions. For several seconds, Zambos remained motionless, his dark eyes locked on Lori's, then he returned the salute, using the palm-down gesture favored by the Lyran Alliance Armed Forces. He held it for a brief second, then snapped his hand down sharply.

Lori's digging had provided even less information on Zambos. Unlike Ciampa, who was a product of the Sanglamore Military Academy, Zambos had graduated from the less prestigious, more practically minded Buena War College. Though he was accounted a good officer, some considered him to be brash, opinionated, and self-centered.

"Welcome to Hesperus, Colonel," he said, and Lori caught the fleeting pause before Zambos uttered her title. Clearly, the man had little use for her. Lori wondered if it was due to a general dislike for paid soldiers or some kind of personal grudge against her or the Gray Death Legion.

"Yes, welcome," Ciampa repeated. "We'd both like to extend our sympathy to you and to your troops. I wish we could have met under different circumstances or that the Alliance could have given you a little more time before shipping you out here. But we don't have that luxury right now."

"Oh?" Lori turned away from the still-glaring Zambos to meet Ciampa's level, open gaze. "We were told the rebels hadn't yet begun to move against Hesperus. Has the situation changed?"

"Not yet, but we expect that to change soon. They've already begun an offensive on Freedom, and the Separatists have never had any trouble recruiting troops. The Free Skye movement has become awfully popular, especially since the Archon split from the Federated Commonwealth. I guess the Separatists figure that if the Alliance can secede from the F-C, then Skye can secede from the Alliance.

"They've got plenty of men," Ciampa repeated. "It's materiel they're a bit short of. A number of native Skye units, like the Fourteenth Skye Rangers, have defected *en masse*. They've got their BattleMechs, fighters, and whatnot, but those few regiments aren't going to be able to force the Archon to give the Isle of Skye its freedom, not against the might of the Alliance Armed Forces. They're going to need to raise local troops, militias almost, to support the main-line combat units. Neither the defector main-line troops nor the militias are going to be able to operate for long without a significant source for 'Mechs and replacement parts, so where does that leave Hesperus?"

"Right in the middle of the biggest bull's eye in the Alliance," Lori answered.

Ciampa laughed bitterly in reply. "That's right," she said. "And, that's why the Archon moved the Legion to Hesperus. The rebels are coming, sure enough, and we want to be ready to meet them when they do. Hesperus is especially important now, since Victor seized Coventry. We're the last major BattleMech production facility still in Lyran hands."

Another man clad in a dark green uniform stepped away from the knot of officers clustered around the jeeps. Slim, with coal-black hair and a thick, almost handlebar mustache, he moved with an easy, springy step that bespoke youth and vigor.

"Colonel Carlyle?" he said, his words spoken in a deep drawl that stretched the name out into "Cah-lyle." "I'm Major James Goree. I'm in charge of the Defiance Self-Protection Force."

"Good afternoon, Major," Lori said, returning the man's salute and shaking his hand, as Alliance protocol dictated. Despite Goree's lanky frame, the handshake spoke of a quiet strength. He held Lori's hand for a moment, then released it cleanly.

"Colonel, I've already made it clear to General Ciampa and General Zambos, and I'd like to make it clear to you." Goree's tone was friendly, with a shadow of formality which, combined with the drawl, gave him an air of old-time gentility that seemed almost quaint in the modern surroundings of the spaceport. "It is your job to defend Hesperus II against any invaders. It is my job to defend the Defiance Industries plant. I understand that your contract allows you to draw from our stockpiles for repairs and reloads. However, that does not give you *carte blanche*, and it does not give you, or these officers"—he nodded toward the Lyran generals—"the authority to commandeer my people to bolster your own strength. My orders come from the board of directors of Defiance Hesperus, not from Tharkad, and not from the Gray Death Legion."

Lori cocked her head, looking closely at the young man

who had obviously shot his bolt and was now waiting for her response.

"Very well, Major," she said quietly. "We can play it your way if you like. Can I ask you a question, though?"

"You may."

"How long have you been with the DSPF?"

"I was here the last time your unit was on Hesperus, if that's what you mean, Colonel," Goree said evenly. "I was part of the Protection Force. I lost my first 'Mech to you people."

"I see." Lori's tone was as neutral as Goree's.

"That's right, Colonel," Goree continued. "I fought you back in fifty-seven. So did a lot of my people. I hope you will understand why we're not keen on seeing the Gray Death Legion again."

"Does that include me, Major?" boomed a voice from the back of Lori's entourage.

Recognizing the speaker, Lori did not turn to see who spoke. Goree looked confused for a moment, but his expression quickly changed to one of quiet respect.

"No, sir, that does not necessarily include you," Goree said, giving the speaker a crisp salute.

"At ease, Major," Daniel Brewer said. "I understand how my presence here, with the Gray Death Legion, puts you in an awkward situation. On one hand, you've got your orders from the board; on the other hand, you've got the CEO of Defiance Hesperus serving with the same mercenary company that attacked your post just a few years back.

"With the Colonel's permission?" Brewer asked, deferring to Lori, who nodded her assent. "Let me make it easy for you, Major. I may be the Duke of Hesperus, I may be the Chief Executive Officer of Defiance Hesperus, but I am also a captain, a company commander in the Gray Death Legion. I will not throw my weight around and overrule the board unless I feel it is absolutely necessary for the security of both DefHesp and the planet's population as a whole."

"May I speak freely, sir?" Goree asked with stiff formality.

Lori watched closely the man who was at once her subordinate in the Legion and her superior in the class-conscious Lyran society. She knew what Goree's formal request meant. He was about to say something that neither she nor Brewer would like. She had been trying not to worry too much about all the complicated undercurrents involved in the Legion's posting to Hesperus II, but maybe they were going to raise their ugly heads on their own.

Brewer stroked one of his braids. "You may speak freely."

"Sir, a goodly number of my men have expressed a certain, shall we say, displeasure, where you are concerned," Goree said in a flat voice, which suggested to Lori that he had rehearsed this portion of his speech until he knew it by rote. "They feel, and I cannot say that I disagree with them, sir, that you have abandoned your responsibilities to both the company and to Hesperus by signing on with the Gray Death Legion. Sir, some even feel that makes you a traitor, sir. I myself do not hold quite so strong a view, but I do feel that your presence here might cause some tension between the Protection Force and the Legion. For that reason, sir, I feel it might be best if you downplayed either your role as a Legionnaire or as CEO of DefHesp. I am afraid sir, that if you try to maintain both, most especially if my men perceive that you are using your position in the company to unduly aid the mercenaries, there may be a bit of trouble within the Protection Force."

"Well," Brewer said, chuckling slightly, "I did give you permission to speak, didn't I? Now, understand me, Major. I have not, up to this date, used my position or my authority to unfairly benefit either myself or the Gray Death Legion. Both I and the Legion believe that merit, not personal influence, should determine reward. I will not try to interfere with the day-to-day operation of your Protection Force. I will not involve myself in the provision of repair and replacement materials. Those are covered in the Legion's contract with the Alliance.

"However, that does not mean I will allow you, the board, or the members of the Protection Force to balk at carrying out their part of those same contracts. And, Major, if push comes to shove, I *will* exert my authority as CEO of Defiance Hesperus, for the good of the company, and for the good of the population of this world, even if that means terminating your employment with the company. Is that clear, Major Goree?"

"Yes, sir, perfectly clear," Goree said. His tone and posture suggested that, though he understood and believed Brewer's words, he would never agree with such an action.

"Well, let's just make sure it never comes to that, shall we?" Lori said, laying a hand on Brewer's arm. "Now, gentlemen, if there is nothing further to discuss, I suggest we see to getting the Legion disembarked and billeted. We've got a planet to defend."

# 4

**Myoo Highlands, Hesperus II**
**Skye Province**
**Lyran Alliance**
**15 June 3065**

**A**s the hover jeep crested a small rise, the road Lori had been following broke out of the thick coniferous forest. She eased to a stop and stepped out of the vehicle. A second identical vehicle coasted to a halt a few meters away. Before her was a broad, pan-shaped valley bordered to the south and east by the next ridge of the Myoo Mountains. A few kilometers to the north ran an off-white, arrow-straight ribbon of steel and ferrocrete stretching from a gap cut and blasted through the mountains straight into the rocky face of the eastern ridge.

Reaching back into the jeep, Lori retrieved a pair of electronic binoculars that she put to her eyes. Touching a control on the device's housing, she set the viewers to four power and scanned the valley. Aside from the occasional scrubby bush swaying in the gentle breeze, there wasn't much movement. Swinging to her left and kicking up the magnification, Lori examined the pale linear structure. From a distance of four kilometers, according to the binoculars' range-finder function, the details of the high-speed maglev rail line were easy to pick out. She could easily see the black line of the "rails" along which the train ran.

Using magnetic levitation, a variant of the principle used to power her *Victor*'s gauss rifle, the train didn't actually run along the "tracks." It floated above them. Lacking the friction of wheels against steel rails or of axles against wheel bearings, the levitating train was capable of speeds in excess of one hundred fifty kilometers per hour.

Swinging the binoculars and feeling the slight drag of the unit's gyroscopic stabilizing device, she followed the tracks to where they intersected with the mountain.

There, she could make out a squat ferrocrete bunker painted gray, green, and brown. It was barely visible. Set back in the rock face above the bunker, sheltered by a thick stone overhang, were a pair of thick doors constructed of the same durallex hardened steel used in her *Victor*'s armored skin. The doors, like the bunker, were difficult to see, since they were cunningly painted to mimic the mountainside that surrounded them. Deep shadows cast by the late morning sun helped conceal the northwest-facing doors from view.

Beyond those doors lay the huge Defiance Hesperus industrial plant. Lori had passed through them once before. Then she had been an aggressor. This time, it had fallen to her to defend those huge portals and the underground factory beyond.

From her vantage point, the external facade of the Defiance plant had changed little. A few more out buildings had been constructed, but not much more. Lori knew there had to have been changes that were not readily visible. Advances in weapon and sensor technology would most certainly have prompted Major Goree and the DSPF to upgrade the factory's defensive systems. That was part of the reason she and her officers were on their way to the plant, to review the changes to those systems. The visit was both a courtesy call—though how much courtesy they'd receive at Goree's hands was a matter for speculation—and a professional inspection. The Legion officers wanted to know what they could expect from the complex's defense grid, in case it might become necessary to use the factory as a base of operations.

A wave of sadness surged in Lori's heart. The last time she'd looked at the entrance to the Defiance factory complex, Grayson was still alive. Everything about this mission seemed timed to remind her of the loss she had suffered and had yet to fully mourn.

"Well, Colonel, are we aye gonna stand here takin' in the sights, or are we going t' move down there and pay our respects?"

Lori started a bit at the soft words in her ear. It seemed almost as though McCall had read her heart, and through that simple question sought to return her to solid emotional ground.

"We're going in, Davis," she said, lowering the binoculars and returning them to their synthetic case. "Nothing seems to have changed, does it?"

"No, lass, it doesn't," McCall answered.

Lori shrugged as she stepped back into the jeep and engaged the drive fans. Though she certainly rated a driver as the commanding officer of the Legion, she had allowed herself the simple pleasure of personally driving the hover jeep. Davis McCall and Captain Daniel Brewer occupied the vehicle's passenger seats. The second vehicle carried Major Rae Houk, Second Battalion's commanding officer, along with Majors Thomas Leone and Megan Powers.

Though some of them had been inside the hollowed-out mountain before, none had enjoyed the luxury of more than a passing observation of the facility's inner workings. Captain Brewer had arranged for the tour. Though familiarity with the inner workings of the plant was not absolutely essential to the defense of Hesperus, Brewer had been able to convince the board of directors that granting the Legion's officers a tour of the facility was the prudent thing to do.

So far, Brewer seemed to be handling the job of juggling his responsibilities to the Legion and his position as CEO of Defiance Hesperus easily enough. Granted, it had only been twenty-four hours. For now, Lori would reserve judgment until she saw how the young man performed under further pressure.

It had taken nearly four hours to make the trip from Maria's Elegy by hover jeep. Lori knew from the briefings supplied by the Alliance that it took the maglev just over an hour to reach the plant, owing to the train's higher speed and the straighter path it traveled. By comparison, the road through the mountains was full of turns and switchbacks, effectively doubling the distance a ground or hover car had to travel. And, because of the treacherous curves, the speed at which ground traffic could travel was severely limited.

As she pulled the ground-effect vehicle to a stop outside the bunker, a guard dressed in the same dark green fatigues Major Goree had worn the day before stepped into the middle of the road. A Gunther MP 20 submachine gun hung from a sling looped over the man's right shoulder. His right hand grasped the weapon's firing grip, though his forefinger lay alongside the trigger guard. Lori had no doubts as to the man's ability to instantly bring the weapon into deadly play, should the situation warrant it.

"Identification?" he rapped out.

Lori handed a small leather case to the guard, who accepted it with his left hand and stepped back from the jeep before opening it to scan the identity documents contained therein. Lori was impressed but not surprised by the level of professionalism the guard displayed. By taking the proffered documents with his left hand, he was able to keep positive control of his weapon, maintaining his ability to hose down the hover jeep and its occupants with thirty heavy eleven-millimeter slugs if any aggressive moves were made. Stepping away from the jeep before giving the identification cards his divided attention provided him with a stand-off space between the vehicle's occupants and himself, should any hostilities arise.

The guard closed the ID case with a snap and stepped back up to the jeep.

"Identification," he said again.

"I just gave you my identification," Lori snapped.

"Yes, you did, Colonel Carlyle," the guard said in a neutral tone. "And I know Mister Brewer by sight. I do not, however, know the rest of these gentlemen, and I cannot allow you to pass until I see their ID."

Lori caught a flicker of motion from the corner of her eye. Turning her attention away from the guard, she looked at the passenger side of the jeep, where two more men in DSPF green, one of them bearing a heavy Thorvald and Koch automatic shotgun, had taken up position. In the jeep's rear-view mirror, she saw that a fourth guard had stepped in behind the other jeep. This man had a TK assault rifle, with an under-barrel grenade launcher, aimed negligently at the vehicle's rear bumper. It was clear that they would not be gaining entrance to the plant or leaving until they had produced the identification the first guard had demanded.

The rest of the officers passed their identification to Lori, who in turn gave them to the guard. Lori glanced in the mirror again just as Tom Leone, who was at the second jeep's controls, also handed over a trio of ID cards.

It took only a few moments for the guards to peruse the documents, return them to their owners, and wave the jeeps through the checkpoint. The Legion officers were directed to follow a white line painted on the tarmac.

"That was a wee bit unfriendly," McCall said. "Ye'd think they were nae happy to see us."

"They probably weren't," Lori said. "Don't forget that the last time they saw a Legionnaire, it was over the wrong end of a gun."

"I hate to burst your bubble, Colonel," Brewer said from the back seat. "That's been the standard security procedure here since long before I was born. When you've been attacked as many times as DefHesp has been, you tend to develop a healthy case of paranoia where security is concerned."

"Och, aye," McCall grunted, but it was hard to tell what he meant by it.

"It's true, sir," Brewer insisted. "That's why the guard said 'where you need to go,' not 'to visitor parking' or anything like that. We don't *have* visitors out here. Most of our workers, including management, even some of the board members, live out here. It's a rare thing for someone not directly associated with the company to be allowed inside."

Lori considered Brewer's words in the light of the Legion's having once been that force attacking the heavily defended factory complex. Perhaps Goree and other members of the DSPF had good reason to mistrust the mercenaries. It would fall to her to win Goree's trust. Grayson always had a knack for dealing with unfriendly people, which she seemed to lack. She sighed a silent regret that more of his charm had not rubbed off on her.

The prescribed white line came to an end on a broad expanse of macadam that anywhere else would have been called a parking lot. Here the pavement lacked any of the lines or divisions that would mark such an area. A massive durallex door, emblazoned with the number two, loomed above the parking area. Lori wondered to herself if she and her officers had been sent to this specific gate on purpose. The last a Legionnaire had seen Gate Two was during a bloody battle of attrition fought back in '57.

A small knot of men wearing a mixture of civilian clothing and DSPF uniforms awaited them. Lori pulled the jeep to a stop and climbed out as Major Goree and one of the civilians approached.

"Colonel Carlyle, welcome to Defiance Hesperus," Goree said in a carefully neutral tone. "This is Mister Samuel Quinn, one of our production managers. If you and your officers will follow him, he will give you the cook's tour."

For the next hour and a half, the Legionnaires were escorted through the subterranean factory complex. The size of some cities, the plant boasted smelting, forging, and casting facilities, electronics and machine shops, powder mills and heavy manufacturing installations of every type and description. Though any tour of the factory could only skim the surface of the colossal operation, Lori was awed by the sheer enormity of it all.

Again, little about the factory and its day-to-day operations had changed. Quinn had at first been reluctant to show his visitors much of the complex's defense systems, but eventually acceded to Lori's requests.

"This is incredible," Lori said as she surveyed the local battery-director's station for an Arrow IV missile system. The guided missiles could be locked on to a target by Target Acquisition Gear mounted in one of the DSPF's BattleMechs or armored vehicles. According to Quinn, the battery and all those like it had enough area-saturation and precision-guided munitions to fight a major engagement without running out.

"Are the rest of the weapon stations like this?" Rae Houk asked.

"Pretty much," Quinn admitted after a moment's hesitation. Lori surmised he was loath to give away too much information about the defense grid's capabilities. "We've got Artemis guided long- and short-range missile batteries, laser and particle cannon installations, autocannon turrets, all tied into a central command and control network. Each emplacement can be controlled locally or through a hierarchy of sector officers, right up to the central control room, if warranted. The systems are guided using all the latest sensor, tracking, and fire-control systems. Each weapon and sensor emplacement is well-protected in hardened pillboxes, and is amply supplied with ammunition and multiple redundant back-up power sources. You'd just about need a WarShip to make a significant dent in the grid.

"We've also beefed up our regular security measures a bit," Quinn continued. "We've increased the number and frequency of regular security patrols, and instituted a number of security checks at every entry and exit point. That was Major Goree's idea. He pointed out that the face of warfare is changing, that special and covert operations are becoming more common. We've got to protect ourselves from sabotage as well as an attacking military force."

Lori declined to comment on Quinn's grandiose assessment of the Defiance defense grid. Then again, given what they'd seen of the installations, she was not eager to test her beliefs.

As the group turned to leave the weapon station, a sharp beep interrupted Quinn's lecture. Pulling a small black comm unit from his pocket, he held the device up to his ear, cupping his free hand over the other to shut out the noise of the factory.

"Colonel Carlyle, we've just received a message from Maria's Elegy," Quinn said at last, returning the unit to his pocket. "Leutnant-General Ciampa wants you to contact her right away."

"Why?"

"They didn't say, Colonel." Quinn shrugged. "Or at least they didn't tell me. There is a comm unit in the battery-director's control booth. Enter code 775 to get an outside line."

Lori slipped back inside the installation. It took a few moments of arguing with the operator before the man would consent to leave her alone in his booth, and then he only agreed after extracting Lori's promise that she wouldn't touch *anything* except the comm. She bit her tongue in an effort to hold her exasperation in check. Would anyone on this planet put aside the past and give the Legion the trust this mission would require?

"This is Colonel Kalmar-Carlyle," she said when the command center at Maria's Elegy came online. "Put me through to General Ciampa."

"Carlyle," Ciampa said with no preamble. "How soon can you get back here? We may be seeing the beginning of this thing. Our space-based early warning system has picked up an IR spike at a pirate point out on the rim."

"We can be back there in a couple of hours, less if you send air transport for us. Have you sent any aerospace assets out to check?"

"Colonel, that's part of the reason you were brought here." Ciampa's voice tightened. "Neither the Fifteenth nor the Thirty-sixth *has* any aerospace assets."

"Dammit," Lori spat, her knuckles whitening on the handset. That was a clumsy mistake. How the hell could she have forgotten that important detail? Coming to Hesperus had stirred up so many old memories that she was finding it hard to keep from being distracted. She knew her grief had its place, but somehow she had to keep it from interfering with the life-and-death decisions that were part of her job.

"All right, General, we're on our way back. What about that chopper?"

"I'll make the call. It will be there within the hour," Ciampa said, and then was gone.

For a moment, Lori glared at the handset as though the inoffensive black plastic instrument was somehow personally responsible for the situation into which the Legion had been dumped. She dropped the unit back into its cradle and started for the control booth's door. Then she turned back to the comm unit again and punched in the access code, followed by the number for the Gray Death Legion's billet at the spaceport. In a few moments, the duty officer answered.

"Lieutenant, get me Wing Commander Vargas," Lori said abruptly, cutting the man off in mid-greeting.

More minutes crawled by before Vargas came on the line.

"Julio, we might have a problem."

"I heard," Vargas said quickly. "I have First Squadron standing by aboard one of our DropShips. All I need is your permission to launch."

Lori permitted herself a quiet sigh of relief. She should have known that Vargas, one of her most capable subordinates, would have taken steps to prepare his unit for battle at the slightest hint of trouble. By leaving the unit's aerospace fighters aboard their DropShips, Vargas had made sure the fighters could be carried out toward the point of the suspected arrival. The savings in fuel and pilot fatigue were enormous.

"Very well, Julio. Launch as soon as you're ready. Just out and back. Two fighters and one *Union* are no match for any kind of invasion fleet. And keep me posted on what you find."

"As you say, Colonel, I will keep you informed," Vargas said. "I will see you when I return."

Lori dropped the handset back into its cradle, this time more gently than before. While her supposed allies seemed prepared to throw every possible obstacle in her way, at least she could count on her own people to conduct themselves with the highest degree of professionalism. Thank god Ciampa was playing things cool, putting aside any personal animosities or resentment in the interests of her duty to the Alliance. Lori stepped from the booth and smiled at the operator.

Ignoring the man's poisonous look, she waved her officers toward her.

"Mister Quinn, I'm sorry, but we're going to have to cut this tour short," Lori told the Defiance representative. "I've been called back to Maria's Elegy as soon as we can get there. General Ciampa will be sending a helicopter for us. Do you think you can find someone to drive our jeeps back for us?"

To his credit, Quinn did not ask questions, but agreed immediately to recruit a couple of drivers for her. Even more to his credit, he excused himself, standing a few meters off while Lori briefed the Legion officers on the situation that had arisen.

"We've got to return to Maria's Elegy as soon as possible," she half-shouted over the clangor of the factory. "It will take Julio some time to reach the pirate point, so let's put that time to good use. I want every Legionnaire ready to mount up on a moment's notice, in case this *is* the real thing."

She turned and waved to their erstwhile guide.

"Mr. Quinn, will you please show us the quickest way out of the complex?"

"Of course, Colonel. This way. I'll take you to the helipad."

Quinn motioned Lori and the others into the pair of electrically powered carts they had been using during their tour of the facility. Taking the controls of the leading runabout himself, Quinn set off through the vast maze of men and machinery that was the Defiance plant. It took almost three-quarters of an hour for Quinn to deliver the Legionnaires to the facility's helipad.

No sooner had the vehicles emerged into the brilliant, late afternoon sun than a low, rumbling drone crept up on the edges of their hearing. Lori looked in the direction of the sound. Off to the northwest, about two hundred meters off the deck, she spotted the boxy, dark gray shape of a *Karnov UR* transport VTOL. While often classified as a helicopter, the Vertical Take-Off and Landing craft was more accurately a tilt-rotored airplane, capable of carrying up to six metric tons of cargo in its belly.

The VTOL flared out, cutting its speed to almost nothing, as the rotors on its wingtips pivoted upward to compensate for the lift that vanished as its speed dropped below that at which the wings would stall. It touched down almost in the center of the landing area, and even before it had come to a complete stop, Lori and her officers were sprinting toward the big transport. In less than two minutes, they were aboard, strapped in, and back in the air.

During the brief flight back to the spaceport, Lori refused to speculate on the nature of the mysterious IR contact. One of the lessons she had learned from Grayson was never to formulate a plan based on partial information. Instead, she directed her subordinates to make sure their units were in top fighting trim for the coming battle.

"Are you sure this is the attack?" Daniel Brewer asked.

"I'd be surprised if it wasn't," Meg Powers put in before Lori could answer. "Who else would come in at a pirate point? A law-abiding merchant?"

"Meg's right," Lori cut in. "If this isn't the invasion itself, it's probably a scouting mission in advance of the main attack force. Either way, we can't take the risk and assume it's some peaceable JumpShip that happened to phase in out along the rim rather than at one of the standard jump-points."

"Sorry, Colonel, I guess I asked a fool question," Brewer said.

"No, Captain, you didn't ask a fool question. That was a legitimate concern I might have expressed myself, thirty years ago." Lori glanced over at Davis McCall, who grinned back knowingly. "The secret is for young officers to ask questions and to learn from the answers."

"Aye, lad," McCall added. "We all had to go through the learnin' process, same as you."

The discussion shifted once more to the logistics of keeping the Gray Death Legion in the field and in battle-ready condition. As McCall began laying out the rather mundane issues of food and ammunition supplies, his words rang in Lori's mind.

*We all had to go through the learning process.*

Well, it looked like she was still learning, she thought ruefully, even after all her years in the field. This time it was the art of command, and it was a subject she could not afford to fail.

# 5

## Interplanetary Space, Hesperus System
## Skye Province
## Lyran Alliance
## 16 June 3065

At a high-G burn, equal to one and a half times that of Terra, the Legion DropShip made a fast run from Hesperus II toward the so-called pirate point out on the system's rim. Most of the ship's crew, veteran spacers to a man, were able to go about their assigned tasks with little difficulty. The fighter crews were even less affected by the higher than normal G loading caused by the high-speed run. Their high-performance aerospace fighters were capable of far more Gs than a DropShip could ever hope to pull. *Union*-Class transports were capable of even higher Gs, but the humans aboard the spherical spacecraft would not be able to function for long under those conditions. Still, the need for reasonable haste was genuine.

Jumping in to nonstandard points was a hazardous undertaking, and not one commonly practiced by civilian captains. Even military JumpShips tried to avoid entering a system along rim points. Only when speed and surprise were necessary would an interstellar craft risk damage to its relatively fragile Kearny-Fuchida drives by entering a system in such a manner. The slang term of "pirate point" bore witness to how effective the use of a nonstandard jump point could be in achieving surprise. Only desperate or dangerous men used them. Given the value of Hesperus II, specifically the Defiance factory complex, any armed force arriving via a nonstandard jump point would qualify under both categories.

Even considering the high-speed run, it took the Legion ship nearly twenty hours to make the trip from Hesperus II to the point where the planetary defense sensors detected the infrared flare of an incoming JumpShip.

Wing Commander Julio Vargas stood before the *Durant*'s primary view screen and studied the electronic chart of the area. He was puzzled. According to the DropShip's sensors, they were right on top of the spot where the IR flare was detected, and yet, the only craft in the area were those belonging to the Gray Death Legion.

Turning to the *Durant*'s Captain, Vargas instructed him to make contact with Legion Command back on Hesperus II.

"I do not know what to tell you, Colonel," Vargas said, once communication had been established. "If we are to believe the sensor operators, we are exactly where they say they saw incoming JumpShips, only there is no sign of any. I suppose it is possible that the inbounds were WarShips that moved off station as quickly as they arrived. But the defense sensors would have been able to track something so large, even all the way out here. It is equally possible that whatever jumped in here used lithium-fusion batteries to make a double-jump out again, and that the sensor operators just missed the exit flare. If that is the case, they may have had enough time to launch their DropShips. And if *that* is the case, then we could have a full regiment of BattleMechs lying doggo out here, just waiting for the right moment to pay us a surprise visit."

Vargas had to wait nearly five minutes before Lori's answer came through. Even with all the technological advances made by man over the past three thousand years, scientists had yet to come up with a method of instantaneous communications between ships in space and ground stations, let alone between star systems. Even the relatively tiny distances between a planet and a ship on the system's rim required a span of several minutes to transmit a message and receive a reply. Given the time lag, military commanders, ship captains, and the like tended to word their messages carefully, trying to cover every possible angle of the issue at hand.

When Lori's answer came through, it was what Vargas had expected.

"Julio, General Ciampa is convinced that her sensor operators' readings were correct. Until we're sure, we've got to assume they picked up something. I want you to launch fighters and quarter and search the area. Hold back half of your squadron to act as a MigCAP in case the searchers run into trouble."

Though the old Russian firm of Mikoyan-Gurevich had gone out of business centuries before, the term MigCAP, for a Combat Aerospace Patrol designed to provide cover for another operation, remained in the military lexicon.

"Sí, Colonel, that is precisely what I have prepared to do," Vargas answered. "It will take several hours to comb just this sector. How far do you want us to expand our search?"

"Just that sector will do, Julio," Lori said. "While you conduct your search, I'll check with the sensor techs and see what else they might have come up with."

As she severed the connection with the faraway DropShip, Lori turned to face Generals Ciampa and Zambos, the latter of whom had just arrived from Maldon, the Thirty-sixth's garrison post on the far side of the planet.

"Well, any ideas or comments?" she asked.

Ciampa shook her head. "None. That is, nothing new anyway. All I can figure is that the sensors might have picked up some kind of ghost image. That, or there really *was* a JumpShip, and it's gone outsystem already. Whether it released DropShips or not remains to be seen. I can't help but wonder why, though. If there really was a ship, it could have carried, what, nine DropShips max? That's assuming it was a *Monolith*, and there just aren't many of that class around. I doubt the Separatists have more than a handful of them. They certainly wouldn't risk sending one on an in-and-out mission like this, would they?"

Lori shrugged slightly. "I don't know. It's too hard to figure out rebels of any stripe. They're so desperate for their independence that they're often willing to take the most extreme gambles to obtain it. At least, that's what

I've seen in the times the Legion has fought alongside various rebel troops."

Just then, an odd shiver ran along Lori's spine. How long ago it seemed that the newly minted Gray Death Legion had taken up arms in the jungles of Verthandi to aid the native freedom fighters against their Kurita masters. She shook off the strange, fey misgiving, and turned to Peter Zambos, who had remained silent during the exchange, but whose fidgety stance proclaimed to one and all that he had something to say.

"Yes, Colonel Carlyle, I have something to add," he said in a low growl, once more emphasizing Lori's rank. "I'd like to know why *you* feel you should take charge of this operation. Leutnant-General Ciampa and I both outrank you. We are both House officers, whereas *you* are just a mercenary."

"She is also Baroness Glengarry," Ciampa reminded him.

"There is that," Zambos snorted. "I don't think an honorary title has much bearing here, does it? What *does* matter here is that this mercenary is giving orders to House troops. That goes against all Lyran doctrine and tradition."

Lori took a moment to force a lid on her rising temper. She was glad that Davis McCall had elected to oversee the preparations of the regiment rather than accompanying her to the command center. Had the big, bluff Caledonian warrior been present, Zambos might well be on his way to the infirmary even now. When she was ready to speak, Lori found she didn't have to.

"Colonel Kalmar-Carlyle—and it's about time you and everyone else on this planet started getting her name right—was *not* giving commands to House troops," Gina Ciampa said. "She was giving orders to her *own* aerospace assets. Or have you forgotten, General, that neither your Thirty-sixth nor my Fifteenth Guards *have* any aerospace units?"

"I haven't forgotten anything, General Ciampa," Zambos hissed. "But it seems that *you* have forgotten *why* your Fifteenth Guards have no aerospace fighter wing. The Gray Death Legion wiped them out the last time these mercenary rats were on Hesperus."

"I haven't forgotten, General," Ciampa shot back. "But that was nine years ago, and nine years is a long time to hold a grudge. If that is not sufficient for you, allow me to say this. We have a larger duty to the Alliance. That duty is to defend Hesperus II against all those whom the Archon designates as our enemy. As of this moment, the Archon has designated the Skye Separatists and the Armed Forces of the Federated Suns as our enemies. She has declared the Gray Death Legion to be our friends. I will grant you that the events of '57 are not so easily put away as an outdated manual. I will admit it was a struggle for me to do so when I first learned that the Gray Death Legion was being assigned to Hesperus. But, I did it, and so must you. We *must* make every effort to override our personal feelings in favor of our duty to the Alliance. If you cannot do that, General, then I suggest you re-evaluate your commitment to the Lyran state.

"Now, General Zambos, I do not intend to stand here and bandy words with you while an invasion force possibly sneaks in on our flank. Have you got anything useful to add to this discussion or not?"

Zambos glared angrily first at Ciampa, then at Lori. "I guess not," he grumbled.

"Humph," Ciampa snorted, turning to Lori. "What do you suggest, Colonel?"

"I'd suggest we proceed as before," Lori answered, not a little confused. If she were going to pick either of the Lyran officers to hold a grudge against her and the Gray Death Legion, it would have been Ciampa. So far as she knew, Zambos hadn't even been *on* Hesperus II when the Legion fought against the Alliance troops here almost a decade ago.

"Let's see what Commander Vargas turns up in his search, though I have the feeling he isn't going to find much. Meanwhile, I'd suggest we pull the *Simon Davion* off station at the nadir point and have her move insystem. From her current position, it would take her a lot longer to reach our phantom contact than it would take any invaders to reach Hesperus II. If nothing else, we might call on her for naval-support fire, if need be."

"I am sorry, Colonel," Vargas apologized a few hours later. "As instructed, we quartered and searched the area. We even pushed into the adjoining sectors, but we still found nothing. No JumpShips, no DropShips, no fighters, nothing. Whatever happened out here was over before we left the planet. I suppose it could have been a quick in-and-out insertion. We don't have the sensors to detect the kind of residual energy traces that might leave. Unless you want to divert the *Simon Davion* out here—she's got the right kind of gear for this job—I think we're finished here."

Lori couldn't help a small sigh. "Very well, Julio. Come on back. I know you did your best," she said.

"If you wish, my squadron can remain on station a little while longer, Colonel. We might get lucky, though I doubt it. Space is an awful lot of nothing to search for a couple of relatively tiny DropShips, or a couple of even smaller fighters."

"No, Julio, you've done everything there is to do short of spending the next year out there searching every hectare of this system. If there was an intruder, he was here for a reason, and I suppose we'll find out what that is soon enough. Come on home."

"Well, Colonel, now what?" Ciampa asked in a neutral tone.

"Now we upgrade our alert status, and then we wait," Lori answered. "I don't quite know what else to do. We know the rebels will hit Hesperus soon enough. All we *can* do is make ourselves as ready for them as possible.

"I might also suggest that we have the sensor techs run a full battery of diagnostics on the early-warning system. Maybe we just ran into some kind of glitch or even operator error. In any event, we need to be sure we can rely on the system one hundred percent. The next time it says we've got an incoming JumpShip, let's be sure that's correct. We don't want to be hunting for the Flying Dutchman."

"Looks like the Legion's fighters are leaving, Colonel," the sensor operator said. "See there? The IR traces are definitely settling in on an insystem vector."

Colonel Francisco de Argall leaned over the bald technician's shoulder to examine the sensor display. Having only a passing familiarity with the device, he was forced to take the word of the tech.

"All of them?" he asked.

"Looks like." The tech gave an odd, jerky nod. "Hard to say for certain. It's a limitation of the passive gear. If you want me to go active, I can do that. Get you a better count. Thing is, I go active and the bad guys are almost certain to spot us."

De Argall straightened up. Cupping his chin in his left hand and his left elbow in his right palm, he thought for a moment.

"No. No active scans," he said arriving at a decision. "Our orders are to slip in undetected. That's why we risked such a fast insertion. If they haven't spotted us yet, we'll let them go on their way without attracting attention to ourselves."

De Argall turned to a thin-faced officer standing at a nearby computer display. "Any idea who they are?"

"Yes, sir," Leutnant-Colonel Don Nix replied, reading from the display. "Radio intercepts suggest that the bogies were elements of the Gray Death Legion. The ground controller kept referring to the aerospace commander as 'Julio.' According to the warbook, the Gray Death Legion aerospace wing, the Death Eagles, is under Wing Commander Julio Vargas."

De Argall resumed stroking his chin, a habit he'd fallen into when thinking. "That's not good, Don," he said. "We knew the Legion was probably going to remain loyal to Katrina. And we figured they would get involved in this business sooner or later. But I did not expect them to be sent to Hesperus. I would have thought their . . . ah . . . history with this world would have dictated they be sent elsewhere."

De Argall stroked his chin for a few moments longer.

"No matter. We must proceed as planned. We really don't have any other choice. Pilot, set your course for Hesperus V Gamma. Ahead dead slow."

"Aye sir, Hesperus V Gamma, ahead dead slow," the DropShip helmsman repeated, confirming the order.

De Argall tromped across the bridge deck toward the lift shaft, his magnetic boots making the process slow and deliberate. As the lift carried him down three decks to the one that held his quarters, he mentally reviewed his orders.

The regiment under his command, the Twenty-second Skye Rangers, had been one of the units to heed the Archon's call to "come home," though they'd really never left the old Lyran Commonwealth. Despite their allegiance to the new Lyran Alliance, the Twenty-second remained, at heart, an Isle of Skye unit. It hadn't taken very long for the regiment to jump ship when Duke Robert Kelswa-Steiner initiated the latest bid for independence for Skye.

Like most officers, de Argall knew that the key to the rebellion lay not in military power, but in political capital. The Separatists didn't necessarily have to win the war; they just had to not lose. They simply had to keep the Alliance tied up in a war of attrition until the Archon sued for peace. The price of that peace would be autonomy for the Isle of Skye.

Of course, fighting such a war was costly in terms of lives and materiel. The first category would have to be handled by Kelswa-Steiner and the rest of the Free Skye politicians. The latter bill fell to the rebel army to fill. The means of filling that bill lay in the Defiance Industries facility on Hesperus II.

Taking the planet with the massive underground factory would not be easy. Direct frontal assault had been tried and had failed more than a dozen times. Duke Robert's plan called for something more subtle. The Twenty-second Skye Rangers had been marched aboard three huge *Overlord*-Class DropShips and been ferried into the Hesperus system mated to the *Invader*-Class JumpShip *Macbeth*. Their orders were simple, in theory, but would require careful timing to carry out.

Once insystem, the Rangers were to make an extreme low-speed run to one of the large, rocky moons orbiting the Hesperus system's fifth, outermost planet. There, the unit would go to ground and wait for the furor that had attended their arrival to die down. Once the search activity ceased, the Rangers would leave Hesperus V Gamma and make another slow run into Hesperus III. Again the unit would go to ground and await the arrival of the main invasion fleet.

Once the primary attack force, under Leutnant-General William Harrison von Frisch, arrived, and the defenders scrambled to meet them, the Twenty-second Rangers would dart out of their hiding place and launch a lighting strike against Hesperus II. De Argall's objective was *not* the Defiance Industries complex, but the spaceport at Maria's Elegy. If his Rangers could seize the port, with its heavy surface-to-air and surface-to-space defenses, the rest of the fleet could land at the port without having to risk a combat drop against a defended world. A parallel objective was the hyperpulse generator station at the spaceport. If the HPG station could be captured, or at least isolated, the defenders would be unable to call for reinforcements.

No communications could be sent to or from the infiltrating Rangers. There was too much risk of interception. De Argall thought the plan somewhat baroque but likely to succeed because of sheer daring, if nothing else. Audacity often won battles where weapons could not.

The only thing about the scheme that did not sit well with him was the lack of information Skye command was able or willing to give him. He knew Hesperus was supposed to be defended by the Fifteenth and Thirty-sixth Lyran Guards, both good, solid mainline combat units in their own right. Not a single intelligence briefing he had seen even suggested that the Gray Death Legion might be on Hesperus II, and the presence of the mercenary combined-arms regiment shifted the balance of power back in the favor of the Lyran defenders.

In retrospect, De Argall thought the move made good sense. The Legion was a famed combat unit, with an astounding track record. Their loyalty to the Alliance seemed solid enough. With regular House units at a premium, and given the uncertainty of their loyalty in the face of the Skye rebellion, the Archon had been wise to take advantage of the well-trained, well-equipped mercenaries. With no means of communication, de Argall had no way to warn the rebels of the increased enemy presence on Hesperus.

He knew, of course, that his own Twenty-second Skye Rangers were part of the invasion force, but he didn't know what other Skye or anti-Katrina units would be coming in with the main body. To a certain degree, he understood the theory behind the secrecy. It was a case of what you don't know, you cannot give away. If he and his men were detected and captured, interrogation would be next to useless. They knew the approximate date of the attack, but they had no information on the size or composition of the main invasion fleet.

If the Rangers were discovered before the invasion fleet arrived, they were to boost immediately for Hesperus II and engage the defenders. One regiment against three was almost certain suicide, but by sacrificing themselves as dearly as possible, the Rangers would hope to weaken the defenders enough for the remaining Skye troops to succeed.

De Argall also knew that the invasion of Hesperus was going to usher in a new, hopefully limited, tactic. The Separatist fleet would be coming in with at least a couple of WarShips. That was good, since intelligence said the cruiser *Simon Davion* had been assigned to protect the vital system. Combat vessels would be needed to deal with that monster. But there was a secondary purpose to the presence of the armed starships. Any transport JumpShips in-system were to be captured or destroyed, thus preventing the defenders from escaping or sending the interstellar craft for help once the HPG station had been captured.

Attacking JumpShips was a rarity in modern warfare. Even the crusade against Clan Smoke Jaguar had seen only a handful of transports taken under fire. Engaging, much less destroying, JumpShips was considered by almost everyone in the Inner Sphere to be an act of criminal barbarism. But Hesperus II had been deemed a prize of the highest importance.

The entire operation was a gamble, but the prize was worth the risk—independence for Skye.

# 6

## Myoo Highlands, Hesperus II
## Skye Province
## Lyran Alliance
## 22 June 3065

"**C**ome on, Boxer Three. Close it up," Captain Daniel Brewer said, with a mild note of reproof in his voice. Roger Karn, the young MechWarrior piloting the *Apollo* assigned to the fire lance of Brewer's company, had been dragging his mechanical feet all day. Brewer wasn't sure why the younger man had been off his game during this patrol. Normally, Karn was squarely on the ball, but something seemed to be affecting the man's performance. Brewer made a mental note to speak with him once the patrol was finished.

Brewer's company had drawn patrol duty the day after the odd "false alarm" was sounded by the planet's early-warning system. That had been six days ago, and nothing more had happened since. The Colonel had ordained that Legion operations continue as scheduled, though with a heightened state of readiness.

There was something else plaguing Brewer, though he couldn't put his finger on it. Perhaps it was the onset of summer, which had brought with it an unexpected warm front. The unusual weather pattern had raised the daytime temperatures to more than thirty degrees centigrade, almost unheard of on the usually cool planet. The uncommon heat, coupled with the completely normal, oppressive humidity, had caused Brewer to consider cutting his thick braids. The style had once been fashionable with Lyran warrior-nobles, but the mode had long since passed. Brewer still wore them, partly as a link to the past, and partly because he liked the look. Several attractive young ladies also seemed to find his braids most appealing. But in the heat of a BattleMech's cockpit, the heavy braids were almost as bad as a head scarf.

But that wasn't really it, he told himself. There was something more, something beyond the war, and the rebellion, and the bloody heat. Or perhaps beneath it.

Then it came to him, the uncomfortable thought that had been like a splinter in his mind.

Daniel Brewer had joined the Gray Death Legion immediately after the mercenary unit's *last* trip to Hesperus II. Then, he had been on the other side, actually fighting *against* the Gray Death. He had "signed up" at the Archon's insistence, as a sort of peace offering, much in the same way Grayson Carlyle had been appointed Baron of Glengarry.

Over the years, he had continued to act as the Chief Executive Officer of DefHesp and to fulfill his role as the Duke of Hesperus. But in spite of those ties, Brewer had noticed a shift in his primary loyalties. Though he still felt the weight of his responsibilities to Defiance and to Hesperus, he felt his first duty lay with the Gray Death Legion. Now that Grayson Carlyle was gone, Brewer wondered what would become of the Legion, and what would be his role in it? Even more, would he be able to divide his own heart and mind enough to judge impartially between the Legion and DefHesp, should matters be put to the test? He knew that some members of the Board of Directors had been less than pleased when he signed on with the Gray Death. Major Goree, who had a non-voting seat on the board as head of the Defiance Self-Protection Force, had certainly not hesitated to express his displeasure. Would some of the voting Directors try to use that against him to have him removed as CEO? So far, no one had exhibited any such tendencies, but Brewer knew that such actions were part and parcel of the corporate world.

With a sigh, he forced down his misgivings and turned his attention back to his command. Boxer Three's *Apollo* had finally regained its position in the patrol formation, and the company continued its patrol.

Moving through the rugged Myoo Mountains was difficult, sometimes dangerous. Loose, rocky soil safe enough for a man to walk across might suddenly shift beneath the multi-ton weight of a BattleMech. The resulting fall could tear a mechanical limb from its socket or even injure or kill the MechWarrior. Brewer knew that his company, second in the battalion still known as Hassan's Assassins, was up to the challenge, and he thought the opportunity to practice mountain operations in a 'Mech would prove valuable for the future.

The operation was not just a security patrol, but a field-readiness exercise. The men and women of Brewer's company would be expected to live in the field during the week-long patrol. Brewer didn't mind that. As a young man, he had spent quite a bit of time camping and hiking in the rocky uplands. Being cooped up for ten to twelve hours a day in the stuffy cockpit of a BattleMech didn't bother him either. What he really hated about these long-range patrols was the pre-packaged field rations.

The packages were labeled "Meal—Ready-to-Eat," though the common joke was that they were none of the three. Other witticisms held that the initials actually stood for "Meals Rejected by Everyone." To Brewer, the bland meals were as tasty as the cardboard and plastic containers they came in. And the dull gray-brown or orange-red food hardly looked appetizing.

The patrol sweep had taken the company first north out of Maria's Elegy along the Caran River toward the Doering Electronics plant, then west into the mountains. Now, they were on their final leg. Their preplanned route would take them through the Myoo Highlands, where they would pass within a few kilometers of the Defiance Industries complex. Colonel Kalmar-Carlyle wanted everyone in the Legion to get a look at the area around the plant, since the facility would be the primary target of an invasion force.

As Brewer guided his company through a narrow cut in the mountains, the broad plateau on which the facility was situated came into view.

"Attention to orders," he called over the company's general-use frequency. "When we move down out of these hills, I want a standard wedge deployment. Cheng, that means recon lance has the point. Fire and command lances will take left and right trailing flank. Let's try to make it clean this time. I don't want lance leaders having to tell their people where they need to be. Everyone clear on that?"

"Yes, sir," said Sergeant Joseph Cheng, fire lance's veteran commander.

Susan Levy, commander of the reconnaissance lance, was far less formal, answering with a cheerful, "You got it, Boss."

"Okay then. Let's move out,"

Brewer saw Levy's *HM-1 Hitman* wave its manlike right arm, motioning the rest of recon lance, codenamed Shepherd, forward. More than most 'Mechs, the thirty-ton *Hitman* had an inhuman appearance. The machine's left forearm was swollen and misshapen, a trio of medium lasers sprouting from where the hand should have been. A pair of downward-curving horns projected from its head, giving the 'Mech the appearance of a gigantic minotaur. Brewer knew those horns were not mere decorations, but housed the emitters and receiving antenna for the *Hitman's* sophisticated electronics package. An almost perfect recon 'Mech, the *HM-1* mounted a Beagle Active Probe mated to Target Acquisition Gear. A Guardian Electronics Counter-Measures unit helped mask its presence from enemy eyes.

As the recon lance reached the plateau, they began to fan out, putting at least one hundred fifty meters between each 'Mech and its nearest partner. Fire lance, codenamed Boxer, went next, fanning out to the left, but keeping a narrower interval to maintain the ability to concentrate their fire if need be. Brewer was happy to see that Karn was right where he should be. He wondered if Sergeant Chou had taken a quick moment to ream out the younger man.

"Command lance, move out," Brewer called when their turn came to go. His lance went by the call sign Doberman, completing the dog motif imposed upon them by Major Devin, the battalion's commander. The first to move was Sergeant V. K. Kaufman's *Hoplite*. Brewer moved his

*Champion* into formation just to Kaufman's left, near the center of the company formation. Lucy Sal and Dale Ross deployed their *Dervish* and *Grim Reaper* out on the right flank, completing the so-called Iron Triangle formation.

It took a bit of doing to keep the formation together as they moved, but again, half the point of the exercise was to give the Legionnaires experience in a time of relative peace. That way, they could do their jobs without having to fret over the details when the shooting started.

Without warning, a sharp tone sounded in Brewer's headphones. A red discrete bearing the word "radar" flared to life on the *Champion*'s center control panel.

"Boss, we're being scanned!" Susan Levy cried. "My whole board is lit up—radar, ladar, MAD, active IR, everything. And I'm detecting fire-control sensors too. Oh, frak!"

"Levy, what is it?" Brewer demanded. There was no reply. Instead, a high-pitched hissing squeal blanketed the comm channel.

"Does anyone have a visual on Shepherd One?" he called to the rest of his company. "Can anybody see if she's still up?"

"Doberman One . . . Four . . . vis . . . act with Shepherd . . . orders, sir?" The message was so broken by the interference that Brewer could not tell who had spoken, let alone what the gist of the message had been.

Brewer pushed his control sticks forward, bringing his birdlike 'Mech into a jerky trot. He aimed the *Champion*'s blunt nose toward recon lance's last known position. In his viewscreen, he saw the rest of command lance accelerate to keep pace with their commander. He could only hope that fire lance, nearly a kilometer to the northwest, had spotted the movement and would follow his lead.

At a speed of nearly eighty kilometers per hour, it took only a few minutes to close ranks with recon lance. As he crested a small rise, he spotted all four BattleMechs, intact and standing still in the shelter of a small copse of scrub oak trees. The whine in his headset grew louder, becoming all-consuming the closer he got. It began to blanket his sensors, even affecting those that provided the images on his viewscreen.

As Levy had reported, discretes for every kind of sensor used on the modern battlefield lit up on his control panel.

Even more disturbing was the THREAT warning that flashed into existence on his heads up display. Someone had just designated his *Champion* with either a Streak missile or Artemis Fire-Control System. He prayed that the threat warning was not the result of a TAG spotter. If it was, the next thing he experienced might well be the shattering impact of a massive Arrow IV missile strike.

But no missiles rained down on the Legion positions. Instead, the squeal of electronic jamming faded a bit, and a familiar, drawling voice spoke in his ear.

"Attention, intruding BattleMechs. You are approaching the Defiance Industries Security Zone. Leave the area immediately or you will be taken under fire."

"Major Goree, this is Captain Daniel Brewer. Shut down your fire-control and your ECM systems. We are Gray Death Legion 'Mechs here on a routine patrol. Scan us. Our IFF signature will tell you who we are."

"Intruding BattleMechs, I know what your Identify Friend and Foe systems tell us, but you know as well as I do that those systems can be compromised." Goree's answer was flat and emotionless. "I suggest you leave the area immediately."

"Major Goree, shut down your targeting and tracking systems. That is an order!" Brewer screamed into his communicator as though volume alone would cut through the electronic clutter. There was no reply. Brewer switched to the frequency set aside for communicating with the Defiance Self-Protection Force, and repeated his message. Again, only the noise of ECM and ECCM jamming.

Movement caught Brewer's eye. He looked up and spotted a *Gunslinger* marching deliberately toward his position. Its camouflage had been so cunningly painted that the barrel-chested assault 'Mech had been invisible to the naked eye, while its position had been masked by the heavy electronic jamming.

Flanking the big machine were other assault-class 'Mechs, a *Banshee* and an *Atlas*, both of which were probably built right there on Hesperus in the Defiance factory. The fourth was a design Brewer had never seen outside of *BattleTechnology* magazine and intelligence briefings. Squat-legged and low to the ground, resembling some great, metallic, predatory beast, a *BGS-1T Barghest* lumbered along on all fours. Paired lasers and a monstrous LB 20-X autocannon sprouted from the quadruped 'Mech's back. Brewer could see other 'Mechs moving toward his command, though he could not identify the types.

A flash of smoke and flame lit the chest of one of the advancing 'Mechs, and a single smoke contrail leaped across the plateau to impact upon Roger Karn's *Apollo*. There was no explosion, no shattering of armor.

Had to be a NARC beacon, Brewer reasoned, deducing that the single missile had attached a missile homing beacon to the torso of Karn's 'Mech. That would fit in with Goree's trying to scare them off.

"Hold fire, hold fire, Dog Company. Weapons are tight. Hold your fire!" Anger rising in his voice, Brewer shouted into his communicator, praying that the warriors under his command would hear and obey. He switched channels and tried again to raise Goree.

"Goddamit, Major, you stand down, or by God, you'll find yourself in more hurt than you ever imagined possible."

Static was his only answer.

Waving the *Champion*'s stubby, winglike arms, Brewer attracted Sergeant Kaufman's attention. As best he could, considering the jamming blanketing the Legion's communication bands, he signaled his subordinate that the company should withdraw. Kaufman signaled his understanding after only a few moments of gesticulating back and forth. Then the veteran sergeant passed the signal along the lines. Slowly, the Legion 'Mechs began to back away. No one seemed willing to turn his or her back to the Defiance Self Protection Force 'Mechs, almost as though each Legionnaire present feared being shot from behind should they do so.

As they withdrew, the ECM jamming began to fade, eventually lifting altogether.

"Captain, they shot at me!" Karn sounded near tears.

"Steady, boy. It was just a NARC pod." Brewer bit back his anger and tried to speak soothingly. Now that the immediate crisis had passed, he had the time to ascertain that the missile fired at Karn's *Apollo* had indeed been one of the magnetic missile-homing beacons. Such pods were only dangerous if the enemy actually fired "war-shots" at a target to which a NARC pod had been affixed. In that case, the beacon would attract any missile equipped with a NARC seeker-head. Brewer knew the effect could be devastating.

Despite his words, he didn't feel the calm he was trying to impart to his warriors. His heart was burning with a barely controlled rage at Major Goree, who had locked fire-control sensors onto friendly BattleMechs. Perhaps the man had felt justified in his zeal to protect his post; perhaps he had been obeying the directives of the Defiance Industries Board of Directors. But, by God, there was no reason to engage in such a dangerous game of brinksmanship with friendly forces.

Of course, as an officer of the Gray Death Legion, Brewer was obligated to report the incident to Colonel Kalmar-Carlyle, who would handle the situation. But as the CEO of Defiance Hesperus, he would have words to say directly to Major James Goree.

**Gray Death Legion Compound**
**Maria's Elegy, Hesperus II**
**Skye Province**
**Lyran Alliance**
**22 June 3065**

Captain Daniel Brewer slammed back his *Champion*'s cockpit hatch and pulled himself from the machine's control cabin. He yanked off his cooling vest and angrily threw the bulky garment into the arms of his chief technician.

"Captain, I . . ." the man began to say, but Brewer spun on his heel and stalked away down the 'Mech gantry catwalk. Though it had taken nearly a full five hours for his company to return to Maria's Elegy from the Myoo Highlands, his anger still burned hot. Ignoring everyone and everything around him, he headed straight for the Legion's command center. He stopped only once, in the 'Mech bay locker room—just long enough to pull a dark gray jumpsuit on over his MechWarrior shorts and to replace his boots with a pair of scuffed running shoes.

When he reached the office set aside for the Legion's commanding officer, he knocked once, loudly, and without waiting for permission to enter, he jerked the door open and passed inside.

"Colonel, I know you probably heard by now but I—."

Brewer almost choked as he finally realized who was in

the Colonel's office. Aside from his CO and Davis McCall, there were two others present, Stanislau Stevens, the president of the Defiance Hesperus board of directors, and Major James Goree.

"Yes, I've heard, Captain," Lori said sharply. "But why don't you tell me *your* side of things? Then we'll try to sort this thing out."

Brewer forced himself to get his temper under control enough to explain what had happened to his command outside the Defiance complex.

"Well, Colonel, I don't know what these gentlemen told you, but from the *Legion* perspective, here is how it went down. As ordered, I moved my company down into the Myoo Highlands, intending to take them on a close pass-by of the Defiance complex. As ordered, I intended to allow my men the opportunity to familiarize themselves with the area, since the accepted conventional wisdom says we will be engaged there by the enemy when he comes. As my unit approached the area around the complex, Sergeant Levy advised me that she had been scanned and then painted by fire-control sensors."

Brewer continued his narrative, making sure to stress the fact that he had attempted to contact Goree to confirm the identity of his company. He especially highlighted Goree's refusal to accept either the IFF or verbal identification of the Legion 'Mechs.

"That's when they fired a NARC beacon at Private Roger Karn's *Apollo*. I don't know if Karn immediately realized that it was 'only' a NARC pod, or if he froze at being taken under fire from what he thought was a friendly force, or if he was merely waiting to hear the weapons-free command." Brewer started to wind down his story. "In any event, that was when I began to pass the word along the lines, by means of visible hand and arm signals, that we should withdraw. I honestly believe, Colonel, that if we had stayed there for another five minutes, maybe less, we would have been involved in a shooting war with the DSPF."

"Well, Major," Lori said to Goree, without commenting on Brewer's report, "how does that square with your version of events?"

"I can obviously not comment on what was going through Captain Brewer's mind during the incident,"

Goree said. "All I can say is that the captain has the meat of the matter correct. Though, from my standpoint, the reasons behind the details are somewhat different.

"It has *always* been company policy of Defiance Hesperus that no unknown military units be allowed to approach to within less than eight hundred meters of the factory complex without being challenged and warned off. In the past, this challenge and warning have come in the form of first a hard scan, then a weapon lock, and then a verbal warning. Captain Brewer surely must have been aware of these regulations, given his position within DefHesp."

"Yes, Captain, I am aware of the regulations," Brewer spat. "I am also aware that the regulations state the DSPF commander on-scene has discretionary authority to implement or to suspend those regulations as the situation warrants."

"Captain Brewer, I am glad to see that you remember the company regulations so well," Goree said dryly. "As DSPF commander on scene, I *did* exercise discretionary authority. I choose to follow the regulations and warn your people away from the complex. Surely, Captain, you can understand my decision, especially given the history between the Gray Death Legion and Defiance Hesperus?

"Now, I understand your side of the issue, Captain, but unless you elect to exercise your power as the CEO of DefHesp and have me replaced, my decision and my orders will stand. And, Captain, I'd have to suspect that the board of directors might have something to say if you try to fire me."

"Major," Lori put in, "need I remind you that the Gray Death Legion is under contract to the Lyran Alliance and that we are here at the Archon's express order?"

"No, Colonel Carlyle. You don't need to remind me of that. But it doesn't change anything." Goree seemed even less impressed with Lori's admonition. "Y'all can send an HPG message to the LAAF Quartermaster Corps and speak directly with General Lisa Steiner if you want. You can send a message straight to the Archon for all I care. The Defiance Self-Protection Force is *not* part of the Lyran Alliance Armed Forces, and as such is not subject to military regulation, review, or oversight. I don't give a damn if you get ol' Nondi Steiner and the whole Alliance army in here. If they get too close to my fences, I'll still lock 'em up on fire-control."

"Now listen here, *Mister* Goree . . ." Brewer growled, in a tone that suggested he was not speaking as a captain of the Gray Death Legion but as the Chief Executive Officer of Defiance Industries on Hesperus. Lori waved him to silence before he could begin warming to his theme once more.

"Laddie, are ye sure of what it is yer doin'?" McCall said, also ignoring Lori's attempts to silence him. "Are ye sure yer' wantin' to be takin' that sorta attitude with th' Legion?"

He gave the Defiance security man a narrow, black look. "I ken ye've got a first-rate unit out there at yer factory, and they're equipped wi' all th' latest technology yer corporation can provide. But they're only what? Battalion strength? If anyone comes in here with more than a troop o' Star Scouts, they'll aye wipe out yer little army and burn yer factory to th' ground—again."

"Davis!" Lori yelled, finally getting her subordinate to hold his tongue.

Goree bristled. "Lieutenant Colonel, you just sit back here in Maria's Elegy and refuse to protect DefHesp when the invasion comes. Then I'll sit back and watch as your careers go straight to hell." His attitude of bored calm had finally broken at McCall's implied threat. "Maybe I should lodge a few complaints of my own. Maybe I should send a message to Hautpmann-General Rainer Poulin. I think the Skye Province Theater Commander might be interested in what you just said. I know Almida Zec certainly would be."

"Major, you are certainly free to send those messages, if you like," Lori said in a conciliatory tone Brewer had never heard her use. "I certainly can't stop you. You realize the Legion will defend itself in a Bonding Commission court as tenaciously as we do on the battlefield. The legal fight may well continue long after we both are gone, and to what end?

"I'll tell you what, Major, let's try things this way. You want an eight-hundred-meter buffer zone around your complex? I'll make it one full klick. But if your people lock up my 'Mechs again, I may not have time to give the 'weapons free.'

"Remember, Major Goree, the Gray Death Legion is onplanet to help protect your facility, the same as the DSPF is. We need to work together on this one, and designating my 'Mechs with fire-control sensors is not exactly conducive to a spirit of cooperation."

Goree nodded silently, evidently satisfied with Lori's offer. He stood and made to leave. As his hand closed on the doorknob, he paused and spoke over his shoulder. "It's all well and good, Colonel Carlyle, to *say* that you're here to protect us. But, until the bullets start flying, and you and your people stand between us and the invaders instead of siding with them, I'll reserve my judgment. I've seen mercenaries turn their coats a few too many times in the past to be comfortable with your assertions."

Without another word, Goree settled his flat-brimmed black hat on his head, pulling the brim down over his eyes, and left the room.

Much to Brewer's surprise, Lori snatched up an empty coffee cup and made to hurl it at the closed door. In the split second it took her to cock her arm back for the throw, he saw her visage change ever so slightly. The anger was still there, but it had been tamed. She slammed the heavy porcelain vessel back onto her desk.

"I don't know how Gray did it all those years, having to put up with jackass officers like that!" she snapped, not looking at either McCall or himself. She tried to continue, but her voice caught in her throat with a sound like a half-strangled hiccup. Like a blind woman, she groped behind her for her chair and collapsed heavily into it. For a moment she sat still, gazing off into the middle distance as if viewing a scene only she could see. Then her resolve broke, and she buried her face in her hands. Brewer could see her shoulders tense as she fought back the tears.

His own anger melted away at the sight of her. She was no longer his commanding officer, but a woman who'd only recently lost her husband and who'd been thrust into this impossible situation with no time to mourn.

He felt McCall's heavy hand fall on his shoulder and turn him away, ushering him out of the room. The big Caledonian officer followed closely, closing the door behind them and leaving Lori alone with her grief.

# 8

**Southwestern Quadrant, Hesperus III**
**Skye Province**
**Lyran Alliance**
**23 June 3065**

"Graves, you see that?" Leutnant Petar Warner called to his flight leader, staring intently at his fighter's sensor console.

"See what?" First Leutnant Ari Graves called back.

"My MAD scans just jumped halfway off the scale," Warner said. "Then it flicked back to nothing. It was almost like we flew right over something big and metallic." Warner pulled his *Seydlitz* into a tight turn, swinging the light aerofighter back across the airless badlands marring the southwestern quadrant of Hesperus III.

"C'mon, Warner, get back in formation," Graves said. "It was probably a hiccup in your sensors. We haven't got enough fuel in these kites to go flat-hatting around chasing down every stray MAD trace."

"I don't think this is a stray trace. It was big. Big enough almost to be a DropShip," Warner argued. The fighter's O/P 3000 electronics package was usually pretty reliable. If the Magnetic Anomaly Detector said he had overflown a big metal object, Warner was inclined to take the machine's word for it. At the same time, Graves was right. If the *Seydlitz* had one major fault, it was the limited amount of fuel the fighter carried. Primarily designed for fast in-and-out raids, the SYD-21 was an old design, dating back to the original Star League. As newer technologies had been developed and newer class fighters began rolling off production lines, the older machines were sent back to second-echelon troops, like the Twelfth Hesperus Militia, of which Graves and Warner were a part.

"One pass, Leutnant, then we'll get on with the sweep."

"All right, Warner. One pass and that's it," Graves agreed reluctantly.

Warner stood his boxy fighter on its starboard wing and dropped toward the surface of the planet. Graves, taking the trailing position behind his wingman, followed him down.

As Warner twisted his ship upright again, he looked steadily at the MAD display. For a second, nothing more than a background trace showed up on the device's screen. Then, as the *Seydlitz* flashed over a narrow canyon, the instrument, which had been showing nothing more than a background level of magnetism, spiked sharply upward.

"MADman, MADman!" Warner cried excitedly, vindicated by the narrow zigzag of light across the black display.

"You were right, Warner," Graves admitted. "There is something pretty big down there. Pull back up to operational altitude, and let's call this in."

"That's it, sir," the tech said, lightly touching the sensor screen with his finger tip. "They made one high-altitude pass, rolled back in, and made a low-level pass. Now it looks like they're climbing out again."

"Did they spot us?" Tension gave Colonel De Argall's voice a harsh edge.

"Can't say for certain, Colonel," the tech replied. "Only one fighter overflew our position. It all depends on how good that net really is."

De Argall considered the implications of having the enemy fly directly over the narrow canyon in which his regiment's DropShips had landed. In theory, the high-tech "ghillie nets" that his 'Mechs had strung up over the grounded spacecraft should keep them well hidden. The infrared suppressive fabric would mask any heat radiating from the ships' hulls. The drab colors and irregular patterns of the net would serve to make visual detection of the ships more difficult. Tiny ECM units built into the fabric would confuse radar return images, giving the impression of a jumbled, rocky canyon floor rather than a cluster of grounded DropShips beneath an expanse of camouflage netting. The only worry had been if any patrol that did stumble upon their hidden landing zone passed directly over their heads with a Magnetic Anomaly Detector running. The nets were wonderful technology, in theory. In practice the concealing properties of the nets sometimes failed. De Argall had never fully trusted the nets. That was why he insisted that a twenty-four-hour watch be kept on the sensor displays. He had also ordered that at least one lance from each battalion be kept ready to deploy against an enemy force, should one present itself. It looked like the need for an alert force was being thrust upon him despite the precautions he had taken.

"Yup, they've seen us, Colonel," the tech said abruptly. "I'm getting coded traffic from the fighters. They're probably calling in our position."

"Weapons officer, engage the fighters. Notify the other ships to hold their fire until ordered to engage. They may not have spotted all of us. No point in tipping our hand to the enemy."

"SAM! SAM! SAM!" Warner bellowed as he spotted the contrails of what seemed to be a hundred missiles streaking up toward Graves' *Seydlitz*. Half of the missiles streaked past his fighter, but the remainder did not. The light aerospace craft was engulfed in a red-orange fireball. When the explosion dissipated, the *Seydlitz* was still there, looking as though it would fall to pieces any second, but still flying, and still under control.

"Warner," Graves gasped over the radio. "Get clear, they've got a flak trap down there. Get back and warn . . ."

A thick bolt of energy streaked upward to impact with the damaged fighter. The lightning-bright stream of charged particles split the *Seydlitz* in two. Graves did not eject. As the halves of Graves' *Seydlitz* fell toward the surface, Petar Warner stomped hard on his rudder pedal, slewing the fighter around in a bid for a high-speed run back to the safety of his unit's base. Struggling against the G forces created by the tight turn, Warner sent out a message that the militia patrol flight was under heavy attack. Rolling out of the turn, Warner began a series of evasive maneuvers, hoping to throw off his enemy's aim.

Another PPC discharge lashed out at him, missing the wildly jinking fighter by less than a meter. He was bracketed on the other side by paired streams of tracers that seemed to originate from the same spot as the PPC discharge.

A DropShip, Warner figured, struggling to avoid the ground fire. It had to be a DropShip. And a DropShip meant 'Mechs, and 'Mechs mean an invasion.

He thumbed the switch on his control column, opening a broadband communication channel.

Before he could utter a sound, a corkscrewing volley of missiles clawed his fighter from the sky.

"Splash Two," the weapons officer said from his console on the other side of the grounded DropShip's bridge.

"Did either of the fighters get a message off before they were destroyed?" de Argall demanded.

"I don't think so, sir," the sensor operator responded. "I think number two was trying to broadband a distress cry or something, but I don't think he had the time."

"This isn't good, Don," de Argall said to his exec. "If the Lyrans know we're here, this operation may be over before it starts."

"So what do we do?" Nix asked.

"We've got two options. Stay and brazen it out, hoping the Lyrans didn't spot us. Or, we displace to Alternate One."

"Are you certain they spotted us?" Nix scowled, an expression de Argall had come to recognize as one of thoughtfulness rather than displeasure on the part of his executive officer.

"I'm afraid I am, Don," de Argall said. "That coded traffic pretty much cinches it for me. Also, we can't be sure that those two fighters were alone. Granted, we have ground sensors out, but you and I both know those things can be unreliable. We didn't spot those two fighters until they were right on top of us. If they come against us in strength, we may not have any more warning than we did this time. I'd rather not jeopardize the ships and the mission."

"If I may, Colonel, I suggest we displace."

"I agree," de Argall said. "It's going to be risky, but we don't have much choice right now. We can't take the chance that the Lyrans know we're here. If we make a clean displacement, they'll waste time and resources looking for us."

"What if they spot us while we're displacing?" Nix asked.

De Argall shrugged. "Depends on the size of the force they send after us. If it's small enough to destroy without losing any of the ships, we'll engage them and then make a run for Hesperus II. And we'll start raising Cain with the defenders, as ordered. If they spot us, and it's too strong a force for us to destroy, we'll find a place to ground on Hesperus III and make life miserable for the enemy here.

"Either way, I doubt any of us are going to survive the fight. If we're lucky, we'll take a good number of those people with us. If we're very lucky, they might think that we were the *sole* invasion force and drop their guard just in time for the main body to arrive."

De Argall sighed heavily.

"How long to get the nets down and stowed?" he asked Nix. "For all the good they did us, I've half a mind to leave the bloody things here."

Lori reviewed the printed copy of the report filed by Hauptmann Leo Moos, the Twelfth Militia's commanding officer. There was little more to the document than she could have gleaned from a newsfax about the incident. Two *SYD-21 Seydlitz* aerospace fighters, on routine short-range patrol over the southwestern quadrant of Hesperus III, had gone down. Neither pilot had given any indication of distress prior to dropping off radar. The Twelfth's communication center had received part of a coded FLASH message, but the transmission had been interrupted before more than a few words came through.

She lowered the pages and looked at the vidcom unit that was part of the computer terminal built into her desk. He was a slight, fair-haired man with several small scars across his cheeks and forehead. Lori knew from the text of the report that Moos had spent several hours flying his *F-*

*90 Stingray* fighter back and forth along the intended flight path of his missing ships. To her mind, such concern for the men under his command made him a good officer. Unlike either Major Goree or General Zambos, Moos seemed to have no problem with the Legion's presence on Hesperus, and less trouble asking for their aid.

"It seems, Hauptmann, that you've done everything that could be done," Lori said, laying the report aside. "What is it you want the Legion to do for you?"

"Colonel, if you could loan us a couple of your fighters and pilots, I'd like to widen the search. Graves was an experienced man, but Warner was still a little green. I suppose it is possible they wandered off course. I just don't have the resources to conduct an extensive search. My men have been down for just about eight hours now. Their survival packs have enough air for twenty-four. They haven't got a lot of time left."

"Why did you wait so long before coming to us?"

"I have nothing personal against you or the Legion, Colonel. I believe in trying to clean up my own mess before going to anyone else."

Lori smiled with the simple pleasure of finding another Lyran officer who didn't seem to hate her and the Legion for their actions in 3057.

Moos continued as though he hadn't noticed. "I would have looked silly coming to ask you to send a couple of fighter lances all the way out here only to find that my men had pranged their ships along their planned flight path. But now, things are different. My men are either *way* off course, or they're down in one of the narrow canyons in the badlands. Either way, I haven't got the manpower or the ships to mount an intensive search. If I have any hope at all of finding my men before they run out of air, it lies with the Legion."

Lori nodded gravely. "Just a moment, Colonel," she said, muting the comm unit's audio pickups.

"What do you think, Julio?" When the report of the missing pilots had come across her desk, Lori had summoned the Legion's wing commander. Vargas sat backward in a ladder-backed chair, straddling the seat.

"I think we should help, Colonel." Vargas scratched his

right ear as he spoke. "Militia or not, no pilot deserves to go out that way."

"That isn't what I meant, and you know it," Lori snapped.

"*Si*, Colonel, I know it." Vargas said contritely. "I can take a couple of lances out there and help with the search. Maybe Major Powers might want to take some of her scouts out too. If those canyons are as narrow as they look on the maps, it will be rough getting fighters in and out safely. If those pilots are down in one of them, we're going to have the devil's own time rescuing them."

Lori switched the comm unit back on and said, "All right, Hauptmann, we're sending some help. I'll send you two fighter lances and a platoon of my armored scouts."

"Good enough, Colonel," Moos said, clearly relieved at the promise of help. "And thank you."

"I just pray we can find your men in time, Hauptmann." With that, Lori severed the connection.

"Well, Colonel, if you'll contact Major Powers, I'll get my boys ready to fly," Vargas said, getting to his feet.

"Not you, Julio," Lori said, bringing him up short.

"What?"

"I said, not you. Give this one to Captain Staedler." Lori held up her hand to forestall any argument. "She can handle the search. I need you and the rest of the Legion brass right here."

Vargas sighed. "*Si*, Colonel," he said finally. He had apparently been prepared to argue the point, but had decided against it.

As Vargas left the office, Lori tapped her intercom.

"Mick, have the battalion commanders meet me in the briefing room in fifteen minutes."

"Right away, Colonel," her orderly replied.

"And please get hold of Major Powers. I've got a job for her."

The sound of a DropShip passing overhead, the roar of its powerful engines barely muted by the building's structure, briefly drowned out all other sounds in the briefing room. The big spacecraft carried four of the Legion's fighters and one squad of infantry scouts, the latter outfitted with the light, highly mobile powered armor the mercenary company developed for the purpose of long-range reconnaissance.

When the deep rushing sound faded, Lori picked up her train of thought.

"So that's all we know," she said, concluding her briefing on the events of the past twenty-four hours.

"What concerns me, Colonel, is the fact that we've had two unexplained and seemingly unrelated aerospace incidents in the past week," Major Thomas Devin said, leaning back in his chair. Devin had taken command of First Battalion, First 'Mech Regiment, only a few years ago, when Andrei Denniken retired.

"I'm a bit concerned about that too, Colonel," Rae Houk admitted. Like Devin, Houk was a Legion veteran who rose to command as a replacement for a senior officer. In her case, it was not retirement that opened up a command slot but the death of Hassan Ali Khalid.

"So am I," Lori said. "It may be a coincidence, but I somehow doubt it. It's all a little *too* coincidental. We'll let Captain Staedler and Lieutenant M'Dahlla conduct their search before we do anything too radical. For now, though, I'm going to up the Legion's readiness status—again. As of now, consider that we are on condition yellow."

"Colonel, are you sure that's wise?" Houk asked. "If we ratchet up our alert status, we may be letting ourselves in for some problems. I mean, things have been pretty intense ever since Goree's boys nearly provoked a 'friendly fire' incident."

"Friendly fire, isn't," Devin muttered quietly, eliciting a chuckle from the Legion officers.

"Maybe not, Tom," Houk continued. "But if we go kicking up our status, and we get into a close-contact situation with the DSPF, or with one of the Lyran units, our boys may be wound so tight that we go over the edge into a real shooting incident."

"There's somethin' else t' consider, Colonel," McCall said. "I never expected t' hear m'self say this. Maybe it's old age creepin' up on me. But if we go on yellow alert, we're going t' be rotatin' pilots in and out of their cockpits by companies, every four to six hours. That kind of schedule is hard t' keep up. Ye ken what I'm sayin'. Th' taut bow loses its strength."

Houk laughed. "Davis, I thought you were a Presbyterian, and here you are quoting Buddha."

"Och, weel," McCall said, allowing his New Caledonian accent freedom to run. "That lad may have been a *sassanach*, a foreigner, but he had a rare grasp o' things fer a' that."

"I take your point, Davis," Lori said, chuckling slightly. "And yours too, Rae. So here's my decision: the Legion *will* go to condition yellow, but only for seventy-two hours. After that, if there are no major incidents, we'll scale things back a bit. If things stay quiet for a week, we'll go back to green.

"Just remember people, the rebels *are* coming to Hesperus. It's not a matter of *if*, it's a matter of *when*. And when they do get here, I want us to be ready to meet them."

Lori looked around at her officers. "Any questions? No? Okay, that's it then. Dismissed."

As the meeting broke up, the Legion officers drifted out in singles, pairs, and trios, each heading off to attend to his or her appointed duties. Within moments, Lori was left alone in the briefing room, praying that she had made the right decision.

# 9

**Badlands, Hesperus III**
**Skye Province**
**Lyran Alliance**
**25 June 3065**

**C**aptain Carla Staedler eased her upgraded *CSR-V12 Corsair* aerospace fighter into a gentle bank to port. She'd seen something glittering in the shadows of a deep canyon. She wanted another look.

Swooping in low over the surface of Hesperus III's badlands, she put her fighter on a course parallel with the narrow canyon. With a flick of the control column, she half-rolled the *Corsair* to get a better view of the ground. Almost immediately, Staedler caught a glimpse of the odd, silver-white gleam that had attracted her attention. Whatever it was, it definitely seemed to have been man-made. Rolling the *Corsair* upright, she checked the fighter's sensors. It was too difficult to tell against the background count of the mineral-rich planet, but it seemed that there was something metallic lying on the ground at the bottom of the canyon.

"Goshawk One to *Phobos*, I have a possible contact at grid six-niner-eight-five-three-alpha. Definitely metallic. My sensors indicate it masses around fifteen tons. It could be what's left of one of those fighters. I can't tell. The contact is at the bottom of one of those damn canyons. We're going to have to use the scouts to check this one out."

"*Phobos* to Goshawk One," came the reply. "We're on our way. ETA your position, ten minutes."

Staedler acknowledged the message as she brought her fighter around for another low pass over the site. Again, the metallic shine caught her eye. In that instant, she made a decision.

"Goshawk Two, remain on station to guide *Phobos* in if they need it," she called to her wingman. "I'm going to land and see if I can figure out what that is down there."

"That isn't part of our mission profile, Captain," Warrant Officer Anson Towsley reminded her. "We're supposed to search from the air and guide the scouts in if we see something."

"I know that, Towsley," Staedler barked. "But there might be a pilot down there."

"Yeah, and if you try to land in that canyon, there might be *two* pilots down there. Maybe two *dead* pilots down there," Towsley shot back.

"I'm going in," Staedler repeated, ignoring her wingman.

Rolling the *Corsair* through a tight turn, she brought the fighter into line with the narrow canyon. With a deft touch on the stick and pedals, she let the craft drift down toward the deep gash in the earth. Had the operation taken place on Hesperus II, such an approach to landing would have been difficult. The *Corsair*, with its relatively tiny wings, had a stall speed of one hundred fifty kilometers per hour. Here on Hesperus III, with its nearly nonexistent atmosphere, the *Corsair* was relying on brute strength to keep itself airborne, making a low-speed approach nearly impossible.

Staedler flew on pure instinct, her eyes never still, constantly flicking between the air-speed indicator and altimeter to the tips of the fighter's narrow wings. She gentled the big GM 200 engines as much as she dared. Even so, the walls of the ground rushed up at her at an alarmingly fast rate, seeming to narrow before her.

"No good," she said, hauling back on the stick and shoving the throttle forward.

"Boss, you okay?" Towsley asked anxiously.

"I'm fine," she said. "That canyon is too narrow for this kite. We're going to have to wait for the scouts."

*     *     *

A few minutes later, the *Phobos*, one of the Legion's first *Union*-class DropShips, swept in low across the badlands, touching down one hundred meters from the spot where Captain Staedler had landed her fighter.

Making certain her suit was sealed against the near-vacuum outside, Staedler popped her canopy and slipped from the *Corsair*'s cockpit. As her feet touched the gritty, tan soil, a small door slid open on the DropShip's hull. One by one, several soldiers swarmed down the ladder and dropped from the hatchway. The first of them, a man nearly the size of a Clan Elemental, sauntered toward Staedler's fighter. His face was masked by the closed faceplate of his light scout armor, but she knew only one individual of that size in the Gray Death armored scouts: Lieutenant M'Dahlla of the first scout platoon.

"Good to see you, Captain," the giant boomed over the short-range communicator mounted in his helmet. "I thought you were supposed to stay airborne and guide us in, not try to make the rescue yourself. Or did you propose to cheat us out of earning our pay?"

"Not a chance, Lieutenant," Staedler said, taking M'Dahlla's extended hand. "I like flying too much, and your job is too easy for a skilled operator like me. It would be a step down."

The scout laughed, a deep rolling sound, and laid a mechanical hand on Staedler's shoulder. "Really, Captain, you should not have risked trying to land in the canyon. That was foolish. You should have waited for us to arrive."

Staedler took no offense. Not only was M'Dahlla right; he genuinely cared for everyone in the Legion. His concern made her a bit uncomfortable. She realized she did not know if M'Dahlla was his first or last name, or even if he had another name. She had never heard anyone call him anything other than M'Dahlla.

"Now shall we go and see what we can see?" he asked, again patting her on the shoulder.

Despite the mass of the powered armor encasing his body, M'Dahlla moved as lightly and gracefully as Staedler did in her pressurized flight suit. As they reached the edge of the canyon, he knelt down, leaning over the rim and bracing himself with his hands. For some time, he gazed into the shadowed depths.

Staedler guessed he was cycling through the various sensors mounted in the scout armor's helmet, trying to get a good look at what lay in the canyon below. Again, she experienced a faint twinge of envy. The only sensors she had to rely on once she climbed out of her fighter's cockpit were a set of "Eyeballs, Mk I," as the soldier's humor referred to one's organs of sight. In the modern combat environment, a warrior's eyes were the least sophisticated viewing device available, and the most critical. If a soldier did not use his eyes—to look around, to observe, to read the displays provided by the electronic sensors—he was not only blind, he was probably dead, and just didn't know it yet.

"Hard to say, Captain," M'Dahlla said, straightening up at last. "Looks like we are going to have to go down there. Have you seen anything resembling a trail or any indication that this canyon opens out onto level ground anywhere?"

"No, Lieutenant. Nothing."

"Ah, well, it looks like we jump."

"Jump?" Staedler echoed in surprise. "Into this, with no clear idea what the floor of this canyon is like? Isn't that going to be a little dangerous?"

"Much like your attempt to land?" M'Dahlla asked mildly. "Do not worry, Captain. We will be fine."

The eight-man platoon formed up on the edge of the canyon and, at a signal from their commander, leapt off into the void. Staedler, along with a few members of the *Phobos'* crew, rushed to the precipice to watch as the flare of jump packs lit the darkening sky. The camouflaged battle armor became harder to discern as the scouts dropped smoothly into the canyon. The dim glow of the jump packs helped the watchers on the rim track the descending soldiers.

Then, the flares died out.

"We are down and safe," M'Dahlla's voice broke from Staedler's communicator. "You can stop worrying about us, Captain."

"What about the wreck?" she asked anxiously.

"We are about fifty meters off. From here, it does look like a crashed aerospace fighter." M'Dahlla was silent for a few moments. Then, "It does appear to be a fighter, though it is in bad shape."

"Can you tell what brought it down?" Staedler asked.

"No, Captain, I cannot. The ship is not intact. It seems to have broken up sometime before impact. I see one section, which may be its engine, lying about twenty meters to the north. This section seems to be the bulk of the fuselage. I cannot see the cockpit. Just a moment . . . Yes, Captain I have some numbers for you. They must be the ship's registration. Are you ready to copy?"

"Hang on a minute." Staedler activated her gauntlet-mounted personal data unit, then said, "Go ahead."

"The number is partial. It reads: seven-tango-whiskey-mike-two." M'Dahlla repeated the alphanumeric string twice more.

"Stand by, Lieutenant." Tapping a control stud on the data unit's keypad, Staedler's heart fell at the information displayed on the tiny screen.

"That's one of our missing fighters," she said. "The pilot's name is First Leutnant Ari Graves. Is there any sign of him? Or of the other ship?"

"I am sorry, Captain. I can see nothing of the pilot or of the other fighter." M'Dahlla's voice was sad. "I will divide my platoon into squads, and we will search along this canyon in both directions. I will contact you if we find anything."

It was only minutes before he spoke again.

"Once again, I am sorry, Captain, but we have found the pilot. He is dead. It appears that he died upon impact with the ground. He is still strapped into his seat, although it looks as if he *did* try to eject. The upper handles have been pulled, but apparently the seat did not fire."

"Dammit!" Staedler cursed. Though Graves had not been a member of the Legion, he was a fellow pilot, one of a band of brothers extending back well over a millennium to the days when men first took to the skies to do battle in fighters of wood and canvas. For a man to die because of something so stupid as an ejection-seat failure was a tragedy greater even than the loss of a valuable, irreplaceable life.

Staedler asked the scout if he could determine what had happened to the fighter.

"Not a clue, Captain. I am looking at a wreck in three large pieces, with many smaller ones scattered across several hundred meters. Even if it were intact, I am not an engineer or a crash investigator. I could be looking right at the cause and not recognize it."

"Can you see the flight data and cockpit voice recorders? They'll be fluorescent, orange metal boxes about eighteen centimeters by ten. If you can find them, they may hold some clues as to what happened here."

"We will look for them, Captain, but we should not spend too much time in the search. There is still one missing fighter out there somewhere. *That* pilot may still be alive."

As it turned out, M'Dahlla's scouts located both recording devices, but they never found Petar Warner's fighter. On the return trip back to Hesperus II, the mood aboard the *Phobos* was solemn.

"I'm sorry Colonel, General," Staedler said wearily. Lori and Hauptmann-General Ciampa had been waiting on the spaceport tarmac for her. "We couldn't find the second fighter. There are too many narrow canyons, ravines, and such. Maybe if we had twice as many people, twice as much time, and half as much area to cover, we would have been able to track him down."

"I'm sure you did everything humanly possible, Captain," Ciampa said in a neutral tone. "Thank you."

"We did find the flight leader's voice and data recorders," Staedler said quickly. "We'll send them over to your command center for analysis. Maybe they'll tell us why the fighters went down."

"Again, Captain, thank you." With that, Ciampa turned away.

"I'm sorry, Colonel," Staedler said plaintively. "We tried. I don't know what more we could have done, short of dropping the scouts into every one of those damnable canyons."

"And I'm sure Lieutenant M'Dahlla and Major Powers would agree with that decision, Captain. You're right. There was little else to be done. I hate leaving people behind as much as you do. And I know that's why you violated orders and tried to land in that canyon yourself."

The sudden swerve in the conversation caught Staedler off guard.

The colonel's expression was stern. "Don't worry, Carla,

I'm not going to bust you—this time. But, if you ever try something like that again, if you ever endanger one of *my* fighters, not to mention the pilot inside it, by disregarding orders, I'll bounce you out. Do you understand, Captain?"

"Yes, Colonel," Staedler answered, relieved to get off so lightly. "So, what do we do now?"

"Well, for the moment, I want you to get yourself a good meal and some sack time," her commander said. "In the meantime, I have a few calls to make."

"Thank you for the warning, Colonel," Major Goree drawled into his end of the line. "Now what do y'all intend to do about this?"

"Major, perhaps you didn't hear me," Lori said, surprised at the Defiance officer's nonchalant reception of her report. "I just told you that two Hesperus Militia fighters have gone down. One is missing, and it looks as if the other may have been *shot* down. I strongly suspect that there is a hostile force present in the Hesperus system. What they are waiting for, I have no idea, but I'm almost positive that they're out there."

"I heard you the first time, Colonel," Goree said. "But, being as how your Gray Death Legion is the only unit insystem with aerospace assets, I repeat, what do you intend to do about it? Until your phantom enemy grounds and launches an attack, there isn't much I can do, now is there?"

"Major why are you being so pig-headed about this?" Lori snapped.

"I'm not being pig-headed, Colonel, I'm being practical. We don't have any aerospace assets beyond the antiaircraft batteries built into our defense grid. You say there is an enemy in system? Fine. Your 'Death Eagles' are going to have to deal with them in space. When the enemy does ground, and when they *do* attack the Defiance complex, then me and my boys will get involved. Until then, I believe it is *your* problem, Colonel."

Before Lori could spit back the rejoinder that was forming on her lips, Goree cut the connection.

"Nice sort o' fella, is he no'?" McCall commented. He had been sitting on the corner of Lori's desk during her conversation with Goree. "And not t' take his side o' things, Colonel, but what *are* we plannin' to do?"

"What *can* we do, Davis? Like he said, we're the only ones on this rock with aerospace assets, unless you count the *Simon Davion*—and they've got their own orders to attend to. I think our only option is to maintain the yellow alert indefinitely. Get hold of Julio and tell him I want a twenty-four-hour Barrier Combat Air Patrol at least over Maria's Elegy and the Defiance plant. I know it's going to put a strain on our pilots, but a BARCAP will give us a little bit of lead time when the attack does finally happen."

McCall nodded and stood up to leave Lori's office. She kept her expression neutral, but in her heart she couldn't help wishing for the hundredth time that day that Grayson had not left her and the Legion to deal with this mess on their own.

# 10

**Gray Death Legion Compound**
**Maria's Elegy, Hesperus II**
**Skye Province**
**Lyran Alliance**
**28 June 3065**

The sound of running feet echoed in the corridor beyond Lori's office. She looked up from the hardcopy report she'd been reading just in time to see her door burst open. Mick Cornwell, her orderly, stood framed in the portal.

"Colonel, a report from the comm center. They just picked up one helluva big IR flare." Cornwell paused to catch his breath. "This time, it's the real thing. They figure at least one big JumpShip, maybe more."

Lori dropped the report. Whatever had downed the militia fighters was now unimportant. She brushed past the young man and headed for the building's front door. Outside, she found Davis McCall and Julio Vargas clambering into a hover jeep. She slid into the front passenger seat and slapped the driver on the shoulder.

"Let's go. Comm center."

The young man engaged the air-cushion vehicle's drive and sped off across the tarmac. Lori hung on grimly as the driver careened around the corner of a 'Mech bay, swerving to avoid hitting a parked Drillson heavy hover tank.

"Take it easy, lad," McCall bellowed from the back seat.

"Yer no in a race, an' there's no prize if ye don't get us there in one piece."

The driver nodded and cut the jeep's speed slightly. Shortly after that, he brought the vehicle skidding to a halt. Lori jumped out, thankful to have solid ground beneath her feet again. Followed by her officers, she darted inside the port's main communications center and ran down a hallway.

Near the end of that corridor, two guards wearing the dark blue and green fatigues of a Lyran infantryman barred their way. Lori flashed her ID at them, eliciting a nod from the young, fresh-faced corporal who seemed to be in charge. As she passed inside the secure communications center control room, she noted the fear in the young man's eyes.

"Thanks, Corporal," she said, pausing for a moment. "You're doing a good job."

"Th . . . thank you, Colonel," the guard stammered. The aura of fear diminished, replaced by a nascent look of confidence.

Lori clapped him on the shoulder and stepped inside the darkened room. "General Ciampa?" she called above the low hum of the voices of the technicians gathered in the room.

A woman wearing the black-ribbed jumper and four Fletching bars of a Chief Warrant Officer came up to greet her. "The general's not here," she said. "I'm Chief Sellars, in charge of this station. General Ciampa is out of position. She's gone into town for the day. We're still trying to reach her."

"Where is Colonel Brennan?" Lori asked, naming Ciampa's second-in-command.

"Don't know, Colonel," Sellars admitted. "I haven't seen her either. We've managed to contact General Zambos at his command center in Maldon. I told him what we've got. He's getting his troops ready for the invasion."

Lori nodded. Zambos' duty station was all the way on the other side of Hesperus II at Maldon, a huge mining installation owned by Defiance Industries. If the invaders stuck to the pattern, the mines would be left alone in favor of an attack on the main Defiance complex. But Lyran command had decided—rightly so, in Lori's opinion—that they could not rely on the Skye rebels to be predictable.

So, Zambos' Thirty-sixth Lyran Guards had been moved to Maldon shortly after the Legion's arrival.

"*Is* this the invasion, Chief?" Lori asked.

"If it isn't, this is the most through-system traffic I've ever seen at one time," Sellars replied, gesturing toward a holographic representation of the Defiance system. "We first picked up the IR flare here at the nadir point. Then, as the thermal radiation began to fade, we were able to discern at least three starships."

As she spoke, various icons in the holographic display lit up briefly.

"It's really too far to tell, but if I had to guess, I'd say at least one of them is a WarShip."

"WarShips?" Lori's thoughts were brought up by the Warrant Officer's calmly spoken words.

Sellars nodded. "Yes, Colonel, WarShips. When the Separatists rebelled, several ships' crews mutinied, some *en masse*. The Alliance lost at least two *Fox*-class corvettes. *And* there are rumors that Victor Davion is lending the rebels aid and technical support. I wouldn't put it past him to be giving them WarShips as well. I've already contacted the *Simon Davion* and given her an intercept vector."

"Intercept vector?" Vargas exclaimed. "Are all the ships moving insystem?"

"Not yet." Sellars pointed to a wedge-shaped scarlet symbol. "But I'm almost certain this is a WarShip of around two hundred fifty thousand tons. That makes it something like a corvette or a destroyer. It could also be a fully loaded *Monolith* Class JumpShip, but I don't think so. This other one might be another corvette. We just can't get a solid reading on it. Either way, we're in one helluva lot of trouble."

# 11

**Bridge, LAS Simon Davion**
**Zenith Jump Point**
**Skye Province**
**Lyran Alliance**
**28 June 3065**

**S**everal hundred thousand kilometers away from the communication center control room at Maria's Elegy, on the bridge of the *Avalon*-class cruiser *LAS Simon Davion*, two other officers had just come to the same conclusion about the uninvited visitors to the Hesperus system.

Leutnant-Kommodore Dieter Bern turned to his executive officer, with a look of grim determination. "Looks like this is it, Speer."

"*Ja, Herr* Kommodore," Kaptain Geron Speer said. "Long-range scans suggest both leading vessels are *Fox*-class corvettes."

"Wonderful," Bern said under his breath. He had heard rumors that a number of the small, agile WarShips had been seized by their mutinous crews and turned over to the Skye rebels. Individually, the tough little *Foxes* would have been no match for the *Simon Davion*. Together, the heavily armed corvettes would be able to dance around his cruiser and pick her apart. To make things worse, both rebel crews were all veteran spacers. "How long until we know for certain?"

"Fifteen minutes, sir. Maybe ten, if we really push the engines."

Bern considered his options. Although the *Simon Davion* was the pinnacle of modern ship design, she was still mostly untested. She had performed admirably during her space trials and shakedown cruise. But even those rigorous days of testing and retesting had been conducted under peaceful conditions. They just could not compare to the stresses of combat.

"All right," he said at last. "Take us to flank speed. If we can reach the invaders before they reach Hesperus II, perhaps we can drive them off before they drop, or at least cut their numbers back somewhat." He looked over toward his communications officer. "Comm, notify General Ciampa that we are moving to engage the invaders."

"Kommodore, General Ciampa is not in command at Maria's Elegy," the young officer replied. "I have been advised that neither she nor Colonel Brennan is on the base. Command has been assumed by the most senior officer present, Colonel Lori Kalmar-Carlyle of the Gray Death Legion."

"You mean Hesperus is in the hands of a mercenary?" Speer barked. "A mercenary who has invaded this planet herself once before?"

"So it seems, Kaptain," Bern said, "but I suppose there are worse choices than the Gray Death Legion to defend Hesperus."

Even as he finished speaking, Bern felt the steel deck vibrate beneath his feet. A low thrum, more felt than heard, rang through the ship as the big maneuvering drives devoured an increased flow of fuel, converting the complex chemicals into flame, heat, and thrust. While it couldn't be said that the *Simon Davion* surged ahead, the acceleration was nevertheless perceptible to a spacer's keen perception.

Bern divided his attention between the ship's clock, the holographic image of the Hesperus system before him, and the constant stream of reports and requests coming his way.

"Kommodore, two of the vessels have begun moving toward us on an intercept course," a sensor tech reported.

"How long until contact?"

"At the current rate of closure? Six minutes."

"Very well. Sound General Quarters."

No sooner had Bern given the order than a loud klaxon sounded throughout the ship. The fluorescent lighting strips set into the *Simon Davion*'s overhead flickered. When they came back on, the diffused white light had been replaced by an unearthly blue glow.

In theory, the blue lights were intended to help technicians and sensor operators read their instruments more easily. The eerie lighting had the additional effect of telling all aboard that the ship had gone to battle stations.

"Kommodore, the ship is cleared for action. All stations report manned and ready," Speer said crisply. "Shall I launch fighters?"

"Not yet, Kaptain. Let's allow them to get a bit closer."

"What do you intend to do, sir?"

"All we can do is try to prevent the enemy from flanking us and concentrate our fire on the smaller target," Bern said.

As if on cue, the sensor tech sang out, "Second vessel now appears to be a destroyer, possibly of the *Whirlwind* Class."

"Distance to target?" Bern asked.

"Distance to lead target now five hundred kilometers. Distance to trailing target is seven hundred kilometers. Both targets now positively identified as *Fox*-class corvettes. The warbook says number one is the *Indefatigable*. Number two is designated the *Illustrious*."

"Weapons officer, prepare a full spread of Killer Whales," Bern ordered. "Get them ready to launch, but do not lock them on target until I give the word. Then I want those missiles out of the tubes in record time."

Deep in the bowels of the WarShip, four huge rotary magazines turned ponderously on their spindles. Each stopped as a fat-bodied antiship missile came into line with the AR-10 launch tubes. Officially designated as ASM-420, the big ship-killer had come to be known by the nickname Killer Whale, for its size and its lethal, explosive bite.

"Killer Whales in tubes one through four, ready for launch," the weapons officer confirmed.

"Range to trailing target?"

"Range to trailing target, now five hundred twenty kilometers," came the reply. "Lead target now four hundred fifty kilometers. Lead target is now within extreme range."

Bern acknowledged the data with a curt, "Very well."

"Detecting fire-control radar. Lead target is attempting to lock missiles."

"Acknowledged," Bern said. "Helmsman, maintain course and speed."

"They are locking missiles," Speer said, his voice tight with excitement and fear. "If we hold this course and speed, they will be in optimum firing range in two minutes."

"Thank you, *Herr* Speer."

"Kommodore, we should lock our missiles as well."

"Not yet."

"Launch detection!" the sensor operator shouted, with a tinge of panic. "Lead target has launched missiles."

"How many?"

"Two, I think. Yes, two missiles. They have acquired and are homing."

"Point-defense online," Bern ordered calmly. "Helmsman, on my command, come to heading two-nine-zero, mark four-five."

Bern watched as two narrow threads of red stretched across the main viewscreen toward the *Simon Davion*.

"Missile impact in twenty seconds," the sensor operator called. "Fifteen seconds . . . ten . . ."

"Helmsman, now!" This time there was none of the easy calm that had characterized Bern's previous commands. "Weapons officer, lock up the trailing target. Be ready to fire on my command."

The helmsman hauled the *Simon Davion*'s control yoke hard to the left and pulled it back into his chest. As gracefully as a vessel massing over three-quarters of a million tons could manage, the cruiser swung away from her original course, turning through seventy degrees to the left and climbing away at forty-five. Bern could see the helmsman struggling against the artificial resistance built into the ship's controls. The resistance had been a feature of spaceship controls from the days of the original Star League as a means of feedback, letting the helmsman know that he *was* turning the ship.

The sensor operator's voice climbed half an octave as he chanted the word, "Impact."

There was no impact. Antiship missiles had the longest

reach of any naval weapon, but at a distance of nearly five hundred kilometers, it was next to impossible to hit a target, especially one taking evasive maneuvers. The missiles slid past the *Simon Davion*'s tail, missing by more than a dozen kilometers.

"Ease your helm," Bern called to the helmsman. "Come right zero-four-five degrees. Weapons officer, lock up the trailing target for a missile strike. Forward gauss and PPC batteries target the leading vessel. Fire on my command."

"Coming right through zero-four-five, sir," Speer said.

"Helm amidships."

"Missiles locked on trailing vessel," the weapons officer said.

"Weapons stand by." Bern gazed steadily at the two tiny holographic images of the enemy vessels. For several seconds, he remained motionless, watching the miniature ships as the battle unfolded.

"Missiles away."

The huge WarShip trembled slightly as four fifty-ton Killer Whale antiship missiles blasted free of their launch tubes. Even as the tubes' outer doors were cycling closed, the huge rotary launchers were moving to bring the next missile into firing position.

"Missiles away, sir," the weapons officer said, repeating an age-old litany dating from the days when men first hunted each other aboard tiny diesel-electric submarines. "Missiles one, two, three, and four have left the tubes and are running hot and straight."

"Forward batteries, fire," Bern rapped out.

This time, there was no perceptible effect on the ship when the monstrous naval gauss rifles and particle projection cannons clustered in the *Simon Davion*'s nose unleashed their lethal payloads. To someone outside the vessel, the only visible sign would have been a flat white flash illuminating the outer surface of two gun blisters where the big mass-driver cannons were located. The PPC discharges were by far more spectacular. Twinned strokes of man-made lightning ripped through space to savage the nose of the approaching *Indefatigable*. At almost the same instant, a pair of nickel-iron slugs, each nearly the size of a small ground car, smashed into the *Fox*-class corvette's thimble-shaped nose, just forward of one of her primary sensor arrays. A second later, there came a pair of bright flashes on the holographic display as two of the Killer Whale missiles detonated against the *Illustrious*'s hide. Though hardly insignificant, the damage inflicted by the big antiship missiles was not enough to penetrate the corvette's tough skin.

The *Indefatigable* looked to be falling off to starboard, but Bern knew better. The nimble corvette was maneuvering to bring the greater weight of its broadside guns to bear.

Ordinarily, he might have been tempted to follow it. Alone, the *Simon Davion* outclassed either of her opponents. But being outnumbered two to one was never a good thing.

"Helm, make for the *Illustrious*. Weapons Officer, weapons are free. Fire on the *Indefatigable* as your guns bear. Give me four more Killer Whales as soon as the tubes are reloaded."

"Whales up, sir," the weapons officer said.

"Launch!" the sensor operator yelled. "Multiple launches from both ships!"

"Helm hard to port! Down twenty!" Bern shouted.

The *Simon Davion*'s deck pitched forward and to the left as the helmsman slammed the control yoke hard over and forward. The big WarShip responded, but slowly, painfully slowly. At least eight missiles smashed into the *Simon Davion*'s nose and port side.

For all her mass, the cruiser shuddered as armor was blasted from her hull. Bern staggered, catching himself against the back of his command chair. Kaptain Speer was thrown off his feet and landed on his hands and knees with a yelp of pain. When he stood up, he was cradling his broken left wrist in his right hand.

"Get to sick bay, *Herr* Speer," Bern ordered.

"With all due respect, *Herr* Kommodore, I will remain at my post," Speer replied, while a bridge crewman wrapped an air splint around his wrist. "I can do you more good here than I can in sick bay."

"More incoming!" the sensor operator called, cutting short any further argument. This time the impacts were less shattering. More conventional, though no less dangerous, naval autocannon and laser fire clawed at the big WarShip's skin.

"Lock the missiles onto the *Illustrious* and fire as soon

as you have the solutions," Bern called to his chief gunnery officer.

"Target locked. Missiles away."

"Helm, reverse your turn. Cut between them."

Speer, his eyes somewhat glazed with pain, goggled at his commander.

"It's a gamble, Speer," Bern said, "but if we break their line and swing around under the *Illustrious*'s stern, we might be able to put her out of action before the *Indefatigable* rounds on us."

"That's a helluva gamble, sir."

"I know, but it's our best bet. Otherwise they'll keep dancing around us, concentrating their fire on one section of our hull and chewing us to pieces."

He turned to the thick-set woman with graying black hair and gave a command. "Launch the fighters. Tell them to try to keep the *Indefatigable* off us until we take out the *Illustrious*."

"Aye sir," the woman responded. She adjusted the lip-mike suspended on a wire-thin boom from her ear piece and said, "Launch all fighters. Target the *Indefatigable*."

Almost immediately, the holodisplay depicted the launch of the first four of the twelve fighters housed in the *Simon Davion*'s hangar bays.

Leutnant-Kommodore Dieter Bern could do little except watch for the next several minutes as the battle raged around him. His officers and crew were among the best the Lyran Alliance had to offer, and they could do their jobs without interference from the *Simon Davion*'s commanding officer.

As the battle cruiser passed between the rebel WarShips, she savaged the *Indefatigable*'s starboard aft quarter and the *Illustrious*'s starboard fo'c'stle. But she took a beating in return.

Damage-control reports began to trickle in to the bridge. Most of the harm had been superficial, though a lucky hit from a Barracuda missile launched by the *Indefatigable* had destroyed two of the *Simon Davion*'s DropShip docking collars.

"Kommodore, the *Indefatigable* has launched her own fighters," the sensor operator said.

"I see them," Bern snapped back. "Air Officer, have

second squadron fall back to cover the *Simon Davion*. First squadron is to press the attack on the *Indefatigable*."

A glance at the holodisplay showed Bern that he had passed between the enemy vessels, and that both were trying to turn to follow him.

"Helm, hard to starboard. Come around under the *Illustrious*'s stern. All starboard batteries, concentrate firepower on her port quarter."

As the *Simon Davion* and the *Illustrious* passed each other at less than thirty kilometers distance, each poured heavy broadside fire into the other. But the greater weight of the *Simon Davion*'s fire told the tale. By the time she completed her dash for the enemy's portside stern quarter, the *Illustrious* had been torn open like a ration can. Flames fed by atmosphere bleeding through shattered bulkheads flared through rents in her armored skin. Another savage broadside broke the destroyer's back and wrecked her drives. The ship began collapsing in on herself.

"Kommodore, they are launching lifeboats," the sensor operator cried. "It looks like they are abandoning her."

Bern ignored the report. If the *Simon Davion* survived the battle, there would be plenty of time to come back and pick up the tiny, brick-shaped vessels crowded with survivors. Otherwise, the rebels would have to look after their own people.

He looked at the holodisplay. The *Indefatigable* hadn't done as he had expected. Rather than rounding on the *Simon Davion* and giving chase, the *Fox*-class corvette had described only a quarter-circle and was even now "crossing the T" directly behind the battle cruiser. Heavy naval autocannon pounded away at the *Simon*'s backside while lasers stabbed deep into the craters left by the exploding shells. A Barracuda antiship missile blasted armor to glittering shrapnel. Still the *Simon Davion* stood the test.

"Kommodore, I'm picking up a number of DropShips launching from the *Indefatigable*," the sensor operator said.

"Show me," Bern ordered.

Immediately, the image in the holodisplay zoomed in to depict a handful of spherical vessels streaking away from the corvette's docking collars.

"I don't believe this. Those are assault ships. They intend to board us!" Bern breathed in shock. "Air Officer, have the fighters target those ships. *Herr* Speer, tell the Marines to prepare to repel boarders."

In the miniature world of the holodisplay, Bern saw a dozen fighters sweep across the *Simon Davion*'s spine to meet the enemy assault craft. But a wave of rebel fighters swooped on the Lyran aerofighters like hunting hawks. Two of the *Simon Davion*'s fighters died under the attack. A third, trying to dodge the fire from the onrushing rebels, pancaked into the cruiser's side. Point-defense lasers and missile launchers swatted down a Separatist *Hellcat*. One of the black-painted assault craft exploded in a yellow-orange fireball. Another spun away, out of control. The rest bore down on the *Simon Davion* like avenging angels. All the while the *Indefatigable* continued to hammer away at the *Simon Davion*'s stern.

"Helmsman, pull her up hard," Bern ordered, hoping to get his ship away from the enemy's line of fire.

The big ship rose until she had pulled up through ninety degrees.

"Now come hard to starboard. Cross over on top of him and roll her ninety degrees to port."

The helmsman wrestled with the controls, which, pushed to their force-feedback limits, were pushing back.

The *Simon Davion* groaned as her spine was twisted by the violent maneuvers better suited to a fighter than a capital ship. As she came out of her spiraling turn, Bern noticed that the *Indefatigable*'s guns had fallen silent.

"Kommodore," Speer said, "I have reports from all sections. The rebels have grappled and are forcing their way aboard."

The rapid crack of gunfire sounded in the corridor beyond the bridge. Bern dashed back to his command chair and snatched a bulky Mauser and Gray flechette pistol from a compartment built into its right armrest. Before he could yank back the charging handle, the bridge doors fell from their mountings with a ringing boom. Smoke and the stink of burnt explosives drifted into the bridge, followed closely by a pair of dark metallic orbs. An ear-shattering bang drove a spike of pain into Kommodore Bern's head, while an incandescent flash assaulted his eyes.

Deafened by the first explosion, Bern did not immediately hear the hollow pop of the second grenade bursting, but he did feel the effects. A foul, pungent odor reached his nostrils, causing him to gasp. In so doing, he drew the incapacitating gas deep into his lungs. The effect was immediate. He began to choke and gasp. The flechette pistol fluttered from his fingers as Bern dropped to his knees. His stomach heaved, and he vomited the remains of his breakfast onto the deck.

As he fought to control his stomach, Bern looked up to see a tall man clad in a Marine combat suit standing over him. The bore of the shotgun he held pointed at Bern's head carried the silent demand.

Bern nodded, unable to speak, and collapsed on the deck.

# 12

Colonel Francisco de Argall watched the mission clock, bolted to a bulkhead on the Twenty-second Skye Rangers' command DropShip, tick down to zero.

"That's it, Don," he said quietly to his exec. "Boost."

Nix relayed the order to the DropShip's captain. A few seconds later, the big *Overlord*-class 'Mech-hauler shook and groaned as the big engines buried deep within her hull fought to overcome Hesperus III's gravity. About a kilometer to either side of the boosting ship, two more egg-shaped vessels began to rise on pillars of fire and smoke.

"Captain," de Argall called across the bridge, "as soon as we're spaceborne, turn us inbound to Hesperus II. Put us on course for our alternate landing zone. And send the signal advising the main body of my decision."

"Aye, Colonel," the spacer acknowledged.

"The alternate, Colonel?" Nix asked.

"Yes. I'm sure that they're prepared for us," de Argall said. "The local militia might not be too clever, but we've got to assume that the Gray Death Legion *is*. Even if that bastard Carlyle isn't in command anymore, his wife is just as much a veteran. She's going to figure that there is a hostile force insystem and put her troops on full alert. That means the aerospace defenses at Maria's Elegy are going to be primed and ready to fire at the first hint of an incoming DropShip.

"If we divert to the alternate landing zone, we won't have to run that gauntlet. All we'll have to face is the Legion's fighter wing. They might be good, but the most they can do is harass us on the way down. I really doubt they'll be able to stop three *Overlord*s, don't you?"

"I agree, Colonel," Nix said, "but I'm a little worried about the damage they'll do on the way down."

"So am I, Don, but we have to risk it." De Argall gave a slight shrug. "And the risk of diverting to the alternate LZ is less than we'd face if we went in against a forewarned, emplaced enemy at the spaceport. At least this way, we should be able to ground and start raising Cain before the main body arrives. With luck, we'll be able to draw the defenders away from Maria's Elegy and the Defiance plant."

"What about the aerospace defenses?" Nix insisted. "They'll be intact when the main force comes in."

"True, but they'll know that, won't they? General von Frisch can divert or follow the plan as he pleases." De Argall smiled grimly as another thought occurred to him. "And don't forget. If the main body makes it insystem past the *Simon Davion*, they'll be bringing in at least one WarShip. I think *that* makes the odds a bit more even, don't you?"

"Colonel, we've got fighters closing on our position, coming in at zero-five-five, mark one-three-five," the sensor operator reported.

"How many?" De Argall looked at the DropShip's tactical display, easily picking out the tiny red dagger icons that represented the approaching attack craft.

"I'd say at least twelve, Colonel," the sensor operator called back. "Mixed weight classes. Looks like they sent up a full wing."

"Launch our fighters," de Argall said to the ship's captain. "Try to keep the enemy away from the DropShips. Our weapons are free."

"Very well, Colonel," the spacer replied. "Gunnery officer, weapons are free to engage the enemy. Flight ops, launch fighters."

The DropShip personnel had been anticipating the commands. A deep, ringing sound vibrated through the huge, ninety-seven-hundred-ton vessel as a full squadron of fighters rocketed out of their launch bays. Immediately, six tiny blue daggers joined the trio of elongated, U-shaped icons representing the Skye Ranger DropShips. An instant later, another dozen fighter icons flickered into existence, six around each of the other two DropShips. Without hesitation, the fighters joined formation and streaked off on an intercept course with the inbound red force.

"Captain, attacking fighters now at three-two-five kilometers," the sensor operator called out.

"Leading attackers targeted," the gunnery officer added. "Engaging now."

Along the *Overlord*'s flanks, a pair of weapon ports snapped open and vomited fire as two volleys of long-range missiles streaked off into space. On the viewscreen, the effect of the missiles was less than impressive. The thin, broken line showing the projectiles' track passed the Ranger interceptors. A second later, the missiles intersected with two of the foremost red daggers, and the tracking lines winked out.

De Argall knew that the reality of the situation was far more devastating, as forty High-Explosive Armor-Piercing missiles guided by sophisticated Artemis fire-control systems smashed into his missiles. He could imagine the silent fiery blossoms engulfing the targets, but he had no illusions that the inbounds would be destroyed or deterred by those HEAP volleys. On the viewscreen, the Gray Death Legion fighters bore in on the invaders.

Wing Commander Julio Vargas flicked his *SL-15 Slayer* heavy fighter into a barrel roll. The nagging tone indicating a targeting lock died. Ahead of him, visible only as targeting discretes on his HUD, he saw the enemy's fighter wing bearing down. He used a thumb control on his fighter's control stick to designate the nearest fighter. His warbook program identified it as a sixty-ton *Stingray*, one of the workhorse fighters of the Lyran military.

The two fighters were almost evenly matched in terms of speed and maneuverability, though the *Slayer* had heavier armor and greater firepower. The *Stingray* did have advantages: a Sunspot particle projection cannon mounted in its nose and a pair of large lasers set into its forward-swept wings. Those weapons gave the *Stingray* the ability to hit at longer distances than the relatively short-range medium lasers and Zeus 56 Type 10 autocannon carried by the *Slayer*. The rebel pilot made his knowledge of his fighter's superior attack-range clear as he laced Vargas' right wing with laser fire, while the man-made lightning of a PPC bolt flickered across the void to smash into the *Slayer*'s tail.

But that was the only unanswered attack Vargas would allow the enemy. He flipped his fighter into another barrel roll, this one in the opposite direction. Coming out of the high-G maneuver, he toggled his controls to bring his *Slayer* into line with the enemy ship. A tap of his right thumb sent a stream of cannon shells ripping into the *Stingray*'s nose. A quintet of medium lasers clawed blackened furrows into its fuselage, one tracing a line of carbon and melted armor up across the cockpit faring.

The rebel pilot jinked, throwing his fighter into a wing-over, then rolling into a split-S. At a combined speed of four thousand kilometers per hour, the fighters flashed past one another and diverged.

Vargas fought the instinct to pitch up into an Immelmann turn and pursue the *Slayer*. He knew his primary targets *had* to be the *Overlord*-class DropShips. It was a difficult decision to make. Left to their own devices, the rebel fighters would swing around on his squadron's tail and begin hammering the Legion fighters to pieces. At the same time, the DropShips' heavy guns would be exacting a serious toll on the defending fighters. Still there was little choice in the matter. The attacking 'Mech-haulers had to be engaged and damaged—destroyed if possible.

The *Slayer* bore in hard on the nearest DropShip, trying to close range as quickly as possible. Taking on a massive, heavily armed spacecraft was a tricky business. The vessels had tough hides and few vulnerable spots. Lasers, PPC fire, and missiles reached out to swat at the inbound Legion fighters. One flight of missiles peppered the *Slayer* but did little more than burn the dark gray paint and knock a few chips off the warbird's tough hide.

Glancing at his displays, Vargas saw that his wingman, Lieutenant Patrick Garrity, was right behind him.

"Come on, Pat," Vargas called. "Let's hit them where it counts."

Vargas hauled back on the stick, pulling the *Slayer* up into a spiraling climb along the *Overlord*'s ovoid flank. As the fighter flashed past the transport's squared-off stern, Vargas eased out of the roll and nosed over, aiming his fighter at the center of the ship's engineering section. Coming in directly behind a DropShip was one way to attack it where it was most vulnerable. The rear armor, though massive when compared to that of a relatively tiny aerospace fighter, was generally thinner and the weapons less powerful. Still, the incredible energies put out by a DropShip's drives could burn an attack craft to a cinder if the pilot chose the wrong moment to fire up his engines.

Vargas braved the possibility of instant extinction and dove on the DropShip's stern. His autocannon and lasers hammered away at the vessel's armor but accomplished nothing. As he pulled away from the ship, Garrity repeated the attack, again with little effect. It would take more than one pass by a couple of fighters to significantly inconvenience the armored monster.

A pair of laser beams from the gun emplacements on the DropShip's stern punched holes in the *Slayer*'s starboard vertical stabilizer, while a PPC blast savaged the fighter's nose. Vargas had been so intent on attacking the DropShip that he'd wandered into a crossfire. Looking up, he saw a battle-scarred *Stingray* bearing down on him.

The Legion's chief fighter pilot whipped the big, delta-winged fighter into a tight bank to the left, turning away from the DropShip's laser fire. He hoped the enemy gunners had read all the textbooks instructing a fighter to turn *into* an antiaircraft battery's fire, because most gun crews could not reverse their tracking quickly enough. The gunners must have been anticipating a textbook evasive maneuver because their next shots ripped through empty space half a kilometer *behind* the *Slayer*.

The *Stingray* pilot was not fooled, however. He rolled his agile craft onto Vargas' tail and blasted a long, smoking gouge in the fighter's body, just forward of its rear-facing laser mount. Vargas lined up the aft gun and let fly with a single bolt of amplified light energy before going into a snap-roll, followed by a tight weaving turn. The *Stingray* hung onto his tail as though tethered by a cable.

"Pat, how about some help?"

"Sorry, sir," Garrity replied. The breathlessness in his voice suggested he was straining against increased G forces caused by maneuvering at high speed. "He's got friends, and they want to play too."

Vargas tagged the *Stingray* with another hit from the aft laser, then kicked the pedal rudder left hard. The stars and planets outside his cockpit canopy suddenly exchanged places as the *Slayer* yawed suddenly to port. Vargas held the stick absolutely still as he fought the centrifugal forces that slammed him against the side of his cockpit. He pulled the throttle back to neutral and gritted his teeth against the G forces tearing at his consciousness.

He again stomped on the rudder pedals, this time snapping the big fighter out of its flat spin, leaving the ship flying *backward* through the vacuum of space. Unlike fighters operating in atmosphere, those in free-fall were able to perform such maneuvers if the pilot were skilled enough and lucky enough to carry it off.

The *Stingray* was directly in front of the *Slayer*'s nose, less than ten kilometers away. Forcing himself to think backward to compensate for the reversed motion of his ship, Vargas lined up his sights on the *Stingray*'s narrow silhouette. His fingers caressed the controls, and a hellstorm of laser and cannon fire poured into the enemy ship.

The *Stingray* shuddered and went into a lazy roll to starboard. Vargas flipped the *Slayer* end-for-end to bring her back into a normal flight profile. Looping back around to engage the battered F-90, he saw there was no need for further attacks. The *Stingray*'s cockpit was gone, its canopy blasted open by cannon shells. Vargas didn't know if the pilot had managed to eject. At the moment, he didn't have time to search for the enemy flier.

Pulling around, he spotted Garrity's fighter. Though sorely abused by the rebel ships, it was still in operation. Vargas dove on the enemy ships, forcing them to break away from the Legion fighter to avoid his attack.

In the momentary respite his dive afforded him, Vargas looked around. The DropShips were over two hundred kilometers away, their lead increasing by the second. Most of the Legion's fighters were still in the battle, but then so were most of the rebels.

Then he saw it.

"Legion One, this is Eagle One," he radioed. "We are not able to stop the DropShips. They are still inbound. I say again, the DropShips are still inbound. And Colonel, I don't think they're headed for the spaceport. It looks like the enemy is headed south and west of the port. I don't even think they intend to ground at the Defiance plant."

"Legion One to Eagle One," Lori's voice said in his ear. "Ground tracking stations confirm inbounds' heading. Any chance you can shadow them and let us know where they land?"

A trip-hammer explosion rocked Vargas' fighter as a pair of *Chippewa* fighters moved to engage him and his mate.

"Negative, Legion One," Vargas said, as he whipped the *Slayer* into a series of evasive maneuvers. He felt leaden disappointment. This was the first time he had so utterly failed his commander. "We are outnumbered and outgunned. If we try to follow the DropShips, we'll lose the whole wing."

"Very well, Eagle One," Lori said flatly. Vargas imagined he could hear a tone of reproach in the simple words. "Break off and return to base. No sense wasting any more lives. I'm sure we'll catch up with them on the ground."

"Colonel, they're breaking off!"

"Yes!" de Argall crowed. He hadn't needed the sensor operator's joyous call. He'd seen the Gray Death Legion's fighter wing turn away from his DropShips.

"Communications Officer, prepare to send a zip-squeal message to General von Frisch. Advise him that we are heading for the alternate landing zone and will execute Plan Bravo upon grounding."

As the youth manning the communications console acknowledged the order and began to ready the compressed-burst transmission, de Argall allowed himself a grin of pleasure. Diverting to the alternate landing zone would change the tenor of the campaign, but beating the Gray Death Legion's aerospace wing was a good omen. The Skye Rangers had a fighting chance to seize Hesperus II. With the fall of that vital world, the entire Isle of Skye would gain its freedom.

# 13

The green-spoked wheel of his targeting reticle floated across the HUD as Francisco de Argall lined up his *Thug*'s right-hand-mounted PPC on a big, prefabricated sheet-metal barn. For an instant or so, he held his fire, feeling a momentary twinge of guilt at the idea of using the assault 'Mech's incredible firepower to destroy a civilian target. Pushing the emotion back into the box he had constructed for it in his mind, he squeezed the trigger.

The coruscating bolt of azure fire ripped through the barn's thin, pressed aluminum wall. For an instant, it seemed that the charged particles had no more effect on the barn than to leave a slagged hole the size of a man's torso in their wake. Then de Argall caught sight of a few thin wisps of black smoke drifting out of the ragged wound in the building's side. Soon, the *THG-11E*'s infrared sensors began to glow as the crops stored inside, ignited by the PPC blast, began to burn. He sent another stroke of artificial lightning into the barn before turning away.

Across the broad, flat valley, he saw at least a score of thick columns of black smoke. Each marked a pyre similar to the one he'd just ignited. This was Plan Bravo, which called for the Twenty-second Rangers to ground here in Melrose Valley, the center of Hesperus II's primary farming area, and begin tearing up everything in sight. Eventually, the Gray Death Legion and the regular Lyran troops onplanet would have to come out to stop the destruction of the planet's main source of food. The hope was to draw the planet's defenders away from Maria's Elegy and the nearby Defiance plant at about the time the incoming Fourth Skye Rangers would arrive at Hesperus II.

It was a risky scheme, but then, everything about Duke Robert's plan to seize Hesperus II and the rest of the Isle of Skye was risky. The likely payoff, freedom for region, was worth the gamble.

Many of the warriors under de Argall's command subscribed to a "liberty at any cost" attitude when it came to the rebellion. To some degree, he agreed with them. Destroying a few farms in the Melrose Valley was intended as a ruse, a ploy to draw the defenders of Hesperus away from their base of operations. De Argall knew it would take more than a few hours to seriously endanger the entire valley's food supply. It was up to him to convince the Legion and the regular LAAF troops that he and his men would not stop destroying farms and crops until the defenders came out to meet them.

"Colonel, this is Owl Six. We've got company." The message came from one of the reconnaissance lances de Argall had deployed along the valley. The recon elements would give the Rangers some warning when the defenders finally massed to oppose them.

"Go ahead, Owl Six," de Argall said. "What have you got?"

"Stand by." The reply was broken by the harsh chatter of machine-gun fire.

"Local miliz, Colonel," the scout said, using the slang term for planetary militias. "Mostly some light and medium 'Mechs, a couple of tanks, and a whole bunch of infantry. Nothing too heavy, but a bit much for just us to take on. We could use some help."

De Argall looked at the electronic map programmed into one of the *Thug*'s secondary multiple-function displays. Owl Six was just a few kilometers east of his position.

"Hold them as best you can, Owl Six," he said. "Help is on the way."

Switching his communicator over to the channel reserved for the regimental command lance, he sent a new message.

"Command Lance, form up on me. We're going miliz-hunting."

As his lance-mates acknowledged the order, de Argall pushed the control sticks forward, setting his *Thug* off in a rolling trot toward the embattled recon lance. As the ugly, almost simian-looking 'Mech loped across the valley, its broad, flat feet kicked deep gouges in the fertile black soil. A pang of regret pricked his conscience. Every barn burned, every field trampled was an injury done to the farmers of the region for which the new Skye government would have to reckon. But such were the costs of a war for independence.

As the command lance crested a low hillock, he caught sight of the skirmish between his recon lance and the local volunteer troops. The miliz were pressing the scout element hard. De Argall could tell that the superior numbers would soon take their toll on the lightly armed and armored recon 'Mechs unless he and his command lance moved to prevent it.

Bringing his *Thug*'s sights to rest on the slab-sided profile of a militia *Enforcer*, de Argall stroked the triggers and sent a pair of PPC blasts into the enemy 'Mech. The temperature in the cockpit spiked upward as the power-hungry weapons spat their deadly bolts at the lighter machine. For several minutes, it was hard to breathe the overheated air until the high-efficiency heat sinks in the 'Mech's legs and lower torso bled away enough of the waste heat generated by the Tiegart PPCs.

The *Enforcer* staggered under the hideous impact of the charged-particle stream. More than a ton of armor had been melted away or blasted off by the star-hot blast. But the miliz pilot was obviously a veteran. The medium 'Mech took a long, gliding step to the side, getting its feet back under it. For a moment, the machine stood still, its posture suggesting that of a man searching for something he could not quite see. Like a pistol-fighter aiming his weapon, the *Enforcer* extended its left arm, and a lance of energy snapped from the extended-range large laser in its hand. The beam was only visible as a bright blue thread where it intersected the thin smoke drifting across the battlefield.

The effect on the *Thug*'s armor was far more palpable. A deep, smoking pit was burned into the hunch-shouldered assault 'Mech's right knee by the laser's invisible touch.

Further reinforcing the illusion of a pistoleer, the *Enforcer* retracted its left arm while extending its right. Flame gouted from the business end of the dual-purpose autocannon. Submunitions showered de Argall's 'Mech, chipping armor across its chest and left side.

Ton for ton, the *Enforcer* had given as good as it got. But de Argall was not willing to settle for an even exchange. He selected the *Thug*'s secondary weapon system, a pair of relatively heat-efficient, six-tube Bical short-range missile racks. At the touch of a firing stud, a dozen missiles rained down on the *Enforcer*. When the smoke and flame of the detonating warheads dissipated, de Argall could easily see the damage he had wrought on the enemy machine. All of the armor was gone from the gangly 'Mech's left leg. Reddish-gray strands of myomer, the artificial muscles that gave a 'Mech its strength and mobility, hung in tatters from the wound, and de Argall could see cracks in the *Enforcer*'s metal leg bones.

Another hit and you're finished, he said silently, carefully aiming his right-hand PPC at the *Enforcer*'s mangled leg. The miliz pilot must have known it, too. Before de Argall could fire, the *Enforcer* raised its arms in a gesture of surrender. Almost simultaneously, the heat signature representing the Magna 250 extra-light fusion plant in the enemy 'Mech's chest began to fade as the pilot powered down his machine.

Accepting the surrender, de Argall set off in search of new prey, but found none. The arrival of his assault 'Mech-equipped command lance had broken the militia's back, as well as their will to fight. What few combat machines remained to them were streaming northeastward toward the imagined safety of the Myoo Mountains.

Well, they would be safe there, de Argall thought. So long as they didn't come back down and try to take him on again.

"Colonel, we have confirmed contact with the enemy," Chief Sellars said, cupping her hand over the in-ear comm unit she was wearing. "They're out in the Melrose Valley, burning crops and destroying barns."

Lori frowned. "It doesn't make sense. They wouldn't drop out in Melrose if they were intent on capturing the planet. They'd hit Maria's Elegy, wouldn't they? Or Defiance, or even Doering? Why would they drop into the planet's biggest farming area?"

Realization followed quickly. "Unless they're trying to draw us away from the spaceport." She nodded to herself. "Chief, keep trying to track down General Ciampa. And send a message to General Zambos. Tell him to expect the main invasion force at any hour. I'll send my Second Battalion out to Melrose. Also, contact Major Goree. Tell him we've got a confirmed hostile force onplanet. I suspect he knows already, but tell him anyway."

The blood drained from Sellars' dark face, and she gripped the back of a chair to keep from falling.

"Chief? Are you all right?" Lori asked, taking the woman by the elbow and helping her into the seat.

"We just lost contact with the *Simon Davion*," Sellars said. "Her last transmission indicated that the rebels were trying to board her. I'm afraid she's been captured."

"Chief, we're getting something on the distress band," a tech cried out.

"Let me hear it."

Sellars leaned forward in the chair, one hand pressed over her ear. Then she sat up and motioned to the tech to cut off the feed.

"That's enough," she said.

"What is it?" Lori asked. "More rebels?"

"No. Nothing so clean," Sellars whispered. "The *Simon Davion* must be in the enemy's hands. She just turned her guns on the *Carolyn*, a Defiance Industries JumpShip. Her engines are out, and she's losing station-keeping. Her captain has ordered her abandoned and is calling for rescue."

"They hit a *civilian* JumpShip?" McCall said, stunned. "Colonel, the *Invidious* . . ."

Lori was half a beat ahead of him. She snatched up a communications headset, ordering the technicians to establish contact with the Gray Death Legion's JumpShip.

"Captain Murad, get the *Invidious* out of this system!" she screamed as soon as the starship commander came on line. Lori knew shouting did little good, but this time she just couldn't help it. The message would take nearly ten minutes to make the long journey out to the *Invidious*'s berth at the zenith jump point.

"Too late, Colonel," Murad said, when her reply came in almost twenty minutes later. Her face was tight with anger and pain. "Right after they shot up the *Carolyn*, those bastards turned their guns on us. The *Invidious* is finished. Her K-F drive core is nothing but a pile of junk, and her back is broken. I'm ordering her abandoned and scuttled. I've also ordered the other Legion JumpShips to surrender rather than be destroyed. I doubt there's any chance of us getting picked up by friendlies, so I guess I'll see you when the war is over."

Lori slammed her fist into the console, swearing.

"Lieutenant Colonel McCall," she growled between clenched teeth, "tell Major Houk to move Second Battalion aboard the DropShips. Send Captain Radcliffe's First Armored Infantry Company with them. I want them to go out to Melrose and pound those Separatist bastards into the ground. And I want their commander's head on a pike."

# ═══ 14 ═══

*Melrose Valley, Hesperus II*
*Skye Province*
*Lyran Alliance*
*28 June 3065*

Rae Houk moved her *Gallowglas* down the ramp from the *Jedburgh*'s 'Mech bay. As she stepped from the reinforced steel runway, she gazed sorrowfully at the columns of thick black smoke rising from the floor of the Melrose Valley to join the heavy black clouds being blown up from the south. Having grown up in a farming region like this one, she could easily imagine the fear, loss, and impotent rage the valley farmers must have been feeling at that moment. Nor were the irony and stupidity of the Separatists' actions lost on her. Under the banner of liberating the oppressed, the first thing the Skye rebels did upon dropping onto Hesperus was to attack farmlands, endangering civilian lives and destroying civilian property

"Legion One, this is Assassin One. We're on the ground and moving in on the enemy positions," she said quietly, as though fearing the invaders might overhear and discern the Legion's plans. Of course, there was no such concern in Rae Houk's mind. Speaking softly had always been her way.

"Captain Radcliffe, form up your troops behind our center," she ordered the armored infantry commander. "Spy One, take the point. Let's move out."

As her battalion spread out in a kilometer-wide wedge formation, four light 'Mechs from First Company's recon lance dashed off to take the lead.

Everywhere she looked were signs of wanton destruction. Barns had been reduced to smoldering ruins; fields had been ripped and trampled by the steel feet of the invading BattleMechs. Only the farm houses themselves remained untouched by the rebels, who apparently had enough sense to leave the people alone. An odd greenish-yellow light suffused the pathetic scene.

A hollow, crackling boom echoed along the valley, accompanied by an electric flash. No weapons fire was responsible. The thunder and lightning were the product of the gathering storm. Raindrops began to spatter against the *Gallowglas*'s cockpit. A glance at a secondary display told her that the temperature outside had dropped to twenty-four degrees centigrade, cooling off by eight degrees in the past fifteen minutes.

"All units, looks like the weather's closing in on us," she said. "The cold rain will help our heat dissipation, but it's going to make the footing treacherous."

Another rumble of thunder echoed along the valley, and the clouds opened, pouring out thick gray sheets of rain. Then a sharper crackle, almost blanketed by the white noise of the pounding raindrops, sounded out of the storm.

"Assassin One, this is Spy One-one. Contact! We have contact with the enemy. Estimate regimental strength. The warbook says they're the Twenty-second Skye Rangers." The scout followed his report with a string of numbers giving the location of the contact.

"Spy One, pull back," Houk ordered. "The battalion is on the way. Let's get 'em, Assassins."

Pushing her heavy 'Mech into a trot, Houk angled a bit to the west, toward the coordinates given her by the scouts. The sound of another rattling burst of light autocannon fire cut through the dripping air, but she thought the heavy downpour might actually work to her battalion's advantage. Though every BattleMech on the field boasted a wide array of sensors, every MechWarrior piloting those machines depended first on his own eyes, then upon the electronic imagers. The pouring rain would diminish the 'Mechs' heat signatures, while the dim light would serve to mask the gray-painted Legion machines from the enemy's sight.

A flicker of movement caught her eye. In one swift, smooth motion, she brought the long-barreled extended-range PPC in her 'Mech's right arm up to cover the ghostly contact. She snapped the weapon off target when she recognized the extra-long legs and squat gray torso of a Legion *Mongoose*.

"Major, am I glad to see you," the recon 'Mech's pilot gasped, skidding to a halt in the thick, slippery mud.

"Where is Sergeant Crown?" Houk demanded.

"About half a klick east, I think," the scout answered. "The rebels haven't pushed us too hard. The sarge is maintaining contact, and they keep potting at us. I think they're afraid we aren't alone out here."

"Assassins, hold position," Houk ordered her battalion. "Sergeant Crown, come in."

"Yeah, Major?"

"Have you got a good fix on the enemy's position?"

"Well, sorta," Crown said. "I know where their front lines are anyway."

"Upload it to me."

In a few seconds, the data gathered by the battalion scouts was transferred to Houk's computer via a secure laser commlink

"Assassin One to all Assassins, the enemy is to our right front. We are going to execute a battalion right wheel and hit them where we find them. That's the best I can do in this soup." She paused long enough for her orders to be passed from company commanders down through the ranks. "All right, move out."

The battalion still known as Hassan's Assassins began a pivoting turn to the east. It took only a few minutes for the first sounds of battle to start echoing along the rain-soaked valley.

Houk held the battalion together, haranguing her company commanders to keep the unit in tight formation. Out of the gloom came the dark blue shape of an enemy 'Mech. With little time to react, Houk let off a snap-shot from her

PPC. The enemy machine, a *Bushwacker,* staggered as the particle stream ate into its right shoulder.

Despite losing most of the armor protecting that vulnerable joint, the tough little 'Mech spun to face Houk's *Gallowglas*. The air split with the deep-throated chatter of autocannon fire and the snap of a laser discharge. The armor-piecing shells stitched a line of destruction across the *Gallowglas*'s right breast, barely missing the twinned over-and-under Sunglow large lasers mounted there. The laser cut half a ton of armor from the 'Mech's left thigh.

Trying to close the range, Houk stepped forward even as the *Bushwacker* danced away. She knew he was trying to increase the distance enough to bring his long-range missiles into play. It was a touchy business. If the *Bushwacker* moved too far off, he and Houk would lose each other in the bucketing rain. But he had to know that the *Gallowglas*'s high-tech ER PPC—unlike the *Bushwacker*'s LRMs or older-type PPCs—had no minimum range. She could practically climb right into the cockpit with her enemy and still be able to hit him with her most savage weapon.

The rebel machine had an edge in speed, and his 'Mech's birdlike construction gave him a lower center of gravity, thus a bit more maneuverability under the poor conditions. The *Bushwacker* managed to gain a few dozen meters on Houk. Spinning on its back-canted legs, the low-slung 'Mech cut loose with a volley of laser and missile fire. The impact rocked the *Gallowglas*, forcing Houk to work feverishly at her controls to keep the tall machine upright. Regaining her balance, she hammered the *Bushwacker* with a blast from her PPC, with follow-up shots from the paired Quasar pulse lasers in the 'Mech's left wrist.

Heat flooded into her cockpit as the core-temperature gauge shot up into the amber band. Fortunately, the *Gallowglas* relied solely upon energy weapons, so there was no ammunition to cook off. But the computer could still SCRAM the engine, shutting it down before it could suffer a catastrophic overheat. An insistent tone in her ears warned of that possibility. Houk slapped the manual override.

The *Bushwacker* had been badly mauled in the last exchange of fire. Most of the armor on its right leg had been torn away, and a deep crater, still glowing faintly, marred its back. The rebel MechWarrior was neither a hero nor a fool, however. He pulled his 'Mech into a tight turn and bolted off into the rain and mist.

For a moment, Houk considered pursuing the damaged machine. But she knew that destroying one 'Mech wouldn't make a difference in the campaign. She had to *damage* as many as possible, in order to put a drain on the invaders' store of reserves and spare parts. She allowed the *Bushwacker* to escape and went off in search of other prey.

The other prey found her first.

A blast of laser fire ripped up her 'Mech's right side and flashed the water-logged ground into muddy steam. A pair of missiles burned so close past her *Gallowglas's* head that she would later swear she could read "Made on Coventry" stenciled on the rockets' fins.

Houk spun, sliding in the mud to face a rebel *Grasshopper*. She speared the heavy 'Mech with a blast from her PPC. Not wanting to risk a shutdown, she peppered the lanky 'Mech with only one of her pulse lasers. The *Grasshopper* absorbed both hits and struck back with lasers and missiles.

For several minutes, the two traded blows. Houk scored a telling hit when her large lasers burned through the *Grasshopper's* right elbow. The enemy 'Mech's forearm dropped into the thick black mud and lay there hissing as the cold goop evaporated against the hot metal of the laser wound and the medium laser mounted in the wrist.

But the rebel warrior would not be panicked as easily as the *Bushwacker* pilot had been. A brilliant blue lance of energy flashed from its Sunbeam extended-range large laser to carve a section of armor away from the *Gallowglas's* belly. Houk tried to turn her relatively undamaged right side to her enemy.

Something smashed against her 'Mech's head, jostling her around inside the cockpit like a die in a gambler's cup. The taste of blood filled her mouth as her teeth lacerated the inside of the cheek. A shiver ran along her spine as a cold, damp wind chilled her skin.

The sudden draft sent a second shudder through Rae Houk's body, this one born of fear. She looked up to see a crack as wide as her hand was long in the wall of her cockpit. Half of the electronic displays around her were dead. Whatever had hit the 'Mech's head had destroyed the *Gallowglas*'s sensors and come close to killing her. Another hit like that, and the Assassins would be looking for a new commander.

Reacting purely on instinct, she pulled back on the 'Mech's control sticks and stomped hard on the pedals controlling the powerful jump jets set into the machine's back and legs. Dark gray steam boiled up around her as the *Gallowglas* shot skyward. Ordinarily, controlling a jumping 'Mech took a delicate touch on the controls. This time she had to wrestle the sticks as though they were the paws of an angry bear.

When the 'Mech touched down ninety meters to the rear of her battalion's lines, Houk felt its right knee buckle. The big machine reeled as the treacherous, greasy black mud betrayed her footing. The *Gallowglas* stumbled, falling to one knee. It took every bit of piloting skill she could muster to get the abused 'Mech back to its feet.

"Rae, you're all busted up," Radcliffe called. "I can see straight through into your cockpit. You can't do any more good here. Fall back to the DropShip."

Houk's first instinct was to protest an infantry captain giving orders to a 'Mech battalion commander, but she knew Radcliffe was right.

"Elias, take command of the battalion," she called to her second. "Keep up the pressure on the rebels, but don't waste any lives. I'm going to fall back to the *Jedburgh* and see if I can call in an air strike."

Feeling like she was abandoning her comrades, Houk found the short trip back to the DropShip particularly lonely. She didn't stop, however, until she and her *Gallowglas* reached the interior of the *Jedburgh*'s 'Mech bay. Without even powering it down or guiding it to its cubicle, she swarmed down the chain ladder she'd deployed a moment before. Still clad in only briefs, boots, and cooling vest, she ran for the bridge.

"Colonel, we're getting pounded out here," she told Lori. "We need an air strike to drive the rebels back to their DropShips."

"How long can your people hold out there, Rae?" the colonel asked.

"It's a slugging match here, Colonel. The rebels have got us outnumbered and outgunned. If we get that air strike, we might be able to hold them or push them back. Otherwise, we'll have to fall back under the *Jedburgh*'s guns. We're facing a full regiment here, Colonel. Even a DropShip won't be able to stand up to that kind of pounding for long. If we get pushed back, we'll have to leave the rebels in command of the field."

"Rae, the air strike is on its way," the colonel said, then hesitated.

Houk wondered if the enemy had begun jamming communications, but then the colonel's voice came in again. "I hate to do this to you, Major. Once the air strike commences, I want your unit to fall back to the *Jedburgh* and return to base. I have reason to believe that the enemy presence in Melrose is a diversion or a secondary force. I want your battalion back here so we can concentrate our strikes against the main invasion force when it arrives."

"Colonel, please confirm," Houk said, unwilling to admit defeat even in the face of three-to-one odds. "You want us to use the air strike as cover for a retreat."

The radio was silent for many seconds. When the colonel spoke again, there was steel in her voice.

"That is precisely what I am telling you, Major. Use the air strike as cover. Break off and withdraw back to Maria's Elegy."

Julio Vargas rolled his *Slayer* onto its port wing, straining his eyes, trying to see the ground. The winds, gusting to more than sixty kilometers per hour, drove the heavy, cold rain against his cockpit canopy like machine-gun bullets. Not so far below, the storm was reducing the battle-scarred soil of Melrose Valley into a sea of mud, though he could not see it. The cloud cover was ten-tenths overcast and seemed to have no lower limit. If not for the *Slayer*'s sophisticated avionics, he would be in real danger of flying the big delta-winged fighter straight into the ground.

Though he could not see the ground with his eyes, the *Slayer*'s computer could, through its sensor array. Three large, metallic shapes gleamed a dull red in his Magnetic Anomaly Detector. Several smaller but still sizable masses surrounded the larger targets. The cold downpour reduced the infrared signatures until his thermal imager could barely pick them out. But Vargas' senses, trained and honed by years in the cockpit, allowed him to translate what he saw on the multifunction displays. The large contacts were the enemy's DropShips, while the smaller ones were his 'Mechs. A score of kilometers to the north was a similar, though smaller, set of contacts. That was where the Legion's Second Battalion was limping back aboard the *Jedburgh*.

Abruptly, the enemy revealed that their sensors could see him, too. A pair of laser beams snapped past his fighter's newly patched left wing, while a brace of missiles traced fiery trails all around him.

Vargas put the *Slayer* into a snap-roll to the right, climbing away from the ground targets. At the top of his loop, he inverted his fighter and pushed it over into a dive. As the red smear of a DropShip swam into the center of his MAD display, Vargas tapped a control stud with his left forefinger. Instantly, the fighter's HUD held a new set of icons. Vargas selected the big magnetic signature to the far left of the cluster as his target. A pale green square snapped into existence around the target, indicating that the *Slayer*'s computer had acquired the DropShip. A targeting reticle, complete with a long "impact line" stretching from the gun sight to the fighter's airplane-shaped velocity vector icon, floated across the holographic sight. Vargas manhandled his fighter against the gusting winds, "caging" the vector discrete inside the target box, and "flying" the reticle along the impact line until the dot in the center of the reticle crossed directly over the combined heading and target icons.

The fighter jerked as the computer's automatic bombing software kicked three five-hundred-kilogram bombs away from the racks under the *Slayer*'s wings and fuselage. Free of the extra weight, Vargas shoved his throttle forward and hauled back on the stick, pulling the *Slayer* out of its dive. Vargas barely heard the trio of flat bangs over the roar of his engine, and the bright white flash of detonating warheads was all but swallowed up by the heavy rain. He knew the effect on the ground would be more dramatic as the free-fall, general-purpose, high-explosive bombs scattered hot shrapnel around the enemy's landing zone. With any kind of luck, at least one of those bombs had actually *hit* the DropShip. Though one five-hundred-kilo bomb was not enough to destroy a DropShip, it would be a serious inconvenience to the enemy.

In reprisal, the enemy fired again. This time, a stroke of PPC lightning shattered the repair plates in his fighter's left wing. The armor patch, still bearing its ugly, red-brown primer, was a legacy of the Death Eagles' fight against the incoming Skye Rangers. Once more, the armor had been blasted away, possibly by the same gunner who'd caused the damage in the first place. There was, to the Legion's wing commander, a certain ironic symmetry to the thing.

As Vargas rolled out of his zoom-climb, he looked around to see the balance of his squadron following him one by one through the attack run on the enemy landing zone. Further north, visible only as blips on a radar screen, Second Squadron was treating the enemy's lead elements to a series of strafing runs.

The whole mission had been laid on so as to allow the Legion's Second BattleMech Battalion to safely break contact with the Rangers, fall back to their DropShip, and return to the legion's base at Maria's Elegy. So far, things were working out according to plan, though Vargas had the uncomfortable feeling that he probably wouldn't be able to say as much in the days and weeks to come

# 15

Major Rae Houk yanked off her cooling vest and threw it onto the floor of her *Gallowglas*'s cockpit in disgust. She treated her neurohelmet with a bit more care, only because the sensitive nature of the bulky unit had been drilled into her when she was a raw recruit serving with the Free Worlds League's Sirian Lancers.

As she pushed the helmet into the storage recess above and behind her command couch, she caught sight of her reflection in the reflective visor. Houk was secure enough to admit she had never been a particularly beautiful woman. She had her father's large, rough features, while her dark olive skin was a legacy from her mother's side of the family. On top of genetics, the privations of nearly two decades of living with too little sleep, poor food, exposure to the elements, and all that went along with military life had further coarsened her appearance.

But it was neither parentage nor a hard life that made the plain visage reflected in the tough, perspex less attractive than usual, even considering the distortion caused by the visor's curved face. It was the anger and shame playing across her features that made her seem ugly in her own eyes. Anger at having her battalion pulled out of the Melrose Valley, leaving the enemy in command of the field. Anger at the Legion's CO for having sent the Assassins into that battle, knowing they were going to be outnumbered. Anger at the Lyran officers who had not been at their posts to send their *own* troops out after the invading rebels. And anger even at Grayson Carlyle, who had died before his time, leaving the Legion to shift for itself.

The shame had almost the identical sources. Houk was ashamed that her battalion could not stand toe-to-toe with the Skye forces and give as good as they got. She was ashamed of having to be pulled out of the firefight and rescued by Wing Commander Vargas and his fly-boys. She was ashamed of being angry at Lori, and even more chagrined because of her anger at Grayson.

For a few minutes, she leaned against the wall of her cockpit, trying to master the destructive emotions boiling in her guts. She knew her troops were probably feeling the same things, and that she, as their commander, had no right to express those feelings, not in front of her subordinates at least. As the commander of Hassan's Assassins, she had to paste a look of confident pride on her face and congratulate her soldiers on a battle well-fought, even if both she and they knew otherwise.

Mastering herself, Houk gave the red-handled lever above the ingress-egress hatch a pull. Hydraulics whined as the portal slid open, and she clambered out onto the gantry next to the *Gallowglas*'s head. Standing in a little knot at the end of the 'Mech-bay catwalk were two of her three company commanders. The missing man, Captain Louis Weatherby, had stayed behind in Melrose Valley, along with the ruins of his *Grim Reaper*. Weatherby had died commanding the rearguard covering the battalion's withdrawal.

"Well, Major?" Edmond Caine said, his tone an open challenge.

"Well, what, Captain?"

"What are you going to say to Colonel Kalmar-Carlyle? And what are we going to say to our men?"

Houk came to a stop in front of the ever-pugnacious
.. to the Colonel is between the Colonel

and me. Complaints go uphill, Captain, and you know that."

The forced calm she had summoned up in her cockpit vanished under the low smolder of her subordinate's gaze. She felt the fire grow in her own eyes. "As to the Assassins, they're not *your* men, Captain, they're the Gray Death Legion's men, Second Battalion's men. That makes them *my* men. If you feel you have to tell them something, tell them *I'll* talk to them after I talk to the Colonel.

"Meanwhile, it is up to you and Elias to keep the men from losing what morale they've got left. In case you haven't noticed, Captain, we've taken some casualties. I want you and Captain Whitlocke to go visit the men in sickbay and see how they're doing. I'll tell Lieutenant Strieger-Pouls that he's in command of Fourth Company now. After that, you and Whitlocke will have to help bring him up to speed. *Then*, all four of us will have to work on getting the battalion back into battle-ready condition. If that means warriors have to get down in the 'Mech-drek with the technicians, well, then, be prepared to get your fingernails dirty.

"That is all, gentlemen," she snapped, and headed for the stairs down to the 'Mech hangar's main floor.

As she descended the steel steps, Houk forced herself to regain the tenuous calm she'd had when she'd exited her 'Mech. She knew it wouldn't do her any good to go before Colonel Kalmar-Carlyle angry and breathing fire. By the time she reached Lori's office, she was in full control of her emotions. She paused outside the door, ran her hands through her coarse, spiky black hair to smooth it down, and knocked three times.

"Come in, Major," Lori called.

Dang, how did she do that? Houk wondered as she pushed the door open.

"I asked the OOD to call me when you arrived," Lori explained, smiling softly. "He said you marched your 'Mech into the repair bay, chewed out your subordinates on the gantry catwalk, and stormed out of the hangar. I figured you were on your way to see me."

"Then the Colonel knows what I wanted to see her about."

"Yes, I do, Rae." Lori's smile faded. "You're honked

off about getting pulled out of Melrose. Hell, you're probably mad that we sent the Assassins out there in the first place. Well, I don't like it any better than you do. It was a bad call on my part to commit less than my total force. And the only way I could counteract a bad call was to make another bad call and pull you out."

"So, what do we do now, Colonel?" Houk asked.

Lori waved Houk into a chair. "Julio tells me that the air strikes drove the rebels back to their DropShips. We're going to keep them under surveillance as best we can, given the crummy weather. We finally managed to track down General Ciampa, and she has rejoined her troops. She made arrangements to relieve the Death Eagles with a rotating series of *Boomerang* spotter planes. They can stay on station a lot longer than our fighters can, which means we'll get a little advance warning when the rebels out in Melrose make their next move.

"On the down side, there is at least one more full regiment of troops on their way insystem. I think we can count on them coming straight into Maria's Elegy and DefHesp, and possibly both, if there are enough of them. To make matters worse, the Separatists have at least two WarShips backing them up now.

"Two?" Houk asked, puzzled. "I thought they came in with two and lost one fighting the *Simon Davion*."

"They did, but they somehow managed to capture the *Simon Davion*. Now it looks like the rebel *Fox* is holding position at the zenith jump point, while the *Simon* moves insystem with their ground troops.

"And to make matters worse, our own JumpShips were also captured by the rebels. That means we're stuck here until this business is concluded."

Lori leaned her elbows on her desk and fixed Houk with a stare. "In the meantime, Major, how bad off is your battalion?"

"Not too bad, considering," Houk said. "Three men killed, five wounded, and two missing. One of the KIAs was Lou Weatherby. I'd like your permission to move Lieutenant Diggsby Strieger-Pouls up into the command slot."

"Granted," Lori said.

"As to my hardware, we lost two 'Mechs, nonrecoverable. One of those was Weatherby's *Grim Reaper*. We also lost a *Bombardier* from First Company. I've got one light and one medium 'Mech that are going to need a lot of work, but I think they can be patched together into something not too embarrassing.

"Otherwise, there's not too much wrong with the outfit that a good night's sleep and a good hot meal wouldn't cure."

"Okay, we'll get right on it." Lori tapped a few notes into her desktop computer. "Anything else?"

"No, Colonel, that about covers it."

"Very well." Lori's expression softened. "Go get some sleep, Rae. You're exhausted."

"Yes ma'am." Houk smiled suddenly, then saluted and turned for the door. Just as her hand was closing on the knob, Lori called out again.

"Oh, Major, that was a good piece of soldiering you did this afternoon. Please don't let it grind on you that you got pushed back today. This was just the first skirmish. After this, things are going to get a lot tougher, and I want all my officers in the best shape possible."

After Rae Houk left her office, Lori leaned back in her chair and stared out at the darkening sky. It was obvious that this night was going to be particularly black. Masked by the gathering clouds, the setting sun was little more than a diffuse glow in the sky. The storm system that had drenched Melrose Valley hadn't burned itself out as the meteorological office had predicted. Instead, it had quartered and ridden up along the Myoo Mountains. It was now closing on Maria's Elegy.

She spun her chair and reached across her desk to activate her comm unit.

"Meg?" she said, reaching the leader of the Gray Death armored scouts detachment. "I really hate to do this to you, but I'm going to ask you to activate your scouts. It looks like it's really going to get nasty out tonight, and I'm thinking the remotes and passive sensors aren't going to be much good to us. I think we're going to need some Model 0 Mark Is on the perimeter."

"You expecting trouble, Colonel?" Major Powers asked.

"Not as such," Lori said. "If I were expecting trouble, I'd have the whole regiment standing to all night long. But if I was the rebel commander, I wouldn't miss an opportunity to sneak some raiders onto the enemy base under the cover of this storm."

"Yeah, it does look like it's shaping up to be sapper weather, doesn't it?" Powers said. She knew as well as Lori that foul weather tended to drive sentries under cover and to interfere with the sensitivity of remote sensors, thus giving saboteurs and raiders an edge in penetrating an enemy perimeter.

"Yes, it does. That's why I want some of your scouts out walking the perimeter tonight. They'll be reasonably well-protected from the weather by their armor, and they'll be able to adjust their suit sensors to fit the conditions. Not to mention that they'll be eyeballs on the scene."

Lori's earlier reference to Model 0 Mark I sensors referred to a trained observer's eyes, backed up by his intuition. Taken together, they would often allow a sentry to detect an enemy presence that mechanical or electronic surveillance devices might miss.

"I'll tell Tom Leone to put his boys on backup and have a company from Devin's Battalion on ready five," she added.

"Okay, boss, I'll get the scouts suited up and on sentry duty. I think we'll go one squad at a time, two-hour shifts," Powers said. "Good enough?"

"Good enough," Lori confirmed. Then she severed the connection. Another couple of taps on the vidcom put her in touch with Gina Ciampa's office on the other side of the spaceport.

"Any movement from the troops out in Melrose?" she asked after the exchange of a few brief courtesies.

"Not much," Ciampa said, "though the bloody cloud cover is making it hard for the *Boomerang*s to see much."

"General, I've been thinking," Lori said, fiddling with a writing stylus as she spoke. "The primary target on Hesperus II has always been the Defiance plant, right?"

"That's been the way of things, Colonel."

"Attackers have seldom gone after Maldon or Doering, or Melrose Valley, for that matter. And when they have attacked those sites, it has almost always been a diversion."

"What are you getting at, Colonel?"

"What I'm getting at, General, is this," Lori went on. "I

want to pull in most of the planetary militias and form them into one battalion. We can use them to keep an eye on some of the secondary targets like Maldon and the valley region. That will free up our forces to oppose the invaders."

"It's a good plan, Colonel," Ciampa said. "With one minor glitch. I haven't got the authority to pull the Thirty-sixth Guards out of Maldon. Not unless the enemy was pressing us so hard that it was a matter of move them or lose the planet."

"General, if you *don't* move the Thirty-sixth, you *might* lose the planet," Lori argued. "Why not be proactive? Move Zambos' boys to Maria's Elegy. Let the miliz take care of the mine site."

"Colonel, my orders are very specific. The Thirty-sixth stays at Maldon. That's why the Gray Death Legion was brought out here, to help defend Maria's Elegy and the Defiance plant." Ciampa stuck to her guns. "The only way I can move Zambos' regiment would be to send a priority HPG to Hauptmann-General Ivan Steiner and get his permission to relocate the Twenty-sixth."

"Then send it, General," Lori said emphatically. "Because I'm telling you, as sure as sunrise, we're going to need the Thirty-sixth right here before this is over."

# 16

**Gray Death Legion Compound**
**Maria's Elegy, Hesperus II**
**Skye Province**
**Lyran Alliance**
**30 June 3065**

The discordant blast of the alarm klaxon startled Wing Commander Julio Vargas out of a sound sleep. He rolled from his bunk, yanked on a set of gray coveralls and boots, and dashed from his room, snatching up his flight bag on the way.

"Attention! Attention!" the intercom loudspeakers blared. "Incoming DropShips! Incoming fighters. All personnel report to ready stations."

Vargas ran to the squat hexagonal building that served as the Legion's command post at the spaceport, dodging a jeep and two hover armored personnel carriers along the way.

"What is happening, Colonel?" he asked, catching sight of Lori.

"The primary sensor station says the rebels' main body has arrived," she answered without breaking her stride. Vargas had to sprint to catch up with her, and then take fast steps to remain at her side. Lori was a half a head taller than he was, and most of that height was in her legs. "They're settling into a geostationary orbit."

"Right over the Defiance plant," he said.

Lori nodded.

"How many?"

"Hard to tell. It could be as many as ten DropShips. We don't know how many fighters." Lori passed Vargas the electronic message pad she'd been holding. He quickly scanned the report displayed on the pad's liquid-crystal screen.

"Well, that's something anyway," he said, pointing to one line in the document. "At least that WarShip seems to be holding back some."

"Yes. It looks like they were just using her to escort their DropShips in system. I guess from here on out, things are going to be pretty conventional."

"What do you want me to do, Colonel?"

"Get your boys airborne right away," Lori said, without slowing her pace. "I know it's just one wing against all those DropShips, but you've got to slow them up, hurt them if you can. I'm sorry, Julio, but aside from the miliz, you're the only fighter wing we've got."

Vargas nodded grimly. "*Sí*, Colonel. I understand." Giving Lori a formal salute, he jogged off in the direction he had come.

Sticking close alongside the building, Vargas came to the spot where his hover jeep was parked. He slid in behind the vehicle's controls and fired up the internal combustion engine. As the jeep rose on its cushion of air, he spun the wheel. He despised the vehicle's sluggish response, so unlike the crisp maneuverability of his fighter.

It was a short drive across the compound to the series of low, hemicylindrical hardened structures that housed the Legion's aerospace fighters. The men and women under his command had gathered in front of the hangar where his *Slayer* was parked. All had already donned their flight gear, complete with the chapslike G-suits. The heavy black garment was full of small, computer-controlled tubes and bladders that would fill with air during high-G maneuvers to force the pilot's blood out of his legs and lower torso, up into his chest and head where it belonged, thus preventing G-LOC, G-induced loss of consciousness.

Vargas skidded the jeep to a halt and killed the engine. Even before the vehicle had completely settled down onto its hull, he slipped from the driver's seat and darted into the hangar. Stepping behind a makeshift screen jury-rigged from heavy corrugated plastic sheeting, Vargas quickly changed out of his coveralls and into his flight suit. He had suffered ridicule about that screen in the past, but Julio Vargas had been raised in a strict, traditionalist Catholic home. Changing his clothing in front of the women of his squadron was something he would not do, even under the threat of an impending attack.

When he emerged again, fully clad in his flight and G suit, he briefed his pilots on the situation.

"It is going to be a hard fight," he said. "We will divide the wing into squadrons. First Squadron will press home the attack. We will concentrate our firepower on a single DropShip at a time. I think that will be the fastest way of destroying them. Once the ship is crippled, we will move on to the next."

He looked toward a taciturn black woman, who stood leaning against the curved wall of the shelter. "Second Squadron, under Captain Carroll, will be the air-to-air element. It will be your responsibility to keep the rebel fighters at bay while we shoot up their DropShips."

Amanda Carroll gave a jerky nod of acceptance.

"One more thing," Vargas said. "The enemy has been escorted insystem by an *Avalon*-class cruiser. As of this moment, the WarShip seems to be holding back. Once we get airborne, there is no telling whether she will get involved or not. If she does, it will most likely be to launch additional fighters or to employ her point-defense weapons against our fighters. In either case, I will make the decision whether we should continue our mission, counterattack the WarShip, or withdraw.

"I needn't remind you that the rest of the Legion, and the regular Lyran forces onplanet, are counting on us to hurt the enemy. If we can cause enough damage, our brothers and sisters on the ground will have a fighting chance. Press in hard, mark your targets, make me proud.

"That is all. Mount up."

As the Legion pilots broke and ran for their ships, Vargas pulled his helmet from his dark green flight bag and tossed the now-empty cordura nylon satchel into a corner of the hangar. He set the thick headpiece on his *Slayer*'s left wing and started his walk-around. Everything was in the proper preflight condition, and there wasn't a red safety tag to be seen. His ground crew had preflighted the fighter and had removed the small warning flags.

Retrieving and donning his helmet, Vargas climbed up the narrow yellow and black steel ladder and swung his right leg over the cockpit fairing. He was careful to place his feet on the ejection seat's armrests, avoiding the control panels to either side of the seat. After dropping into the cockpit, he reached under the seat and pulled the last remaining red-tagged safety pin, the one preventing the *Slayer*'s ejection system from arming. He carefully tucked the cotter key with its scarlet label into one breast pocket. With smooth, practiced movements, he activated the controls that brought the heavy aerospace combat ship to life. At his touch, the fighter's three primary multi-function displays flickered to life. Gauges immediately began to monitor the condition of his engines, fuel state, and weapons load.

He reached across his body with his right hand and depressed a shielded red stud. Immediately, a low-toned whine filled the cockpit, and the ship began to vibrate strongly. The noise spooled up in both pitch and volume as the *Slayer*'s powerful Shinobi 320 engines gathered rpms until there came a noise like a shotgun going off in his ear. The engine caught and began to run on its own as Vargas pushed the throttles open, feeding fuel to the ravening steel beast behind him. The noise increased. He pulled the switch that dropped and locked the canopy. The sound level abated to a dull, throbbing hiss.

Following his crew chief's hand and arm signals, Vargas taxied the big fighter out onto the tarmac. From there, the air-traffic controllers in the spaceport tower took over. Vargas received clearance to launch almost immediately. He rolled the *Slayer* out onto the runway and stood hard on the brakes while he ran the engine up to its maximum revs. The ship squatted on its nose wheel, straining against the brakes, almost as though it was a living creature eager to get into the air.

He let the brakes off with a jerk, and the big, delta-winged fighter began to roll down the runway. The nose wheel came clear of the ground as Vargas kicked in the over-thrusters, causing the *Slayer* to leap into the air.

Climbing rapidly, Var

wing assembly point, where he went into a slow counter-clockwise orbit over Maria's Elegy. His wingman, Lieutenant Patrick Garrity, dropped into his accustomed place, off Vargas' left wing and half a kilometer behind. When the last gray fighter fell into formation, a *Corsair* flown by Ensign John Monty, the son of a retired Legion pilot, Vargas checked his instruments and called out a vector for the pilots under his command. The Death Eagles dropped quickly into formation and followed their commander in a fast, zooming climb toward the edges of space.

The dark blue of the morning sky quickly faded into a deep purple, then the velvet blackness of space as the fighters left the atmosphere. Vargas consulted the navigational information currently being displayed on the left-hand MFD. He corrected his course ten degrees to the right and signaled his squadrons to follow suit.

It took less than five minutes for the Death Eagles to catch sight of the enemy DropShips. At first, the big armored 'Mech-haulers resembled only a cluster of shooting stars. It became rapidly apparent that the tiny glittering dots were nothing so innocent or so beautiful.

The DropShips, mostly spheroid *Union*s and *Overlord*s, with a few aerodyne *Leopard*s in the mix, bore large swatches of roughly laid-on paint where the Lyran Alliance's mailed fist emblem had been obliterated. In its place, the rebels had painted the crudely rendered image of an ancient Scots warrior wielding a claymore. Alongside the almost cartoonish figure was the blue and green map-of-England crest of the Fourth Skye Regimental Combat Team.

"Here we go," Vargas said aloud. "First Squadron, target the closest *Leopard*. Second Squadron, give us cover."

The Death Eagles swooped down on their prey.

Vargas locked the brick-shaped *Leopard* Class DropShip in the center of his fighter's HUD. As he bore in, he watched the range indicators on the lead computing optical sight tick down. An IN RNG discrete flashed across the bottom of the heads up display. Vargas squeezed the trigger, and the fighter's Zeus 56 autocannon stitched a line of sparkling explosions across the target vessel's forward, portside 'Mech-bay door. His lasers ripped deep furrows in the transport's thick skin. Then he was past her. A jagged bolt of PPC fire slashed past the *Slayer*'s belly, a parting shot from one of the *Leopard*'s gunners. Vargas pulled his fighter up into a half loop, rolling out at the top. Below him, he saw a pair of *Stuka*s whip around the DropShip, leaving her with serious damage to her port side.

A series of bright green darts pounded his fighter from above and behind. Vargas pitched out, dropping through a wing-over into a split S. When he rolled upright again, he saw an enemy *Lucifer* clinging to Garrity's tail.

"Hang on, Fox. I'm coming!" Vargas shouted to his wingman. "Break left when I tell you. All right, now!"

Garrity, whose dark auburn hair and sharp features had earned him the vulpine nickname, pushed his *Shilone* into a tight bank. The *Lucifer* tried to stay with him, but lacked the maneuverability of the Legion ship. Instead, the rebel found himself nose to nose with Vargas' *Slayer*.

The rebel pilot tried to turn away, but it was too late. Fire spat from the *Slayer*'s guns, shredding armor and shearing the *Lucifer*'s left wing from the fuselage.

The *Slayer* flashed past the enemy ship as the *Lucifer* went into an oddly slow and unbalanced barrel roll. Vargas half-twisted in his seat to watch the rebel fighter spiral away, out of control.

"*Su madre!*" he yelled at the doomed enemy ship.

"First Squadron, sound off," he ordered as he brought the *Slayer* around. He had briefly lost contact with the rest of his pilots during his spoiling attack on the *Lucifer*.

"One-two, right here, boss, coming back onto your wing," Garrity called.

"Two-one and -two okay."

"Three flight okay." That was Carla Staedler.

"Four-two here," Ensign Keith Williams said sullenly.

"Where's Johnston?" Vargas asked sharply, already knowing the answer.

"Bob's gone, Commander," Williams answered dully. "The *Leo* got him, but he took the DropShip with him."

"Very well," Vargas said, keeping his voice equally monotone. They couldn't afford to stop now to mourn their comrade's loss. "Reform, and let's get on with our jobs. Second Flight, you're on lead. Head for that big, fat *Overlord* at five-low. Come in under his stern, and let's see if we can chew him up some."

"We're all over him, boss," Lieutenant Saul Dietrich sang.

A moment later, Dietrich's *Corsair* was bearing down hard on the ship, blazing away with its powerful lasers. Dietrich pulled out seconds before he would have slammed into the *Overlord*'s stern quarter. "Jaybird" Batsa followed his wingman, making an identical attack, but breaking away to the left, where Dietrich had evaded to the right. Staedler and Towsley rolled in next, followed by Vargas and Garrity.

Even the concerted attack of six aerospace fighters had not breached the *Overlord*'s thick armor. As the fighters swung around for another pass, a shout rang in Vargas' ears.

"Eagle One, this is Eagle Two. We've got trouble, Commander," Amanda Carroll said, the harshness in her voice the result of tension compounded by an old throat injury. "We've already got our hands full, and it looks as though the *Cruiser* is launching more fighters. In about two seconds we're going to be purely defensive here."

"Can you give us one more pass on the *Overlord*?" Vargas asked.

"Not a chance," Carroll gritted. "If we don't get some help up here, I'm going to lose the squadron."

"Dammit," Vargas spat. "First Squadron, form up on me. Let's go bail them out. Williams, fall in on my right wing, one klick back. We'll go with a three-ship element, staggered wedge formation."

The superbly trained pilots wasted no time. They dropped into formation, even as they angled off to join their comrades.

Vargas lined up his sights on the bizarre, lopsided shape of an *RPR-100 Rapier* fighter, and caressed the trigger. The *Slayer* quivered as his main gun spewed out a volley of armor-piercing high-explosive shells. The rebel fighter weathered the storm and flipped into a Shandel turn, climbing back to the left to meet its attacker. A few hundred meters away, a similar craft executed a near mirror-image wing-over, diving away to the left.

Vargas knew the rebels weren't trying to break contact, not in the first few seconds of the engagement. What they had just executed was called a defensive split. Under ordinary circumstances, his flight would have pursued one of the *Rapier*s, leaving the other free to maneuver against the attackers. But this time, as so often before, the commander of the Death Eagles had an ace up his sleeve.

"Pat, Williams, break low. Go after the wingman. I'll take the leader." The extra fighter in his element gave Vargas an element of surprise.

Vargas pulled his *Slayer* into a steep climb, cutting in the over-thrusters. Above and ahead of him, the *Rapier* pilot was reversing his turn. He reversed again, just as Vargas was maneuvering to follow the original course. The two ships fell into a pattern called a vertical rolling scissors. The *Rapier* was fractionally more agile than the *Slayer*, but not so much that he could easily evade Vargas. At the same time, the *Slayer* could not line up for a killing shot on the twisting enemy fighter.

Suddenly, the *Rapier* chopped his speed and flipped his fighter over onto its back. The off-balance-looking machine pushed over into a dive and lit off its thrusters. Vargas tried to follow the tight evasive maneuver, but before he could pull the *Slayer* around, the rebel pilot cut his engines back and executed a skidding end-for-end turn, almost identical to the one Vargas had used against the Separatist flyer a few days earlier. Instead of letting his fighter fly backward for a few minutes and hammering the pursuing *Slayer*, the *Rapier*'s pilot once again engaged his thrusters and rocketed forward into a high-speed head-on pass.

Twin strokes of lightning flashed from the *Rapier*'s paired particle cannons. The savage energy bolts ripped into the *Slayer*'s nose and left wing. A flight of missiles hammered the *Slayer*'s portside vertical stabilizer and cracked fuselage armor.

Julio Vargas was far from out of the fight. He again blasted the *Rapier* with all of his forward weapons, slagging away armor and leaving deep, carbon-blackened scores in the enemy's skin. He side-slipped his fighter, setting it off to one side of the *Rapier*'s collision course. The fighter shook as the paired PPCs blasted into his ship.

As the enemy broke away, Vargas whipped his fighter into a tight, knife-edge turn, which he held through a complete three-hundred-sixty-degree circle. He rolled out on the *Rapier*'s tail and fired. He heard the deep, musical hiss of the lasers firing, but for some reason, the autocannon did not fire. Vargas scanned the main weapons console. A small red bar was blinking calmly, proclaiming to the Legion pilot that the Zeus type 56 autocannon had been destroyed, probably in that last exchange of fire before the *Rapier* turned into the scissors.

The *Rapier* pilot came around for another pass. Vargas laced his enemy's uneven wings with his lasers, but he knew it was only a matter of time before the *Rapier* was able to pick his heavy armor to pieces.

Now it was Vargas' turn to dive away. He hoped the rebel pilot would be as eager for a kill as he had seemed to be so far. He prayed the other fighter would follow him through the dive.

"Pat!" Vargas yelled into his mike. "I've got a *Rapier* on my tail. I need you to scrape him off."

"Coming, Mother," Garrity quipped. "I've got you in sight. Level off and come hard right, and you'll bring him right to me."

Vargas kicked the right-rudder pedal and pushed his stick to starboard. He felt his G suit tighten against his legs as the air bladders inflated against the centrifugal force generated by a high-speed turn.

In that instant, the *Rapier*'s PPCs found the *Slayer* once more.

The wedge-shaped fighter shook under the high-energy discharge. Warning lights flared on the control panel, telling of armor loss and the destruction of the aft-facing laser. Missiles widened and deepened the damage, clawing deep into the *Slayer*'s guts to reduce its engine to a pile of wreckage.

"That's it. Eagle One is out of the fight. Carla, take the Squadron," Vargas called, locking the ring collar of his flight suit into the lower edge of his helmet to turn the garment into a vacuum-proof survival garment. He reached up to grab the yellow and black rings of the "face-blind" ejection handles.

"This is Eagle One-One requesting rescue. Eject, Eject, Eje—"

Carla Staedler watched in helpless horror as the *Rapier* dove in on Vargas' shattered fighter, its heavy Ranger autocannon walking a line of tracers up the *Slayer*'s spine and straight into the fighter's cockpit.

**Gray Death Legion Compound**
**Maria's Elegy Spaceport, Hesperus II**
**Skye Province**
**Lyran Alliance**
**30 June 3065**

Lori stared at the communications console in dumbfounded shock. In an instant of time, the life of a man she'd known for almost forty years had been snuffed out.

"Colonel, we can't hold them," said Carla Staedler, her voice breaking from the speakers. "We've got to withdraw or we're going to lose the whole wing."

"Pull out, Captain," Lori ordered. "You can't do any more good up there. Save the rest of the wing. We're going to need it."

"Colonel," a sensor tech called. "We have established a track on the inbounds. Analysis indicates they are *not* on course for the Defiance complex. Course and speed suggest the inbounds are heading for the Caran River basin."

Lori looked questioningly at Gina Ciampa.

"Doering," Ciampa said. "They're headed for the Doering plant."

"General, if I may," Lori said, remembering Grayson's lectures on maintaining proper military protocol, especially when dealing with house troops. With a nod from Ciampa, Lori called up a map of the area north of Maria's Elegy.

The Caran River basin was a broad, relatively flat area about two hundred kilometers north of the spaceport. The river itself was a fairly deep and wide watercourse, flowing roughly north to south from an out-jutting spur of the Myoo Mountains, through Maria's Elegy and on toward the sea. The Doering Electronics factory was situated on the Caran's west bank.

"You leave one of your battalions here," Lori said. "The other two and my regiment will immediately head for the Caran basin. With luck, we can bounce our DropShips out to the Doering plant before the rebels get there. If we have time to dig in, they will need their superior numbers to root us out."

"And what about Defiance?" Ciampa asked. "What if the inbounds divert to the factory complex while we're flying out to Doering? And what if those troops out in Melrose Valley move against the plant while both of our outfits are pinned down in the Caran basin?"

"Then, General, we have to trust Major Goree's Self-Protection Force to hold the rebels while we divert ourselves." Lori shrugged. "Or we recall General Zambos and the Thirty-sixth from Maldon. No matter how we cut it, we're still going to have to cover this whole planet with only three BattleMech regiments."

Ciampa took a few minutes to digest Lori's analysis of the situation.

"Very well, Colonel. Here's how we'll play this. You take the Gray Death Legion, my Second 'Mech battalion, the Second Armored, and Second Infantry regiments. My adjutant, Colonel Brennan, will have field command of the Lyran troops, but you'll have operational command. I'll keep the rest of my outfit here in Maria's Elegy. We'll stay ready to respond as the situation develops. If the Separatists move against Defiance, we'll hop out there to stop them. If the thrust at Doering is the genuine article, then we'll be ready to back you up if need be."

"Fair enough, General," Lori said grimly. "One other thing. I suggest you get an HPG message off to Hauptmann-General Poulin. See if you can get him to send us some support."

"I've already taken care of that, Colonel," Ciampa said

good-naturedly. "Just because we aren't mercenaries doesn't mean we're stupid."

"I never thought you were, General," Lori said lightly, then touched her fingertips to her forehead in a casual salute. "Now if you'll excuse me?" Not waiting for a reply, she ducked out of the communications center.

"Davis," she said to her second in command, "get the troops aboard the DropShips. We're going to war."

"Colonel—on your nine!"

Lori spun her *Victor* sharply to the left in response to Dallas MacKensie's warning cry. On instinct, she brought the assault 'Mech's right arm into line with the dark red metallic form of a *Maelstrom* closing with her at a lumbering run. The Dragon's Fire gauss rifle cracked, sending a basketball-sized sphere of nickel-iron streaking across the field to punch into the out-jutting torso of the enemy machine. Armor shattered under the impact. The *Maelstrom* staggered, but quickly regained its balance as it raised both its arms and let fly. A dazzling stream of charged particles ripped into the *Victor*'s left arm, burning away a ton of hardened Durallex armor. Simultaneously, a laser beam sliced into the 'Mech's plastron, cutting dangerously close to the quartet of missile tubes in its left breast.

Lori recovered quickly and fed a volley of those missiles at the hunched-over enemy machine. The four-kilogram shaped-charge warheads detonated against the *Maelstrom*'s tough hide, gouging divots in the Kellon Heavy armor. Lori fired the paired medium pulse lasers set into her *Victor*'s much-abused left vambrace, and touched off the gauss rifle again for good measure. The pale green energy darts chewed into the enemy machine's legs, while the gauss rifle's hypersonic slug smashed into almost the same spot as the first shot.

The rebel pilot seemed to take no notice of the gaping hole in his 'Mech's center torso. Defiantly, he unleashed his PPC again, this time lacing the *Victor*'s right leg.

The guy had courage, Lori thought. And tenacity. She had to admire him for that. Then again, he was fighting for his homeland against what he perceived as a foreign power. That often tended to make a man brave.

A sharp, warbling tone pierced Lori's ear, and a scarlet warning light flashed on her control panel. Someone, possibly the *Maelstrom*'s pilot, had illuminated her *Victor* with Target Acquisition Gear.

Not waiting around to find out if the designator had been linked to an artillery or Arrow IV missile battery, Lori stomped on the pedals controlling her *Victor*'s jump jets. Smoke and flame spilled out of the nozzles in her 'Mech's back and legs as the eighty-ton war machine rose into the air. The *Maelstrom* tried to track her with stuttering blasts from his pulse lasers, but was unable to score a hit. As Lori eased off on the jets, the warning tone fell silent. The TAG lock had been broken.

Feathering her jump jets, she brought the *Victor* back to the muddy banks of the Caran River. The Separatist 'Mech had turned to pursue her, but, before it could close with her, she hammered it again with laser and missile fire. The *Maelstrom* squatted back on its birdlike legs as the attack savaged its football-shaped body. With remarkable grace for a seventy-five-ton lump of metal and composites, the rebel machine turned away from Lori's *Victor* and loped off to the northwest, in the direction of the invaders' grounded DropShips.

Though her instincts told her to pursue, Lori knew there were other targets to contend with. The combined Legion and Lyran counterstrike force had arrived in the river basin only a few minutes before Skye Separatist DropShips burned their way across the sky above the Doering Electronics plant. The Fourth Skye Rangers had come in hot and hard, dropping two companies' worth of light and medium 'Mechs almost directly on top of the manufacturing center. Lori detailed the Lyran tank and infantry regiments under her nominal command to engage those forces, while she directed the full Gray Death Legion and the Fifteenth Lyran Guard Second 'Mech battalion against the invaders' main thrust.

The attackers grounded their DropShips on both sides of the Caran River, forcing Lori to further divide the units under her command. She sent the Lyran troops across the rain-swollen watercourse to engage the invaders there, while she led her mercenaries against the enemy forces on the west bank, where the Doering plant was located.

Scanning the *Victor*'s damage display, Lori saw that the fight with the *Maelstrom* had left her 'Mech's left arm and right leg with dangerously thin armor. The rest of her armor was relatively intact.

The combined Lyran and mercenary force seized and held the upper hand early in the battle, killing several lighter enemy 'Mechs with concentrated firepower. But the Skye Rangers' greater numbers began to tell, and the advantage shifted to the invaders. Lori's troops had been pushed back almost to the chain-link fence surrounding the Doering manufacturing center before she was able to stabilize her lines. On the far side of the river, Colonel Nana Brennan was faring about the same. Her battalion had contained the invaders in their landing zone until a fighter strike had torn up her lines and killed her executive officer. In the confusion that ensued, the Lyran Guards were pushed southward several kilometers before Brennan could restore order.

Sweeping her eyes across the main viewscreen, Lori picked out a fresh target and settled the red cross hairs of her primary gun sight across the tall, humanoid machine's armored spine, keyed in her gauss rifle, and stroked the trigger.

She felt no compunction at shooting an enemy from behind. After all, as an old Terran gunfighter once said, "His back was to me."

The dense metal pellet collided with the enemy machine's left calf, and the armored giant turned to face its attacker. As it came around, Lori was startled at the almost human appearance of the 'Mech's faceplate. The short tube of a small laser jutting from the cooling fins beneath the slitted, horizontal viewscreen added to the illusion by giving the impression that the machine was smoking a cigar. Only one BattleMech in the Lyran arsenal had such an appearance, the *HA1-O Hauptmann*, an OmniMech.

Lori knew that the 'Mech had been developed by the Lyran Alliance a few years earlier in an attempt to create the same class of adaptable war machines as were fielded by the Clans. Still fairly rare, a few *Hauptmann*s had been sent to Skye Rangers units. How ironic that those units were now using the new model machines against the same Lyran Alliance that had designed them.

Lori knew from intelligence briefings that the *Hauptmann* OmniMech had three variants, but she wasn't sure which one this was. When a flat actinic glare lit the business end of a thick cylinder perched on the *Hauptmann*'s right shoulder, and a silvery gray streak flashed past the *Victor*'s head, Lori saw that she was facing the "A" variant. Armed with a gauss rifle and an array of lasers and short-range missiles, the 'Mech could strike effectively at any range, while its thick armor would give it the capacity to endure for a long time on a modern battlefield.

Lori aimed her *Victor*'s full weapons complement at the rebel machine, then pressed the trigger. Streams of laser fire spattered against the *Hauptmann*'s legs. An instant later, the heavy gauss slug delivered a stunning body-blow to the OmniMech's left side. The short-range missiles, by far the lowest-velocity weapon carried by her 'Mech, wreathed the *Hauptmann*'s torso in smoke and flame, but did little more than chip its heavy armor.

The Lyran pilot was no rookie. Despite the barrage his machine had just taken, he returned Lori's fire without hesitation. Two ruby threads of laser energy speared the *Victor*'s left leg, while a slug from the shoulder-mounted gauss rifle punched into its belly. As Lori fought the controls, struggling to keep her machine upright, she heard an urgent warble being generated by her Matabushi Sentinel sensor system. Then a red MSSL warning light started flashing on her 'Mech's center control panel. She looked up in time to see the *Hauptmann* slightly extend both arms and launch a dozen short-range missiles. Guided by the *Hauptmann*'s Artemis Fire Control System, the missiles homed in on her battered *Victor*, the warheads bursting all around her. Some burrowed into the ground before exploding, throwing great clods of dirt into the air. Most found their targets, blasting away much of the armor remaining on the *Victor*'s right arm and leg.

"I could use a little help here!" Lori yelled into her headset mike.

"On the way, Colonel," a voice replied. "Are you still mobile?"

"Affirmative," she answered.

"Great. Jump out of there backward, to your seven. Make it about a hundred meters."

Lori stomped on her jump jet control pedals, boosting the massive, eighty-ton assault 'Mech into the air. Hauling back on the control sticks, she steered the jet nozzles to propel her backward and to her left.

The *Hauptmann* pilot must have known the *Victor*'s limited jump range, because he kicked his machine into a lumbering run, seemingly eager to finish off his opponent.

As Lori's *Victor* landed with a bone-jarring thud, she heard the deep, groaning squeal of metal stressing. The *Hauptmann* was almost five hundred meters away and closing fast. She brought her gauss rifle up, took careful aim, and fired. The slug bounced off the enemy's plastron, leaving a deep gouge in its wake. Instinctively, she waited for the weapon's breech to cycle another of the one-hundred-twenty-five-kilo spheres of nickel-iron into the firing chamber. Again, she took careful aim and squeezed the trigger.

The weapon failed to fire. Instead, it produced a hollow, buzzing thunk. There was no projectile to fire. The intense fighting had emptied Lori's gauss magazine, robbing her of her most effective weapon. She cued up her short-range missiles and watched the range to the target tick down until it entered the weapon's two-hundred-seventy-meter effective range.

"Where's that help?" she called. "You better get here quick."

A flight of missiles arced over her position to shower down upon the enemy 'Mech. The *Hauptmann* shifted its stance as the rebel at the controls turned his attention to the new foe. Before the enemy pilot could bring any of his weapons to bear, Lori heard the chattering roar of an autocannon and the hissing crack of gauss-rifle fire. Tracers stopped a few meters from their target, as proximity fuses detonated bursting charges. Submunitions battered every part of the *Hauptmann*, while the gauss rifle's solid shot blasted armor away from the 'Mech's left breast.

Lori searched the display for her rescuer, and caught sight of the elegant, birdlike form of a Clan *Cauldron-Born* alongside her. Its dark gray Legion paint job was hard to see in the waning light of the day, but she could make out the words "Faudgh an Bellagh" painted in gold lettering over a green field across the OmniMech's narrow body. There was only one such 'Mech in the Gray Death Legion.

The Gaelic slogan, meaning "Clear the way," was the motto of Major Thomas Devin.

Taking advantage of the Clan-designed and -built weapons, Devin savaged the *Hauptmann* with laser and missile fire. The rebel 'Mech replied with its gauss rifle. The slug broke armor on the *Cauldron-Born*'s left leg, causing Devin to stutter-step in his deliberate advance. The enemy split his fire, using his extended-range lasers to again claw armor from Lori's *Victor*.

Both Legion 'Mechs turned their fire on the *Hauptmann*. Though the big assault 'Mech was tough, it could not stand up to that kind of a combined pounding. Its right leg snapped off above the backward-acting knee joint, and the proud war machine toppled. Even as it fell, Lori saw the bright flash as the pilot ejected from his crippled 'Mech.

"Thank you, Major," Lori said, panting from the heat of her cockpit and the stress of the moment. "How is the rest of the regiment faring?"

"Not too bad, Colonel," Devin said in his clipped St. Ives accent. "We've been pushed back onto the Doering factory grounds. The rebels keep pushing, but so far we've been able to hold them off. If they get organized instead of coming at us piecemeal, I don't think we'll be able to hold them."

"What about Colonel Brennan?" Lori asked. "Where are the Lyran guards?"

"To hell and gone," Devin spat. "Brennan tried to hold the buggers on her side of the river, but there were too many of them. The Guards fell back and got scattered. It will be morning before all of them find their way back home. The Separatists have pulled back and are probably reforming out there in the dark. When they get on track, they're going to try to do the same thing to us."

"Well, Major, let's get back to the Legion and see if there is any way we can prevent that."

"Legion One, this is Assassin One. We've got a breakthrough in our sector."

Lori looked at the map of the Doering Electronics complex and its environs displayed on a secondary monitor in her 'Mech's cockpit. The tiny blue triangles marking the

Legion's second battalion were arrayed in two staggered lines along the Doering Electronic complex's northern perimeter. A spear of scarlet icons was now penetrating the line. It had taken the Skye Rangers some time to get "on track," as Major Devin would say. Then, just before midnight, they launched a new attack.

"Major Devin, get your battalion into the line to support Major Houk," Lori barked into her communicator. "Davis, we'll move the command company into the center of the complex and form a mobile reserve."

"Colonel, it's no good. They're coming at us in full strength," Houk yelled. "I don't think we can hold them."

"You've got to hold them, Major," Lori snapped. "Devin is on his way to support you. I'm moving—"

A triphammer series of explosions thundered into her cockpit, ending her message prematurely. Lori scanned her primary viewscreen, catching sight of four heavy BattleMechs moving in on her right. None of the humanoid war machines responded to her communication system's automatic Identify Friend or Foe interrogation. The enemy had somehow managed to flank the Legion's positions.

Lori slammed the control sticks hard over. In response, her *Victor* twisted at the waist. She jerked the triggers, snapping off a hasty volley at the attackers. Her lasers dug into the tough, armored hide of an enemy *Black Knight*, but the short-range missiles all fell short, scattering chunks of pavement across the 'Mech's feet. The *Knight* responded with a blast from its PPC that ripped away the last of the armor on her *Victor*'s left arm. Lori heard the groan of overstressed metal as the endo-steel of the 'Mech's chassis all but collapsed under the particle beam's savage caress.

A *Cataphract* and an *Orion* stepped up beside the *Black Knight*, while the fourth 'Mech, all but invisible in the moonless night, hung back. Lori's computer rendered the machine as a *Banshee*, making it the heaviest enemy machine they had seen yet. Lori suspected that the *Banshee* might be the Skye Ranger command 'Mech.

Dallas MacKensie and the rest of the Legion's command lance closed ranks with her *Victor* and opened fire on the new arrivals, but they stood little chance against the armored monsters.

"Legion command, pull back," Lori called to them, though the order almost stuck in her throat. "All Gray Death units, fall back on the DropShips."

One by one, the Legion's company commanders registered their compliance with her orders. Each voice carried with it its own note of anger, reproach, or disgust. The Legion had lost battles before. This was something different. It was almost as though the Gray Death Legion was admitting defeat. To Lori's mind, it seemed that each bitter-toned acknowledgment was an accusation. This was her first big fight as the commander of the Gray Death Legion and she'd been found wanting. She'd let the Legion down and failed Grayson's memory.

Pushing those despairing thoughts into the back of her mind, she guided her badly damaged *Victor* away from the Doering plant, leaving it in the hands of the enemy.

# ═══ **18** ═══

*Gray Death Legion Compound*
*Maria's Elegy Space Port, Hesperus II*
*Skye Province*
*Lyran Alliance*
*01 July 3065*

Lori sat in her office chair, leaning on the top of her desk with her chin cradled in her hands. The only source of light in the room was the digital clock on the wall. She stared at it as it clicked from 0329 to 0330.

Another minute of her life gone, she thought, feeling the first edges of despair touching her heart. She tried to tell herself again that the battle at the Doering plant was not the first engagement the Gray Death Legion had lost, nor was it likely to be the last. But here on Hesperus II, in the early morning hours of the first of July 3065, it felt like the world was beginning to wind down for her. Grayson, her husband of forty years, was gone. Before she had had time to properly mourn his passing, the Legion had been sent off to war. Then, Julio Vargas, that smiling, daredevil Spaniard, was taken from them. It seemed the Legion's phenomenal luck in battle was running out. Who would be next? McCall? Devin? Dan Brewer? Maybe she herself.

Lori felt the weight of the years pressing in on her. She had been a warrior all of her life, and a long, hard life it had been.

*Yes, you have been a warrior all of your life,* a voice in

her head said. *And a warrior doesn't sit in the dark and mope. Now, pull yourself together, go out there, and* lead *your troops.*

The words and tone of the silent voice were so familiar that Lori shot from her chair, turning it over in the process. She slapped on the desk light, and glared around the office, as though she expected to see her husband standing in the corner, looking at her with that infectious, crooked grin.

But she was alone. Lori righted her chair and thought about dropping back into it. But the words kept echoing in her head, "Go out there and *lead* your troops."

She snapped off the desk lamp and made her way to the door in the dark. She *would* go out there and lead her troops. She'd lead as Grayson had always done, by example. Right now, the example her troops needed was one of a sensible commander, and a sensible commander would go try to get some rest.

The Legion would patch itself up and begin again in the morning, just as it always had done.

Lori made her way through the darkened corridors of the Legion officers' quarters until she reached her suite. Keying in the combination to her door, she slipped inside. Without turning on the lights, she passed into the bedroom. Pausing only long enough to remove her jacket and to pull off her boots, she threw herself onto her bunk. Almost at the same instant, the comm buzzed.

She sighed and sat up, slapping the answer stud.

"Yeah?" she mumbled. "And this had better be important."

"Colonel, I'm sorry to disturb you." It was Chief Sellars. "General Ciampa wanted you to know that it looks like the rebels in Melrose Valley are preparing to boost. We're getting real-time feeds from the *Boomerang*s. We've got heat blooms in the power plants of all of the enemy's DropShips. Yep, there they go. One, two, yeah, all of their DropShips are boosting."

"Where are they headed, Chief?" Lori asked.

"Don't know," Sellars answered.

"What about the force up at Doering?"

"Don't know," the chief sensor operator repeated. "We don't have sensor coverage of the Caran basin. We tried to over-fly the site, but the Separatists shot down the *Boomer-*

*ang*. We sent out a few Skulkers, but they haven't reached the site yet."

"And the WarShip?"

"Holding position outside lunar orbit."

"Hmmm," Lori grunted. "All right, Chief. Please tell General Ciampa I'm on my way. I'll be there in about ten minutes."

In less time than she had predicted, Lori strode into the communications center. When she entered, Gina Ciampa was leaning over a map table, speaking animatedly over a comm. From Ciampa's agitated state, Lori silently bet that the person on the other end of the line was General Zambos.

"Wait one," Ciampa said into her lip mike. "Colonel Kalmar-Carlyle just walked in." She rounded to face Lori. "So, Colonel, what is *your* opinion?"

Lori studied the tracks plotted for the departing DropShips. All of the broken red lines seemed to be arching up and away from Hesperus II in the general direction of the *Avalon*-Class cruiser parked in geostationary orbit, just outside the orbit of the planet's sole moon.

"Still nothing on the Fourth Skye Rangers?" Lori asked, tapping the section of the electronic map representing the Caran River basin and the Doering Electronics factory.

"Nothing." Ciampa shook her head. "The Skulkers should arrive there within the hour. We'll know more then. Those scout cars carry about the same sensor packages as the *Boomerang*s, so our feed will be almost as good."

Lori frowned as she walked around the map table, tapping her front teeth with a stylus she had taken from her pocket. She completed two circuits before she spoke again.

"I don't think this was just a raid-in-force," she speculated aloud. "There were too many 'Mechs for that. Nobody pulls that kind of a raid with two full Regimental Combat Teams. Even if they did, these guys barely inflicted enough damage to slow down anybody's plans."

"What about your fighter wing, Colonel? Could you send some of your pilots out there to track the enemy's movement?"

"I could, General. The question is, should I?" Lori gave a single bitter laugh. "The Eagles are shot up pretty bad.

I doubt we could field five undamaged ships. We go chasing after their DropShips, and we're liable to lose the rest of the wing. I'd rather not risk that, General."

"I understand and appreciate your concern for your men," Ciampa said. "But we really need to know what the rebels are up to. If the Skye Rangers are displacing, we need to know where they're going, so we can be ready to meet them in case they're not leaving. We may risk a few of your pilots, but in the long run it will be a greater risk to all of us if we lose track of the enemy."

Lori gave Ciampa a cool look while she digested her words. Ciampa was right. The only way of knowing for sure what the Separatists were up to was to assign some of her pilots to fly reconnaissance.

"Very well, General," Lori said at last. "I'll arrange for a recon flight."

"Owl One to Legion One, we've just picked up the Rangers on our scanners," said Lieutenant Saul Dietrich, his voice crackling over the ear piece of the communications headset Lori wore over her left ear. "They are no longer outbound. The targets have assumed a GSO and are just sitting there. They have not deployed fighters. If I had to guess, Colonel, I'd say they were waiting for something."

"Confirmed," a technician sang out. "Sensor track indicates the rebels have left the atmosphere and have settled into a geosynchronous orbit."

"Lieutenant, can you remain onstation and keep us advised?" Lori asked.

"Yes, boss," Dietrich replied. "Either the bad guys haven't spotted us yet, or they don't care if we spy on 'em. Unless they launch fighters or try to get frisky with their DropShips, we should be able to remain onstation for . . ."

Dietrich paused, and Lori reasoned he was computing his fuel consumption versus the remaining fuel in his tanks.

"We can remain onstation for one-eight-zero minutes at present rate of fuel consumption," he said finally.

"Very well, Owl One. Remain onstation for one-four-zero minutes, then come back home," Lori ordered. "Maneuver at your discretion. If you think you can get us a better look without getting your tail shot off, that's fine, but do not place yourselves or your aircraft at risk. I'd be just as happy if the two of you stayed out of gunnery range."

"Don't worry about us, Legion One." Lori recognized the cheerful voice of Dietrich's wingman, Ensign Jason Batsa. "The first rule of being a mercenary is live to spend your paycheck."

"Roger that," Lori said flatly. Too many of her friends had died recently for her to appreciate that comment. She turned to Gina Ciampa.

"There you have it, General. Apparently the rebels are forming up to make another push."

"Yes, and God only knows where it's going to come down."

"We have three places that are likely," Lori countered. "I doubt they boosted just to turn around and hit Doering or Melrose again. That means they're going after Maldon, the Defiance complex, or Maria's Elegy."

"They haven't been behaving like a typical invasion force," Ciampa said as she studied the holographic plotting board. "They've hit two secondary targets."

"Strategic deception," Lori said, shrugging. "They know their battle plan and their timetable; we don't. They can strike when and where they please. We either have to keep our forces consolidated in one place and respond to their moves or try to be proactive and guess where they're going to hit next, which leaves the rest of the targets onplanet relatively unprotected. It's a good plan."

Ciampa gave a noncommittal grunt. "It's almost to be expected."

"Oh?"

"Yeah, I know the Fourth Rangers' commander, Lieutenant-General William Harrison von Frisch. He was a year ahead of me at Sanglamore."

"I thought Sanglamore took only Isle of Skye natives," Lori said, staring at Ciampa.

"For the most part, they do. I'm a daughter of Skye. I was born on Alkaid and graduated from Sanglamore with honors in twenty-nine. Don't be suspicious of me, Colonel. I don't agree with what Duke Robert is trying to do. Like it or not, the Isle of Skye is part of the Lyran Alliance. We can't quit just because we feel like it."

Lori blinked in surprise at Ciampa's quietly impassioned

statement, although she knew that such was the cost of any civil war. Men and women would be forced to turn their backs on home and family in order to follow the dictates of their conscience.

"You were saying about von Frisch?" she prompted, thinking to turn Ciampa away from what was obviously a painful subject.

Ciampa gazed through her for a moment, then returned to her theme.

"He's a maverick, always has been. I remember him mouthing off at one of the professors about the stale old we-always-did-it-this-way attitude of the Steiner officer corps. He was always in trouble for going his own way, but his record in field exercises was undeniable. He fought more like a Fedrat than a Lyran. I lost touch with him after he graduated, but I kept seeing his name on promotion and decoration rosters and kept hearing rumors that he was in trouble with the higher-ups.

"He was one of the first generals to hand over his resignation when Duke Robert declared Skye to be independent. Again, that's hardly surprising. And it's hardly surprising that Robert would pick him to lead the assault on Hesperus."

Lori pulled up a chair and sat back to digest what Ciampa had just told her. An unorthodox officer in command of the enemy forces would make predicting his next move difficult and would limit the defenders' options.

"Well, General," she said at last, "the Gray Death Legion has a reputation for being unpredictable too. Once we get von Frisch on the ground, we'll do everything we can to keep *him* guessing."

That drew a chuckle from Ciampa that was cut short by the voice of one of the communication techs.

"General, Colonel, we've got a sensor feed from Sage Five."

The officers jumped to their feet. Sage Five was the code name of the three-vehicle unit of Skulker Wheeled Scout Tanks that had been dispatched to the Caran River basin.

"Sage Five, this is Warrior One Actual," Ciampa said, adjusting her headset. "Where the hell have you been? We expected to hear from you over an hour ago."

"I know, Warrior One," the scout replied. "We got into

position right on time, but we had to lay low for a while. We were just about to start sending you telemetry feeds when a couple of bad guys came and camped right on our doorstep. One was a *Hermes*. If we'd started sending, they'd have spotted us right away. We went into complete shutdown. Even then, we were afraid his Beagle probes would pick us up. They just now moved away enough for us to risk transmitting."

"Never mind that now," Ciampa cut him off. "Where are the rebels?"

"They've left a holding force at the Doering plant, and it looks like the rest of the enemy are boarding their DropShips. They can't be bugging out, or they'd all be leaving."

"How much of a holding force?" Lori asked.

"Looks like an armored regiment, maybe two regiments of infantry," the scout answered. "Stand by. Telemetry coming your way."

A technician pointed to a monitor where the data being fed to the communications center was displayed. The installation's powerful computers read the encrypted electronic signals and rendered a graphic, three-dimensional picture of the tactical situation. Lori didn't need to strain her eyes to pick out the image of a dozen or so armored vehicles parked inside the chain-link fence surrounding the Doering complex. At least two of those were Demolisher II heavy tanks. The smaller shapes of infantrymen moved among the tanks.

"Not good," Ciampa said. "It looks like they mean to hang on to the factory."

"Actually, the news isn't all that bad," Lori contradicted. "It's only bad if we plan on taking the factory away from them. As far as I'm concerned, they can have Doering, for now at least. What's good for us is the fact that they've weakened themselves a little without our having to fire a shot. One tank regiment and two regiments of PBIs may not seem like much when you compare them to what von Frisch has left, but every little bit helps. Once we beat the heavy assault forces, we can go back and mop up at Doering."

Ciampa snorted at Lori's use of the acronym for "Poor Bloody Infantry," knowing the Legion's reliance on ground-pounders who were specially trained and equipped for anti-Mech tactics.

"You may be right, Colonel," she said. "I hope you are." Then she spoke into her mike. "Sage One, continue your surveillance. Let us know the minute the enemy boosts. But do not put yourself at risk. If it looks like they've spotted you, pull stakes and run for cover."

"Wilco," the scout commander replied, signing off.

It was over an hour before any new information came into the comm center. When reports arrived, they heralded the next phase of the battle for Hesperus.

"Sage One to Warrior One, the bad guys just boosted. Tracking indicates that they're headed for geosynch. They're probably going to rendezvous with the rest of the rebels before they move on their next objective."

"Roger," a tech responded. "We've got them on our screens now. We'll take it from here."

"Sage One, what about the holding force?" Ciampa asked.

"Looks like the holding force is digging in."

"Very well. Hold position and maintain surveillance." Ciampa turned to Lori, who had been dozing in her chair. "Well, Colonel?"

"Whatever is going to happen next is about to happen," Lori said. The nap seemed to have left her more tired instead of rested.

"General!" the shout came from the woman manning the center's primary long-range scanners. The unit had been aimed into space to keep track of the WarShip lying doggo just outside Hesperus II's orbit. Lori's fatigue vanished in a burst of adrenaline triggered by the tech's panic-tinged shout.

"What is it?" Ciampa demanded sharply.

"The WarShip is on the move. Sensors indicate she is moving insystem."

Before either woman could respond, a third voice rang in Lori's ears.

"Legion One, this is Owl One, FLASH! The *Simon Davion* is underway and heading insystem. The DropShips are still onstation."

"Owl One, bug out," Lori barked. "We have the

DropShips and the *Simon* on scanners. No sense in getting yourselves killed."

"We're long gone, boss." In her headset, Lori heard the powerful engines of Dietrich's fighter cut in. On the tracking board, the tiny blue daggers representing Owl Flight's *Corsair* aerospace fighters began moving away from the clustered red circles of the enemy DropShips. A number of scarlet daggers blinked into existence on the board as the rebel fighters gained enough separation from the ships to be detected by the planetside sensors. There was no string of alphanumerics attached to the enemy fighters because the rebel craft were too far away for identification.

"Owl Flight, you've got at least six fighters in pursuit," Lori said into her microphone.

"Thanks for the tip, Legion One," Dietrich said with a touch of sarcasm. "We can see them. They aren't gaining, and they aren't falling behind."

"Owl Flight, can you adjust your vector to bring them across the spaceport defenses?" Ciampa asked.

"That's what we're trying to do." The Legion pilot's voice was tight, with a raw edge. He sounded as if he was straining against the G forces generated by aerospace combat maneuvers. The scale of the tracking board was too small to show that.

The icons representing Owl Flight began to veer away from their original course, as Dietrich and Batsa vectored in toward Maria's Elegy.

Ciampa moved to the opposite end of the communication center, talking animatedly with a technician. Lori couldn't hear what was being said, but she had some idea. The plaque above the tech's station read Primary Weapon Control.

The tiny pointed crosses representing Legion fighters crept across the tracking board, slowly descending to twenty-five thousand meters. Their heading change had cost them some of their lead, but they were still outside the maximum effective range of the pursuing fighters. As she watched and prayed, silently urging her pilots to hurry, a wedge of amber light flashed across the tracking board. Her fighters were just crossing the boundary of the yellow fifty-degree arc. The rebel ships trailed them by less than a finger's width.

"Wait for it," she heard Ciampa mutter.

The attacking fighters crossed the verge of the wedge.

"Wait," Ciampa said.

Another twenty seconds ticked by.

"Now," the general said.

Across the spaceport from the command center, a set of massive doors set into a large hardened ferrocrete building swung open. For a moment, the air was filled with a high-pitched rumble, followed by quiet, then an earsplitting crack resounded across the spaceport as a megawatt pulse of laser energy ripped into the sky.

The lights dimmed in the comm center as the huge defensive laser drew power from the rest of the base.

"Miss," the weapons officer spat. "Charging for another shot. Those fighters are too small for the system to target accurately."

"Keep firing," Ciampa growled. "You might not hit the rebels, but you'll give them something to think about."

"Weapon on line. Firing." The tech thumped his fist against his console. "Dammit."

"How long until the missiles can be brought to bear?" Ciampa asked.

"We have a hard Artemis lock. It will be a few minutes until they enter missile range," the tech said, fiddling with his controls.

"General, it looks like the enemy is breaking off pursuit."

Ciampa turned to the sensor operator who had spoken. "Confirm it."

"Confirmed. General. The fighters are breaking off, but the DropShips have started an in-run. It looks like they're headed for the Defiance complex." The tech leaned in toward his display. "Wait one . . .oh, no."

"What?" Lori snapped.

"The *Simon Davion*. She is *definitely* moving insystem. I think she's going to pull into orbit."

**Myoo Highlands, Hesperus II**
**Skye Province**
**Lyran Alliance**
**01 July 3066**

"Thank you, General. We'll be ready for them," Major Goree said. "But we need you to come and help us. If both rebel units *are* headed this way, I don't think the DSPF can hold them off alone."

Without waiting for Ciampa's reply, Goree switched off his comm unit. He looked at the two men seated across his desk, then spoke first to the man in civilian clothing.

"Mister Quinn, I think you had better shut down as many of the plant's facilities as you safely can. Seal up the ammunition bunkers, and get your people into the shelters."

Samuel Quinn, the Defiance facility's production manager, nodded, then got up to do as he was bid.

Goree addressed himself to the remaining man. "Pres, get the troops mounted up. If the Separatists are really on their way here, we don't have a whole lot of time. Get the defense grid powered up. We might not be able to knock any of their DropShips down, but we can seriously inconvenience them."

"Yessir," Captain Preston Minh responded, turning to leave.

"Wait a second, Pres." Goree stopped his executive officer. "Shut the door. There's something else General Ciampa told me. I didn't want Quinn to hear it, for fear of starting a panic."

"What is it, Jim?"

"Ciampa said the Separatists are moving a battlecruiser into orbit. We know this mountain is big enough to withstand any conventional weapon. I don't know if it can stand up to naval gunfire, especially anti-ship missiles. Detail a squad of infantrymen to help Quinn get everyone into the hardened shelters. Try to get them as deep as possible. But don't let word of this leak out, Pres, or we're liable to have a panic on our hands."

"Major, you're full of good news," Minh said sarcastically.

"I am that," Goree said, with a thin, humorless smile. "Get a move on, Captain. Our guests will be here soon."

As Minh left the Major's office, Goree got up and pulled a large nylon duffel bag from a wardrobe. Then he stepped into the hallway, out of habit slapping a wall-mounted switch, killing the lights. For a moment, the irony of his action tugged at the corners of his mouth. Here he was, about to go into a desperate battle against long odds in which incredible amounts of energy would be expended, and he was concerned about saving the company a few ergs worth of draw on its electrical generation system.

Goree walked quickly through the corridors toward the 'Mech hangar. He was now so familiar with the maze of passageways that he could walk them blindfolded. When he first arrived at DefHesp, he'd been overawed by the sheer enormity of the facility, with its cracking stations, fractionating towers, blast furnaces, smelters, and rows of warehouses. Now when he passed through the complex, he barely noticed them. That was not to say he was unmindful of the huge automated and manual fabrication systems. He was supremely aware of them. Indeed, protecting the underground complex had become Major James Goree's overwhelming reason for living.

As he entered the 'Mech hangar, Phil Bertrand, the head of his personal technical crew, hurried across the bay to meet him.

"Major, we just completed the diagnostics and pre-start sequences. Everything checks out fine. You've got a full load of ammunition, and you're ready to go."

Goree took the electronic note pad Bertrand was holding. With an elegant hand more suited to a scholar or poet than a warrior, Goree signed the status report without reading it. If Phil Bertrand said his 'Mech was ready to go, then it was ready.

Goree looked at the men and women standing around the bay. All of them were skilled warriors. Many had once been part of the armed forces of one Great House or another. A few were veterans of the war of annihilation against the Smoke Jaguars.

"They are coming, people," he said simply. "Let's mount up."

As the MechWarriors of the Defiance Self-Protection Force scattered toward their BattleMechs, Goree headed for his *GUN-1 ERD Gunslinger*. The 'Mech was the product of a joint Davion/Kurita design team. Intended to cripple Clan 'Mechs at the stand-off ranges the genetically engineered Clan warriors seemed to favor, the *Gunslinger* mounted a pair of gauss rifles, one in each forearm. A half-dozen medium lasers, two of them pulse models, completed the assault armament.

Goree was as familiar with the 'Mech and its capabilities as he had been with his ex-wife, but unlike her, the big machine had never let him down. He sprinted up the steep metal stairs to the catwalk that ran shoulder-high to most of the 'Mechs in his battalion. When he reached the open ingress/egress hatch set into the back of his *Gunslinger*'s head, he placed his duffel on the perforated steel decking and knelt beside it. He pulled a coverall from the bag and exchanged the MechWarrior combat suit for his normal clothing.

Like a cooling vest, the MCS helped counteract the effects of the waste heat generated by a 'Mech's fusion plant and weapons. Unlike the vests, the combat suits covered the whole of a warrior's body, increasing their effectiveness. They included a hardened armor vest and a special light combat neurohelmet, which could be sealed against a hostile atmosphere. With practiced fingers, he fastened the suit's armored plastron in place over his chest and shoved his civilian clothing into the duffel. He pulled the light combat neurohelmet from its padded compartment in the bag, tucked it under one arm, and ducked into the cockpit.

Then Goree dropped into his command couch and fastened the seat's five-point harness around him. He made sure his combat suit, with its all-important cooling tubes, was not pinched or constricted by the heavy nylon straps encircling his waist and crossing his body down from his shoulders and up between his legs. Once he was satisfied with the fit of the harness, he pulled the neurohelmet over his head and attached the control leads. For a moment, he experienced a flash of vertigo as the sensors in the helmet attuned the big gyrostabilizer in the 'Mech's belly to his own sense of balance.

"Enter password and security code now." The computer's synthesized voice was a neutral contralto.

"Password: Floodgate," he said clearly. Unlike many MechWarriors, Goree's password meant nothing to him personally. He had chosen it at random from a dictionary. "Security code: In good time."

"Password and security code accepted. Voiceprint match confirmed." The computer's tone never changed. "Welcome aboard, Major Goree."

Goree returned the greeting. He took hold of the control stick with his right hand. With his left, he flipped a switch on an overhead panel. A dull thump penetrated the thick armor covering the cockpit, an indication that the locking clamps that held the *Gunslinger* to the gantry had released.

"All Defenders, this is Seawall," he said into his helmet's integral microphone. "Move out according to the numbers. Form up just outside the hangar. It's time to earn our pay."

Two of the 'Mechs of his command company exited the hangar before Goree was cleared to leave. He guided the big 'Mech through the hangar door out into the open space beyond. Quickly, the 'Mechs of the Defiance Self-Protection Force fell into ranks behind him.

"Attention to orders," he said when the last 'Mech stepped into place. "We have a large force headed this way. On a 'Mech-for-'Mech basis, we outweigh and likely outgun most of them, but overall, they've got us completely outclassed. So, this is how we're going to handle it. We'll move down to our prepared emplacements, we'll fight from cover wherever possible, and we'll stay within range of the defense grid. If the enemy comes at us in force, and I expect he will, we will displace to our fallback positions, and then, if necessary, withdraw inside the factory itself. If you must withdraw, keep to the clear lanes. Do not stray into the minefields.

"I do hope it will not come to that. General Ciampa and Colonel Kalmar-Carlyle are mustering their forces to come and relieve us. We've got to hold the enemy back from our gates for as long as possible. If we're forced back into the mountain, they will lay siege to the gates and eventually batter them down. We've got the advantage if the fight goes inside the facility, but I'd rather avoid that sort of battle. The damage it would inflict on the plant is too great. Further, if the enemy troops are inside when Ciampa and the Legion arrive, they'll have to root the enemy out, just the same as the rebels would have to root us out.

"We must be tough today, people. Mark your targets. Make every shot count. That is all. Now, company commanders, move your troops into position."

A flurry of orders blanketed the communications net as the commanders of each of Goree's five companies barked out orders to the warriors under their leadership. Goree and the 'Mechs of his command company held back, giving the rest of his troops time to deploy to the improved fighting positions that had been prepared for this day. All around him, studding the sides of the mountain, were low camouflaged pillboxes, each housing a powerful laser, particle projector, autocannon, or missile launcher. Some of the bunkers contained Long Toms or Arrow IV launchers, heavy artillery units that could rain destruction down upon the invaders before the attackers could get close enough to hit back.

Even with all that firepower at his disposal, he wondered if he could hold until the combat units arrived from Maria's Elegy. It was less than an hour by DropShip, but Ciampa had told him that the rebels had moved the *Simon Davion* into position above Maria's Elegy. The presence of the capital ship would make transporting ground units by suborbital DropShip flights risky in the extreme. Therefore, it would take the relief force most of the day to traverse the rough Myoo Mountains. With luck, they would arrive in time to interrupt the Separatists' victory celebration.

"Major, we've got a feed from the spaceport," a technician said via the command net. "You should be able to see the inbound DropShips any second, coming in at one-five-eight degrees."

Goree touched a control, setting the magnification on his main viewscreen to its highest level. He twisted the *Gunslinger*'s torso to the right, and within seconds, the 'Mech's sensitive targeting and tracking equipment picked up the relatively tiny black spots of the incoming DropShips.

"Command center, I have the inbounds on my scope," he called. "It looks like it's just DropShips. Have they launched their fighters yet?"

"Not yet, Major." The sensor operator sounded as perplexed as Goree felt. The larger, more powerful fixed sensor systems that were part of the Defiance Industries defense grid should have been able to detect such fighter craft had they been deployed. "They may be waiting until they're closer, to give their fighters less of an in-run to the target."

"Well, keep your eyes open," Goree said. "I want to know the minute they launch."

"You don't have to wait, Major. The lead ship just deployed its fighters. It looks like heavies, and they're inbound high and fast."

Goree relayed the warning to his troops and ordered the command center to switch the defense grid to its antiair role. He watched as the fighters appeared on his viewscreen, first as tiny specks, then as miniature, aircraft-shaped blotches. In a matter of seconds, the spots resolved themselves into the flying-wing shape of *Chippewa* aerospace fighters.

The first pair flashed over the Self-Protection Force's dug-in 'Mechs, bypassing even the command lance before they rolled out. The lead *Chippewa* held its dive for a full five seconds before releasing a stick of bombs. The deadly packages of steel and high explosive slammed into the mountainside and blossomed into a gout of smoke and flame. From his position, Goree could not see what the attackers were aiming at, but he could guess. Their target was either one of the heavy artillery emplacements or a sensor radome. The second fighter made its run even before the smoke of the first bomb salvo had dissipated.

Missiles, laser, and autocannon fire reached up from the

defense grid to claw at the rebels, but the swiftly darting fighters made difficult targets. Most of the attacks hit nothing but empty air.

Two more fighters swooped in, aiming for a different point on the mountainside. They weren't quite so lucky. The heavy ground fire swatted one *Lucifer* out of the sky and left the second with a badly perforated wing.

A warning tone screeched in Goree's ear. A small red square flicked on in the top-left corner of his viewscreen, bracketing what appeared to be a rebel *Stuka* aerofighter. Beneath the viewscreen glowed a threat light labeled TAG. The ship must have been one gained from House Davion during the time of the Federated Commonwealth. The big fighter was boring its way in on the command lance's position.

Goree called a warning to his lancemates even as he snapped the *Gunslinger*'s twin gauss rifles into line with the attacking fighter. Both shots missed the relatively tiny, fast-moving target. Laser fire from the defense grid slashed at the *Stuka*'s skinny fuselage. Missiles and particle bolts fired by the command lance also tore at the attacking ship. But still he came on. A new alarm sound joined and clashed with the first as the threat light labeled MSSL lit up.

The *Stuka* pulled up and away from the command lance, but left two streaks of fire arrowing in toward the DSPF commander's position. One of the big Arrow IV missiles smashed into the *PPR-5S Salamander* artillery 'Mech piloted by Livia Lassiter. The explosion drove the hunched machine back a step, blasting half the armor away from its chest. The second Arrow IV drove into the stony ground between the *Salamander*'s feet, scattering shrapnel and bits of shattered rock for thirty meters around, and causing the staggering 'Mech to fall to one knee.

Then, as suddenly as it began, the air attack was over.

"All units, check in," Goree snapped.

"Alpha Company, checking in. We took some damage, but we're all still here."

"Bravo Company here, Major. They didn't touch us at all."

"Major, this is Lieutenant Nystrom, Charlie Company. Captain Harris is dead. His *Nightsky* took two Arrows square in the chest. They damn near cut him in half, sir."

"Take it easy, son," Goree said, hearing the unsteady note in Nystrom's voice. "How is the rest of C Company?"

"We're okay, I guess," Nystrom said, clearly trying to master himself. "We took a few hits, but the rest of us can still fight."

"Good man," Goree said. "Delta Company, report."

"Delta Company got banged around some, Major, but we're mostly intact."

"Good. Now, all commands, look sharp. The rebels are on the ground, and I don't think they're going to give us much time to recover from the air strike."

"You're right about that, sir," Nystrom yelled across the comm net. All traces of sorrow or fear were swallowed up in anger and the anticipation of battle. "Here they come."

Goree looked out across the plateau and spotted a broken line of 'Mechs carefully picking their way across the uneven ground.

"Command Center, we have 'Mechs on the ground," he said, catching some of Nystrom's excitement as he spoke. "Patch me through to the Fire Direction Center."

"FDC," were the next words he heard.

"Fire Mission," Goree told the officer controlling the defense system's artillery assets. "Grid: Lima-India-Five-Seven-Two-Niner. Target: BattleMechs moving in the open. Request spotting round."

"Confirming, Grid: Lima-India-Five-Seven-Two-Niner. 'Mechs in the open." There was a pause while the big Long Tom artillery pieces aligned themselves. "Spotting round on the way."

Goree heard the thump as the massive cannon spat out its projectile. Several seconds later, the shell landed one hundred meters in front of the advancing 'Mechs.

"Splash," he said, telling the Fire Direction Center he could see the shell impact. "You're short. Up fifty and fire for effect."

"On the way."

Again, the thump of the big gun shook the mountainside. Before the echoes of the blast could fade, a trio of similar reports roared out. The first projectile arrived right on target, bursting directly between two of the invaders' 'Mechs. One reeled and fell. The other took a stuttering step, recovered, and kept on coming. A split-second later, three dirty

black-gray flowers bloomed over the battlefield, slightly in front of the advancing line. Under maximum magnification, Goree could see the sparkling flashes of submunitions exploding against armor as the shells burst, showering the enemy 'Mechs with smaller antiarmor bomblets.

A second volley of artillery shells boomed overhead. But the rebel commander was too smart to just stand in the open and take the fire. No sooner had his 'Mechs recovered from the pounding of the first barrage than they sped up their advance, heedless of the uneven ground. Goree called a correction in to the FDC, and a third set of shells dropped into the advancing ranks.

At almost the same time, a half-dozen bolts of azure fire, barely visible in the late-morning sun, lashed out at the attackers from his partially concealed 'Mechs. The Separatists hit back with PPC, laser, and missile fire, pausing only long enough to target the half-hidden DSPF machines.

"Take aim. Mark your targets," he called across the comm net.

Lasers and autocannon fire joined the charged-particle streams and antiarmor missiles.

"Major, do you want another volley?" the artillery officer asked over the command channel.

"Negative, the enemy are at 'danger close,'" Goree shot back.

"Can you give me a TAG paint for the Arrows?"

"Stand by." Goree switched to the general net. "Can anyone TAG any of those 'Mechs?"

"Charlie One-four, TAG, TAG, TAG."

"Fire Control, TAG one." Goree pressed a switch, relaying the targeting data to the Fire Direction Center.

Within a few seconds, four missiles screamed down into the enemy lines, blasting a rebel *Vindicator* to pieces.

"Seawall, this is Bravo One-One," Marty Cross bellowed. "We're about to get overrun here."

"All Defenders, this is Seawall," Goree yelled into his mike. "Pull back. Displace to your secondary positions."

Below his position, he saw roughly half of the surviving DSPF 'Mechs slip out of their revetments and dash across the open ground toward their fallback emplacements. A rebel fighter, a *Stuka*, possibly the same one that had attacked the command lance, rolled in on the withdrawing

BattleMechs. Lasers tore up the ground as the big fighter flashed along the lines at less than a hundred meters above the battlefield.

A Defiance *Centurion* pitched headlong into the rocky soil, its left leg severed neatly at mid-thigh. A barrel-chested *JagerMech* and a stocky *Bombardier* stood their ground, blazing away at the attacking fighter, which was trailing a thin streamer of black smoke as it pulled up out of its strafing run. The *Stuka*'s wingman, seemingly undaunted by the ground fire, followed his leader, making a point-attack with his missiles and autocannon against the *JagerMech*. The antiaircraft 'Mech took the withering fire, hitting back as best he could, as did the missile-armed *Bombardier*, but luck was against them this time. The *Stuka* escaped without serious damage.

Even as the big fighter climbed away from the battlefield, the rest of the defending 'Mechs bolted from their original fighting positions and made a mad dash for their fallback stations.

The enemy, seemingly emboldened by the withdrawal of the dug-in 'Mechs, leapt forward. For the most part, the Skye Rangers were keeping good order, but a few 'Mechs, mostly light, fast reconnaissance-types, pulled a bit ahead of their slower, more massive fellows.

A loud, flat bang echoed among the rocks, followed by a second, then a third. Geysers of rocky earth were flung into the air as heavy anti-vehicular mines detonated beneath the feet of the onrushing 'Mechs. When the smoke cleared, a *Raven* lay on the ground trying to get back to its feet, both of which had been blown off by the mine. A second 'Mech, a type Goree did not recognize, lay full length on the ground, twitching as though it were some living colossus that had been shot through the spine.

The sudden knowledge that they had blundered into a minefield caused the attacking 'Mechs to pause. The defenders used that hesitation against the rebels. Three more light and medium 'Mechs were smashed to the ground by accurate fire coming from the entrenched 'Mechs. The Defiance troops began to select their targets carefully, massing their fire by lance against a specific target. A fireball blossomed in the enemy ranks as a rebel 'Mech suffered a magazine explosion.

Then the invaders surged forward again. This time, the heavier 'Mechs led the way. More mines detonated under the feet of the attackers. A few were damaged, but not enough. They closed on the defenders, losing a few of their number in the process, but still they came on.

Goree brought up his powerful gauss rifles, dropping the targeting reticle over the center-mass of a slightly damaged Ranger *Flashman*. The basketball-sized nickel-iron slugs smashed into the stubby 'Mech's torso and left leg, shattering armor and cracking the enemy's metallic shin bone. The rebel must have spotted Goree's camouflaged *Gunslinger*, for he raised both arms and touched off the Radionic large lasers that replaced the 'Mech's hands. The radiation-intensified light beams ripped across the *Gunslinger*'s breastplate, leaving deep, blackened scars on the 'Mech's belly and left side.

The enemy didn't get a chance for a follow-up shot. Three flights of twenty long-range missiles from Lassiter's *Salamander* completed the work Goree, along with some unknown Defiance MechWarrior, had begun. Armor-piercing warheads savaged every portion of the *Flashman*'s body. Its left leg parted company with its body, and the machine toppled to the ground, snapping off its right arm at the shoulder as it tried to break its fall with that weakened limb.

Still, it was not enough. There were far too many rebel 'Mechs for the DSPF to destroy one at a time. Facing odds of better than six-to-one, Goree's valiant warriors could not hold out.

"All defenders, this is Seawall," he said, the words sour as bile in his mouth. "Recall, recall, recall. Pull back into the mountain. If we cannot hold them here, we'll make them shoot their way in and pick them off as they try to secure the factory."

Again, the Defiance 'Mechs began an orderly retreat into their mountain home. Goree sighed heavily. He had done his best. Now it was up to General Ciampa's Lyran Guards and the Gray Death Legion to save Defiance Hesperus from the hands of the enemy.

*Gray Death Legion Compound*
*Maria's Elegy Spaceport*
*Hesperus II*
*Skye Province, Lyran Alliance*
*01 July 3065*

**"C**'mon, Davis, get 'em moving," Lori bawled into her communicator. She stood on the corrugated and louvered roof of a massive boxcar, which was hitched to a powerful engine. Both floated a handspan above the ferrocrete and steel trackway of the Maria's Elegy/Defiance maglev rail line.

On the tarmac below her perch, Davis McCall was doing a little yelling of his own.

"Dammit man, can ye no follow directions?" He glared up at the towering form of a Legion *Wraith*, shouting into the small, short-range communicator he held before his lips. As always, when he was angry or in the grip of any other strong emotion, his Caledonian accent came out in full force. "Ah said the fifth car, can ye no count? Noo take that micklin' monster o' yours doon tae th' *fifth* bloody car and get aboard the bloody damn train!"

The *Wraith*'s pilot somehow got his 'Mech to give an almost-human apologetic shrug. As the machine turned away, McCall turned to the next one in line, favoring the pilot with a blast of vituperation more fit for a Master Sergeant than a Lieutenant Colonel.

A husky man clad in civilian clothing called out to Lori as he pulled himself atop the freight car.

"What is it, Mister Cooper?"

"Well, Colonel, as I've been trying to tell you, this train isn't going to be able to carry *all* of your 'Mechs, *and* your tanks, *and* your infantry." Cooper removed the drab green baseball cap emblazoned with the Defiance Hesperus logo, and wiped his bald pate with a handkerchief. "The best you'll be able to cram aboard her is two 'Mech battalions and a couple companies of infantry. We can't haul anymore weight than that."

"What if we hook on another engine?" Lori asked.

"We can't couple on more engines. This maglev line was designed to carry a specific amount of weight. There is a margin of error built into the system, but we're already pushing *that* limit." Cooper stuffed the handkerchief back into his pocket and replaced his cap. "I've been the chief engineer on this line for the past twenty years, and you're going to have to take my word for it."

Lori nodded. "All right, Mister Cooper, I'll take your word for it. Get this thing ready to move. We're almost done loading."

"We're ready whenever you are, Colonel," Cooper said, and started forward, jumping across the gaps between the maglev rail cars.

"Davis, get the last of our Mechs aboard," she yelled to McCall. "And cram in as many of our infantrymen as you can. The Lyran Guards will have to wait until the next time around."

"Aye, Colonel," McCall shouted back. "And when might that be?"

"As soon as possible. That's all I can get out of Cooper," Lori said disgustedly. "He says there are safety margins built into the maglev system that just can't be tweaked, no matter how hard we push. From what I gather, Second Battalion will be thirty minutes behind the first."

"That's too long, Colonel," McCall said.

"I know that, Davis, but what are our alternatives? Use the DropShips and have that blasted battle cruiser up there burn them out of the sky?" Lori could not control her exasperation. "We're out of choices."

"Aye, and I hope Major Goree isn't."

Lori grabbed the back of the engineer's chair, steadying herself as the maglev train rocketed around a bend in the track. Had the Legion been aboard a normal train, the curve would have been noticeable but not inconvenient to the passengers. Aboard the maglev, which reached speeds in excess of one hundred fifty kilometers per hour, the centrifugal forces generated were enough to knock passengers off their feet if they weren't holding on to something.

Lori cursed as her right hip smacked into a bank of instruments running down the center of the magnetic-levitation engine's control deck. Cooper laughed softly at her swearing and at the reason for it. He had warned her about the dangers of pushing the safety margins on the maglev. But she had insisted, browbeating him into taking it beyond its normal operating speed to a dangerous velocity.

Recovering her balance, she looked at her watch. Cooper said it would take about forty-five minutes to make the direct, high-speed run from Maria's Elegy to the Defiance complex. If the engineer's estimates were accurate, they would be pulling into the giant manufacturing complex in less than fifteen minutes.

Cooper caught her checking the time. "We've got one more tunnel. Then we'll drop out of the mountains into the highlands. From there, it's about ten minutes to the factory."

"Right," Lori said, and pulled her communicator from her pocket. "Attention, all Legionnaires. We are about fifteen minutes out. You all know the drill. We'll stop the train short of the mountain and come in on the enemy's flanks. That's all I can tell you until we get some eyes-on assessment of the battlefield. Mount up, and good luck."

"No worries here, Colonel. I'll bring you to a nice gentle stop," Cooper promised with a smile.

"Thanks," Lori said. She clapped the engineer on the shoulder and headed for the narrow hatchway leading from the control deck back toward the freight cars.

"Fifteen minutes," she yelled at the Legionnaires gathered in the first car. The MechWarriors responded by clambering up the chain ladders to their 'Mech cockpits.

A few infantrymen and technicians, along with a couple of train crewmen, remained on the floor of the freight car.

The cargo carrier was essentially a flatbed, with heavy, corrugated steel sides locked into place once their payload was loaded. Each car normally held two BattleMechs chained on their backs to the bed. Lori had managed to coerce the railyard workers into an alternate means of boarding the Legion 'Mechs. Every car held four 'Mechs, each in a kneeling position, fastened to the car by several sets of heavy chains. When the train arrived at the Defiance complex, the techs and crewmen would flip off the brake pawls of the "come-along" chain tensioners, and the 'Mechs could rise, free themselves of their chains, and join the fight.

Most of the soldiers in the next car were Tom Leone's armored infantrymen. They were jammed in so tightly Lori was tempted to scale the roof-access ladder next to the hatch and walk across the car on their armored shoulders. But the men jostled and pushed each other enough to clear a path for their commander. As she reached the far end of the car, she advised Major Leone of their imminent arrival.

"As soon as this thing stops," she told him, "I want your boys off the train. Establish a secure perimeter for us. If the enemy spots us, do your best to keep them at bay until the rest of the battalion gets activated."

"You got it, Colonel," Leone smiled.

Lori smiled back and ducked into the next car, where she repeated her order to Meg Powers. The third car held her *Victor*. Her technician took the bulky gray coveralls Lori wore over the dark gray body-stocking of her cooling suit, and passed across her combat neurohelmet. After fastening the lightweight, but awkward helmet in place, Lori started up the chain ladder to the *Victor*'s cockpit.

MechWarrior Corporal Valdis Koll scanned his *War Dog*'s sensors for enemy activity. It had been almost twenty minutes since the Defiance Self-Protection force 'Mechs had retreated inside the mountain factory complex, and his superiors in the Skye Rangers had yet to figure out what to do about the dug-in defenders.

Koll's company had been deployed on the Fourth Rangers' right flank to help protect the Separatists' main body from any flanking attack. Koll was certain such an attack would come as soon as the regular Lyran forces and the Gray Death mercenaries could figure out a way to make the run to Defiance without the use of their DropShips. General Ciampa was no fool, and that bitch Carlyle was far too clever for her own good. To make matters worse, she had inherited most of her husband's infernal luck. Taken all together, it was a dangerous combination.

Then he spotted the train. The maglev cargo-hauler was headed straight for the Defiance complex, but there was something odd about it. The train was capable of over one hundred twenty kilometers per hour, but it seemed to be slowing. Koll locked his Garret O2j tracking system onto the high-speed transport, watching as the computer translated the impulses fed into it by his motion sensors, radar, and laser-rangefinders. The train's speed was rendered as a set of holographic numbers in the lower left corner of his HUD. One-twenty, one-ten, one hundred kilometers per hour. The train was definitely slowing, though it was still a dozen klicks from the mountain. That made no sense. Who would send a vulnerable maglev train into a battle?

He kicked up the magnification on his viewscreen and instantly recognized the squared-off, lopsided head of a *Grasshopper* BattleMech. The mottled light and dark gray paint job on the *GHR-5J*'s head was a bit more difficult to discern, but Koll realized immediately what it meant. The Gray Death Legion was trying to reinforce the Defiance Self-Protection Force by rail.

A grim smile curled his lips. Carlyle's luck in battle was about to change.

Koll brought the *War Dog* into a rolling, apelike run. The 'Mech took a bit of getting used to, both in terms of piloting and in appearance. Its small, egg-shaped body suspended between legs that appeared to go all the way up to its shoulders made it one of the ugliest 'Mechs on the modern battlefield. The legs made for a long, jolting stride, and the right arm supported half again as much armor as did the left, making for some tricky gyro-balancing. But once you learned how to handle the quirky 'Mech and ignore its odd appearance, the *War Dog* was an excellent fighting vehicle.

Koll raced across the plateau, hearing but ignoring the calls of his lancemates and the orders of his company commander to rejoin the formation.

"There's something I've got to check out," he said by way of explanation.

When he'd closed to within a half-kilometer of the maglev line, he pulled up in a skidding halt.

Quickly, he brought up the Grizzard gauss rifle mounted in his 'Mech's right arm and the large Blankenburg pulse laser set into the left. The targeting reticle drifted a bit on his HUD, but he quickly locked the weapons onto the target, the train's engine. With no hesitation, he fired.

A shudder raced through the maglev. Lori's *Victor* jumped and thrashed against the steel tie-downs, causing the chain ladder she was climbing to sway sharply. As the ladder slammed into the *Victor*'s side, catching her fingers between the steel rungs and the 'Mech's armor, Lori heard the deep boom of an explosion. Again, the train shivered. Lori fought to hang on to the madly gyrating ladder.

There was a sickening crunch and the awful high-pitched shriek of metal being twisted and pulled asunder. One of the chains holding Dallas MacKensie's *Trebuchet* snapped, flailing around the compartment like a striking metal snake. It caught one of the Legion techs squarely across the back, whipsawing halfway through the man's body and hurling him to the deck in a bloody heap. The *Trebuchet*'s left arm wrenched free and punched a hole in the thin metal side of the car.

There was another explosion, and more sounds of tearing, stressed metal. The railroad car pitched violently to the right. The combination of her bruised fingers and the unexpected sideways movement of the car broke her grasp on the ladder. Rather than falling straight to the bed of the car, Lori found herself flying through space, but only for a fraction of a second. Her brief flight was arrested by the ridged wall of the cargo carrier. Lori gasped in pain, and stars shot across her vision when her head bounced off the steel.

She slid down the wall as a terrible, high-pitched scream that could only have come from a human being echoed through the car. She looked up to see her *Victor* suspended in its chains *above* her. The last conscious thought she had was a hope that the giant assault BattleMech would not break free and crush her.

# 21

**A** dull throbbing sighed in Daniel Brewer's ears as he lay on his back.

Whoever is making that noise, I wish they would stop, Brewer thought, wondering if the party last night had been worth the hangover. Then his aching, befuddled mind latched onto reality. He tried to open his eyes, but found they were glued shut by some thick, sticky fluid. He wiped the viscid matter from his eyes, and gazed at his fingers. They were coated with blood. He touched his head and found a long, jagged gash in his forehead. Startled, he pushed himself upright and immediately regretted it. He felt as though his head had been clamped in a vise. He grabbed an out-jutting metal bar to steady himself and waited for the nauseating dizziness to pass.

As his mind began to clear, Brewer remembered the colonel's order to mount up and prepare for battle, but there was little after that. He knew he had begun to climb up the chain ladder to his cockpit when something happened to the train. He looked up to see his *Champion* kneeling above him, still held in place by the heavy chains. To either side crouched a *Hoplite* and a *Grim Reaper*, the number

two and three 'Mechs of his command lance, likewise secured to the rail car's deck.

Lying next to him, his left arm twisted around backward, was Gene Deloray, chief of his tech crew. Brewer pressed his fingers into Deloray's neck and felt the slow, steady throbbing of a carotid pulse. Dimly, Brewer became aware that others were moving about in the rail car.

"Captain," Dale Ross rasped, "what the hell happened?"

"I don't know, Dale. It almost felt like we hit something."

"Yeah, or something hit us."

A wave of cold realization swept over Brewer. Fighting the nausea, he pushed himself to his feet and headed for his 'Mech. As he approached the kneeling giant, he realized that the machine was leaning to its right. As a matter of fact, the whole car seemed to be listing.

"Dale, I'm going to get powered up. You check on Sergeant Kauffman and the techs. Once I'm ready to go, I'll need you to pop the chain locks. Can you do that?"

The MechWarrior nodded.

"Good," Brewer said as he climbed toward his cockpit. "If anyone else in the company is fit to fight, get them powered up and unhooked from this damn train. I'll find a rally point and try to get things organized." He stopped just long enough to pull himself into the *Champion*'s cockpit.

"And send someone to find the Colonel and McCall," he tossed out as he slammed and dogged the hatch.

Running quickly through the startup sequence, he wondered if whatever had happened to the train had also damaged his 'Mech. The *Champion* came on line as readily as ever.

A touch of a button keyed in the 'Mech's external speakers and sound pick-ups.

"Dale, what's the scoop?" he asked.

"Better than I'd hoped for, though Deloray and Pe are hurt pretty bad." Ross picked his way through the debris littering the car floor as he spoke. "The sarge has a big gash in his leg, but he's patching it up now. Everyone else seems to be okay. I sent a couple of runners to try to find Colonel Kalmar-Carlyle and Colonel McCall."

"Good. If there are any fit techs, have them cut me loose, and then you get mounted up. I have a feeling we're about

to walk right into the biggest firestorm this side of Huntress."

Even as Brewer spoke, he saw a couple of men and women dressed in gray coveralls begin to worry at the heavy locking devices holding the chains that secured his 'Mech. As the restraints gave way, he had to lunge for his controls to keep the *Champion* from toppling sideways off the rail car. Carefully, he pushed the big 'Mech to its feet and stepped away from the listing transport.

The sight that met his eyes was incredible. The maglev's engine was gone. In its place, a heap of twisted metal lay burning alongside the tracks. The first two freight cars were in a similar condition, though they were not afire. The rest of the cars had been derailed. Brewer could see bodies lying on the ground beside the wrecked train. He had no idea if those people were dead or merely unconscious. Two BattleMechs were also sprawled alongside the first car, looking like gigantic human casualties. Brewer knew the Colonel's 'Mech had been loaded into the third car. That cargo-carrier sat almost upright on the tracks, though the wreck had spun it around ninety degrees so that it rested *across* the rails. Here and there, armed men and a few BattleMechs were beginning to disembark from the train.

"Attention, all Legionnaires," he called over the Legion's general-use channel. "This is Captain Brewer. Until a superior officer can be found, I am taking command of the situation. All Legionnaires able to fight, form on my 'Mech."

"Cap, this is Kauffman, I've got most of the company mounted up. We'll be ready to go in a minute or two."

"Good to hear your voice, Sage," Brewer said to his company sergeant. "You said most?"

"Yes, sir. Warner is dead, and McNab has a broken back."

"Dammit!" Brewer spat. "All right, Sergeant, you take the company. Move them out a klick or so east. I don't know what caused the crash, if it was an accident or enemy action. Whichever it was, the Skye Rangers have to be aware of it, and they aren't going to pass up an opportunity to shoot up the Gray Death Legion while we try to recover. When they come up, you make the call whether you should hold or fight a delaying action. Whatever you do, Sage,

you're going to have to buy us a long hour or two. Give us time to get things sorted out. I'll send you reinforcements as they pull themselves out of the wreck."

"You've got it, sir." Kauffman said confidently. "All right, boys and girls, let's move out: company wedge formation."

As the 'Mechs began to fall into place, Brewer wished Kauffman and the men and women under his command good luck.

"Thanks, boss, you too," Kauffman replied. "We'll see you when it's over."

As the 'Mechs of Second Company, First Battalion, moved off, Brewer started his *Champion* at a slow walk toward the front of the train. He peered as best he could into the wreckage of the colonel's car, but the twisted structure prevented him from seeing much. The Colonel's *Victor* and Dallas MacKensie's *Trebuchet* were still firmly anchored to the canted car deck. Paul Hansen's *Bombardier* had broken its restraints and toppled over sideways, tearing through the thin sheet metal sides. It lay half on and half off the car, with its right shoulder half-buried in the stony soil.

"Colonel Carlyle?" he called through his external speakers. "Colonel? Sergeant MacKensie? Anyone?"

"Who is that?" The *Champion*'s sensitive external microphones picked up a voice outside his 'Mech.

Brewer felt a flash of excitement, believing for a moment that someone inside the car was alive and conscious. Then he realized that the call had come from his right, closer to the front of the train. He turned to see Major Leone and a handful of the armored infantry standing beside the wrecked car. Further along, more armored troopers were crawling out of the wreckage. Apparently the hard-suited troopers had been protected from the worst of the crash. Brewer even spotted a few of the light scout suits among the survivors.

"It's Dan Brewer, Major," he answered. "I've sent my company east to act as a screening force against the rebels should they come up. Sir, I can't see if the Colonel is alive or not. And I don't know where Colonel McCall is."

"Never mind that now, son," Leone said. This time, Brewer heard the words in his headphones. Leone must have switched on his communicator. "You take command of the Legion's 'Mech forces. My troopers and I will handle the rescue operation."

"Major, you're the ranking officer—"

Leone cut him off. "Captain, *you're* the only 'MechWarrior officer I've found. Now, if Major Devin, or Colonel McCall, or Colonel Kalmar-Carlyle can be found, then you can hand off the command. Until then, you're it. And in case you want to push the matter, Captain, that's an order."

Brewer backed off in the face of Leone's blistering retort.

"Very well, Major. In that case, as you get 'Mechs or any other combat unit free of the wreck, send them to me over . . ." He paused, then pointed with one of his *Champion*'s stubby arms. "Over by that little stand of brush."

"Will do, Captain." Leone turned and began directing his armored infantrymen through the rescue effort.

Brewer moved away and took up station near the patch of low, scrubby bushes he had chosen. In a few minutes, a quintet of 'Mechs—three of them wearing the cloaked-assassin emblem of the Second 'Mech Battalion, the other two showing the Death's Head insignia of the First— approached the rallying point. Each of the machines showed light damage from the train wreck.

"Listen up," Brewer said. "Second Company, First is out there about four klicks east. I want you to form an *ad hoc* reinforced lance and move in on their left. Keep your eyes open, and don't let any of the enemy get past you. I've put Sergeant Kauffman in charge of the line until an officer shows up. Any questions? No? Then get moving."

As the five BattleMechs headed off to do Brewer's bidding, the young captain heard the whistle and crack of weapons fire coming from the approximate position occupied by his company. For a moment he wrestled with the impulse to go and join his comrades. But he knew doing so meant abandoning his post.

"Captain, this is Kauffman," his company sergeant called. "We just got dropped into the kettle here. Estimate one battalion, maybe more, of mixed-weight BattleMechs headed your position. We have taken up position on the reverse slope of one of these little hillocks, and are attempting to slow the enemy. We cannot hold him. I repeat, we cannot hold him."

"Hang on, Sarge," Brewer sent back. "Help is on the way. You've got a reinforced, mixed lance coming in on your left. I'll send you more troops as they become available. Do whatever you think is best, Sergeant."

Twice more, small clusters of 'Mechs came to him for orders. He sent them to the combat area, each time praying that he had assessed the situation correctly.

Just as the second group set off, Brewer heard a loud, flat boom and saw a rolling cloud of black smoke curling up over the uneven, rolling hills of the Highlands. He wondered if it had been a rebel or a Legion machine.

As he watched the smoke dissipate in the light wind, Brewer saw another BattleMech moving slowly toward him.

"All right, trooper. Here's how we're going to play this," he said, turning to face the new arrival. He'd given the same speech a dozen times in the past fifteen minutes as Legionnaires filtered into the rally point from the wreck. "I don't care what company or lance you belong to. As of now, you go where I send you."

"Aye, lad. Where is it ye'd be havin' me go?"

"Colonel!" Brewer shouted, relieved that at least one of the Legion's senior officers had survived the crash. "Dang, sir, I'm glad to see you. Where have you been? Have you heard anything about Colonel Kalmar-Carlyle?"

"I'm all right, boy," McCall said. "Th' *Bannockburn* got tossed clear off th' bloody train." A burst of static interrupted McCall's narrative. ". . . ter I woke up from m' nap, it took me a coupla minutes t' find her, clear her hatch, and get her back on her feet.

"Noo, what's th' situation?"

"The situation is a bit confused, sir. I don't have a clear picture of what's happening out there. We've got about three companies on the line right now, but they're all mixed up. Everything we have out there is ad hoc except *my* company. Near as I can figure it, the Separatists are pushing our people hard. We're holding a line along the reverse slope of a couple of low hills about two klicks east-southeast of here. The line seems to be holding, but that won't last unless we can get a lot more 'Mechs into the fight pretty quick."

"Very well, lad. Ye've done well, considerin'," McCall said approvingly. "Noo, where *is* the Colonel?"

"Unknown, sir," Brewer admitted reluctantly, superstitiously feeling that if he said anything negative about Lori, she would not be found alive. "No one has heard anything from her since before the wreck. I've got some of the GDAIs looking for her and the rest of HQ company. But her car is in a precarious situation. At least, that's what Major Leone told me about ten minutes ago. I guess the car is stuck on about a forty-five degree list, but some of the structural members are jammed against the ground and against the car behind hers. Leone is afraid that if they go hacking around with their suit lasers, trying to cut their way in, or if one of the scouts bounces in on his jet-pack, they may upset whatever is keeping that car in place, and bring the whole thing crashing down on whoever is inside."

"Then we'll leave that operation in the hands of the infantry. They're better suited to it than we are." Again, McCall's words were squelched by static. ". . . ant you to take command of the battle line. I'll stay here and keep th' reinforcements comin'. Just see to it y' don't waste any o' them. If things get too bad, pull back, and we'll live t' fight another day."

"But Colonel, you're senior here. You should take command on the line and leave me here to play traffic cop."

"Aye, ah should," McCall said reasonably. "But I canna. M' poor wee *Bannockburn*'s had her commo gear shaken loose in th' wreck. I dinna trust it tae hold tegither under the stress o' battle. If I try t' take command o' the battleline, what happens if m' communicator goes out completely? Nae, lad, 'tis better if you go. Th' minute we find either Major Devin or Major Houk, I'll aye send 'em up t' relieve you. Assumin' they're fit for duty."

"Very well, sir," Brewer said. "Please keep me informed on the search for the colonel."

"Ah'll do that, lad. Dinna ye worry."

# 22

**B**rewer spun his *Champion* on its heel and started off at a low trot for the battlefield. The irony of the situation struck him. He had been feeding small units into the furnace of war just beyond the low, rolling hills. Now he had been tossed into the flames.

Following the deep gouges left in the rock soil by the feet of passing 'Mechs, Brewer moved parallel to the ruined maglev tracks for a short distance. The trail diverged. Most of the tracks angled off toward the south, while a smaller set of gouges, made by three or four 'Mechs at most, continued to follow the tracks. Someone in the Legion must have tried a flanking maneuver. He wondered if the impromptu tactic had succeeded.

Rather than running into an ambush set by his own troops, Brewer followed the Legion's main body, if it could be called that. There had been no rhyme or reason to the manner in which he had assigned 'Mechs to the battlefield, beyond the desperate need to get combat forces deployed between the invading Skye Rangers and the crippled Gray Death Legion.

As the *Champion* loped across the uneven rocky ground,

Brewer started to hear the whistle and crump of gunfire. Shrapnel, clods of dirt, and bits of stone blasted up by exploding warheads peppered his Mech's legs. The missiles had not been aimed at him. They were strays. Despite not being intended for him, the projectiles nearly found a mark.

Brewer angled away from the spot where the missiles had fallen, hoping that a follow-up volley would land in roughly the same place. As he ran the *Champion* up the short, steep slope, he felt the loose ground shift beneath his armored feet. He had to wrestle briefly with the controls in order to get the big machine back underneath him. His balance recovered, Brewer sprinted across the crest of the hill in order to minimize the time he would be silhouetted against the sky.

The scene in the broad, pan-shaped valley beyond the rise might have come straight from Dante's *Inferno*, had the poet lived in the thirty-first century. 'Mechs wearing the mottled gray camouflage of the Legion were intermixed with those in the red and black colors of the Skye Rangers. There was no semblance of order or of battle lines. 'Mechs fired at one another at point-blank range. They punched and kicked. Those armed with hatchets or improvised clubs bludgeoned their foes. Off to his left, a pair of warriors who had ejected from their ruined 'Mechs grappled with each other, kicking and gouging. Both were so covered in dust and blood that it was impossible to tell who belonged to which army.

One temporarily gained the upper hand by pounding his opponent's head against a rock. He rolled to his feet, groping for the pistol hanging at his side in a flapped holster. But his foe recovered, dragging a long combat knife from its sheath. As the latter surged forward, his blade scything upward, the former drew his weapon from its buttoned-down carrier. The dagger caught the pistoleer low in the belly. Pain or the shock of the wound caused the man to jerk the trigger, sending a bullet into his enemy's brain. The warriors collapsed across each other.

Brewer tore his eyes away from the horrific sight just in time to see an enemy *War Dog* blast the leg from a Legion *Panther*. Before the rebel could lift his weapons to finish off his helpless foe, Brewer unleashed his autocannon on the ungainly enemy 'Mech. Submunitions ripped into the

*War Dog*'s legs and belly. The Ranger shifted his aiming point and sent a flickering blast of laser fire into the *Champion*'s torso.

Brewer shook off the damage and tried to lock his Harpoon short-range missiles onto the target. The discordant warble of the Artemis IV Fire Control System linked to the missile rack growled in his ears as the specialized infrared targeting unit struggled and failed to illuminate the *War Dog*.

That was when Brewer realized the other 'Mech must have an ECM suite. Dropping his reticle across the enemy machine, he triggered the missile rack. Even unguided, there was a good chance some of the half-dozen rockets would hit. A sharp buzzing report tore across the battlefield as bullets clawed most of the unguided missiles from the air. A single warhead struck the Separatist 'Mech in the left ankle.

"C'mon, you mercenary bastard," a taunting voice rang in his ears. "You're gonna have to do better than that."

The *War Dog* savaged the *Champion* with another blast of laser fire, this time adding the medium pulse lasers mounted in its right arm and chest. His 'Mech absorbed the attack. It seemed strange to Brewer that the *War Dog* had not yet brought his gauss rifle into play. Perhaps the weapon was either out of ammunition or had been damaged. Either way, he didn't want to risk taking a slug from the powerful railgun. He struck back at his tormentor with a blast of cannon fire, adding its medium-beam lasers to the mix.

"Ah, that's better," the jeering voice sang. The Skye MechWarrior must have scanned the radio frequencies to find out which one the Legion was using. "But it's still not good enough. C'mon, man, hit me. You're going to have to kill me, or I'll burn you down just as surely as I blew up your train." Brewer knew that rants like this were common among warriors from the Isle of Skye, being a tradition of the Celtic warriors from which many claimed to be descended.

Brewer felt a chill. This was why the maglev had jumped the track. The *War Dog*'s pilot had fired upon the vulernable transporter, destroying the engine. This was the man who had killed Marion Warner and crippled Fal McNab—

the man who also might have killed Colonel Kalmar-Carlyle.

An icy finger trailed along Brewer's spine, despite the heat of the cockpit. Feeling oddly detached, he started forward at a fast, deliberate walk. He dropped the targeting reticle of his autocannon down over the *War Dog*'s torso, squeezed, and held the trigger. A muzzle flare a meter long belched from the gun's maw as shells ripped into the enemy 'Mech. The cannon's breech thunked, locking open as the last cassette of cluster ammunition was expended. With a flip of a switch, Brewer charged the weapon with standard anti-armor rounds from the *Champion*'s second ammunition bin.

From the corner of his eye, Brewer saw a Legion *Hatchetman* bound in behind the *War Dog* on jets of superheated reaction mass. Against Colonel Carlyle's orders, this 'Mech had retained the heavy axe-like club for which it was named. That meant it could only belong to Captain Brian Scully of the Legion's Third BattleMech Company. Scully swung the huge axe, striking the *War Dog* across the ball of its right shoulder. Armor crumpled under the terrible impact. The rebel 'Mech was driven to one knee. Before it could recover, another Legion 'Mech, a *Hunchback*, blew its left arm off in a hail of exploding cannon shells.

Apparently, the Skye Separatist's taunting admission had been heard by every active Gray Death warrior. Every 'Mech that was not engaged and any of those that could break away from their foes descended upon the unfortunate *War Dog*. Willie McBride's captured *Thor-B* Omni-Mech shouldered Brewer aside in its haste to close with the enemy. The powerful 'Mech, built with Clan technology, grabbed the *War Dog*'s shot-riddled right arm and ripped it from its socket.

Distantly, Brewer heard a voice yelling in his ears.

"I said, cut it out, dammit!"

The voice was his own. Pushing Legion 'Mechs aside, he waded into the fray in an attempt to save the life of the *War Dog*'s pilot. He was too late. By the time Brewer dragged McBride away from the rebel machine, it was nothing more than a smoldering pile of twisted metal.

For a few seconds, none of the Legion 'Mechs moved. Brewer felt a sick emptiness in the pit of his stomach. Killing an enemy in combat was the purpose of an army. But this was something different. This was savage butchery.

"Get back in the fight," he said, finding his voice at last. "Scully, you, Royce, and McBride flank out left. I'm going to go find the center of this mess and see if I can straighten things out."

Without waiting for Scully to respond, Brewer turned away, putting the grim reminder of what savagery every man is capable of behind him.

As he turned his 'Mech south, Brewer called up a tactical map of the battlefield on one Multi-Function Display. The map gave only the grossest representation of the battle, but it truly was the mess he had called it. The stunned Gray Death Legion had deployed along a broad, ragged front, and had engaged the enemy as the rebels came up, but there was no order to the formation whatever. Nor did there seem to be any logic to the pattern of the enemy's attacks. So far, every 'Mech they had encountered had been from the Fourth Skye Rangers, as evidenced by the map-of-Britain crest worn by those machines. But they seemed to be from at least three different companies.

The fighting had slipped into a lull following the destruction of the *War Dog*. Brewer wondered if the pilot had been a company or battalion commander. If so, he must not have been particularly well-liked by his troops, because the Rangers had fallen back, leaving his brutal death unavenged. Or perhaps he *had* been well-liked. It often happened that the fall of a beloved commander caused morale to collapse.

Whatever the case, Brewer was not going to allow the hiatus to slip by. Using the tactical map as a guide, he emplaced the troops available to him as best he could. He had no time to reform individual companies. There was no indication of when the rebels would return; however, he was certain they *would* return. Several of the units under his command were badly damaged. He ordered them to the rear, filling their places with fresh units coming up from the wreck site.

"*Here they come!*" was the cry that rang along the Legion's front.

Brewer spotted a mass of red and black war machines bearing down on the Gray Death lines. Without the benefit of tactical reconnaissance he would have to guess at their strength, but it seemed to him that the aggressor force was at least a full battalion, probably more.

"Stay calm," he said, opening the Legion's general-use channel. "Mark your targets. Don't be in a hurry. Wait for them to come into range."

He watched as the distance between the advancing rebels and the emplaced Gray Death Legion diminished.

"Stand by with LRMs."

The Separatists drew to within six hundred meters.

"LRMs . . . Fire!"

All along the line, missiles trailing fire and smoke leaped away from their launchers to fall among the enemy ranks. A second volley of missiles followed. The first azure strokes of PPC fire reached out to savage the onrushing enemy 'Mechs, followed by lasers and autocannon shells. But the damage was not enough to slow the enemy attack.

The Skye Rangers slashed into the scattered Legion formations. A lance of heavy 'Mechs smashed into the center of the lines, right where Brewer was standing. One of the rebel machines caromed off a Legion *Dervish*, flattening the lighter 'Mech. Brewer pumped a burst of high-explosive shells into the *Exterminator* before it could recover its balance. The *Dervish* came back up to its knees, and blasted the rebel's relatively thin dorsal armor with lasers and short-range missiles.

Caught in a crossfire, the *Exterminator* tried to back away, to bring both Legion 'Mechs into its front arc. But Brewer hung with him, circling around to his left, forcing the rebel to turn or have the powerful *Champion* move around his flank. The *Dervish* got to its feet and moved to encircle the enemy on the other side. The tall enemy machine split its fire, sending a rack of missiles into the *Dervish*, while it laced Brewer's *Champion* with bolts of coherent light from its medium lasers. Armor melted and ran under the fierce caress as the lasers carved a ton of fiber-reinforced steel away from the Legion 'Mech's skin.

Heat swept into the *Champion*'s cockpit as Brewer loosed another flight of missiles and triggered his medium lasers at the same time. The Harpoons homed in on the Artemis system's infrared designator. Unlike the *War Dog*, the *Exterminator* had no ECM suite to protect it, but it did boast a Buzzsaw anti-missile machine gun. Two missiles were swatted out of the air by the nearly solid stream of thirteen-millimeter slugs. The rest got through to rip armor off the rebel's legs and belly.

At the same time, the *Dervish* hammered the heavy 'Mech with four flights of missiles, wreathing the *Exterminator* in flame and smoke. When it cleared, the enemy 'Mech stood frozen in place, its back ripped open by the brutal assault it had suffered at the hands of the Legion *Dervish*. From his perspective, Brewer could see the dull silver-gray of the 'Mech's internal structure. Heat spilled from the open wound like blood from a severed artery. He guessed that the missiles had shredded the *Exterminator's* reactor shielding. The rebel 'Mech's head split open as the warrior punched out of his ruined machine. Making a cursory scan for the Separatist pilot, Brewer spotted the man steering his ram-air parachute toward the Skye lines.

"You okay, MechWarrior?" Brewer called to the *Dervish* pilot.

"Yessir," a woman's voice answered. "I'm good to go."

As Brewer turned back to the battle line to seek out a new target, his eyes widened in fear and awe. What he had taken to be a battalion had swelled until it seemed that a full regiment of BattleMechs and supporting infantry were bearing down on his thin, disorganized line.

"Colonel McCall, if you have anything left to send me, you'd better send it now," he bellowed over the command channel, "'cause the whole damn rebel army is about to land right on my head."

"Hold fast, lad," McCall answered breathlessly. "Devin and Houk are on their way. They've got aboot a company each in tow. They ought to be there any time noo."

"I'll hold on as long as I can," Brewer said. Concern over McCall's winded tone filled his mind. The Legion's exec was no youngster, and he had suffered a number of severe wounds over the course of his career. Was the stress of battle finally catching up with him?

The enemy gave him no more time to speculate. A lance of energy skewered his *Champion* through a gap opened in the fight with the *Exterminator*. He looked up to see a hunched-over *BGS-1T Barghest* loping across the battlefield toward his position.

A newer design, the quadruped 'Mech outweighed Brewer's badly abused *Champion* by ten full tons. Its powerful long-range lasers and massive Defiance Disintegrator Class Twenty dual-purpose autocannon gave it a definite edge in both long-range and close-quarters fighting. Ironically, the armored monster's big gun had been manufactured in the factory complex the *Barghest*'s pilot was attacking.

The Separatist warrior snapped off hastily aimed twin bursts of laser fire. One of the beams slashed across the *Champion*'s faceplate, which turned black to protect Brewer's vision from the burst of light. Nonetheless, the amount of energy leaking through the nearly opaque shield was enough to painfully dazzle him.

As his eyes recovered, Brewer realized that nearly all of the armor protecting his cockpit had been burned away. Another hit from even the lightest 'Mech-mounted weapon was likely to kill him.

The other laser bolt inflicted even more telling damage as it tore into the *Champion*'s left breast. The light energy punched deep into the 'Mech's innards. Brewer heard a loud, hollow pop as the laser blew one of his own lasers to shreds. The fragments of the exploding laser ricocheted around the *Champion*'s torso, severing wires and rupturing the tube on its second medium laser.

Brewer unleashed his autocannon on the *Barghest*, but accomplished nothing beyond denting the 'Mech's thick armor. A flight of missiles blasted a few more shallow divots out of the doglike machine's forelegs. The rebel 'Mech came on, scorning the light damage inflicted by Brewer's weapons. When it had closed to within three hundred meters, the turret-like weapons mount swung around to present the gaping maw of its autocannon. Brewer slammed his battered *Champion* into a flat-out run.

A sharp crack rippled through the air, causing Brewer to flinch and jink his running 'Mech to the left. As he centered the controls, a *whang* echoed in the wake of the gunshot. Then it dawned on him that the report had not been that of an autocannnon, and that it had come from the wrong direction. He turned to see a pair of 'Mechs in Legion gray standing side by side, savaging the *Barghest* with missiles and gauss rifle slugs. He immediately recognized the pair as McCall's *Highlander* and Major Devin's captured *Cauldron-Born*.

"Are ye a'right there, laddie?" McCall's brogue was a most welcome sound in Brewer's ears. "Yer lookin' a wee bit worse fer the wear."

"I have taken some abuse, Colonel," Brewer said. "I'll be okay if we can convince these party-crashers to go home."

"Step back and catch yer breath a bit. We'll look after these *sassanach* fer ye."

Without another word, McCall turned his 'Mech's full fury against the enemy. The *Barghest* gave way under the combined fire of the *Highlander* and the *Cauldron-Born*, but other Ranger 'Mechs came up to take its place.

Brewer, despite the damage to his *Champion*, rejoined the fray, sniping at enemy 'Mechs and tanks with his autocannon and Artemis guided missiles. For a moment it seemed that, even with reinforcements, the Legion might be overwhelmed by the rising tide of Skye Rangers. Then a familiar voice broke from the communicators.

"Legion One, this is Seawall." The slow, broad accent could only belong to Major Goree. "I wonder if we might get an invite to this party."

"Join in, lad, and welcome," McCall sang out.

"Roger that, Legion Two." Brewer was not surprised that Goree recognized Colonel McCall's voice. "We've got them by the seven. Maybe together we can push them back to their DropShips."

Brewer felt a sudden surge of confidence. He targeted a rebel *Kintaro* with his last flight of missiles and let fly. The Harpoons peppered the chest and chimpanzee-like face of the enemy war machine, causing it to stumble and fall. Whether the pilot had been wounded or merely startled by the exploding warheads, Brewer couldn't say, but the long-legged 'Mech rose swiftly to its feet, only to be swatted again by a flight of long-range missiles from another Legionnaire.

"Skull Two-One-One is winchester missiles, winchester guns," Brewer called to his comrades, the code phrase "winchester" signifying he was out of ammunition. "Skull Two-One-One is falling back on the train."

"Go ahead, lad. Yer no in any condition t' continue this fight. We'll carry it from here," McCall said.

As Brewer turned his war-torn *Champion* away from the battle, the Skye Rangers began doing the same. First, the *Kintaro* and a few other lighter machines that had suffered damage at the Legion's hands or the hands of the DSPF, pulled out of the enemy line. Then, some less damaged machines withdrew. Finally, the rebel lines collapsed under the two-pronged attack of the defenders of Hesperus II. Both the Gray Death Legion and the Defiance Self-Protection Force surged after the retreating enemy.

Brewer heard McCall's order to stop the pursuit as he was pulling his 'Mech to a stop beside the wrecked train.

"Gray Death Legion, this is Legion Two," McCall said. "Recall, recall, recall. Let 'em go, lads. They'll be back soon, and there's no sense in chasin' them under the guns o' their DropShips. Enough. We've done enough for one day."

# 23

**Myoo Highlands, Hesperus II**
**Skye Province**
**Lyran Alliance**
**01 July 3065**

**B**rewer pushed his bulky neurohelmet into the compartment above and behind his command couch, feeling as though that action had depleted the last of his strength. He wiped perspiration from his forehead with a kerchief pulled from his kit-bag, but he might have spared himself the effort. The *Champion*'s cockpit was so stiflingly hot that new streams of sweat poured forth almost the instant the cloth passed over his skin.

That was one of the *Champion*'s few flaws. Compared to a PPC, its Lubalin LB 10-X autocannon generated little waste heat for the amount of damage it inflicted, nor did its missile launcher or the individual medium and small lasers produce much thermal energy. No, the problem was in the 'Mech's heat sinks. The *Champion* carried only ten of the critical radiator-like devices, and those were the old "standard" models rather than the newer high-efficiency units. That meant that, in any long-running battle, weapons fire and the increased demand for power on the 'Mech's Vlar 300 power plant would result in an increased core temperature.

Reaching for the handle of his ingress/egress hatch, he

told himself that maybe when this thing was over, he could get the sinks replaced with the new model. He smiled at the thought. After all, this was Hesperus. Maybe he should just take the *Champion* up to Defiance and have the tech boys at the plant swap them out for him. After all, what was the good of being a CEO if you didn't exercise a few prerogatives now and then?

Brewer pulled the handle. A long, hissing pop accompanied the opening of the hatch, as the pressures inside and outside the cockpit equalized. Though toxic chemical weapons had been outlawed by the Ares Conventions, such laws were not always observed, especially during a civil war, when old hatreds often overshadowed the maudlin "brother-against-brother" nonsense spouted by the media. Chemical agents had made a ghastly reappearance during Sun-Tzu Liao's bid to thrust the Capellan Confederation to preeminence. Thus it had become standard, though perhaps reactionary, practice to pressurize 'Mech cockpits to one hundred ten percent of a planet's normal atmosphere where such a move was practicable. The technique kept even the most insidious chemical weapons outside the cockpit, where they could do the pilot no harm.

As the hatch slid open, he took in the scene below. The fires that had been blazing in the ruins of the maglev train when he marched off to battle had been extinguished or had burned themselves out. Technicians, train crewmen, and Legion warriors moved like ants along the train, freeing those trapped by the wreckage and trying to salvage what gear they could. A large canopy made of several camouflaged tarps had been strung up near the tail end of the train. A white flag bearing the ancient symbol of a red cross marked the tarps as an aid station.

Brewer activated a control that should have dropped a chain ladder from its compartment beneath the hatch. When he did not hear the familiar rattle of steel on steel, Brewer looked down to see that the compartment, along with the armor that surrounded it, had been blown away during the fighting. Brewer leaned back inside the cockpit and picked up the communications headset. A tap of a control keyed in the 'Mech's external speakers.

"Hey, anybody down there got a ladder?"

A man in civilian clothing looked up at the *Champion*'s open hatchway.

"A ladder? Anything to get me down from here?" Brewer repeated. "Mine's been shot away."

The man nodded and trotted off. In a few moments, he returned and flung a coil of heavy yellow nylon rope up to Brewer.

"The best I could find," he hollered.

"It'll do. Thanks."

The man waved and jogged off while Brewer took some moments to find a suitable piece of equipment to which he might secure the rope. He knelt and looked into the gash in the armor where his ladder used to be. Fortunately, one of the anchoring bolts and a few links of chain remained in the ruined compartment. Cautiously, so as not to over-balance and end up making the eight-meter trip to the ground without the benefit of the rope, he tied the line to the ring bolt that had supported his ladder. He hoped he had made a good knot. He tugged hard on the rope several times to make sure. He leaned as far down as he could and dropped his kit bag to the ground, tossing it back a bit so it would land under the 'Mech, where it would not impede his landing. Then, checking to make sure that no sharp metal edge was in contact with the line, he wriggled over the edge of his cockpit and started to climb down the rope. As his feet cleared the bottom of the *Champion*'s out-thrust hull, his grip on the slippery nylon failed. The rope slipping through his hands peeled the skin from his palms.

He landed on his feet, but stumbled in the loose, rocky soil and fell forward, catching himself on his hands, causing further damage. Feeling embarrassed by the clumsy display, he got back to his feet, looking around. Fortunately, everyone seemed to be occupied with their own concerns.

Wiping his abused palms on the front of his cooling vest, Brewer caught up his kit bag. Swiftly he pulled off his cooling vest, donning a set of gray coveralls instead. He exchanged his boots for a pair of lightweight jogging shoes, then stuffed his combat gear into the bag and set off toward the canopy.

He'd only gone a hundred meters or so when Davis McCall's *Highlander* pulled into the Gray Death's impromptu lager. Brewer stopped and waited while the Legion's exec shut down his 'Mech and also climbed down to the ground.

"That was aye a good piece o' soldierin' ye did today, lad." McCall laid his hand on Brewer's shoulder. "It'll go on yer record."

"Thank you, Colonel," Brewer said, appreciating the rare compliment. He gestured to the wrecked train and the shot-up legion 'Mechs still straggling in from the battlefield. "Do we have any idea of the butcher's bill?"

"Not yet, lad." McCall shook his head sadly. "Though I'm afraid it's gonna be high." He shook his head again, and sighed deeply. "Now, let's go see the colonel."

"The colonel?" Brewer exclaimed. "She's alive?"

"Aye, lad. She's alive," McCall said with a haggard smile. "Did ye nae know? She's alive, but she's hurt her back. We dinna ken how badly. They found her in the wreck out cold. The medics strapped her to a bit of siding with gaffer's tape, not havin' a backboard available. Doc Sweney says she's in good shape, but that's all I know right now."

Brewer felt some of his weariness lift at the news that Colonel Kalmar-Carlyle was alive. Grayson's death had been a major blow to the unit's morale. He wasn't sure the Legion could survive losing her as well. He mustered a tired smile, and suggested that he and McCall go find out how their commander was doing.

The aid station was a nightmarish scene, reminiscent of a long-gone age when men fought with muzzle-loading muskets, bayonets, and swords, rather than BattleMechs, lasers, and particle cannons. Wounded men and women lay on the ground, covered by blankets or field jackets. Wounds had been roughly dressed, some using strips of cloth torn from the casualty's own clothing. Mercifully, most of the wounded were unconscious, either from shock or from medication.

A short distance away, outside the tarps that sheltered the injured from Hesperus' blazing sun, lay a row of bodies shrouded in poncho liners. Brewer was surprised at the number of the huddled forms. Modern battles were far from bloodless, but powerful energy weapons and high-explosive warheads usually didn't leave much of a body to bury. The sight of the aid station, and the men and women who had been wounded in combat and injured by the train wreck, left Brewer feeling nauseous.

McCall tapped him on the arm and pointed toward the back of the aid station. Brewer followed his gesture and spotted Lori sitting up against the side of a packing crate, her forehead and cheek masked by an expanse of self-adhesive bandage. What could be seen of her face was pale. She held a black-cased noteputer in her hands.

As Brewer and McCall made their way to her, she caught sight of them and her face broke into a smile.

"I heard you both survived," she said, her voice a bit thick from painkillers. "But they won't tell me anything else. What happened? How is the unit?"

"Th' Legion's fine, lass," McCall said gently. "It's you who're pointin' south."

"Now, Davis, don't you start," she snapped, exhibiting sickbed temper. "My back just went out on me, that's all. Doc Sweney gave me some muscle relaxants and some painkillers. I'll be fine. Now what happened out there?"

McCall and Brewer exchanged glances, silently agreeing that McCall would speak.

"Well, Colonel, first thing off the mark, I want to put Captain Brewer here in for a commendation. He was aye one of th' first to recover after th' wreck. He got mounted up and threw out a screen t' keep th' *sassanach* away from us while we pulled ourselves tegither."

"Is that true, Captain?"

"Well, mostly true, Colonel," Brewer said. "I just did what I thought was best. Then when Colonel McCall relieved me, I went up to the main battle line as he ordered and helped direct our defense. They pushed us a couple of times, but we pushed back. That last time, I don't think we could have held them if it weren't for Major Goree."

"Yes, I heard." Lori tried to shove herself into a more upright position, wincing at the pain in her back.

"I came to about the time the DSPF got into the fight. I wanted to mount up and go out to play with you boys, but they had me duct-taped to that damn board, and the Doc wouldn't let them cut me loose."

"You're dang right I wouldn't," a tenor voice said behind them. Brewer recognized it as belonging to Doctor Gregg Sweney, the Legion's regimental surgeon. "You were in a train wreck, Colonel. Your back isn't broken, or sprained, or dislocated, and you can thank blind, dumb luck for that.

But I didn't know that then, did I? If I'd sent you off to battle with a cracked vertebrae or a dislocated disc or two, or ten, you might have ended up paralyzed. Or have you forgotten how rough a 'Mech's ride can be?"

"No, doctor, I haven't forgotten. How can I? You keep reminding me every fifteen minutes or so," Lori snapped. She turned back to her officers. "You both did a good job out there today, especially you, Captain. And you made the right decision not to pursue the Rangers back to their DropShips. Maybe if the Lyran Guards were here, or if we at least had the full Legion, things might have been different. As it was, getting too close to the DropShips would have been stupid, maybe even suicidal.

"And I suppose I owe Major Goree an apology."

"Y'all don't owe me anything, Colonel," Goree said coldly, stepping unexpectedly into the aid station. His face was still streaked with sweat from the heat of his cockpit, but his dark green coveralls were neat and clean. "If I did not join the fight when I did, the Separatists would have overrun your battle line, and probably the train as well. Then, they would have turned right around and attacked Defiance again. It was a matter of military expediency. We were both just doin' our jobs."

He looked squarely into Lori's eyes. "How are you, Colonel?"

"I've been better, Major," she said. "And I've been worse."

"I see." Goree's tone gave nothing away. "Are you going to be fit to lead your troops, or should I be talking to Mister McCall?"

"Give me a chance to x-ray her back and find out how bad she's hurt before you go shoving her back into the cockpit," Doc Sweney said harshly.

Lori ignored him. "I'm still in operational command of the Legion. Colonel McCall and my battalion commanders will have tactical control. So you may address your questions to me."

"Very well, Colonel. I was just wondering what your plans are now." Goree's tone was as brusque as ever. "Will you salvage your unit and return to Maria's Elegy, or do you intend to stay on here in the Highlands?"

"I've been thinking about that one myself, Major," Lori said. "I don't think we can defend both Maria's Elegy and

Defiance. The distance between them is too great. With the maglev out of commission, it just got a little greater. As important as the planetary capital and the spaceport are, the Defiance complex is this planet's primary asset.

"What I'd like to do is recover what 'Mechs I can from the battlefield and from the wreck, move the Legion into the complex, and use it as a base of operations. General Ciampa can either stay in Maria's Elegy or move out here with us. I assume, Major, that your 'Mech facilities can handle another regiment or two?"

"My facilities? No. But the overall complex can handle a full brigade and then some," Goree answered, with a cold glance at Brewer. "And, I think the *Board* will agree to let you use the facilities."

Brewer caught the stress Goree placed on the word "board." It seemed that, for all Goree's help on the battle-field, the DSPF officer still hadn't much use for a CEO-turned-mercenary. He decided he was too tired to make an issue of Goree's prejudices, and let the matter pass with only an exasperated sigh for a comment.

"Good," Lori continued, ignoring the byplay between the officers. "We'll use the Defiance plant as a base of operations for this area. If the rebels go somewhere else, which I doubt, we'll figure something else out."

"Beggin' yer pardon, Colonel," McCall interjected. "I shouldn't need t' remind you of what happened to th' German army during the Second World War on Terra, when *they* allowed themselves t' get trapped in a factory complex."

"I know what happened at Stalingrad, Davis, but I have no intention of sitting back and waiting for the enemy to mass enough troops to grind us down. Nor do I intend to wait for the Rangers to launch their next attack. As soon as the Legion is all in one place and we finish our repairs, I plan on going on the offensive."

# === 24 ===

**Defiance Industries Complex**
**Myoo Highlands, Hesperus II**
**Skye Province**
**Lyran Alliance**
**01 July 3065**

**O**ver Doctor Sweney's objections, Lori pulled herself to her feet. A sharp lance of pain shot through the muscles of her back, and the world side-slipped and took on a reddish hue. She lashed out with her left hand, grabbing McCall by the front of his jumpsuit. The bluff Caledonian stepped forward, catching her under the arms, which set off a new wave of dizzying pain.

"That's it, Colonel! I'm taking you off combat status," Sweney barked.

In that instant, Lori's vision cleared. She glared at the Legion's chief medic. "No, Doctor, you are not," she growled. "I have far too much work to do. When this is over, if I'm still alive, you can take me off combat status, but until then, leave me alone."

"Colonel, if you go out to fight, you're going to end up paralyzed, maybe permanently."

"Understood."

"Colonel—"

"That will be *all*, Doctor," Lori blazed.

"Maybe ye should listen t' him, lass," McCall said mildly. "We can nae afford t' lose you."

"Leave me be, Davis." Lori shrugged off his arm, gritting her teeth as agony ran along her spine.

"Colonel, I can summon a hover jeep to take you to the factory," Goree offered quietly. "One of your men can pilot your *Victor* in for repairs once they get it free of the wreck. I guarantee you'll be more comfortable in our hospital than you'll be out here on the cold ground, waiting for them to cut your 'Mech out of the rubble."

"Major Goree . . ." Her voice trailed off like the hiss of an angry cat, and she felt her anger getting the better of her. She took a moment to get herself under control, but could still feel the anger burning inside her.

She gazed around the circle of officers, all of whom looked worried. "Major Goree, I appreciate your offer. I think I should accept it. Can you arrange for your technical people to come out here with some heavy equipment— 'Mech-recovery vehicles if possible—and help my technical crew with the recovery process?"

"Of course, Colonel." Goree executed a short, formal bow and stepped out of the shelter tent to contact his base.

"And once we get back to Defiance, I'll need an office to work from. And I'll need a secure landline connection to the spaceport at Maria's Elegy," Lori said, thinking out loud.

"After you're checked out by their docs," Sweney told her firmly.

For a second, her anger blazed again. She forced it back down, locking it away in a secure corner of her mind.

"All right, Doctor. I'll wait until the DefHesp pill-pushers have had a chance to poke and prod me."

Sweney nodded. "Good enough, Colonel."

"Davis, you and Dan stay here and get the recovery operation going. Have Devin and Houk move their troops over to the Defiance plant. One of Major Goree's officers will direct them?" The last was more a question aimed at the DSPF commander, who had just returned to the aid station.

Goree nodded. "Of course, and I've also called for ambulances for your wounded. We have a small but excellent hospital facility at the plant. Any serious cases can be air-lifted to Maria's Elegy once they're more stable."

"Thank you, Major. We're indebted to you."

Goree just smiled politely.

"One question, Major Goree," Brewer said sharply. "Why this change in attitude? Before, you were almost ready to take on the Legion, regardless of the fact that I'm the company CEO and Duke of Hesperus. Now, you're the poster boy for helpful cooperation."

"That was before the Legion proved its intentions." Goree's tone was flat and unemotional. "The difference is that now I know they can be counted on to fight in our corner. It's nothing more or less than that."

It was several hours before Lori was given access to the office she'd asked for. In the meantime, the doctors gave her the good news that her back was neither broken nor sprained. The bad news was that she had a couple of cracked ribs as well as bruises from the base of her skull to her hips. The doctors told her she would be extremely sore for several days, but there had been no lasting damage.

She'd also been assigned an orderly, a slight young woman named Sarah Trotter, who Goree promised was a top-flight assistant. "I'm sorry, Colonel, but we can't get you a phone," Trotter was saying now. "When the Separatists took out the maglev, they also knocked out the land-lines because they were strung along the underside of the rail bed. We've got techs out working on the problem, but it may take several days to fix. Can you make do with wireless?"

"I guess I'll have to," Lori said with a shrug so painful that she immediately made a mental note to avoid doing that again until her back had healed. Trotter withdrew, saying she'd be just outside the office door should Lori require anything.

It took a minute or two for the call, which was essentially a long-range radio signal, to be bounced between relay stations, before someone at the other end finally picked up. Lori directed the operator to connect her to the Legion's compound. A moment later, Captain Joan Monti, her tank commander, was on the line.

"Joan, listen," Lori said, cutting off Monti's polite, concerned greeting. "I need you to get the Armored Battalion and the rest of the infantry mounted up and moved out here. We're setting up shop at the Defiance plant. We're going to need every available Legionnaire."

"Right away, Colonel," Monti said. "Does that mean what we heard about the maglev line getting cut and your guys getting all shot up is true?"

"Partially. The maglev line *is* out, and some of the Legion did get hurt, but for the most part, we're in good shape. We fought one honking battle up here earlier today. If we're going to continue operations, we're going to need the rest of the outfit."

"Yes ma'am. You want us to bring the DropShips out there?"

"No!" Lori said loudly. "Leave the ships on the tarmac. The Separatists have moved that captured WarShip insystem. I'm afraid she'll shoot down any non-rebel aerospace craft she sees leaving the planet. You're going to have to hump it overland."

"Okay, Colonel," Monti said in a strange tone, which Lori guessed was an overlay of apprehension at moving the balance of the Legion through the mountain passes. "It might take us a day or so, but we'll be on our way in a couple of hours."

"Good," Lori said, satisfied with the estimate. "Transfer me back to the switchboard. I need to make some more calls."

"We'll be on our way as soon as possible, Colonel," General Ciampa told Lori. "It may take a while, especially if you don't want us to use the DropShips. Don't forget that not using them also makes it impossible to recall Zambos' Thirty-sixth Guards from Maldon."

"I know that, General, but I don't think we should risk using the ships until we figure out how aggressive the rebels are planning to be with that WarShip. They've already disabled and captured our JumpShips. I'd rather not risk losing our DropShips and crews, too. And that goes for your Lyran troops as well."

"No we don't want to risk that," Ciampa said. "It will

take a couple of days for us to get the whole Regimental Combat Team moved out to Defiance, but we'll make the move as quick as we can."

"One more thing, General," Lori said before breaking the connection. "If you haven't made that call we discussed, I think now would be the time to do it."

Lori knew that most units the size of those she was facing boasted sophisticated electronic surveillance equipment. It would be easy for the rebels to intercept the conversations she'd just had and act upon them. But short of sending one of the civilian passenger VTOLs belonging to Defiance Hesperus back to Maria's Elegy with written instructions, she had little choice.

Trusting the chopper to deliver the messages would be just as risky. The Skye Rangers had already proved that they were willing to fire upon civilian transports, even ones as vital as the maglev train. If they detected, intercepted, and destroyed the VTOL, not only would she lose the message, but she would lose the aircraft and its crew. There was also the chance of the VTOL being forced to land, resulting in the messages falling into the enemy's hands. As much as she hated the idea of sending a call for reinforcements over an unsecured communications link, she didn't see any other choice.

"Have you got all that?" Gina Ciampa asked, having gone personally to the small business office attached to the ComStar HPG station located at the northern end of the Maria's Elegy spaceport.

"Yes, General," the ComStar technician replied. "Priority One HPG message to Skye. Addressed to Hauptmann-General Rainer Poulin. Message reads, 'Hesperus II under heavy attack by Fourth and Twenty-second Skye Rangers. Request immediate reinforcements.' Signed Gina Ciampa, Leutnant-General, Fifteenth Lyran Guards. Message ends. Is that correct?"

"That is correct, Adept," Ciampa said, turning to leave. "Please make sure it goes out pronto."

A call for William von Frisch came in from the captain who'd been given the captured Lyran WarShip. "General, this is Kaptain Cerlenko," she said. "We've just picked up an electronic signal coming from the spaceport at Maria's Elegy."

The general looked at the map a technician had called up on the mobile HQ van's primary viewscreen. The graphic representation of the area of space around Hesperus II showed a small golden blip where the *Simon Davion* stood in geosynchronous orbit above the planetary capital. Fitted with the most advanced electronics available to the Federated Suns, the ultra-modern *Avalon*-class cruiser was easily able to detect ground-bound electronic emissions from space.

"Any idea what they are?" he demanded.

"Oh, we've got a real good idea what they are," Cerlenko said. "It's an HPG-carrier signal. It looks as though someone on the ground is getting ready to send out an HPG message."

"It's that bitch Carlyle," von Frisch spat. "Or Ciampa, or Zambos. They're trying to call for help.

"Can you shut it down, Kaptain?"

"Not from here, sir. Perhaps a commando team might, but we haven't got any commandos. The best we have is a couple dozen Marines. But even if we sent them to the surface, they'd never arrive in time."

"Then destroy the source," von Frisch said arrogantly.

"General, that's a ComStar facility down there."

"That it is, Kaptain," von Frisch spat back. "And that ComStar facility is about to call in reinforcements. I'd bet my life on it. And if that's what they're doing, then they're no longer neutral but are taking sides in this war. Destroy it. We'll settle with ComStar later, after the Isle of Skye is free."

"But General . . ."

"That is an order, Kaptain."

"Yessir."

Kaptain Elena Cerlenko stepped away from the communications console and looked across the *Simon Davion*'s bridge. In one corner of her mind, she told herself they'd really have to rename the ship. Perhaps that honor would go to her crew. If so, she thought it would be a wonderful gesture to name her the *Bartlett*, after Private Roy Bartlett, the first of her Marines to board the cruiser during her capture, and the first to lose his life in the attempt.

"Helmsman, begin a spiral descent. Take us down to three hundred kilometers and park us right over the spaceport."

"Aye, Kaptain."

As the ship nosed down into a long, slow, spiraling dive toward the planet, Cerlenko spent the time studying the maps and radar images of the Maria's Elegy spaceport stored in the *Simon Davion*'s computer banks. She wanted to make certain her fire-control systems could positively identify the ComStar HPG facility before she ordered her gunners to open fire.

The ComStar facility was a technically neutral site. As the organization's military also formed the heart of the Star League Defense Force, it had taken no official stance in the matter of the Skye rebellion. That was bad enough, though Cerlenko understood the necessity of stopping any military communication from leaving Hesperus II. She also knew the terrible risk in bringing her ship's guns to bear on a relatively tiny ground target. If her gunners' calculations were off by even a few degrees, the deadly barrage could hit a civilian area of the city. She decided that she would call von Frisch and tell him the target could not be clearly identified if there was even a chance of that happening. Let him clean up his own mess.

For a few moments, she even considered disobeying his order, but quickly realized that he was right. If Skye was ever to throw off the yoke of Steiner domination, risks would have to be taken. In that instant, she made the fateful decision to carry out William von Frisch's orders.

A few minutes later, the helmsman called out that they were in position.

"Helmsman, give me a slow roll to starboard, ninety degrees." She peered closely at the chart depicting the spaceport. "Gunnery Officer, bring your starboard antiship weapons to bear on Grid Whiskey-Romeo-Niner-Seven-One, by Alpha-Lima-Three-Zero-Six, and fire one broadside."

Gina Ciampa was walking across the spaceport tarmac with her aide, Colonel Nana Brennan, when the Chief Warrant Officer in charge of the spaceport sensor and communications station called on her portable comm unit.

"General Ciampa, this is Chief Sellars. The *Simon* has settled into a new orbit. It looks like a geosynch, about three hundred kilometers up." Sellars had been feeding her reports about the WarShip's movements for the past ten minutes. "Wait a minute . . . Holy Mary, Mother of God, we're picking up fire-control signals. I think they're about to start—"

A clap of thunder ended Sellars' message, followed by an incandescent beam of light shooting through the darkening sky. The laser bolt flashed from sky to earth in the northeast corner of the spaceport. Before Ciampa's stunned mind could begin to grasp what had happened, a second beam snapped into existence with an eye-hurting intensity. A second thunderclap shook the air, followed by a hollow boom. A ball of flame boiled into the air at the far end of the port, followed by a series of laser blasts slashing into the ground. What were they shooting at?

Realization dawned in an instant—the HPG station. Ciampa was sure no one could have survived the attack. The urgent request for reinforcements would not be sent.

"General, the cruiser has altered her course. She is now heading two-eight-five, true," Sellars said tensely. "That will bring them right over the spaceport. And we're still picking up fire-control sensors."

Before Ciampa could react, a laser blast tore into the empty building that until recently had been the primary barracks facility for the Gray Death Legion. The structure was blown apart, then set ablaze by the laser's fiery touch. Another blast gouged a strip out of the tarmac, leaving thick, oily smoke and dark greasy flames in its wake.

Not another second passed before Ciampa threw herself to the pavement and rolled under a ground jeep as an ear-splitting crack sounded. Half a second later, an *Atlas* assault 'Mech crumpled in on itself as the blast of a naval gauss rifle swatted it to the ground. More savage blasts followed, the ground shaking from the incredible energies being unleashed on the spaceport. A laser bolt smacked into the tarmac twenty meters from Ciampa's hiding place, sending ash and burning tar-based pavement showering down on her. Three Gray Death Legion fighters died in a fireball created by naval autocannon shells.

"What the hell is going on?" Brennan yelled over the

cacophony of exploding ordnance and massive energy
discharges.

A hunk of misshapen metal clanged off the hood of the
ground jeep. Debris skittered across the hood, landing on
the pavement not far from Ciampa's face. In one of those
odd moments of clarity that sometimes occurred during
combat, Ciampa realized that the pieces had once been an
ammunition cassette for an autocannon.

"Naval bombardment," she screamed back. "Those
bloody bastards are bombarding us."

No sooner had the words left her lips than the attack
lifted. For long moments, Ciampa stayed where she was.
Across the spaceport, an ammunition bunker had been
struck, blanketing the base with both exploding and unex-
ploded ordnance. Smoke from a burning fuel tank hung
low in the sky, blotting out the sunset. Over the noise of
the fires and detonating ordnance, she could hear the
screams of the wounded and dying and the high, thin ulula-
tion of sirens.

Slowly, she got to her feet, then stood staring empty-
eyed across the devastated spaceport. The battle for
Hesperus had taken a new, ugly turn.

**Fourth Skye Rangers Landing Zone**
**Myoo Highlands, Hesperus II**
**Skye Province**
**Lyran Alliance**
**02 July 3065**

Leutnant-General William von Frisch leaned his elbows on the edge of the tiny desk in one corner of the mobile head-quarters van. For long moments, he remained like that, his eyes shut, silently cradling his head in his hands. He was aware of the anxious glances cast his way by the command truck's crew, but they were not his primary concern right now. His worry was for the future of the rebellion, and for the reputation of the Isle of Skye once it gained its independence from the Lyran Alliance.

Kaptain Cerlenko's report troubled him deeply. He had expected a single, surgical attack on the ComStar installation at Maria's Elegy, not a wholesale naval bombardment of the spaceport. Such attacks were not the common order of the day, nor should they be. The destructive energy released by a WarShip's guns was greater than that of an entire 'Mech battalion, and was, on the whole, less accurate.

Though Cerlenko told him she had targeted the ComStar HPG station, he knew that the damage caused by the bombardment would not be limited to that building alone. If the WarShip's guns were off by even a fraction of a degree, it could endanger a civilian area of the city. Von Frisch had ordered the attack, and if even one shot went awry, the responsibility for it was his.

The surest way to reduce the political ramifications of the attack was plain. He had to *win* the fight for Hesperus.

One other aspect of Cerlenko's report troubled him. The Kaptain didn't know if her bombardment had destroyed the HPG station before any messages could be transmitted. If a message had gone out, though, von Frisch wasn't sure Katrina Steiner really had units to spare for reinforcing Hesperus. And even if she did, would she risk sending them? The event that had triggered the rebellion in the first place was the relocation of mainline combat units to worlds within the Isle of Skye. Would the Archon risk inciting additional worlds to revolt by sending more combat troops into Skye? For the sake of his command, von Frisch had to assume so.

Pulling himself up, he activated the computer terminal and quickly tapped in a carefully worded message that he saved onto a datachip. A second message followed, and was likewise copied to an offline storage device.

Then he called in his orderly with instructions. The young officer would rush the first chip to the captain of one of the Ranger DropShips, with orders that the man take the chip via a high-speed burn to the *Sharuq*, the JumpShip that had transported the Rangers to Hesperus. The *Sharuq*'s captain would then jump immediately for the Skye system, taking the chip to Duke Robert's second in command, General John Dundee. Von Frisch made it clear that the *Sharuq*'s captain was to deliver the chip directly into Dundee's hands.

Then he handed the second chip to his young aide. "This one goes to the *Nomad*'s skipper," he said. "Tell him to run it up to the *Simon Davion* and place it directly into Kaptain Cerlenko's hands. Is that understood?"

"Yes, General," the lanky, tow-headed youth answered.

"Good. Now get moving."

Von Frisch sighed. Sending a message via DropShip might take longer, but it would be almost impossible for the enemy to intercept. The first message was to Skye Command, asking for reinforcements. The second instructed

Kaptain Cerlenko to place the captured *Simon Davion* in orbit above Hesperus III. Both were precautions against reinforcements from the Lyran Alliance.

The message to Cerlenko held a slightly more dire set of instructions, however. He directed that she engage *any* JumpShip coming into the system via a pirate point, regardless of whether it was a WarShip or a transport. Military ships were to be destroyed. Civilian vessels were to be disabled and seized. Likewise, she was to destroy *any* DropShip launching from those JumpShips.

Like the attack on the HPG station, ordering the *Simon Davion* to attack all starship and spaceship traffic was a calculated risk. By destroying or capturing any vessel that entered the system, von Frisch hoped to convince Archon Katrina and Nondi Steiner that Hesperus was too expensive to hold on to.

He knew that might be a vain hope because of the importance of Defiance Industries. But it was a hope.

"Colonel, you need to see this." A technician wearing the green uniform of the Defiance Self-Protection Force passed a portable data unit to Lori. "One of your pickets recorded this and transmitted it back to us. It's less than five minutes old."

Lori pushed the playback stud set into the unit's casing as the tech retreated to stand near the door. She watched as the screen displayed a clear night sky. Suddenly, the starfilled heavens were illuminated by two bright streaks rising up from beyond the horizon.

"DropShips," McCall said, looking over her shoulder.

"DropShips," she confirmed. "But it looks like only two of them."

"Aye." Her exec's tone was speculative. "And why would only two o' the *sassanach* be leavin'? They're up t' something."

"Yes, and I intend to find out what." Lori waved the tech over to her, with orders to find Meg Powers and bring her here. Within ten minutes, the tall, dark-haired major joined them.

"I've got some night work for you," Lori said, handing the data unit to her scout officer. Powers watched the recording, then placed the device back on Lori's desk.

"You want me to see why only two DropShips boosted."

"That's right," Lori said. "The problem is that we have no hard intelligence as to exactly where the rebels landed. The Defiance scanners followed them down until they dropped into the ground clutter. We can give you a general idea where the bad guys are, but you'll have to scout around to locate their LZ. I need to know where they've gone to ground, how seriously they've been hurt, and whether they're in any shape to launch another attack on Defiance. And I need to know as soon as possible.

"This will be dangerous, Meg. If von Frisch has any sense, he's studied up on the Legion and knows about our scout platoons. He's likely to be prepared, so take all reasonable precautions. If you run into trouble, beat it out of there. The best report in the world isn't going to do us any good if there's no one left to deliver it."

Powers nodded absently. Lori knew she was already kilometers away, searching for the enemy's base of operations.

"El, take a look down there," Meg Powers whispered to Sergeant Elron David, her platoon sergeant. She kept her pointing hand close to her light scout armor's plastron. Though they had yet to see enemy soldiers, scout training said to keep your gestures small and close to your body, because the enemy didn't need to know what you knew.

Elron David followed his commander's gesture, his eyes widening behind his armored visor.

The scouts had tracked the retreating Skye Rangers northward for thirty kilometers after their departure from the Defiance factory complex. Till now, a blind man could have followed the ruts the Rangers had carved in the rocky turf of the Myoo Highlands. As the trail began to ascend the slopes of the next ridge, the ground cover changed from loose, stony earth to solid rock only thinly covered by soil, making the tracks more difficult to follow.

To meet the conditions, Meg Powers had divided her scout company into two platoons, with Lieutenant M'Dahlla in command of one and she of the other. The two units fanned out to search for the enemy's trail, and it wasn't long before her platoon located the enemy's tracks.

The path angled away to the east, running a few kilometers deeper into the mountains before leading to a broad, relatively flat alpine meadow. Powers' team slipped into the rocks along the trail like mechanical ghosts. Below them was laid out the entire enemy bivouac.

She activated the recording gear built into her suit, panning the sensors across the rebel encampment. She saw dozens of BattleMechs, most of them being serviced by mobile repair trucks, and at least a score of aerospace fighters. Of the enemy DropShips she saw not a trace, and every engine, be it a fighter, tank, or 'Mech, was shut down cold.

"Maybe they bounced their DropShips back to an alternate LZ," Elron David opined. "Maybe they're setting up a fallback position."

Powers nodded slowly. "Could be. I don't know what to make of it. If they boosted the rest of their ships, why didn't we see them? And if they didn't, where the hell are they?"

"Camouflaged? Back there among the rocks?" David pointed toward the far end of the meadow where the steep escarpments of the mountains came down. "If they strung up some of those big electronic ghillie nets, we might not be able to detect them. Or maybe they've got some kind of ECM."

"I don't know, El. It just doesn't feel right." Powers stared searchingly at the enemy camp, mulling over the odd disquietude she felt. There was something not right about the bivouac.

"Okay, El," she said, abandoning the attempt to figure out what was bothering her. "Let's flank out to the left and move along their perimeter. Maybe a new perspective will tell us something."

Moving carefully and quietly, the platoon slipped from shadow to shadow, dividing their attention equally between the rebel camp, their path through the rocks, and potential enemies. In this manner, they made a quarter-circuit of the landing zone before Powers signaled another halt.

"Still no sign of the DropShips," she murmured.

"No, and we'd best be getting back," David said. "We've got about two hours of darkness left, and there's no telling how long these fellas are going to wait before they kick off whatever plan they've cooked up overnight."

Powers looked at him with a sudden feeling of certainty. "You feel it too?"

"Yeah. It's like they're about to start something."

Powers checked her chronometer. She wanted her scouts to be out of the area before dark.

"All right, let's pull back," she said. "We'll head for the spot where the trail swung east before we recall First Platoon. That'll give the enemy less chance of picking up our signal."

"Halt!"

Instinctively, the scouts froze.

"Identify yourselves."

The voice was coming from ahead of them and to the right. Moving as slowly and smoothly as she could, Powers lifted her heavy Thunderstroke gauss rifle out of its assault sling, pointed toward where she'd heard the picket's voice, and fired.

A sharp crack echoed among the rocks, followed by a yelp of pain.

"Second Platoon, break contact!" Powers bellowed across her company's general frequency. There was no need for stealth. The enemy surely knew that her scouts were there. The general broadcast, which was automatically encrypted, was for First Platoon's benefit. At least they would know that Powers' team had engaged the Skye Rangers and would be pulling back.

"Escape and evade," she said. "Rally Point Tango."

She and David opened fire, blanketing the area where the sentry's voice had been heard with a fusillade of steel slugs intended to keep the enemy pinned down. When they withdrew, the next pair of scouts took up the suppressive fire. One of them was using the platoon's semi-portable machine gun. As Powers and David bounded past the third pair of armored scouts, Powers saw that one of them was preparing a directional antipersonnel mine. The other had a man-pack PPC aimed along their back trail.

Fifty meters distant from their original position, Powers and David stopped, slid into cover, and spun to face the way they'd just come. Two of her scouts dashed past them, moving another ten meters before likewise falling into defensive postures. In less than thirty seconds, the rest of the platoon had fallen back, and the night was quiet.

Powers strained her ears, expecting to hear the bang of the mine going off or the crack and rattle of enemy small-arms fire. What she heard instead was the loud whine-thump of a moving BattleMech.

"Dammit," she muttered. "They must have had a 'Mech on low-power standby and we didn't spot it."

The deep-throated chatter of a heavy machine gun ripped through the cool night air. Mangled bullets whined off rocks as the sentry *Vulcan* hosed down the area. By a stroke of good fortune, the 'Mech's burst touched none of the armored scouts. In response, a deep, crackling boom was followed by the jagged stroke of charged particles plowing into the cylindrical joint of the *Vulcan*'s left hip.

The 'Mech took a stutter-step, probably more from surprise at being attacked by a heavy weapon than because of the minor damage done to his armor. As the pilot recovered his footing, the Legion scouts bounded away on their suit-mounted jump packs.

At the top of her arc, Powers flipped her visor over to thermal, and spotted the heat signatures of at least three more 'Mechs. She couldn't tell what model each individual machine was, but she figured that all were lighter recon-types.

Coming to earth again, she switched her viewer over to its light-amplification setting. A ghostly vista of green, white, and black stretched out before her. There was no immediate sign of the enemy 'Mechs, but that could change any minute. The rebels might be satisfied with driving them off, but Powers didn't want to risk it. If she ordered her men into a general withdrawal, it would let them move out of the enemy's zone of control more rapidly. But if the rebels were in pursuit, the odds were against her troops if 'Mechs caught them in the open.

"Second Platoon, keep your eyes open," she radioed to her team. "There are at least three more 'Mechs out there. If you see one, sing out. Everyone is free to displace or engage at his discretion, but let's not get hung up out here. We've got intel for the colonel, and it won't do her or us any good if we all get greased before we can get it back to her."

She switched comm channels and made direct contact with Lieutenant M'Dahlla. "Pull your people back to Rally Point Tango and execute Plan Whiskey," she instructed. "Just make sure your people know that Second Platoon will be moving back through their field of fire. Tell them not to grease any of us along with the bad guys."

"Affirmative," was the taciturn M'Dahlla's only reply.

"Second Platoon, displace one hundred meters back right."

The other scouts flitted off to the southwest. No sooner had they gone to ground than the spindly form of the *Vulcan* reappeared. Moving carefully among the rocks, its slow speed made it a perfect target.

"Okay, boys," Powers said. "We'll fire in volley. Aim at his head." She gave her men a few seconds to bring their guns to bear on the enemy 'Mech. "Ready. Fire."

Lasers snapped out at the *Vulcan*, the report of the infantry fire lost in the deeper boom of the platoon's M-PPC. Armor spalled away from the *Vulcan*'s spherical cockpit, making the skinny 'Mech stagger drunkenly. The pilot quickly recovered and fired his machine gun into the area from which the man-made lightning had come. Even before the echoes of the chattering burst had faded, the *Vulcan*'s right arm lifted, displaying the flared, blackened muzzle of its most fearsome antiinfantry weapon. Flame vomited from the handless wrist. A scream made of equal parts terror and agony beat against Meg Powers' ears as the flamer washed across the position occupied by one of her men.

"Hit him again!" she roared.

Again, the platoon's lasers reached out to claw at the *Vulcan*. This time, the man-portable particle cannon failed to speak, but its deadly work was done. The Skye 'Mech's left arm bore deep, blackened scars.

"And again!" Powers barked before the *Vulcan* could recover enough to turn its flamer on another of her scouts. A loud, rushing crackle sounded across the battlefield as the renewed attack ripped through the tissue-thin armor remaining on the *Vulcan*'s left arm, severing myomer bundles and frying a vulnerable actuator package in its shoulder. The arm dropped to hang limp at the 'Mech's side.

"Fall back!" Powers yelled. "Fall back to the rally point."

The *Vulcan*'s pilot declined to pursue the retreating scouts. But the rest of his lance came on, nipping at the Legionnaires' heels with laser and machine-gun fire.

The broken terrain made it an even race. The scouts in their jump-capable power suits could vault over large impediments, which their pursuers had to go around. Still, the 'Mechs were faster and their pilots were fresh, whereas the armored scouts had been on the move all night.

"Lieutenant M'Dahlla, are you in position?" Powers called.

"Yes, Major. We are ready," he replied.

"All right. We'll be coming through your ambush zone hell-bent-for-leather, with two 'Mechs behind us. Think you can scrape them off for us?"

"We are ready," M'Dahlla repeated.

Second Platoon dashed through the narrow pass designated as Rally Point One and went to ground. A few moments later, the ground began to tremble as their hunters approached. The lead 'Mech, a hunch-shouldered *Watchman*, stepped into the notch. He slowed, as though sensing an ambush, but it was too late.

Powers heard M'Dahlla shout, and eight armored scouts swarmed from their hiding places. Darting forward, the platoon clambered up the *Watchman*'s legs. Powers saw a scout shove a bulky canvas bundle into the 'Mech's well-protected knee joint. Another trooper, bolder or more consumed with battle lust, clambered higher to lodge his satchel charge in the 'Mech's more vulnerable hip joint. A second later, both scouts bounded off. Their companions likewise scattered as the *Watchman* blazed away fruitlessly with its machine guns and lasers.

A flat bang echoed through the dark pass. Half a second later, a louder explosion dwarfed the first. Powers lifted her head to see the *Watchman* take one last step. Then its right leg parted company with its body, severed above the knee by the explosive charge.

As the medium 'Mech toppled onto its face, a second 'Mech entered the killing zone. Powers' scalp tightened when she saw its right arm swing up, revealing a Class 10 dual-purpose autocannon.

"Second Platoon, hit him!" she bellowed, bringing the sights of her gauss rifle up across the eye-like viewscreens of the enemy *Enforcer*. Lasers and slug-throwers alike hammered the 'Mech but inflicted little damage. One of First

Platoon's troopers skidded to a halt, knelt, and set a bulky short-range missile launcher against his shoulder. The first of those deadly projectiles streaked away into the night.

Powers watched in horror as the *Enforcer* cocked its head while raising its left arm, with its powerful 'Mech-killing laser. She waited calmly as the SRM launcher's semi-automatic mechanism brought the second missile around to the firing position. Her trooper took careful aim and fired. So did the *Enforcer*. The rocket tore through the air, even as the laser snuffed out the life of him that launched it. Instead of bursting upon impact with the 'Mech's armor, the projectile split open a few meters before it struck, showering the *Enforcer*'s legs with burning petrochemical fuel.

Ignoring the flames, the pilot hosed down the pass with a thundering burst of autocannon fire. Submunitions sparked and banged against the rocky sides and floor of the pass, and against the tinfoil armor of two armored scouts. Shrapnel and rock fragments filled the air, wounding more of her men.

Meg Powers took careful aim on the *Enforcer*'s cockpit and fired as one of First Platoon's other troopers sprayed the already burning 'Mech with a man-pack flamer. A single bolt from the 'Mech's laser felled the flamer-man.

"Time to go!" she yelled, knowing there was nothing more they could do here. "Everybody pull out!"

As she scrambled from her hiding place in the lee of a large, flat rock, something hammered into her power suit's back, knocking her sprawling. The breath was driven from her lungs as her chest slammed against the inside of the scout armor's plastron.

As she lay there gasping for breath, she heard a loud, rippling explosion. She tried to get to her feet, but her suit would not respond. The low-light viewer she'd been using ever since Second Platoon had vacated their first position flickered and went out. Cursing, Powers tried again to bring the suit to its feet, but to no avail. Her scout armor was dead.

Suddenly she heard a sharp hiss and felt a cold breeze against her sweat-soaked skin.

"Major, are you all right?" Elron David asked.

"I think so, El," she answered, shrugging off her armor's inert carapace. Her subordinate must have tripped the suit's manual latches. As she pulled herself out of the disabled armor, a chill shook her limbs. The thick metal backpack that had once housed the scout armor's power cell, electronics suite, and infantry jump jet was a ruined tangle of metal. The smell of highly volatile fuel stung her nostrils. Whatever had knocked her to the ground had destroyed the suit's vital systems and ripped open the jump-pack's fuel cell. Only luck had kept that fuel from igniting and turning her into a living torch.

Of the *Enforcer* there was no sign other than a smoking hulk where the fifty-ton 'Mech had stood. Powers guessed that his profligate use of the heat-generating laser, combined with the effects of the flamer and inferno rounds, had caused the rebel's ammunition to cook off and destroy the 'Mech.

"El, take command," Powers said, looking up at her battle-armored sergeant. "I can't lead the company like this. I've got my survival pack. I'll call for pick-up and see you back at the base."

"Major, I can assign—"

"Sergeant, there are more rebels out there. You take command, and get the scouts home safe. The colonel needs the data you're carrying."

"Major—"

"That is an *order*, Sergeant!"

"Yes, sir." David saluted and was gone.

Meg Powers flipped open a metal case attached to her power suit's left hip. After shrugging into the pack's thin camouflaged coveralls and fastening a web belt with its holstered pistol around her waist, she activated her recovery beacon. The fist-sized device would continue to transmit a coded radio signal until she was picked up or its batteries ran out.

Following Legion doctrine, she performed one last operation before jogging off into the night. She knelt beside her ruined armor, placed a stubby cylinder over the ruined power-pack, and yanked a ring-pin free. Grabbing her survival pack, she hauled ass away from the downed power suit.

The incendiary grenade detonated with a harsh *whoosh*, igniting the spilled fuel.

She jogged a hundred meters in the general direction of

the Legion base before going to ground. The rescue beacon would guide the rescuers to her, and it would be easier for them to home in on her position if she sat still. Crouching in the dark, she listened as the sounds of the battle grew fainter. The noises moving away to the south told her that Elron David was doing as she had ordered—attempting to return the scout company to the Legion HQ at the Defiance complex.

Then she heard the scuffing of a footstep in the loose, stony soil. She looked up and to her right to see a young woman clad only in a cooling vest, briefs, and moccasins standing over her. A holstered pistol rode on her left hip. The patch of the Twenty-second Skye Rangers sewn to the vest's front left no doubt as to the newcomer's identity. For a moment, the women stared at each other in surprise, each waiting to see what the other was going to do.

Then, as though on a signal, each clawed at her holster. Both weapons came free at the same moment. In a corner of her mind, Powers felt scorching pain rip up her left arm, followed by the stench of seared flesh. But her attention was focused on her pistol's luminous sights. As the front blade came up over the Ranger's chest, she squeezed the trigger rapidly three times. A trio of nine-millimeter slugs tore into the other woman's body, and she collapsed abruptly.

After making sure that her enemy was truly dead and recovering her laser pistol, Powers shoved back the collar of her jumpsuit to inspect her wound. The beam of amplified light had burned a neat pair of holes in the sleeve of the jumpsuit, leaving a shallow, charred gash in her upper arm. There was no blood, but the pain seared along her arm.

Zipping up the jumpsuit, Powers recovered her pack and slipped off into the darkness, praying that a Legion recovery team would find her before the Skye Rangers did.

**Defiance Industries Complex**
**Myoo Highlands, Hesperus II**
**Skye Province**
**Lyran Alliance**
**03 July 3065**

"**C**olonel, your scouts are back," her new orderly reported.

Lori instantly dropped the hard copy reports she'd been reading, grateful to leave off perusing the butcher's bill from the train wreck and the battle that followed. Reading casualty reports was one of the most difficult jobs she had to perform. Only writing the letters that those reports generated was more painful.

It was a short walk from the office Defiance Industries had given her to the large 'Mech bay. As she stepped onto the surprisingly clean concrete floor, Lori saw Lieutenant M'Dahlla sitting back in a folding plastic chair, his face pinched with fatigue and streaked with sweat. His bullet-scarred scout armor, spattered with thin, sandy mud, lay on the floor beside him. Davis McCall, Tom Devin, and Major Goree stood close by. Their postures told Lori that they had been waiting for her.

When M'Dahlla spotted Lori, he put aside the plastic bottle of water from which he'd been drinking and got wearily to his feet.

"Colonel . . ."

"Sit down, Lieutenant," Lori said kindly.

"Thank you, Colonel," he sighed, dropping heavily into the chair. Sighing once more, he launched into his narrative. "We located the enemy bivouac about thirty klicks north, northeast of us. They are set up in a broad meadow right up against the foot of the next ridge. We counted at least three trails leading back from the meadow into the mountains. As nearly as we could tell, they have got two regiments of BattleMechs, plus about a brigade of support troops. We saw one full wing of aerospace fighters, but no DropShips."

"No DropShips?" Lori interrupted.

"No, Colonel. They may have moved them farther back into the mountains," M'Dahlla continued. "Or they may have sent them away, though it did not feel like either of those. I cannot quite put my finger on it. Major Powers took First Platoon—"

"Wait a minute," Lori cut in again. "Did you say Major Powers was with you?"

"Yes, Colonel, the major was with us. She always liked to get a firsthand look at things and . . ."

"Well, if Major Powers was with you, why isn't *she* making this report?" Lori's voice froze in her throat, even as she spoke the words.

"We lost contact with her on the way out, Colonel." M'Dahlla's voice was quiet and even, but he appeared to shrink in on himself. "Lieutenant David was the last one to see her. He says she was in good shape and was going to activate her distress beacon as soon as she got clear of the combat zone. He says she *ordered* him to leave her, that she said the intel was more important than any one life.

"You know the Major, Colonel. You know what she was like. The job at hand always came first."

Lori felt her heart do a slow forward roll at the thought of another friend gone. Meg Powers was irascible, irritating at times, but she was a professional, and she did her job very well. Ordering a subordinate to leave her in order to ensure the timely delivery of an intelligence report would be just like her.

"Has anyone gone out to look for her?" Lori asked, turning to McCall. "Have we picked up her beacon?"

"As soon as we heard that Major Powers was on foot,

and missing, we borrowed a couple of Major Goree's VTOLs," he said. "They were able t' make a couple passes over the area, but th' *sassanach* began pottin' at them almost as soon as the choppers started inta their search pattern. They weren't able t' pick up her beacon. It's startin' t' look as if Major Powers is either dead or a prisoner."

"I see," Lori said, steeling herself. "And where is that report?"

"It's bein' analyzed," McCall said. "We should have a clear strategic picture in an hour or so."

Lori turned to M'Dahlla. "Well done, Lieutenant. Please pass that along to your scouts. Until we determine Major Powers' status, you will be acting company commander. I'll move Captain Monti into battalion command."

Lori turned away from the exhausted scout. "Lieutenant-Colonel McCall, Major Goree, if you'll accompany me please?" She led them into the safety of her office, where she sagged against the edge of the desk.

"I'm getting too old for this."

"Aye, lass, we all are," McCall agreed. "But that gives us the advantage. 'Age and treachery' and a' that."

"Maybe so, Davis." Lori snorted at his use of the old adage which held that age and treachery will always win out over youth and enthusiasm. "But I'm all out of treacherous thoughts right now."

She stretched, easing the aching muscles in her neck. "Until the intel boys get done playing with the raw data, we have to go on instinct. What do we make of what M'Dahlla said?"

With a murmured apology, Goree reached across Lori's desk. "Well, Colonel, if I'm understanding your scout correctly, then I'd guess the Skye Rangers are about here." Tapping a few control pads, he called up a map of the Myoo Highlands on a wall-mounted viewscreen. A small red dot flashed the location where M'Dahlla said the Skye Rangers were to be found.

"If your man is correct, and I have no reason to assume otherwise, the Rangers are probably right here. Now, I know these mountains. They're riddled with trails, passes, and meadows. They're also full of box canyons, cul-de-sacs, and dead ends. So that makes me wonder if the rebels are getting some kind of local support. God knows, there are

just as many Separatists on Hesperus as you'd find anywhere else in the province, except maybe on Skye itself."

"That may be so, lad," McCall said, stepping up to study
the map. "But I still dinna see why the *sassanach* would
put themselves inta a box like that in th' first place."

"The why of it is a concern," Lori said. "What really
worries me is where are their DropShips? I suppose
M'Dahlla could be right, that they may have diverted the
ships to some alternate landing zone, but again, why?"

McCall stood before the map, studying it carefully. "Well,
they made a feint twice before, once in Melrose, and once
at Doering. Both times, we had t' leave them in possession
of th' field, and they abandoned it, moving on to another
place, where they launched another attack."

"Is that what you think is happening here?" Lori asked.

McCall shook his head almost sorrowfully. "Truthfully,
lass, I dinna ken. But t' quote our lad M'Dahlla, that
doesn't feel right."

"So what does feel right?" Goree asked.

"Well, I'm only guessin', y' understand. But were th'
roles reversed, and th' Legion was sittin' oot there in th'
hills with aboot even odds, but facin' a dug-in enemy, I ken
what I'd be doin' wi' me DropShips. I'd have them boost
and burn hard for my JumpShips, and I'd be sendin' some
pretty strongly worded messages back to Skye askin' fer
help t' crack this nut."

Lori nodded thoughtfully at McCall's assessment of the
situation.

"But why boost their ships at all?" Goree wondered
aloud. "Why not just send the message to the *Simon Davion*, and have them relay it back to their JumpShips?"

"The same reason I've got a couple of your repair crews
out hunting for breaks in the land-line between here and
Maria's Elegy," Lori said. "The same reason General Ciampa is sitting at the spaceport waiting for her regiment to
dig itself out and get itself patched up, instead of being on
the march."

She stood up and began passing in front of her desk.
"Security. It's far too easy to intercept anything other than
a hard-line signal, and the only reason that's hard anymore
is the job takes a human to tap into the line and listen in.
With electronic signals, like a radio message, there's just

too much chance of interception. So, if the rebels wanted to shout for help and didn't want us to know about it, they'd have to hot-up their DropShips."

"That would only take one DropShip, or two at most," Goree said, pensively scratching his cheek with his right forefinger. "Where are the rest of their ships? They couldn't have boosted without us seeing them. Unless they stayed low, below our radar. If so, they could have dispersed their ships to alternate LZs. That's the only possibility, unless the Skye Rangers have come up with a way of making DropShips invisible."

"If they've done that, Major, we're in a lot more trouble than we think."

"So what *do* we do?"

"We wait for the intel to come back, then we hit the Rangers—hard." Lori's tired eyes took on a new light as she spoke of the coming battle. "We don't have enough strength to wipe them out here. We'll need Ciampa for that, and it's going to take a few days for her to get here. I propose we make a raid in force, concentrate on their fighters and their support structure. If we can kill or cripple some of their 'Mechs or heavy tanks, so much the better. But our primary goal is to clobber their fighters and to take out their repair and refit equipment. We'll burn or blow up whatever stores we can find, and destroy their repair facilities."

She shrugged lightly. "If we can't out-gun them, maybe we can outlast them.

"Meantime, Major Goree, I'd like to use your facilities here to effect repairs to my unit."

"I was about to make that offer," Goree said with a smile. "In fact, I'll go you one better. I will loan you whatever 'Mechs you need to replace any that have been destroyed or damaged past repair. Even better, I'll place myself and my battalion under your command for this fight."

"That is a most generous offer, Major, but why . . ."

"Why the change of heart, Colonel?" Goree smiled at her surprise. "It isn't really a change of heart. It's like I told you before. I'd start trusting the Legion once I was sure you could be trusted."

His smile broadened. "Besides, if I didn't offer, Captain

Brewer would have changed his clothes, and CEO Brewer would have ordered me to help."

Lori smiled for what felt like the first time in months.

"Major, thank you for your offer. We will gladly accept the repairs and replacements, but I'm afraid I'll have to decline your unit's company on this raid. Not because I don't think they can fight, and not because I think we're any better soldiers than you. It's just that I'd rather have you hold the Self-Protection Force in reserve, right here at the Defiance complex, in case the Separatists manage to evade or eliminate the Legion."

"All right," Goree said, his voice heavy with reluctance. "I understand what you're saying. It's the best tactical option, but I have to say that I don't like being kept out of a fight."

"Don't worry," Lori said, turning her eyes toward the big map. "This war's not over yet."

**Myoo Highlands, Hesperus II**
**Skye Province**
**Lyran Alliance**
**04 July 3065**

Lori watched with rapidly eroding patience as a tiny blue dot crawled across the electronic map displayed on one of the *Victor*'s secondary monitors. The electronic indicator marked the location of the recon lance attached to the Legion's headquarters company. Despite Lieutenant M'Dahlla's insistence that the armored scouts were ready to make another run at the encamped Skye Rangers, Lori insisted that the exhausted men and women of his company sit out this fight. That meant any pre-battle surveys would have to be done the "old-fashioned" way, using light, fast BattleMechs for the job.

"Buckskin, this is Roan," Lieutenant Christine Wellerman, recon lance leader said, using the call signs Lori had assigned before they left the Defiance plant. "Roan group is in position. Everything is as reported." Though she spoke quietly, her voice came clearly to Lori's ears, thanks to the sophisticated communications equipment built into Wellerman's captured *Koshi-A* OmniMech.

"Roan, Buckskin. Stay on station. Report any changes. We will advise before the bull runs."

Lori pressed a switch on her left-hand joystick, selecting the Legion's general-use radio frequency.

"Herd, this is Buckskin. Form up."

Immediately, the Gray Death Legion swung into action. In a few minutes, all company commanders had reported their readiness. Taking a deep breath, Lori gave the order to move out.

A slight push of the joysticks settled the *Victor* into a slow walk. To either side, the 'Mechs of her command lance kept pace. About three hundred meters ahead of her were the 'Mechs of First Battalion's Second and Third Companies. They were arrayed in two blocks, with Second Company in front of Third. First Company was detached, moving parallel to its comrades, a kilometer distant to the east. Elements of Second Battalion were drawn up on First Battalion's left in a mirror-image formation. Far out on the flanks, broken into two roughly equal forces, were the Legion's conventional armor and armored infantry forces. Surprisingly, given the rough, broken terrain, the detached wings of the Legion kept the rough formation as they closed on the enemy's position.

Minutes passed, and the distance shrank. Twice Lori had to change the scale of the electronic map as the icon representing the Legion threatened to merge with the scarlet marker of the Skye Rangers.

"Buckskin, this is Sorrel," Daniel Brewer said in her earpiece. "We have contact with the enemy. We are engaging." His level tone failed to completely mask the fear and anticipation felt by every soldier going into battle.

At a word from Lori, the advancing line came to a halt. From her position, she could see little of the fighting. Only the snap and thunder of gunfire and the occasional arcing contrails of missile volleys revealed the spot where the deadly contest was being waged.

She switched display modes, and the scrolling electronic map was replaced by a graphic tactical representation of the battle. Tiny blue icons stood against advancing red markers as the Legion and the Skye Rangers sought to annihilate one another. One scarlet triangle blinked out, followed by an azure pyramid. A 'Mech from each side had just died, and possibly the human being at the war machine's controls. Lori knew that damage was beginning to

mount on both sides, but still she held her wings and reserves back from the battle.

Two more blue icons faded, and a third began to blink
as a severely damaged 'Mech fell out of line, heading for
the rear.

*Now! It's time,* her heart screamed. Her mind agreed.

"Sorrel, this is Buckskin. Pull back."

Immediately, the blue icons began moving back the way
they had just come, giving up the ground they had won.
The red enemy pursued. The volume of fire marking the
battlefield increased in intensity.

Just a few hundred meters, Lori prayed. That was all
she needed.

Then, the rebel 'Mechs stopped.

"Sorrel, what's happening?" she snapped into her mike.

For a few seconds there was no reply. When Brewer
came on the line, his voice had a strained, breathless quality. "They aren't going for it. They've pulled up short.
Stand by, One."

The line went silent for a few moments. When Brewer
came back on, his voice was steadier. "They've broken contact, Colonel. The rebels are falling back on their bivouac."

"Dammit!" she howled.

"Do you want us to go back in?"

"Stand by, Sorrel."

For only the briefest moment or two, Lori mulled over
the failure of her plan. She had intended that the Rangers
pursue Brewer's retreating 'Mechs as the company withdrew. Then, once the rebels had overextended themselves,
and had been drawn in against the heavier 'Mechs of the
command company, the bulk of the Legion would swing
around and hit the enemy in the flanks.

Either von Frisch had recognized the ploy and refused
to be taken in, or he simply did not want to be pulled away
from his base of operations. Whatever his thinking, his refusal to fall into her trap left Lori with two options. She
could either concede that the raid in force had failed, withdraw from the field, and hope to launch an attack at some
later date, or revise her plan on the fly and press the attack
already underway.

"Herd, this is Buckskin," she said, arriving at a decision.
"Reform. We're going to hit them again. This time nobody

pulls back, nobody stops. We all go in." In a few precise phrases, she laid out her impromptu plan of attack.

"Now, any questions?"

"This is Palomino," the commander of a tank company called. "No questions, Buckskin, but I've got some good news. One of my hover tanks just picked up Major Powers. She's cold, hungry, and exhausted, but she's alive."

Lori sighed, feeling a portion of the burden lift from her shoulders. Finding Meg Powers alive was a small victory in itself.

"Very well, Palomino," she said with a slight chuckle of relief. "Tell off one of your light hover tanks and get her back to the base. Meanwhile, the rest of you, let's try this thing again. Form ranks."

Again, the Legion surged forward, aiming at the heart of the Rangers' camp. Again, the rebels came out to meet them.

"Contact!" Brewer shouted. "Sorrel has contact with the enemy and is engaging!" His voice was almost joyful in the wake of the previous failure.

"Lean into them!" Lori shouted back. "Keep the pressure on."

The din of battle filled the air, as the headquarters company rolled forward. Lori spared no glance for her map display now. Only the tactical situation held any significance.

A *Grand Dragon* sent a fan of missiles ripping through the air, only a few meters above her head. She targeted the 'Mech and fired, staving in its metallic ribs with a gauss slug.

Undeterred, the Separatist warrior struck back with PPC and laser fire that ate away at the armor on her *Victor*'s chest and ribs. Lori traded blow for blow, punching through the weakened armor with a flight of short-range missiles, and ripping armor from the beast's legs with twin blasts from her pulse lasers.

Leigh Cooper, warrior number four in the HQ lance, stepped up alongside the *Victor*, beams of amplified light snapping from her *Exterminator*'s wrists. The *Grand Dragon* rocked back on its heels, recovered, and began to withdraw from the fight, its armor gouged and torn by the assault it had just suffered.

"Let him go, Leigh," Lori said, but not before Cooper savaged the rebel once more with a flight of long-range missiles. The *Grand Dragon* shuddered under the fiery onslaught and measured its length in the stony soil of the meadow. As she rushed by, Lori saw the dazed pilot drag himself from the disabled 'Mech's cockpit. In a futile act of defiance, the rebel pulled himself to his feet and peppered her *Victor* with small-caliber pistol rounds. A few dozen meters down the line, she saw McCall's *Highlander* lower its shoulder to bowl over an enemy *Wraith*.

"Herd, this is Buckskin," Lori panted as her heat sinks labored to bleed away the heat generated by her weapons. "Break, break, break."

Immediately the foremost elements of the Gray Death Legion divided in two, and flowed around the Skye 'Mechs that had marched out to oppose them. The supporting ranks stepped into their places, raining shells and missiles onto the enemy machines. The companies far out on the Legion's wings extended their lines deep into the rebel bivouac before turning to hammer the partially encircled enemy.

"Buckskin, this is Sorrel," Brewer called. "We're running the bypass, but I'm not sure the Rangers are falling for this one, either. If they don't, we're going to be in a world of hurt."

Lori consulted the electronic map. Indeed, many of the rebel units had not turned to follow the encircling Legion 'Mechs. One cluster of red icons, about a reinforced company's worth, seemed to be massing for a counter-charge against Major Devin's flank.

Cursing, she yelled an alert to Devin, but could do no more.

"Colonel, look out!"

Lori never learned who shouted the warning, for in that very instant something collided with her *Victor* in a loud, ringing crash. The eighty-ton assault 'Mech was knocked sprawling on its face. Lori's neurohelmeted head bounced off the heads up display. Stars shot across her vision, and her ears were filled with a throbbing rush of sound.

With limbs suddenly as unresponsive as house cats, she tried to get the *Victor*'s arms under it. The pulsing roar in her ears rose in pitch and cadence as a gray haze swam across her vision. Dimly, she was aware that the green silhouette on her Mech Status Display had taken on large patches of amber, proclaiming damage to those sections of her armor. A loud stuttering roar, followed by the harsh electrical crackling of a PPC discharge tortured her ears despite the noise-attenuation systems built into both the neurohelmet and her 'Mech's cockpit. Again, something struck her 'Mech a heavy blow, this time across the backs of both legs. Again, she was hurled forward against the straps of her restraint harness as the *Victor* was once more knocked to the ground.

"Colonel? Colonel?" a distant voice called in her ears. "Colonel, are you all right?"

Lori shook the cobwebs out of her head, and took stock of her situation. She was hanging face down from her safety harness, but seemed to be uninjured. Her MSD showed moderate damage to her *Victor*'s head and left shoulder, and light damage to both lower legs, but all of its systems seemed to be operational. Still, she could not bring the big machine to its feet.

"Colonel!" the voice yelled again, this time much closer. She was finally able to distinguish it as belonging to Dallas MacKensie.

"I'm all right, Mac," she said. "Just please stop yelling."

"Hang on a second, Colonel. That Skye bugger has got you pinned."

"What?"

The only immediate reply was a short, "All together now," followed by heavy metallic scraping.

"Okay, Colonel, you're free," MacKensie said.

Lori tried again to get the *Victor* upright, and succeeded with only a modest amount of effort.

As she regained her ·bearings, she saw the burned-out carcass of an enemy *Starslayer* lying on its back at her feet. Its cockpit had been crushed by a blow of horrific force.

"That son-of-a-buck jumped on you, Colonel," MacKensie explained. "Just jumped right over our lines and landed on you with both feet. He was about to back-shoot you when we brought him down. When he dropped, he fell across your legs and kept you pinned. We had to roll him off."

Lori looked around to see three watchful Legion 'Mechs, besides MacKensie's *Trebuchet*, standing close by. One was Captain Brian Scully's *Hatchetman*. In that moment, Lori was grateful that the ex-Lyran warrior had chosen to ignore Grayson's order to discard melee weapons in favor of more armor or ranged weapons.

"Thanks, people. There will be something special in your paychecks this month," she said with weary humor. "Now, let's get back to it."

She checked the map display again, mindful of what had happened the last time she took her mind off the ebb and flow of the battle around her. She saw that her carefully crafted plan, interrupted by the Rangers' reluctance to follow her withdrawing 'Mechs, had fallen completely apart. In just those few minutes, the battle had degenerated into a street fight between two armed mobs. Both armies were so intermixed that the Legion no longer enjoyed the all-too-fleeting advantage of enfilading fire that the flank moves had given them. Only Scully's Third Company and the command lance remained lightly engaged.

"Form your company up on the command lance," Lori said to Scully. "We're going to push through this mess and do what we came for."

In moments, the small task force was driving into the heart of the melee. A *Whitworth* and a *Tempest* stood together to bar their way, but a heavy volley of fire reduced both 'Mechs to scrap, but not before they had destroyed a *Commando* from Scully's combat lance. Penetrating deeper into the Rangers' bivouac, the Legion 'Mechs broke clear of the main battle area. A few Skye Rangers turned away from the fighting to oppose them.

"Scully, hold them back," Lori directed. "Command lance, start tearing this place apart."

As Scully's company moved to intercept the pursuing rebels, Lori turned and aimed her pulse lasers at a slab-sided truck with a "cherry-picker" sprouting from its back. In seconds, the repair vehicle was in flames. She turned and served a second, similar vehicle the same.

At the same time, MacKensie poured laser fire into a parked ammunition carrier, adding to the fireworks display by setting off a tanker truck loaded with highly volatile aviation fuel. Paul Hansen and Leigh Cooper walked along a line of parked aerospace fighters, methodically hammering each attack craft into smoking rubble.

A squad of infantrymen dashed from the shelter of a tracked armored personnel carrier. One dropped to his knees and slammed a brace of short-range missiles into the *Victor's* chest. The others raced forward. Lori saw a green canvas bag clutched in the hands of the leader.

She took a long step backward and sprayed the group with darts of energy from her pulse lasers. The foot soldiers died under the megajoule caress of the lasers, their knee-capping satchel charge falling harmlessly from the sergeant's lifeless hands. To ensure that no further close infantry assaults occurred, Lori blasted the APC with her gauss rifle, punching a head-sized hole through the transport-passenger section. A burst from her pulse lasers set the vehicle ablaze.

"Buckskin, this is Pinto," McCall yelled. "The *sassanach* are startin' t' gain th' upper hand here. I think it's aye time to go."

"All right, Pinto," Lori called back. "Pull 'em out. Herd, this is Buckskin. Your signal is Bridle. Pull out, and head back to base."

As the Legion 'Mechs slipped away from the field, the rebels drew back into their encampment, perhaps fearing another trap.

More likely, they were just as tired as she was, Lori decided as the last Legion 'Mech withdrew from the meadow.

# 28

Myoo Highlands, Hesperus II
Skye Province
Lyran Alliance
05 July 3065

**L**ori stopped in the wide doorway to the main floor of the 'Mech hangar that housed the Gray Death Legion. She leaned wearily against the steel doorjamb, watching the Legion's technical crews, augmented by volunteer workers from Defiance Industries, crawling around on scaffolds and gantries as they serviced or repaired the Gray Death's battered 'Mechs.

She avoided looking at the handful of empty 'Mech bays scattered throughout the hangar. Each of the seven vacant stalls represented a wrecked machine and a dead or wounded warrior. The losses to her tank and infantry battalions were not so graphically illustrated, though they were more severe. Her mechanized and jump infantry platoons had lost more than a quarter of their two hundred thirty men. The tankers came off a bit better, though not by much. The worst damage had befallen the Gray Death armored infantry. The dozen men taken out of action represented a third of the GDAI's strength.

Far in the distance, she heard the sound of the massive durallex steel doors of the 'Mech hangar sliding open on their runners. Looking toward the far end of the hangar, she saw a cluster of blue and white 'Mechs enter the facility. Leading the group was a *BNC-5S Banshee*. The assault 'Mech's face, normally a grinning mask of death due to the contours of its faceplate, had been painted to resemble the hideous visage of an angry ghost. Only one such machine existed in the Fifteenth's Table of Organization and Equipment, the one piloted by Leutnant-General Gina Ciampa.

"It's about time," Lori said to herself. There were many in the Gray Death Legion who shared that sentiment, and who were less reserved in expressing it. Those people, warriors and technicians alike, had begun to complain that Ciampa's troops were sitting back at Maria's Elegy—fat, dumb and happy—while the Gray Death Legion beat its brains out against three full regiments of Skye Rangers. Few seemed willing to remember that the Guards had been heavily engaged by the Rangers at Doering. They likewise failed to mention the hammering the Lyran troops had taken when the Separatists turned the *Simon Davion*'s guns on the spaceport.

Lori remained where she was and watched as the 'Mechs of the Fifteenth Lyran Guards made their way into the hangar. A low, orange-painted truck with a lighted sign reading "Follow me" led the way. The Guard 'Mechs were dusty, but the layers of grit could not disguise the fact that a number of the machines had places where their paint jobs did not quite match. In those spots, areas of the blue and white colorings were brighter, unfaded by the sun and rain. Lori recognized the patches for what they were, scars of earlier battles and of the bombardment. Many of the Legion's 'Mechs sported similar markings.

She counted a total of sixty-eight 'Mechs as they filed into the hangar. Only a few were light models. Most of the lighter machines had been destroyed, along with a goodly portion of the Fifteenth's conventional armor.

As the armored doors began closing behind the last Guard 'Mech, Lori commandeered one of the small electric carts used to negotiate the kilometers of passageways, manufacturing spaces, and living areas of the underground factory complex. Putting the vehicle into gear, she headed off in the direction the Lyran troops had gone. She rounded a corner a bit too fast, causing the cart's tires to chirp in protest. Though she had used the carts during the Legion's previous visit to Defiance, she was still unused to the powerful motors possessed by the relatively tiny vehicles.

By the time she reached the section of the hangar assigned to the Lyran Guards, Gina Ciampa had backed her 'Mech into a repair gantry and had climbed out onto the *Banshee*'s left shoulder. She was leaning against the 'Mech's cheek, pulling off her thin felt slippers.

"It's good to see you, General," Lori shouted up from the hangar floor, forcing herself not to add "at last" to her greeting.

Ciampa replaced her slippers with a pair of heavy black combat boots and grinned down at Lori.

"We're glad to be here, Colonel. I'm just sorry we couldn't have made it sooner. It's a long hike overland. I gather you've been having a pretty tough go of it."

"That's putting it mildly, General," Lori said with a touch of bitterness. "And it's going to get worse."

Ciampa climbed down the steel ladder from the ingress/egress catwalk to the floor of the 'Mech hangar before continuing the conversation. As she strode across the bay floor, Lori saw the strain of the last few days on Ciampa's face. New lines seemed to radiate out from the corners of her eyes and mouth, and the old ones seemed deeper, more pronounced. Lori could have sworn that the general had more gray in her hair than the last time they spoke, less than a week before.

My God, I hope I don't look that bad, she thought.

"You said things might be getting worse," Ciampa said. "How so?"

Lori explained how the Legion scouts had been unable to locate the enemy DropShips and her fears that the missing vessels suggested the Separatists had sent them to fetch help.

"I'm afraid you might be right, Colonel. One of the last things the ground sensors picked up before those muck-eaters blew the monitoring stations all to hell was a DropShip, probably a *Leopard*, burning hard for the zenith jump point."

Lori mulled over what Ciampa had just told her. Though she had suspected the rebels had sent for reinforcements, she'd nursed the hope that *all* of the Ranger DropShips had been dispatched to some remote alternate landing zone in the hopes of preventing their capture or destruction by the Gray Death Legion.

"If the ground-side sensors are out and the monitoring station has been blown away, what kind of early-warning system do we have in place?" Lori asked.

"None," Ciampa said. "The Separatists could come in here with half the Star League Defense Force, and we might not know about it until their DropShips were already in the atmosphere."

"Any idea what kind of a timetable we're looking at?" Lori asked. "How soon we might expect reinforcements to arrive, ours or theirs?"

"Six weeks ago, I'd have been able to give you a pretty accurate guess," Ciampa said with a bitter laugh. "Now? I haven't got a clue. Things have been so screwed up by both the rebellion and by Prince Victor's war of aggression, that I don't have any idea where the nearest friendly units are stationed, or where any units who have turned their coats for Skye might be. I don't even know if there *are* any more rebel units. For all I know, Kelswa-Steiner and Dundee have committed all of their forces to this one operation. That would be too risky for my blood, but history shows that, in a rebellion like this one where you've got a numerically and technologically inferior rebel force, fortune does often favor the brave."

Ciampa sighed and thrust her hands into the pockets of her fatigues. "And that leads us to the question of what do we do now?"

"Well, the first thing we do," Lori said, escorting Ciampa to the waiting cart, "is not discuss it out here on the hangar floor. There are too many prying ears."

"You don't think there are spies among our own people, do you?" Ciampa asked, looking around suspiciously.

Lori waited until they were seated and the cart was in motion before answering.

"Among the Legion? No, not a chance. All of our people are loyal. I can't speak for your troops. That's got to be your call. What concerns me are the civilians. All of the workers and most of the supervisors, even the low-level managers, are Skye natives. A few of the Board members are Skye-born and bred too. How many Defiance employees are secretly rooting for the Separatists?"

"Does that extend to your own Captain Brewer?"

"No," Lori snapped with a fatigue-induced flash of temper. "Dan is as loyal as McCall, or Powers, or any other Legionnaire. No, it's the lower-level people I'm questioning."

"Colonel, you've got a nasty, suspicious mind there," Ciampa said without insult in her voice.

"Occupational hazard," Lori said wearily. "Haven't you heard the old mercenary's adage? Somewhere, sometime, there will be an employer who teaches you the meaning of the word paranoia."

"Has the Archon ever given you reason to be paranoid?" It was Ciampa's turn to bristle.

"No," Lori said flatly, making the conscious decision not to be drawn into an argument. "We've only ever really had one employer who tried to rake us over the coals, and *that* was a long time ago. But you don't survive as a mercenary unless you have a healthy sense of self-preservation."

Lori refused to discuss her plans for defending the Defiance complex and Hesperus until they reached her office.

"How do you know this place is secure?" Ciampa asked.

Lori pulled a small black box from the top desk drawer.

"Bug detector," she said, switching on the unit. "And I had Major Powers sweep the place as soon as we took up residency. If you think I'm paranoid, you ought to talk to Meg. She suspects everyone until they've *proven* themselves trustworthy. According to my little friend here, we're still the only ones listening. So, General, what do we do now?"

Ciampa dropped into the chair Lori offered her and sat back to think for a moment. "Well, the way I see it, we have two options: one, fort up and hope our reinforcements arrive before the rebels'. If that happens, we can run the enemy to ground in short order. If the Separatists get help first, then we're trapped here. We can call Zambos in from Maldon, but I'd rather not do that unless we have to. I don't want to give the rebels that kind of undefended target. Remember what they did to the Doering plant."

"I remember," Lori said quietly.

"Our second option is to combine our strength and launch an all-out assault on the Rangers. If we win, we can pull back to the mountain for repairs and wait for reinforcements to arrive. That takes us back to our first consideration. Whose reserves will get here first?"

"That's just about the way I read it, General, with one additional question. Was our call for help sent before the rebels blew up the HPG station?"

Ciampa shook her head. "I don't know. The station was totaled. Everybody inside was killed. There were a few ComStar personnel away from the installation when the attack came, but they couldn't say for certain if the message got through."

Lori sighed. "In that event, we have to assume a worst-case scenario. We have to assume that the Separatists have fresh troops on the way, and that Theater Command has no idea what we're facing here."

"So what do we do then? Fort up?"

"No," Lori answered. "I've never liked being in a cage. I propose we take the fight to the Skye Rangers while we have the chance. We know where they are. I have a scout platoon keeping tabs on them. If we pull back, and 'fort up' as you say, we'll lose contact with them. The rebels will be free to maneuver around the planet, shooting up secondary targets until we're forced to go after them. If that happens, we'll be fighting on ground of the enemy's choosing.

"In addition," Lori continued, "if we allow the Rangers to break contact now and go after them later, the strategic situation would allow the enemy to strike at Defiance while we're trying to track them down."

"So what do you propose we do?"

"What I propose, General, is risky. We'll leave your Lyran Guards here at Defiance. Like you said, it's a long march from Maria's Elegy. Your troops are tired. You'll stay here and bolster Major Goree's defenses. I'm going to take the Legion on a night march to the east through the mountains and see if we can come in on the enemy's flank. If we can take them by surprise at night, we might be able to hurt them enough to put them on the defensive. Then, once your people are ready to go again, we'll trade places. Your Guards can harry the Rangers into the ground."

"Not a bad plan, Colonel," Ciampa allowed. "Not bad at all. Still, I hate the idea of putting your people on the firing line again. If I'm not mistaken, they've been fighting almost constantly since you arrived at Defiance. Why not wait a few days and launch a combined assault on the Rangers? Or let my Guards make the flank attack?"

"I thought about that too, General," Lori said. "'Mech for 'Mech, your Guards are heavier and in better condition than the Legion."

"But?"

"But if I'm not mistaken, you are primarily a main line-of-battle unit. You haven't got a whole lot of experience in this kind of operation, nor does your TO&E allow you the kind of operational flexibility necessary for such a mission." Lori spoke as diplomatically as she could, reinforcing her position with a thin, polite smile. "I mean no offense, General. I just think the Legion is more adept at being sneaky and underhanded."

For a moment, Ciampa stared at Lori, who wondered if Ciampa was going to simply command her to allow the Fifteenth Lyran Guards to make the flank march. She knew Ciampa had a reputation for micromanaging battles or even whole campaigns. She hoped the other woman would see the sense in allowing the Legion to do the job for which it was most suited—guerrilla tactics.

"Very well, Colonel." Ciampa's neutral tone gave away nothing of her thoughts. "We'll play this one your way."

Lori smiled, but didn't show that she was relieved. "Thank you, General. Now, if I might ask one thing of you. It is entirely possible that when we hit the Rangers, we may flush them out of their bivouac toward you. If we do, you might want to have some of your lighter, faster elements standing by to take up the pursuit."

"I was already planning on that, Colonel," Ciampa replied.

Lori tapped her intercom.

"Major Powers, would you please report to my office?"

Within minutes, the scout commander was leaning over Lori's desk studying a hard-copy map of the region surrounding the Defiance complex. While Lori could read a map as well as any other officer in the Legion, Meg Powers seemed to have a second sight that could see beyond the lines of ink on paper to discern the exact lay of the land.

She also seemed to have a preference for the archaic printed map rather than the sophisticated electronic version. At last, she looked up with a slow nod.

"I've got it, Colonel," she said, pulling a handful of colored markers from the breast pocket of her fatigues. "This will be the best way." With swift strokes, she began drawing a route through the rugged Myoo Mountains. The lines and arrows started at the Defiance complex and arced away to the southwest, then ended behind and above the Rangers' bivouac.

"It's the most direct path you can take and still keep the mountains between you and the enemy. It's not going to be especially fast or especially easy, particularly for the armor and mechanized infantry. In fact, I'd suggest that you leave those units here. This right here"—she circled a patch of jumbled brown squiggles—"looks like it's moraine boulders. It'll be nearly impossible to move anything other than 'Mechs or leg infantry through that."

Powers marked out another trail in green. "Now *this* would be easier, and you should be able to take the armor with you. The ground looks more even. You can avoid any major hazards, *and* you'll still be out of sight of the bad guys. Unfortunately, it's going to take you at least five days to make this march. The first route will be just under two days, barring any accidents or terrain-to-map anomalies."

Using a red marker, Powers laid out a third road through the mountains.

"This would be the fastest, though you'd have lots of rough ground to cross. Some of the heavier 'Mechs might not make it."

Ciampa leaned over the map and whistled. "She's not kidding, Colonel. One of my battalions tried to move through this gap during an exercise last year." She pointed to a narrow pass through a steep-sloped ridge. "It was so full of loose rocks, some of them almost the size of a house, that they had to turn back. One of their scout 'Mechs, a *Javelin*, tried to make it through. The 'Mech is still there. The pilot fell into a gap between boulders and snapped both of the 'Mech's legs off. We had to abandon the 'Mech, and airlift the pilot out with a VTOL. The rest of his battalion had to back off and go around."

"I was going to point that out, Colonel," Powers said,

irritation in her voice. "If you're forced to circumvent any obstacles, particularly here or here, you'd probably be spotted by the Rangers, especially if they have recon teams out."

Lori studied the lines and arrows.

"I don't like going into a major fight without my support troops. But I don't think we can take five or six days to launch this attack." She sighed and rapped the chart with her knuckle. "I guess it's the middle road."

She looked at Meg Powers. "Major, we'll have to pull your scouts out of the observation posts. Please hook up with Captain Radcliffe. Find out which of his leggers or mounted infantrymen have experience to see if we can free up your people for route reconnaissance."

Then she turned to Ciampa. "General, might I prevail on you to run a similar check on your troops? I'd like to keep the rebels under surveillance, just to make sure they hang around long enough for the Legion to throw them this surprise party."

Ciampa agreed and set off to comply with Lori's request.

"I'll brief my scouts," Powers said. "We'll be on the road in an hour or so." She saluted smartly and also turned to leave Lori's office.

"Meg, I can't let you come on this one," Lori said.

"Colonel?"

"I can't let you come on this mission." Lori held up her hand. "You're the best scout the Legion has. I know that. I also know you haven't got a power suit right now. Granted, there are a couple of spares back at the spaceport, if the Separatists didn't blow them up with the naval bombardment. But there isn't time to send for one, except by air. We did knock out a few of the Rangers' fighters, but we didn't get all of them. If we launch a VTOL now, there's a good chance the Rangers will spot it and launch an intercept. I know you don't want to risk the air crew's lives just so you can go on this mission."

"I can borrow a suit from one of my scouts," Powers said.

"Which one, Meg? Which one are you going to order to stay behind so you can risk your neck?" Lori shook her head, laying a hand on the younger woman's shoulder. "I know it rankles, but you're just going to have to sit this one out."

Powers started to speak, but Lori shook her head and smiled ruefully. "Call it the price of command," she said.

# 29

*Myoo Highlands, Hesperus II*
*Skye Province*
*Lyran Alliance*
*08 July 3065*

The chronometer built into the *Victor*'s center control panel declared the time to be 0254 when the Legion's armored scouts sent the message that they had made contact with the rebellious Skye Rangers. The difficult roundabout trek through the Myoo Mountains had taken longer than originally expected. Nearly three days had passed since the Legion's 'Mech, jump, and armored infantry units had slipped out of the Defiance factory complex. Now they sat in silence on the edge of the enemy's bivouac, waiting to launch their attack. Lori did not keep them reined in for long.

"Ghost group," she said quietly over an encrypted comm channel, "commence your run."

Sergeant Elron David did not hear Lieutenant M'Dahlla. Rather, the scout officer lifted his hand and flashed a few signals to his armored scouts. Moving as silently as the haunts for which his group had been code-named, the scouts slipped into the enemy's encampment. They dispersed by squad. In addition to a personal weapon, each man carried a single Mark Forty demolition charge.

David guided his troops through the thin, low scrub trees lining the perimeter of the enemy bivouac. A score of meters into the camp, a lone sentry stood in their way. To his eternal misfortune, the guard was facing the wrong way.

David held up his left hand to call a halt. Drawing a specially modified pistol from the holster strapped to his armor's right thigh, he settled the weapon's self-luminous sights over the picket's spine and squeezed the trigger. The handgun jerked in his grip, emitting a low, harsh cough instead of a loud bark. The sentry collapsed. The clatter of his rifle falling from nerveless fingers was louder than the suppressed pistol shot.

David scanned the area, taking advantage of the advanced sensor systems built into this scout armor's helmet. No one seemed to have noticed the sentinel's death. He beckoned his men to follow him.

A hundred meters away stood a *ZEU-9S Zeus*. David caught the attention of the two scouts nearest him, tapped his left leg with the base of his left fist, and pointed at the red and black assault 'Mech. The troopers crossed to the big machine. One scuttled up its leg to stuff his satchel charge into the machine's vulnerable knee joint while the other stood guard. In short order, an *Axman* was served the same way.

David scanned the area, noting that the enemy's 'Mechs had been parked haphazardly. He decided that the apparently random order was a result of the Separatist officers trying to reform some of their broken and depleted units by stripping 'Mechs away from others. He saw a particularly valuable target: the towering shape of a captured Clan *Loki* OmniMech.

He signaled to his squad to cover him, then began to move quickly and quietly across the encampment. It was a long hop from the ground to the top of the *Loki*'s arched left foot, and he reached up to grab the out-jutting flange covering the front of the knee joint like a hardened steel patella. The drag of the thirty-kilo block of pentaglycerine explosive he carried made the climb difficult.

Gaining a stable place to stand, he unslung the big demolition charge. He studied the *Loki*'s knee joint. The scarlet paint was greasy. Chips and scratches showed where the lower-leg armor slid up and down across the plating of the thigh. He had to lean far over, supporting himself with his hands braced against the knee shield, to see the place where the upper and lower legs actually joined.

He unslung the satchel charge and rested it against the trapezoidal kneecap. Contorting himself into an uncomfortable angle, he braced his feet against the lower end of the 'Mech's thigh and his back against the inside of the shield. Grabbing the demolition block, he shoved it deep into the *Loki*'s knee joint, securing it in place with hooked elastic straps. Finally, he flipped a switch set into a small box attached to the top of the pentaglycerine block by a few thin wires, then jumped down.

Rejoining his squad, Elron David selected the next target. The squad had barely begun to move across the 'Mech park when the rattle of a submachine gun pierced the night. The deeper roar of a light machine gun drowned out the small-arms fire.

"Do it," David barked at his scouts, then dropped back into the shadow cast by an enemy *Catapult*. His automatic shotgun came up to a low-ready position. Behind him, two of his scouts dashed off to sabotage the nearest enemy machine, a fifty-ton *Centurion*.

Spotting a woman clad only in a pair of spandex shorts and a cooling vest running toward him, he downed her with a single blast from his shotgun.

His night-vision visor suddenly flared to intolerable brightness. Involuntarily, his pain-wracked eyes screwed shut against the blinding glare. David keyed in the normal visible-light viewer but was still unable to see anything but bars of light dancing before his eyes. Until his vision cleared, all he could do was crouch in the shelter of the *Catapult*'s foot. The deep roar of a heavy machine gun assaulted his ears. He heard the thin crack of the transsonic bullets as they passed overhead, and the banshee shriek of mangled metal as they ricocheted off some hard surface.

As his vision cleared, he saw the twisted, bleeding bodies of his scouts.

A beam of light swept across his hiding place, and he barely shielded his eyes in time. When the light passed, he was able to see the grotesque shape of a *Guillotine* moving through the enemy bivouac, its searchlight probing the dark. Another 'Mech, smaller, but unidentifiable in the dark, lumbered beside it.

"Ghost Group, this is Vampire One. Pull out," he called to the rest of his squad. "The big boys are in there to play." Springing from his hiding place, he sprinted for the edge of the 'Mech park.

His movement must have attracted the attention of the enemy MechWarriors. The searchlight panned across his trail, briefly illuminating his armor. Machine-gun bullets followed, the heavy slugs tearing up the ground beneath his feet. David zigged sharply, turning in toward the enemy machines. In the backwash of the *Guillotine*'s light, he saw a *Bushwacker* shifting on its feet as though trying to track him.

As he broke out of the searchlight's illumination, he made another tight turn, heading back almost the way he'd come. He hoped the sudden, jerky changes would prevent the Rangers from spotting him again.

Suddenly, a blow harder than any punch he'd ever experienced struck David between the shoulders. He pitched forward, dead before he hit the ground.

"Vampire, we've lost Ghost Two," M'Dahlla yelled over the communicator. "We're pulling out. Suggest command detonation of charges."

"Confirmed, Ghost One," Lori responded. "Get out of there. Save yourselves. Vampire One will detonate charges in one-zero seconds."

She watched intently as the chronometer scrolled off ten seconds, then she punched a small red button on her right-hand control panel. A handful of white flashes, subdued by the tamping effect of the armored joints into which the charges had been stuffed, lit the darkened encampment. Lori didn't know if any of the enemy machines had been crippled by the knee-capping charges. At the moment, she had more important worries. Her *Victor*'s thermal viewer showed four enemy 'Mechs up and running, with more powering up every second.

"Wraith Group, Vampire Group, looks like the plan's gone to hell. Hit 'em where you find 'em. Charge!"

Lori flung the *Victor* into a lumbering run, closing the

distance. At two hundred meters, she pulled up short, skidding to a halt in the loose soil. She snapped up her gauss rifle and pumped a dense metal slug into the *Guillotine*. The Separatist 'Mech was half-twisted at the waist by the impact of the nickel-iron pellet, which splintered the armor on its right forearm.

A lance of laser energy speared Lori's 'Mech through the belly, while missiles flamed out of the *Guillotine*'s chest. It was Lori's turn to stagger as the warheads savaged the *Victor*'s torso and leg. Leigh Cooper slipped up beside her to blast the rebel 'Mech with lasers and short-range missiles. Only the pulse laser scored a telling blow, burning a line of smoking divots in the Ranger's right leg.

All three 'Mechs fired again, almost simultaneously. Cooper's anti-missile system whined, reaching out to swat the Separatist's missiles from the air. The stream of machine-gun bullets tore through empty air. When the smoke cleared, all three 'Mechs were still standing. The *Guillotine* had taken the worst of the exchange, though Lori's *Victor* wasn't far behind. The missiles had blown armor away from her Mech's left torso and leg.

Before either of the Legion 'Mechs could act, the *Guillotine* turned and fled back into the bivouac.

Lori surveyed the damage done to her *Victor*. The armor, though badly damaged on the left arm, had not been breached.

"Let's keep moving," she said to Cooper. Her lancemate said nothing but moved off into the night, seeking a new opponent. Lori and the rest of the command lance followed close behind.

A stroke of man-made lightning streaked out of the night, followed by a volley of short- and long-range missiles. Lori's sensors displayed a trio of attackers, who had taken the Legion's command lance into a crossfire. She selected the nearest machine, a *Lancelot*, and blasted the heavy 'Mech with her full weapons complement. Heat flooded into her cockpit as the lasers and short-range missile launchers discharged.

"Mac, take the *Assassin*. Leigh, you're on the *Dervish*. Paul, can you hit the *Lance*?"

Cooper and Paul Hansen, the fourth man in the Legion's command lance, shouted their acknowledgments and turned their weapons on the enemy. Dallas MacKensie was strangely silent.

"Mac?" Lori called again. Still there was no answer. The *Lancelot* dragged her attention back to the fight as its large laser slashed away armor from her left arm. The endo-steel bone creaked dangerously as the laser bit deeply into its metallic structure.

Lori fired back, her gauss rifle blowing away all but a fragment of the armor protecting the *LNC25-01*'s right arm. Darts of verdant energy from her pulse lasers also clawed at the enemy 'Mech. One stuttering blast spent itself ripping into the ground behind the *Lancelot*. The other burst melted away more than a third of a ton of armor from the rebel machine's right breast.

A flight of long-range missiles arched over the *Victor*'s head, falling on and around the Separatist *Assassin*. When the firestorm from Paul Hansen's *Bombardier* died, the Skye 'Mech was still on its feet, but its splendid paint job was now more black than crimson.

"Mac?" Lori yelled again as she waited for the gauss rifle's breach to cycle. She received no answer other than static.

Gamely, the *Lancelot* stayed in the fight, striking at Lori's 'Mech with a one-two punch from its lasers. She could only imagine the fiery heat the rebel pilot must be experiencing, despite the high-efficiency heat sinks in his 'Mech. One azure beam flickered past the *Victor*'s head, but the other left a deep, carbon-edged score in its right shoulder.

Lori fired her jump jets, vaulting high over the enemy machine. Flexing the *Victor*'s knees, she brought the 'Mech back to earth, then fired her gauss rifle. The heavy slug blasted into the rebel 'Mech just below one armored shoulder, splintering armor and internal structure. A loud bang echoed across the battlefield as fragments of armor and nickel-iron projectile mangled the rebel's Kinslaughter particle cannon. Pulse lasers and missiles tore through the Ranger's shattered armor. In an instant, the 'Mech's thermal signature blossomed from a dull red to a brilliant orange-yellow as shielding was stripped from its power plant.

The *Lancelot*'s head split open as the pilot ejected. Looking around, Lori saw that Leigh Cooper and Paul Hansen were pursuing the *Lancelot's* companions deeper into the rebel encampment. Ominously, Dallas MacKensie's *Trebuchet* was standing frozen where it had been when the fight began.

"Mac?" Lori said in a small, hopeless voice. "Dallas, answer me."

Stepping closer to the immobile machine, she saw a jagged hole burned through the middle of the 'Mech's eye-like viewscreen. She leaned in as close as she dared, trying to peer through the dark opening. She could see nothing.

"Command Lance, this is Vampire One. Mac's dead."

No one answered Lori's simple declaration. Neither did the warriors of the Gray Death Legion slow their deadly work. The *Dervish* and the *Assassin* died within seconds of each other.

"C'mon, people," she yelled to the surviving members of her lance. "Reform on me. We've got to get back in the fight."

As Cooper and Hansen fell into formation, Lori looked over the situation on her tactical display. The Legion was holding formation better than she had expected. The Rangers seemed to be disorganized, but were relying on their superior numbers to make up for unit integrity. They had closed with the Gray Death 'Mechs and were wreaking havoc.

"Colonel McCall, what is your situation?" she said, trying to pick out the *Highlander* amid the mass of 'Mechs.

"It's nae sae guid, lassie," the bluff Caledonian replied. "Th' *sassanach* are aye makin' a fight o' it. We're tangled wi' 'em, proper. They're pressin' us hard. I'm tryin' t' turn their flank, but there's sae bluidy many of 'em, I'm in danger o' losin' both m' own flanks."

"Hang on, Davis. I'll see what I can do," Lori shot back.

The command lance had been pulled further north than Lori had intended, and now she formed her lance into a wedge with her *Victor* in the lead. The darkness before her was lit by brief, flickering gouts of flame and energy discharges, showing exactly where the area of hottest fire was.

"Paul, Leigh, we got pushed so far north, it looks like we're coming in across the end of the lines." Lori squinted at the tactical display, trying to decipher the jumble of information. "We're going to try to roll up the Rangers' flanks. Pick your targets carefully. You're just as liable to run into a friendly as you are an enemy. Let's try not to kill any Legionnaires.

"All right, here we go."

Lori pushed the *Victor* into a slow forward trot, bringing her lance in squarely perpendicular to the main line of battle. In that moment, a red and black *Zeus* loomed out of the darkness. All three 'Mechs of the command lance fired. The assault 'Mech absorbed the damage and split his return fire, blowing armor off Cooper's *Grim Reaper* and Hansen's *Bombardier*. But at three-to-one odds, the fight could not last long. Another volley from the command lance finished off the rebel machine.

Moving south, the next 'Mech they encountered was a boxy-looking *Cataphract*. The machine's blue icon on Lori's tactical declared it a friend. A blast of laser fire lanced out from the heavy 'Mech's wrists. One went wide. The other sliced into the *Victor*'s left thigh.

"Dammit, Lieutenant, we're friendlies!" Lori howled into the communicator. "Use the damn IFF! That's what it's there for." Her IFF showed the *Cataphract* as belonging to Lieutenant Andrei Denniken, a Legion veteran.

"Identify yourselves," the stubborn pilot snapped back. "Name and codeword."

"This is Colonel Kalmar-Carlyle, you moron! Codeword Stingray," Lori fumed.

"I'm sorry, Colonel," Denniken said apologetically. "My IFF is out and so are about half of my sensors." Then he gave Lori the tactical situation in his sector.

"We've lost three 'Mechs so far, Colonel: two lights, one heavy. I've got four seriously damaged, but still able to fight. They come up close, hit us a couple times, then back away."

"Okay, let's—" Lori started to say, then paused as movement flickered in the corner of her viewscreen. She twisted her 'Mech's torso so she could see.

"Sappers!" she shouted, catching sight of a dozen infantrymen running forward, lugging large canvas satchels over their shoulders.

One of the ground-pounders dropped to his knees and fired a pair of missiles from the man-portable launcher on his shoulder. Another peppered the *Victor*'s faceplate with automatic rifle-fire. The rockets missed their mark, bursting at the feet of Denniken's 'Mech. The dull orange glare of burning napalm illuminated the darkness.

"They're using Infernos!" Leigh Cooper yelled, turning her *'Reaper*'s pulse laser on the crouching infantryman. The stuttering blast of energy flickered green where it passed through the smoke of the battlefield. But the pulse laser had not been designed to kill infantrymen. The missile-man abandoned his weapon, diving for cover. He escaped the laser bolts unharmed.

Half a dozen Skye foot soldiers broke from cover, dashing straight toward the *Cataphract*.

"Andrei, look out," Lori shouted. She fired the twin pulse lasers affixed to the back of her *Victor*'s left arm, though with little effect. Denniken's 'Mech executed a half-bow as he tried to bring the dual-purpose autocannon into play, but the ground-pounders were too close. They swarmed up the *Cataphract*'s back-acting legs. Lori looked on in helpless horror. She could not fire on the infantrymen without hitting the 'Mech itself.

Denniken swatted one trooper away with a clenched steel fist, but then time ran out for the Legion vet. The infantrymen dropped away and dashed off into the night. Lori felled one with a laser blast just as a pair of loud explosions tore through the *Cataphract*'s reverse knee joints.

Denniken's machine sagged, the mangled right knee giving way as the 'Mech toppled. The *Cataphract* thrust out its arms, trying to catch itself. Because of the twisting fall, the swollen vambrace housing the rapid-fire Nova-Five ultra autocannon on its right arm hit the ground first. It gouged deep into the gravel-laced dirt before finding purchase. The seventy-ton machine came down hard on that spindly limb, snapping it off at the elbow. Lori saw Denniken drop to the ground, apparently unhurt. He pulled a heavy automatic pistol from his holster, jerked the slide back to chamber a round, then waved at the Legion command 'Mech.

Before Lori could call for a rescue unit, tracers reached out of the night, punching Denniken against the shoulder of his fallen 'Mech. He collapsed to the ground, leaving a long, bloody smear on the *Cataphract*'s armor.

Lori fired long blasts from her pulse lasers in the direction from which the shots had come. She didn't know if they had any effect. She didn't get time to find out.

A knot of medium and heavy machines bearing the crest of the Skye Rangers came up, pushing hard against the Gray Death lines. Lori ordered her soldiers to push back. For a few moments, both lines wavered. Then a rebel 'Mech vanished in a roiling fireball. The ill-fated warrior's friends fell back in disarray.

All along the lines, the Skye Rangers were pulling out of the fight. Lori slouched wearily in her seat, knowing the Legion had broken the rebels' back. The realization jerked her upright. She had to make a fast decision. Pursue or call it a day?

If she gave chase, the Legion could likely destroy the bulk of the Separatist force before sunup. But doing so would scatter the Gray Death throughout the passes and valleys of the Myoo Mountains, and it would cost her still more damaged and destroyed 'Mechs and wounded or killed pilots. She didn't think she could afford either. She had to assume that there were more Skye Separatist troops on their way to support the invasion of Hesperus. She had to conserve enough strength to oppose them until Lyran loyalist troops arrived to bolster her defenses.

"Bloody hell!" a baritone voice yelled in her headset.

"What is it?" she snapped. "Report."

A loud, rolling series of explosions accompanied by strobing flashes of detonating ordnance were the only answer.

"Command Lance with me," Lori barked, kicking her *Victor* into a lumbering run. She aimed the battered 'Mech for the spot where the explosions were coming from.

Cutting around a stone outcropping, she saw three 'Mechs locked in a death struggle. McCall's *Highlander* snapped a shot from its gauss rifle into the body of an enemy *Rakshasa*. The big 'Mech, an Inner Sphere version of the Clan *Mad Cat* OmniMech, took the devastating hit and struck back with a volley from the boxy missile launchers set high above its shoulder joints. A score of warheads rained down on and around the *Highlander*.

From another angle, an ugly *Guillotine*, which could have been the twin of the 'Mech Lori had fought earlier, savaged the big Legion 'Mech with laser and missile fire.

Lori watched as McCall tried to step backward so he could keep both opponents in his front arc. The Rangers moved to keep the *Highlander* in a crossfire. She brought up her gauss rifle, the only weapon she had that could reach the machines harrying McCall's 'Mech. The crosshair targeting reticle floated across the *Rakshasa*'s form, and she stroked the trigger.

The basketball-sized, metallic sphere missed the rebel by centimeters. She waited for the solid, satisfying *clunk* of another round settling into the weapon's breech, but it never came. She stared unbelievingly at her master armament panel. The night's fighting had exhausted her ammunition supply.

If the Skye MechWarrior had noticed the shot that streaked past his war machine, he paid it no mind. Instead, he kept his attention focused solely on McCall. He poured laser fire into the already damaged 'Mech, while his partner, the *Guillotine*, did the same. Lori threw the *Victor* into a shambling run, screaming for Cooper and Hansen to engage the rebels with their long-range missiles. Her headlong charge began too late.

The *Rakshasa* stepped in close to McCall's *Highlander*, firing its large lasers point-blank into a rent in the big machine's side. The Legion 'Mech reeled like a drunk, and Lori realized that they'd gotten his gyro. She fought her swaying 'Mech as she desperately tried to close range with the enemy.

The *Rakshasa* clubbed the *Highlander*, sending the massive assault 'Mech sprawling. A second later, the *Guillotine* took a long step forward and smashed its foot into the side of the bigger 'Mech's boxy head. The *Highlander* convulsed. Again, the rebel machine lashed out. Armor crumpled and broke. The Legion 'Mech's right arm flailed blindly. A third savage kick, and the *Highlander* lay still.

Lori shrieked an inhuman cry of rage and anguish. She fired her lasers and missiles as she ran, with little hope of hitting either of the enemy 'Mechs. The *Rakshasa* turned to face her. Its extended-range large lasers burned away the remaining armor on her right leg and cored deeply into the *Victor*'s breastplate. The *Guillotine* likewise opened up on her charging 'Mech. Its powerful laser hacked through the exposed endo-steel bone of her left arm, severing it just above the laser mounts.

Something huge moved in the darkness behind McCall's killers. Lori's mind screamed at her to pull out, but her heart clamored for revenge. The shape resolved itself into a *Banshee*. Something in the sight of its hideously grinning faceplate snapped Lori out of her berserk rage. She slammed the *Victor* to a skidding halt and touched off her jump jets, just as the *Banshee* unleashed its particle cannon. The man-made lightning struck the ground where she had been standing in an explosion of dirt and stone.

Riding the jets, Lori extended her backward leap a bit longer, then allowed the crippled *Victor* to settle back to earth.

"Colonel, we gotta pull out. Now!" she heard Hansen yelling at her.

"All right, Paul. Give the order."

"There ain't no order to give, Colonel," Hansen said, moving his *Bombardier* up to support his commander's battered machine. "The Legion is retreating. The lines broke when they heard Colonel McCall was dead. Let's try not to lose you, too."

"Okay then, Paul, get me out of here," Lori said dully.

McCall had been her oldest friend in the world beside Grayson, and now they were both gone. Lori fought against the black, enveloping grief that tried to invade her mind until the Legion was clear of the combat zone.

A dozen kilometers away from the battlefield, she called a halt, ordering the least damaged units to form a rearguard while her battered command rested. Then, switching her communicator off, she tore her neurohelmet from her head, buried her face in her hands, and gave in to the grief.

# 30

**Defiance Complex, Myoo Highlands**
**Hesperus II**
**Skye Province**
**Lyran Alliance**
**10 July 3065**

Repairs to the Gray Death Legion's BattleMechs were proceeding. Lori could see that from her perch on the catwalk running around the outside of the huge 'Mech bay deep inside the DefHesp underground complex. Rebuilding the unit's morale would be much more difficult. More than half of the slots assigned to the Legion stood empty. In most of those cases, the vacant cubicles meant a vacant bunk in the Legion's barracks. The feeling that she had let the Legion down, and had failed Grayson's memory, writhed through her heart like a venomous snake.

"Stop it," she whispered angrily to herself. "You did your best and that's the most anyone, including Gray, could ever ask for."

"Colonel, I hope I'm not disturbing you," someone said, coming up behind her.

Lori jumped at the voice intruding upon her gloomy thoughts. Feeling the flush of embarrassment spread across her face and neck, she turned to see Gina Ciampa standing behind her, a steaming cup of coffee in each hand.

"I don't know how you take it," Ciampa said, handing

one of the cups to Lori. "I hope cream and sugar is all right."

"That's fine, General." Lori smiled, taking the cup. If Ciampa noticed her embarrassment at being caught talking aloud to herself, she had the grace not to mention it. "Thank you."

Ciampa took a sip a coffee. "That's something else. We've been calling each other 'General' and 'Colonel' ever since you got here. Don't you think it's about time you started calling me Gina, Lori?"

"Probably," Lori allowed. "Thank you, Gina."

"Well, Lori, what now?"

"I wish I knew," Lori said wearily. "The Legion is in bad shape. I've lost over half my strength, including all of my armored scouts. I've lost some key people, too. The warriors I have left are exhausted, dispirited . . . Hell, I'm feeling kind of demoralized myself."

A long, bitter sigh escaped her. She shook her head in deep sadness. "I don't know how Grayson stood it all those years. I thought I felt the losses the same as he did. But now? Now I feel like I killed each one of them as surely as if I had pulled the trigger."

Ciampa snorted softly. "I know what you mean. Lori, please don't take this wrong, but I *do* know exactly how you feel. The last time you people were on Hesperus II, you killed and wounded an awful lot of my soldiers, destroyed an awful lot of my 'Mechs. I had to write 'those' letters. I always hate doing that. And I blamed the Legion. In time, I got over it. I rationalized to myself that the Legion was just doing its job, following its own conscience.

"Then, when I heard the Archon was sending the Gray Death to Hesperus, I discovered how angry I still was. There I was carrying around all that guilt for having lost my men in battle, only to be told that I had to accept the presence of the people who killed my troopers on the very world we'd fought to protect."

Ciampa stopped to take another gulp of her coffee. Lori knew that having the Gray Death Legion posted to Hesperus must have been hard to take, not only for Ciampa, who hid it well, and for Zambos, who took no pains to conceal his feelings, but for the men under their command. How would she have felt if Katrina had posted the

Fourth Skye Guards on Glengarry, given that unit's participation in the invasion of the Legion's land-hold during the rebellion of 3056?

She would have felt angry, would have felt betrayed by the Archon, to whom the Legion, in the person of Grayson Death Carlyle, had pledged loyalty. To be completely honest with herself, she'd probably have taken an attitude similar to that displayed by Peter Zambos.

"I had to make a decision," Ciampa said at last. "I had to decide if my devotion to the Archon was greater than my devotion to my own feelings. That always has to be the first consideration for a soldier, wouldn't you say? Loyalty to the greater cause. I know some say the first duty of a commander is to his or her troops. I think that by maintaining loyalty to the Alliance, and to the just causes it pursues, I am serving the best interests of my men."

Ciampa looked down at her mug, thinking for a moment. "They know I'm not about to throw away their lives in a hopeless fight, because, in the end, that harms the Alliance and dishonors the Archon."

She glanced up again, a strange light in her eyes. "I think, Colonel . . . Lori, you have a decision to make. I think you've already made it, but your mind hasn't notified the rest of you yet. Are you going to take this kick in the teeth, roll over, curl up, and die? Or are you going to pull your unit together—for the good of your unit, if for no other reason—stand up, dust yourself off, dig in your heels, and fight?"

Lori regarded Gina Ciampa over the rim of her cup, masking her turbulent emotions behind a long pull at the steaming beverage.

"Point taken, General," she said, intentionally using Ciampa's rank rather than her given name. "Of course we're going to dig in and fight. I suppose I should notify myself first and then the rest of my warriors, eh?"

"Those were the first two things I did when I decided to accord the Gray Death Legion the respect and consideration it deserved as one of the Archon's premier combat forces, rather than treating you like a bunch of murdering cut-throats." Ciampa smiled to rob her last few words of any offense. "I made up my mind first, then I went about making up my soldiers' minds."

Lori nodded slowly, taking the other woman's words to heart. She looked out over the 'Mech bay again. The empty berths still caused her heart to ache, as did the stack of "those letters" waiting on her desk, but the despair had faded to a dull throb. There was something else growing in its place, a new, refreshed determination. The Legion had known defeat, but it had never been beaten.

"So, Lori, I'll ask you again, what now?"

Lori saw an odd light of triumph in Ciampa's dark eyes, and she understood. This was a different kind of victory, one over an insidious inner enemy more dangerous than any enemy from without.

"Well, I'd like to say the Skye Rangers are finished, but I know better than that," Lori said, pushing herself erect. "They still have enough 'Mechs onplanet to make up an effective combat force, and they still have that WarShip floating around up there. That is one helluva force equalizer."

"I'd have to say it is a force *multiplier*," Ciampa said. "They don't even have to bring her into direct action again. All they have to do is keep her onstation, and we have to assume they *are* going to use her, either for fire support or to keep our DropShips and fighters on the ground."

Lori nodded. "Right. That will limit our ability to make rapid shifts in troop deployment while giving the Rangers the freedom to move their forces around with impunity. I don't really think they'll play it that way, but it might be a good idea to put General Zambos' men on the alert. We've given the rebels a couple of solid defeats here in the north. They might decide that cracking Defiance isn't worth the risk and move on to other, less heavily defended sites. I guess we'll have to send some of your troops back to Maria's Elegy, just in case the rebels try to take the spaceport."

Ciampa smiled. "Well, at least my people are getting in their cockpit time for the month."

"Then they're getting some good out of this mess," Lori said, a bit of humor creeping back into her tone. "The rest of us will fort up here until reinforcements arrive or until the Rangers make their next move. I'll have some of my armored infantry work with the few scouts I have left to keep track of the them. I don't want to lose contact with the bad guys again. This planet is too big to track them down without aerospace cover, and if we don't keep an eye on them, there are too many places the Rangers could crop up to cause us trouble.

"I'd also propose we alternate sending out lance-strength patrols in maybe a three-kilometer radius sweep around the plant. That will give us some warning if the Separatists try it again."

Lori sat staring off into the middle distance for a time, as though it would let her see the entire Isle of Skye in a single glance. "The key to this rebellion is Defiance. The Separatists need 'Mechs to carry the thing through. If they don't get this factory, they'll have to try to buy them from someone, but I don't know if they've got either the money or the time to count on doing that.

"As for Katrina Steiner, with Coventry in Victor's hands, Defiance is the Alliance's only major source of Battle-Mechs. I don't believe she can afford to lose this world.

"The Archon will *have* to send us reinforcements, and soon."

# 31

*Defiance Complex*
*Myoo Highlands, Hesperus II*
*Skye Province*
*Lyran Alliance*
*12 July 3065*

In the days following her talk with Gina Ciampa, Lori found her mood gradually brightening. The pain of losing Davis McCall was still there, along with the overshadowing grief of Grayson's death. However, the fire of determination that had been nearly quenched during the disastrous night attack on the Rangers' bivouac was beginning to blaze again.

Now, as she paced along the catwalk high above the Legion's assigned area of the Defiance 'Mech bay, watching as the repairs on her beloved regiment's BattleMech and armor assets neared completion, her heart was warmed with the beginnings of a new pride and a new resolve. The Legion had always bounced back from a defeat, and it would do so again.

Most of the Gray Death 'Mechs that had survived the battle had been reparable, including her own *Victor*, whose armor had been patched and its left arm replaced. A few, however, were too damaged for anything but the scrap heap. The pilots of those 'Mechs had worried that they'd be thrown into the ranks of the Dispossessed, an old term for MechWarriors who'd lost their mechanical mounts. Considering that the Legion was now ensconced in one of the biggest 'Mech production facilities in the Inner Sphere, the notion was almost laughable. Still, the old stigma of losing one's 'Mech was difficult to erase.

Her troops needn't have worried. It took only the barest of urgings by Daniel Brewer, backed up by General Ciampa, Major Goree, and herself to see her 'Mech-less warriors given replacement machines fresh from the Defiance production lines. They were so new that, when Lori inspected the *NGS-4S Nightsky* replacing Lieutenant Brian Scully's junked *Hatchetman*, the cockpit still had the odd aroma of whey that often pervaded the control deck of new machines.

She couldn't help thinking that it wasn't so easy to replace human losses, but she crushed the mordant thought almost at the same instant it flashed across her mind. Lori wouldn't permit herself to slip back toward the paralyzing grief that had threatened to immobilize her. She owed it to the men and women of her command.

"Colonel Carlyle?"

She turned at the sound of a runner barking the abbreviated version of her name. The young woman's footsteps rang on the metal walkway as she jogged her way across.

"Colonel, Major Goree wants you to join him in his office right away. He sent for General Ciampa, too," the runner panted.

"I'm on my way," Lori said. "Did he say what this is about?"

"No, ma'am. He just sent me to fetch you."

Lori quickly descended from the catwalk to the bay floor, where her commandeered electric cart was waiting. Taking the wheel, she raced the little vehicle through a maze of passages and concourses until she reached what the DSPF referred to as "the officer's block." Lori's temporary quarters and office, along with those assigned to Gina Ciampa, were housed in the same building as Goree's permanent accommodations. She parked the cart in a layby carved out of the living rock of the mountain for just such a purpose, and ducked inside the block.

"I'm here, Major," she said, striding into Goree's office. "What's up?"

"I'll tell y'all when General Ciampa gets here," Goree drawled. "We've got that much time."

The coda to Goree's simple sentence piqued Lori's curiosity, but filled her with apprehension as well. "Reinforcements?" she asked.

Goree nodded.

"Ours?"

"Theirs."

"Theirs what?" Ciampa asked as she entered the room.

"Reinforcements," Goree said. "I've just received word from Maria's Elegy that the technicians there have managed to restore at least a basic level of the aerospace warning system. They detected a massive burst of tachyon energy at a pirate jump point out on the system rim. Without sophisticated scanners, the spaceport has no means of knowing either the size or the heading of the incoming force. We'll have to wait until the enemy enters orbit to make that kind of guess. About all they can tell us is that it's a massive intrusion into this system, and there has been no response to their radio signals. Therefore, we must assume the new arrivals are hostile."

"Is there any way to get a feed from the spaceport sensors out here?" Ciampa asked.

Goree shook his head. "Not anymore. The Rangers took care of that when they blew up the maglev line. All of the data-transmission cables ran along the rail bed."

"You said it was a massive intrusion," Lori said. "Do we have any idea how big the incoming force is?"

"I asked them the same thing. All they could say is that it was big. That could mean it was a single big JumpShip or several smaller ones. It could even be another WarShip, for all we know."

"I doubt it," Lori said.

"Why's that, Colonel?" Goree asked sharply.

"The rebels already have one WarShip insystem. They haven't really used her since they leveled half the spaceport. Why would they move a second combat ship into Hesperus when they haven't been using the assets they've got?"

Lori turned to look at the chart of the Hesperus system displayed on the back wall of Goree's office. A small red light blinked at the estimated position of the newly arrived force. "I suppose it's possible that the Separatists are expecting the

Archon to send in a relief force to break up the invasion and secure Hesperus II for the Alliance. In that case, they might send another WarShip to try to stop the relief force.

"But, even then, why would they deploy a WarShip without sending some kind of ground forces as well? We know von Frisch boosted a couple of his DropShips. We know one rendezvoused with the *Simon Davion*. That was right before they started bombarding the spaceport. As for the other ship, we're reasonably certain it went to meet the other Ranger JumpShips and that one of those jumped out-system. Why do that? The only reason I can think of is to call for reinforcements."

Goree nodded agreement. "I just wonder why the rebels haven't sent reinforcements before now."

"Probably because they didn't have any to send," Ciampa said, speaking up finally. "Aside from the Fourth, the Seventeenth, and the Twenty-second Skye Rangers, the Separatists haven't got all that many troops. They might be able to raise a few militia companies here and there. But unless a Lyran unit jumps to their side, wholesale, or if Kelswa and Dundee manage to scrape together enough money to hire a mercenary outfit or two, what we see on Hesperus right now is what they've got."

"So, what we've got inbound then is the Seventeenth Rangers?" Lori asked.

"Probably. Though, last I heard, the Seventeenth was way to-hell-and-gone out on Lost, barely managing to keep their 'Mechs operational." Ciampa looked up at the chart. "If I remember the latest strength estimates correctly, the Seventeenth is supposed to be down to one regiment only. If the tachyon burst was as big as the techs are saying it was, then there's more than one regiment coming in."

"What if this isn't the Separatists?" Lori asked in a grave voice. "What if this is Victor renewing his offensive against the Alliance?"

It suddenly grew very quiet in Goree's office.

"If that's the case, we're in deep trouble," Ciampa said. "We can recall the Thirty-sixth Guards from Maldon, but given our losses, that will only put us at, what, six full 'Mech battalions, if we combine our strength. If that *is* Victor out there, he's coming in here with a helluva lot more than two regiments. All we'll be able to do is pull back inside the mountain and suffer through the siege until help arrives. But I don't think it's Victor."

"Why not?" Lori asked.

"Because he was sitting on Freedom last I heard." Ciampa worked the controls to change the chart of the Hesperus system to a map of the Lyran Alliance. "Then he pulled back from the Skye border. Some think he was repositioning his troops for a strike into Skye, and some think he's going to circumvent the province and hit another target. A few think he's going home."

Ciampa looked back at Lori and Goree. "I don't have an opinion either way. But, if I were Victor, I'd leave the Isle of Skye alone. We all know firsthand what a nightmare it's become. Why expend lives and resources capturing the region when he can let it become a sinkhole into which his sister ends up pouring time, money, and 'Mechs?"

"You're probably right, General," Lori said quietly. "Nonetheless, I'd still suggest having General Zambos and the Thirty-sixth stand by to be recalled, just in case the enemy comes in too strong. If they drop into our laps, we're going to need all the help we can get."

*"Ja, Herr General,"* Leutnant-General Alice Day said nearly ten minutes after William von Frisch sent his initial message. The transmission time-lag made communication between the Skye Separatist forces already on Hesperus II and the reinforcements clumsy. "We have already begun launching DropShips. We will be in position to commence combat drops in a few days."

"Good," von Frisch said, refusing to lapse into the stilted German used by the Lyran Alliance. He was an officer of the Isle of Skye—if anything, he should be speaking Gaelic.

"When you're twelve hours out, you will signal me and have your ship captains bring your Thirty-second Lyran Guards in for a low-altitude drop directly on top of the Defiance complex. I will move what is left of the Fourth and Twenty-second up to support your landings. We will then go straight in against the factory complex. Divert the Seventeenth to Maldon. I don't want Ciampa and Carlyle calling up the Thirty-sixth Guards as reinforcements."

*"Jawohl, Herr General,"* Day said, sticking to her formal tone. "We are on our way."

**Defiance Complex**
**Myoo Highlands, Hesperus II**
**Skye Province**
**Lyran Alliance**
**18 July 3065**

Almost a week later, Lori, Gina Ciampa, and James Goree were back in Goree's office, watching a short-range sensor feed on the wall-mounted display screen. The device showed Hesperus II as a large, green-brown disc, with Maria's Elegy and the Defiance Hesperus factory marked in white. The mining complex at Maldon was not displayed, as it was on the far side of the planet. If desired, a command to the screen's map system would change the view to reveal Maldon and the other sites now hidden.

It was not the details of the map display that interested the officers. Their concern lay in the half-dozen or so tiny, U-shaped red icons closing on the planet.

"Any idea where they're headed?" Lori asked with a sigh.

"Specifically, no," Goree answered, tapping the screen with his forefinger. "It's too hard to tell until they've entered the atmosphere. This group *might* be headed for Maldon. The larger group seems to be headed straight for Defiance."

"Have we gotten an ID on them yet?" Ciampa asked.

"Not yet." Goree shrugged, shaking his head. "They've

been observing strict radio silence ever since they entered Hesperus orbit. Unless Colonel Kalmar-Carlyle wants to launch a fighter to go take a look, we're going to have to wait until these ships are on the ground to find out who they are."

"Well, we know they're hostiles," Lori said. "If they were friendlies, they wouldn't have come in under radio silence. They would have contacted somebody by now, either at the spaceport or here at Defiance. I'm willing to bet that Zambos hasn't heard anything from them either."

"Not a peep," Ciampa confirmed.

"Then I guess we're still playing the waiting game," Lori said tensely.

A *CHP-5W Chippewa* heavy fighter blazed in low over the Defiance complex. Though lasers and missiles reached up to tear armor from the flying wing's nose and belly, the *Chippewa* gave as good as it got, its guns blasting at the underground factory's defensive gun emplacements. The whole mountain seemed to vibrate as a long-range missile turret was destroyed. The blast of the emplacement's destruction rippled back through the ammunition-feed tunnels, touching off that launcher's magazine. Fortunately, the defense grid's designers had had the foresight to isolate each launcher's ammunition supply.

As the battle unfolded, Lori, Ciampa, and Goree watched from a room off the main 'Mech bay, which offered a display screen similar to but somewhat smaller than the unit in the DSPF commander's office. Pulling out of its attack run, the *Chippewa* rolled to one side, displaying the red arrow-and-bloody flag emblem of the Thirty-second Lyran Guards.

Gina Ciampa swore when she saw that crest.

"I'd heard that the Thirty-second was negotiating with Robert Kelswa-Steiner," Goree said, his voice cutting across Ciampa's hissed expletives. "I had no idea they'd struck a bargain."

"Obviously, they have," Lori said evenly. "I wonder how many Lyran units Duke Robert managed to subvert." The comment triggered a new round of cursing from Gina Ciampa.

Goree ignored her and reset the viewscreen to display a

larger, tactical picture of the battle. DropShips were grounding on the plateau a few kilometers from the front gates of the Defiance complex.

"General," Lori said, laying her hand on Ciampa's shoulder, "if you're about done, it's time for us to get to work."

Ciampa's vituperations ceased immediately. She stared at the tactical display, nodded, and stalked silently out of the office. Goree shrugged, smiled, and gave Lori a courteous half-bow.

"After you, Colonel," he said as Lori headed out the cart that would take her to her troop area.

Bringing the cart to a skidding halt, she leaped from the vehicle and ran toward the stairs leading to the catwalk. By now, the rest of the Gray Death Legion's MechWarriors had heard the news and were already sealing themselves into their cockpits. Not far off, diesel internal-combustion engines throbbed to life as Legion tank crews buttoned up inside their armored fighting vehicles. The surviving Legion infantrymen made last-minute preparations for battle.

Smoothly, Lori swung into the *Victor's* cockpit, and quickly connected the 'Mech's cooling and power systems to her combat suit. Next, she settled her combat neurohelmet over her shoulders, feeling the familiar wave of vertigo sweep over her. Far beneath her feet, the *Victor's* huge gyroscopic stabilizer spooled up, its settings fine-tuned and matched to Lori's sense of balance through the helmet interface.

She scanned all of the *Victor's* primary displays. The Defiance repair technicians had carefully patched her battered 'Mech back together, and every component was functioning as it should. Hardly surprising, since Defiance Hesperus was the company that had designed and assembled the 'Mech.

As the ready signals filtered in, Lori passed her orders to the Gray Death.

"Take up position on the left wing," she said into her neurohelmet mike. "We'll deploy in battalion order: Major Devin on the right, Major Houk on the left. Devin, you'll hook up with General Ciampa's left flank. Major Goree's DSPF is going to take close-in defensive positions, in case the enemy pulls off a successful end run.

"Tom, stay in contact with the Guards. Make sure there

are no breaks in the line. Command Company and the infantry battalion will form the tactical reserve. The armored battalion will form up at a right angle to Second Battalion's left. Meg, you'll be the flank guard. Don't let any of them get past you."

"Count on it," Powers said tightly.

"That's it, then," Lori said. "You know, people, I have a feeling Hesperus will either stand or fall on this battle. If things start to go sour, we all pull back in good order to the mountain—the Legion, the Lyran Guards, everybody. We don't retreat as separate units.

"All right. Form ranks and move out."

As Lori struggled to wheel the Gray Death Legion's left wing forward, she spiked an *Orion* that got in her way with a blast from her *Victor*'s newly refitted pulse lasers. By now, the Gray Death lines were overlapping the fresh rebel troops' formation by several hundred meters.

Lori snapped off a message to General Ciampa that the Legion was going to attempt a flanking maneuver. As she urged Rae Houk's troops forward, the Lyrans spotted the attempted end run and moved to oppose it.

The *Orion* sent a short burst of autocannon shells into the *Victor*'s right leg, and also peppered it with long-range missiles. Lori scanned her 'Mech Status Display, noting that she'd suffered only moderate damage from the attack. According to Ciampa, many of the Thirty-second's 'Mechs and vehicles were older models, lacking the upgrade kits. That gave her a triple advantage over her opponents.

Lori knew she out-gunned and out-armored the enemy machine and, judging from the Skye warrior's clumsy movements, it looked like she also had a lifetime's worth of experience over him. The enemy warrior surely realized it, too.

Lori settled her targeting crosshairs over the *ON1-K*'s center of mass and squeezed the trigger. A loud crack followed as the nickel-iron slug sped from the barrel of the *Victor*'s gauss rifle, making the rebel machine jerk convulsively as it smashed into its right arm. The damage wasn't fatal, but it was bad. Lori brought up the *Victor*'s left arm, following up with a double blast of laserfire into the enemy machine's chest and right arm.

Undeterred, the *Orion* hit back with autocannon and missile fire. The echoes of the exploding warheads had yet to fade when a pair of laser beams carved chunks of armor off the *Victor*'s left arm.

"Dammit," Lori cursed, her damage display showing that she'd lost nearly two-thirds of the armor protecting that limb. That arm had just been replaced, and she wasn't going to let some rebel son-of-a-buck rip it off again.

She fired the gauss rifle again, hammering the *Orion*'s left arm. Missiles and lasers added to the injuries already suffered. Still, the enemy machine came on. Missiles sprang from the big, triangular missile launcher set into the *ON1-K*'s shoulder, showering Lori's 'Mech with a hail of fire. She weathered the blast, but the missiles chewed vital armor from her machine's legs and belly. She'd forgotten how tough some of these old machines were.

Lori traded a few more blows with the pilot before Paul Hansen finished off his long-range dance with a rebel *Stalker*. Stepping up to his commander's side, he leveled a double volley of missile fire that left the *Orion* with its entire front torso burnt and blackened. The pilot started backing away from the fighting, and his tormentors pursued. The enemy machine burst through the main rebel line, but the Legion was unable to pursue as the Skye troops closed ranks around their damaged comrades.

The rebel forces delivered a barrage of weapons fire that swatted two Gray Death machines to the ground. Neither got up again, nor did either of the pilots escape.

Lori picked out a target and pumped a gauss slug into the *Quickdraw*'s left shoulder as fire erupted along both lines. 'Mechs on both sides staggered and fell. Behind her lines, Lori heard an explosion, the sound of a Legion tank taking a solid hit from an enemy weapon. The Striker's ammunition had cooked off, turning the wheeled tank into a funeral pyre.

Just then, Lori spotted an infantry squad moving among the feet of the enemy 'Mechs. Fearing that the enemy might be turning the anti-'Mech tactics Grayson had invented against her people, she bellowed a warning. It wasn't needed; Legion 'Mechs turned their weapons on the darting foot soldiers. A few squads were shattered, but not before they got their own bite in. Antiarmor missiles, flamers, and machine guns all struck out at the Gray Death, claiming another victim down and three more damaged.

Flame blossomed from the *Quickdraw*'s left breast. Missiles pummeled Lori's *Victor*, shattering armor on the assault 'Mech's legs and torso. She returned fire, hitting the round-headed machine in the chest with a gauss slug. Lasers ripped up the rebel's left arm and opened a gash in his right leg. The *Quickdraw* gamely hung in the fight, returning Lori's fire, but only succeeded in scrubbing away some of the *Victor*'s tough armor.

Then a PPC blast nearly knocked the *Victor* off its feet. As Lori fought to recover, a flight of missiles tore up the ground around her feet. Rocked by the near miss, the *Victor* fell to its knees.

The *Quickdraw* pilot strode forward, raising his 'Mech's clenched fists high above its head. Lori struck out with her right-arm gauss rifle, jolting the *Quickdraw* to a stop with a punch to the belly. The *Victor* was jolted too, as its handless arm rammed full force into its sixty-ton opponent. Instinctively, Lori jerked the trigger, sending a chunk of metal into the rebel 'Mech's torso. The impact sent the *Quickdraw* sprawling.

Lori glanced around to see a *Vindicator* wearing the colors of the Thirty-second Lyran Guard lining up for another PPC shot. She snapped off a twin blast from her pulse lasers, carving armor from the *Vindi*'s chest and right leg, and spoiling his aim. The bolt of charged particles ripped through the air a meter above her head.

Leigh Cooper stepped up and grasped the *Victor* by the right arm, helping Lori get back to her feet.

"You okay, Colonel?" Cooper asked.

"Yeah, I just got knocked off my feet," Lori paused to lace the *Vindicator* with her pulse lasers. Cooper did the same to the *Quickdraw*. The lighter 'Mech fired its jump jets, bounding away to the rear. The *Quickdraw* froze in place as the pilot ejected. A second later, the 'Mech blew itself apart in an ammunition explosion.

"What about the rest of the Legion?" Lori asked. "And what about Ciampa?"

"The Legion is holding for now. So are the Guards," Cooper replied.

Another voice cut across the Legion's command channel at that moment.

"No, we aren't," Ciampa yelled. "We aren't just facing the Thirty-second. They've brought up the remains of the Skye Rangers and have thrown them into our section of the line. We're going to have to fall back."

"Very well, General. We knew it might come to this." Lori switched to the Legion's general communications frequency. "All Gray Death units, this is Legion One. Fall back. Fall back on the factory."

A flurry of acknowledgments flooded Lori's ears as the Gray Death Legion began pulling away from the enemy. The turncoat Lyran Guards and Skye Rangers pressed the attack. Occasionally, a lance or a company would turn and fire a few volleys at the enemy to discourage pursuit. Often, the only thing that was achieved was a waste of ammunition.

Once, the rearguard action cost the Gray Death dearly. Fifth Company's combat lance was one of the last to withdraw, lagging behind to guard the end of the retreating formation. As they turned to fall back after one of their discouraging volleys, a Skye Ranger piloting a damaged *Salamander* unleashed three flights of long-range missiles at the withdrawing Legion 'Mechs. All three flights seemed to home in on the back of Private William McBride's captured *Thor-B*. The OmniMech's anti-missile system whined, clawing a third of the missiles out of the air, but the sheer volume of fire overwhelmed the radar-aimed machine gun.

The missiles slammed into the big machine's back and left arm, chewing through the thin dorsal armor. The *Thor* was engulfed in a fireball as the warheads set off an ammunition locker. A second explosion followed the first, as another magazine went off in sympathetic detonation. The *Thor* collapsed, toppling onto its side, its left arm and shoulder blown away by the explosions. Orange flames and greasy smoke boiled from the huge gash in the ferro-fibrous armor. McBride didn't escape.

The death of the OmniMech seemed to be a signal for both sides, and the defenders' resolve seemed to collapse. They fell back with only the barest semblance of order, while the Skye Separatists, emboldened by the destruction of such a formidable opponent, rushed forward.

Lori and the Legion command company found themselves in the rearguard facing the onrushing rebels. Having seen McBride's fall, she targeted the *Salamander*, punching a gauss slug deep into the missile-armed machine's right shoulder. The damage didn't seem to deter the artillery 'Mech's pilot, who launched a spread of twenty missiles at Lori's *Victor*. The warheads cracked armor and widened the gap left in the machine's left breast by the *Vindicator*'s PPC. Like hyenas worrying a wounded lion, other rebel 'Mechs closed in on the *Victor*. A *JagerMech*'s autocannons ripped armor from the *Victor*'s greaves, while an old-model *Zeus* savaged it with laser and missile fire.

Warning lights flared all over the *Victor*'s cockpit as systems failed. Most terrifying of all were the twin scarlet bars in the center of Lori's main control panels. One read FIRE and the other CORE. With flames growing in her 'Mech's belly and severe damage to her reactor core, she had no choice. She reached above her head and yanked a pair of yellow and black striped handles.

An instant later, the ejection seat rocketed her clear of the dying 'Mech. Lori felt the bump as the seat pan separated from her safety harness and the parafoil deployed to bring her back to the ground.

Not wanting to be taken prisoner, she aimed the 'chute at the open 'Mech bay doors. She had no illusions that she could fly the steerable canopy through the opening. She just prayed she could get it close enough to allow her to dash inside the mountain before the doors were sealed. She hauled down on the front risers, spilling air out the back of the canopy as fast as she believed was safe. The ground rushed up to meet her. Her right foot hit first, sending a jarring pain the length of her spine. She tumbled forward.

Rolling to her feet, Lori took stock. The last of the defending units, a mixed bag of Legion, Lyran Loyalist, and Defiance 'Mechs, were still a hundred meters from the doors, backing slowly up the grade toward the 'Mech hangar. The enemy was right on top of them. In her heart, Lori knew those last five defenders were going to die and that their sacrifice would be in vain. Lighter, faster Separatist 'Mechs swept around the flanks of the collapsing battle lines, heading for the 'Mech bay doors.

Lori broke into a shambling run, favoring the right leg that, though uninjured by the marred landing, still pained her from the heavy impact. She dodged inside the open bay door and ran for one of the many side rooms opening off the hangar. On foot and armed only with the Mydron autopistol she preferred as a sidearm, Lori would only get herself killed if she stayed in the 'Mech bay. The first store-room door she tried was locked.

An explosion rocked the 'Mech bay. Shrapnel rang and clattered off the rock walls and floor. One fragment of steel tore through the sleeve of Lori's combat suit. A gout of coolant fluid spilled from the rent. Lori spun, dropping to her knees. Instinctively, her pistol came up to follow her eyes. A *Flashman* painted in Legion colors lay on its back across the threshold of the hangar bay doors. She watched as Elias Whitlocke climbed from the smashed 'Mech's cockpit. The legs of his uniform were soaked in blood. He ran a few steps, then collapsed. Lori didn't know if he was dead, and she couldn't reach him to find out.

Four Skye 'Mechs, led by a scarred *Banshee*, entered the 'Mech bay, followed closely by a quartet of Maxim heavy hover transports. The screaming howl of the armored personnel carriers' lift fans cut through the din of battle. The 'Mechs pressed deeper into the 'Mech bay, firing their weapons at targets Lori could not see. More giant war machines followed on their heels, fanning out across the bay, penetrating deeper into the factory complex.

The Maxims dispersed throughout the bay. One settled onto its skirts about twenty meters from Lori's position. She scuttled across the bay and tried the next door she came across. It too was locked. The third opened. Lori dodged inside, allowing the portal to close behind her. Stacks of armor plating cluttered the room. She pulled herself up across one of the pallets and dropped into the narrow space beyond.

There, she pulled her emergency radio from her combat suit. She didn't know if the device would work in the underground environment of the Defiance factory complex, or even if there was anyone listening to the Legion's search-and-rescue frequency.

"Lifeline, Lifeline, this is Skull One-one."

There was no response.

"Lifeline, this is Skull One-one. I do not know if you receive, but I send. Skull One-one is down. I am inside the complex, under cover. Do not attempt rescue. I am behind enemy lines. I will attempt escape and evasion. I will attempt to return to friendly lines soonest. Do not attempt to contact me, as I may be compromised. Skull One-one out."

Before she could return the radio to her pocket, the door to the storeroom rattled violently. Lori flattened herself against the rock wall. A blast of gunfire, muted by the thick door, sounded in the small chamber. Five armed infantrymen dressed in the uniform of the Skye Separatists dashed into the room, sweeping the area for any signs of resistance. Lori remained still. The men turned to leave.

Then a woman's voice called out, "Hey, Sarge, looky here. This looks like coolant. It stinks like coolant, too. There's someone back there. Hold it, you!"

Lori saw a female soldier lifting a rifle to her shoulder. In that instant, she snapped up her own weapon and squeezed the trigger.

The Mydron belched out a stream of nine-millimeter slugs that smashed the female rebel in the chest, punching her backward. Lori rode her weapon's recoil, allowing the gun to rise, stitching a line of bullets up the woman's body, past her flak vest, and into her neck and face. She died messily.

Lori then swung the pistol toward the other Skye infantrymen. She got off a short burst at the nearest one, a staff sergeant. She never knew if she hit him or not, for in that moment two rifles spoke in unison. One bullet ricocheted off the wall behind her. The other smashed into her left shoulder. She dropped to the floor behind the armor plate, her pistol falling to the floor as she clutched her wounded shoulder.

Something clanked against the wall above her, then rattled down to the floor. It was a grenade.

# 33

**Defiance Complex**
**Myoo Highlands, Hesperus II**
**Skye Province**
**Lyran Alliance**
**18 July 3065**

"I'm on it," Captain Daniel Brewer shouted into his neurohelmet microphone. He'd seen the Colonel's *Victor* go down and the Skye troops sweep into the 'Mech bay. Ignoring Lori's instructions to delay rescue, he led his company in a fierce countercharge that temporarily split the attacking rebel forces. One section of the invaders pressed deeper into the Defiance complex. The other, smaller force withdrew to reform. Brewer's men were able to establish a weak perimeter, closing off one section of the 'Mech bay, the one near which Lori's 'Mech had been destroyed.

A red-and-black-painted *JagerMech* broke cover, charging the open 'Mech bay doors to make it inside. Brewer carefully settled his *Champion*'s targeting reticle over the rebel machine and squeezed the trigger for his autocannon. The armor-piercing shells ripped into the big fire-support 'Mech, stitching a line of cratered and broken armor across the *JagerMech*'s barrel chest.

The Skye warrior tried to turn to face Brewer. As he did, a pair of missiles streaked out of the shadows of a huge automated milling machine. The rounds burst, showering the rebel 'Mech with burning napalm. For a few seconds, the *JagerMech*'s pilot hung on, firing his autocannons first at the missile team, then at Brewer's *Champion*. Finally, he ejected in a cloud of smoke and flame.

Brewer appreciated his enemy's desperation. If there was insufficient "head room" inside the bay, an ejecting warrior might be slammed into the stone roof or find that he didn't have enough altitude for his parachute to open. Even if the 'chute did deploy, the canopy could get fouled on projecting machinery, leaving the pilot hanging in space. It could drift into an active machine or an open crucible full of molten metal. Fortunately for the *JagerMech*'s pilot, his chute opened properly. He drifted to earth just as his 'Mech's ammunition cooked off.

The fall of the heavy 'Mech seemed to dishearten the rebels crouching outside the bay, but Brewer knew it wouldn't last long. Soon they would drive Second Company out.

"Lieutenant, you'd better hurry the hell up," Brewer grated.

"We're going as fast as we can, Captain," Lieutenant Morgan Graham shot back. "Most of these doors are locked, and we've got to break them down. Stand by . . ." The armored infantryman paused for a long moment, then Brewer heard an anguished moan. "Oh, no."

"Graham, what is it?" Brewer demanded. "Answer me, Lieutenant!"

"Captain," Graham said in a strangled voice. "The Colonel . . . the Colonel is dead. Looks like she tried to hide in a storeroom. There's one dead rebel in here, so she took at least one of the bastards with her."

"All right, Lieutenant. Pull back." Brewer felt an icy weight in the pit of his stomach. As he stared hopelessly around him, he noticed that none of the original Legionnaires remained. The heart and soul of the Gray Death Legion was gone.

A volley of missile fire rocked his *Champion*. In that instant, the despair vanished in the bright, white-hot flame of anger and the thirst for revenge.

He snapped his 'Mech's weapons into line, tripped the targeting interlock circuits, and fired. Heat flooded into his cockpit. He could hardly breathe. The computer screeched a shutdown warning. He slapped the manual override. Down-range, a Separatist *Kintaro* wearing the red arrow of the Thirty-second Lyran Guards reeled as cannon, missile, and laser fire shredded its armored hide.

The apelike machine recovered its balance and dispatched a volley of short-range missiles. The rockets hammered the *Champion*'s right arm and side, and blew shallow craters in the ferrocrete floor of the 'Mech bay. Brewer ignored the damage and fired again, this time using only his heat-efficient Lubalin LB 10-X autocannon and short-range missiles. The *Kintaro* struck back with its lasers, both of which missed the mark.

Suddenly, the rest of the Skye Separatists charged the bay doors. Michael Taylor and Roger Karns stepped up beside their company commander, showering the enemy 'Mechs with long-range missiles. Jason Fry's *Panther* blasted a rebel *Assassin* with its PPC and semi-guided short-range missiles. A howl of rage cut across the comm channel. Brewer looked up just in time to see Dale Ross' *Grim Reaper* charging the onrushing rebel 'Mechs. That seemed to be a signal. Almost as one, Brewer's MechWarriors flung their machines into a wild assault on the enemy.

The *Kintaro* tried to stand in Brewer's way, but he lowered his 'Mech's shoulder and smashed into the lighter machine's broad chest. The *Kintaro* went over backward, grappling with Brewer's *Champion* as it fell. Brewer struggled with his controls, but failed to keep his 'Mech upright. The birdlike machine fell half on top of its victim. Before either machine could move, a steel arm and fist lanced past Brewer's cockpit, and the massive hand of Joseph Cheng's *Apollo* splintered the *Kintaro*'s faceplate. Cheng drove his fist into the fallen 'Mech's head twice more before he stopped. As Cheng helped Brewer's *Champion* to its feet, he saw the ruin of twisted metal that had once been the *Kintaro*'s head. The Skye warrior was dead in his cockpit.

An *Axman* in the blue and white of the Lyran Guards but bearing the Skye crest, strode forward, cocking its massive double-bitted weapon back over its shoulder. Brewer fed it a burst of autocannon fire, while Cheng launched a double volley of missiles. The enemy 'Mech was too close for the LRMs to be effective, but the autocannon shells slashed across the *Axman*'s left knee. A stroke of man-made lightning flashed over the *Champion*'s head, as Fry pummeled the tall rebel machine with his *Panther*'s particle cannon.

The axe flashed down, shearing through the *Apollo*'s shoulder. As the Separatist wrenched his weapon free of Cheng's crumpled armor, he unleashed his monstrous Luxor Devastator autocannon. Anti-armor hollow-charge shells blasted into the *Apollo*'s chest. Even over the din of battle, Brewer heard the rackety whir of a damaged gyro. Cheng's crippled 'Mech reeled under the impact and crashed to the ground.

Before the downed *Apollo* stopped sliding, four of Brewer's 'Mechs combined their fire to destroy the *Axman*. As the big machine fell, Brewer searched for another target but found none. The rebels who had been caught outside the 'Mech bay were on the run.

A platoon of Legion infantrymen dashed out of the open 'Mech bay to check on their fallen comrades and to round up any rebel warriors surviving the destruction of their 'Mechs. Brewer watched dispassionately as three ground-pounders rushed up to the wrecked *Axman* and dragged a half-conscious female pilot from the cockpit. Then he caught sight of the scarlet shirt beneath her cooling vest, and a flash of silver on her shoulder.

"Sergeant, take good care of her," he ordered through his 'Mech's external speakers. "That's a senior officer you've got there."

The squad leader looked up and waved his assent, but the expression on his face looked like he'd rather knife her.

Summoning his troops, Brewer moved his company back inside the 'Mech bay.

"Third Squad," he called to one element of his infantry support. "You guys stay here," he said raggedly. "Stay with the Colonel's body. The rest of you, form up. We have more rebels to kill."

"Lucy, take him!" Brewer shouted.

After leaving the 'Mech bay, Brewer's existence became a series of ambushes and counter-ambushes as his company fought their way through the cavernous tunnels and factory spaces of the Defiance complex. In one of the large armor-fabrication shops, his depleted company ran into a disorganized mob of Separatist 'Mechs.

Lucy Sal brought up both of her *Dervish*'s misshapen hands and launched her last four short-range missiles. The Streak semi-guided weapons crashed into the ribs and hip of an enemy *Hunchback*. The Separatist machine staggered as half a ton of armor was blown away, but it was not out of the fight yet. Raising its arms in return, the rebel 'Mech flashed beams of laser energy from its wrists. The huge 'Mech-killing autocannon that gave the *Hunchback* its name remained silent. Brewer figured it was out of ammo.

The lasers melted through the remaining structural members holding the *Dervish*'s left arm to its body. The limb crashed to the ground, leaving Sal's 'Mech crippled. Brewer cut loose with his own medium lasers. The *Hunchback* turned to face him, giving Sal a shot at its back. Her lone medium laser severed the rebel's leg at the knee. The *Hunchback* fell onto its face, tried once to rise, then lay still. Brewer's sensors told him that the rebel warrior had shut down his power plant.

"All Legion warriors, this is Legion Two-one," said Major Devin over the general channel. "The enemy is withdrawing. Let them go."

With Lori's death, Devin had assumed command of the Legion, though the scattered small-unit actions deep in the bowels of the factory complex required little in the way of overall command.

Brewer looked around the armor mill. One rebel 'Mech, an old model *Dragon*, stood next to the door, smoke pouring from a huge gash in its chest. A Skye Ranger *Penetrator* lay on the ground, its armor breached in a dozen places. There had been two more 'Mechs in the area.

"They bugged out, boss," Sergeant Kauffman told him. "Just before you guys polished off that *Hunchback*. It looked like they were headed for the exit, so I just let them go. 'Sides, my *Hoplite* isn't in any condition to chase 'em."

Three of his Mechs lay on the armor mill's floor, beside the fallen rebel machines. Roger Karns' *Apollo*, Susan Levy's *Vulcan*, and Dale Ross' *Grim Reaper* had been reduced to scrap, as had most of his company.

Brewer slouched forward in his seat, leaning his elbows

on the armrests of his command couch. He felt old, tired, and sick. He forced himself to sit erect.

"All right, Sarge, Lucy, let's head back toward the 'Mech bay and see what's left." He sighed. "Keep your eyes open. There may be a few die-hards lurking in the shadows."

Making the journey to the 'Mech bay was not long or difficult, but somewhere along the way, Brewer used up the last of his strength. When his *Champion* stepped into the cavernous room, his flagging spirit sank even lower. Less than a dozen Gray Death Legion 'Mechs were still operational. Of those, only a few would be able to be repaired. Brewer focused his will on the task of backing his mangled *Champion* into its cubicle. Unlatching his neurohelmet and shrugging out of his safety harness seemed to burn up the last of his strength. He could not bring himself to slip out of his seat and crack the hatch.

He sagged in his seat, unable to move. Then he heard a loud, hissing pop as the seal on his cockpit was broken.

"Captain? You okay?" a young man's voice said behind him.

Brewer made a concentrated effort to turn his head. A freckle-faced youngster in the green coveralls of the Defiance technical crew crouched in the open ingress/egress hatch.

"Yeah," was all he could muster.

"Captain, lemme help you," the boy said. Brewer felt strong hands lifting him out of his seat and gently guiding him toward the hatch.

"How many?" Brewer mumbled, dreading the answer.

"I don't know, sir," the technician admitted. "There are about a dozen of your 'Mechs here in the bay. I don't know for sure about any others elsewhere."

The cool, fresh air of the 'Mech bay brought a little life back to Brewer's weary body. He thanked the boy for his help and walked stiff-legged to the catwalk's safety rail. A few meters away, he saw Major Devin clutching the rail with exhaustion. Across the bay, he noted that the Lyran Guards and the Defiance Self-Protection Force had not escaped the carnage. He wondered what would become of the Gray Death Legion now that Lori was gone. He supposed it would be up to Alexander, Grayson and Lori's son, to decide. But Alex was on Tharkad with the First Royal Guards

Regimental Combat Team. It would be some time before he could rejoin the unit, let alone start to rebuild it, if it *could* be rebuilt.

Leaning heavily on the rail, Brewer dragged himself across to Devin.

"Good to see you're still alive, Dan," Devin said, exhaustion shadowing his voice.

"You too, sir," Brewer replied. "How many of us are left?"

"No idea. Twenty MechWarriors, maybe less." Devin shrugged. "Tankers and PBIs? Who knows?"

For a long moment, the officers remained silent, then Brewer spoke again.

"I guess Ciampa will have to call in the Thirty-sixth now."

"Probably. Though I don't think there's going to be a whole lot for them to do once they get here. I'd have to say the Separatists are broken. Major Goree tells me that our infantry captured Leutnant-General Alice Day and some of her command staff. So, the Thirty-second is minus its leaders. The Separatists will probably retreat into the hills. They're finished as a threat to Hesperus. All the Thirty-sixth will be doing is mopping up."

"If she'd called them in last week, none of this would have happened," Brewer said, fighting to damp the consuming rage threatening to overwhelm him.

"Maybe," Devin allowed. "But we can't know that. If she'd brought in the Thirty-sixth, we'd have been able to keep the rebels at bay, but von Frisch might have called in the *Simon Davion*. A naval bombardment would have ripped the hell out of the Legion just like the Separatists did here today, and there would have been no way to hit back. That would have been harder to take."

"Yeah, but that doesn't make it easy," Brewer said, shaking his head.

"No, it doesn't," Devin said.

"So where do we go from here?"

"We do what the Legion has always done. We pull ourselves together, make repairs, bury our dead, and keep the faith." Devin gazed out over the empty 'Mech cubicles in the legion's troop area. "But unless Alex has inherited all of his father's spirit and grit, we've seen the end of an era."

He shook his head.

"I think the Gray Death Legion is gone forever."

# Epilogue

*Royal Palace*
*Avalon City, New Avalon*
*Crucis March*
*Federated Suns*
*25 August 3065*

Katrina Steiner leaned back in the high-backed leather chair and closed her eyes. For a long while, she remained that way in silence. Behind her, just outside the office windows, the trees and shrubs of the palace grounds were in full leaf.

The "real time" HPG image of her aunt, General Nondi Steiner, watched Katrina carefully for any clues to her reaction to the report she had just finished reading.

Katrina drew in a deep breath, blowing it out again in a long sigh.

"Do we have anything available to send to Hesperus?" she asked, without opening her eyes.

"We have a few regiments we can transfer," Nondi answered. "Mostly ad hoc units assembled out of the remains of those shattered by the fighting against Victor."

Katrina's eyes flashed open at the mention of her brother. "Move one regiment to Hesperus to bolster their defenses," she said, mastering her anger with what felt like a supreme act of will.

"I will, Highness, though I doubt Robert has much left to devote to his bid for Skye independence."

"Be that as it may, General"—Katrina stressed her aunt's rank, as a means of putting the older woman in her place—"we cannot leave Hesperus II open and undefended. The remnants of two Lyran Guard RCTs and one mercenary regiment are not going to suffice should my brother return to attack that planet, damn him."

"And what of Hauptmann Carlyle?"

"What of him?"

"He has requested leave to attend his mother's funeral and to set things in motion for the rebuilding of the Gray Death Legion."

Katrina thought for a moment before answering. "Ordinarily, I might be inclined to release him. But, with Victor knocking on our gates, I do not think I can spare him or any other man of the Royal Guards."

Nondi opened her mouth as if to protest, but closed it again as Katrina continued.

"Tell him that, once the war is over and this matter between Victor and I has been settled, then he may have a leave or even a discharge if he wants it. Once this war is over, he can go rebuild the Gray Death Legion, not before."

"If he survives," Nondi said guardedly.

"There is always that, General," the Archon allowed. "If he survives."

# PRAISE FOR *THE SOOF*

"As a Navy oceanographer, I have firsthand experience supporting the missions of Navy submarines and SEALs. The critical importance of the environment in such operations is almost always overlooked in military novels. Samuel Tooma gets it right in *The SOOF*. If you are with me on this, you will thoroughly enjoy reading this terrific adventure story."

—**Rear Admiral Tim Gallaudet**, PhD, US Navy (ret), Former Deputy Administrator, National Oceanic and Atmospheric Administration, and Assistant Secretary of Commerce for Ocean and Atmosphere

"Tooma has an uncanny and thrilling ability to transport the reader through time and thousands of miles. *The SOOF* is an engaging and exciting front row seat for a dramatic look at the secret world of classified military operations. A nail-biter and heart thumper, this tale reveals complex human dynamics in characters who will remain in our hearts for years to come."

—**Bea Wray**, Best-selling Author, Motivational Speaker, and Business Woman

"It was a page-turner. Couldn't put it down! And it's cool that one of the underlying themes is the basis of the work that my colleagues and I have spent our careers working on: 'Whoever understands the environment the best will win the day.'"

—**Bruce Northridge**, United States Naval Academy, Naval Postgraduate School, Oceanographer at the Naval Research Laboratory, and Program Manager for the Commander, Naval Meteorology and Oceanography Command.

"Hold on to your Dixie cups as you read this fast-paced, high-stakes drama about a brilliant civilian female environmental scientist, Dr. Samantha Stone, who suddenly finds herself working in the male-dominated nuclear submarine world to prevent Armageddon. The team has very little time and only one chance to develop and execute a complex plan using Navy SEALs, a nuclear submarine, and Samantha to save the world from a threat hidden beneath the Sea of Okhotsk."

—**Dawn P. Erlich**, Environmental Scientist, retired

"*The SOOF* is an outstanding military thriller. I loved that the protagonist was a female scientist and was at the top of her game at every turn. This book is a must-read for any man or woman."

—**Robyn Zimmerman**, Press Secretary for Former
South Carolina Governor David Beasley

"After reading *The SOOF*, I was disappointed. I was disappointed because it ended. I wanted it to keep going. I can't wait for the sequel."

—**Rob Cushman**, Retired Senior Executive of a Major
American Steel Company

*The SOOF*

by Samuel G. Tooma

© Copyright 2021 Samuel G. Tooma

ISBN 978-1-64663-379-1

Published by

**köehlerbooks**™

3705 Shore Drive
Virginia Beach, VA 23455
800-435-4811
www.koehlerbooks.com

# THE

SOOF

## SAMUEL G. TOOMA

VIRGINIA BEACH
CAPE CHARLES

*As the Hawkbill inched away from the pier, Admiral Flaxon and Captain Forrest Jenkins stood on the pier in silence. Finally, Roger said to Forrest, "That's a beautiful boat that's going in harm's way. I absolutely love the people on her, and I pray to God that we see them again."*

**The momentous and extremely dangerous journey had finally begun.**

# PART 1

## DISCOVERY

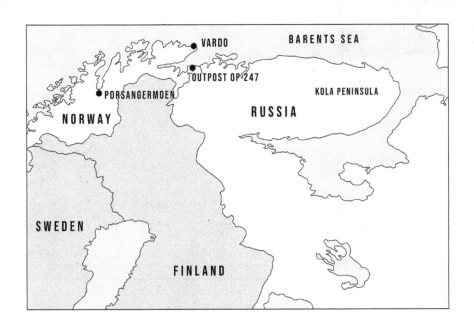

# CHAPTER 1
# NORWEGIAN OUTPOST-247

## (8 MARCH)

**LIEUTENANT ODD BERGSTROM OF THE** Royal Norwegian Navy studied the latest set of data once again, shook his head in dismay, and decided it was time to brief his commanding officer on his observations over the last two weeks. Assembling the information into a folder marked *SECRET*, he punched in Lieutenant Commander Lars Skarsgaard's number on his phone.

"Hey, Odd. What's going on?"

"Lars, I've been tracking some interesting Russian activity here for over two weeks, and quite frankly, it's a little troubling."

"Do you want me to call you back on a secure line?" asked Lars.

"No. I need to show you my data and some summaries I've put together. I'd like to discuss this and brainstorm a little bit. Are you free now?"

"Yes. Bring your stuff."

Odd made sure that he had shuffled together all the data he needed and began the long trek down the 508 stairs from his observation post on OP-247.

The mission of OP-247, Norway's primary station for monitoring Russia's military activities in the Arctic Ocean's Barents Sea, was to observe and identify anything new or unusual. They intercepted Russian communications, maintained visual records, and more recently, recorded underwater acoustic events. The station was located in northern Norway at the highest elevation overlooking the area where Russia's northern fleet exercised and tested its latest military systems and tactics.

Lieutenant Bergstrom had been assigned to OP-247 nearly six months ago as an underwater acoustics expert, specifically as it applied to Russian submarines. While this duty assignment was initially extremely boring for Odd, that had suddenly changed two weeks earlier.

It took about fifteen minutes for Odd to descend the long stairway down to the spartan command center building. The cold March winds were unusually brisk. Finally, Odd arrived to the welcome warmth of the lieutenant commander's office.

"Hey, Odd. That was quick. You should have worn your hat. Your hair is all messed up."

"I should have. I was afraid it would blow away. The wind is vicious out there today."

"Coffee?" asked Lars.

"I thought you'd never ask."

Lars poured Odd a cup, then asked, "What have you got, Odd? You've got me curious."

Odd sat, took a few sips of coffee, and began spreading his data on the table. "Lars, as you know, the Russians were doing a lot of testing of their submarine-launched hypervelocity cruise missiles. I was assigned here to monitor this testing and to gather submarine acoustic signatures of their firing subs. Well, when I got here, there was no activity going on. It had suddenly stopped. I was bored to tears."

"I know what you mean. I was actually wondering if we needed

OP-247 at all. But I know that you've been busy and preoccupied lately. What's going on?"

"I didn't want to stir things up until I was sure there was something to what I was starting to see, but about two weeks ago there were several reconnaissance aircraft flights over the pack ice. About a week after that, a nuclear icebreaker shows up on the scene and stations itself about fifty miles north of here and begins conducting all kinds of helicopter operations. I am certain they've established one or two manned camps on the ice."

"For what purpose?" asked Skarsgaard.

"I really can't say for sure, but I have some strong suspicions. After the ice camps were set up, I detected a submarine operating in the area. The acoustic signature is very consistent with that of the Akula. But I keep getting snippets of an acoustic source that I don't associate with an Akula. The signal is of a higher frequency, very faint, periodic, and very difficult to detect and hold on to once I think I'm locked onto it."

"Could it be a new source from the Akula? Or could it be a new-class submarine?" asked Lars.

"Possibly. I thought of both those things. So I searched the databases, and I came up with nothing on either possibility. However, I'm starting to get a handle on the strange signal. As I said, it comes and goes. But now I can detect harmonics of the main signal, and they're helping me a bit. It's very difficult to hold, but I'm more and more confident that it's from a submarine, a new one."

Skarsgaard said, "So, in summary, missile testing has disappeared, there was a several-month period with no activity, but now operations have begun again. And you think that there may be a new type of Russian submarine involved in this activity. Right?"

"Yes, sir."

Lars then asked, "What about the Akula? What's it doing?"

"My best guess is that the new sub, if it is a new sub, is conducting sea trials, and the Akula is working with it to develop tactical capabilities."

Lars's brow furrowed as he pondered that possibility. Finally, he said, "Odd, keep up your surveillance and especially focus on the possible new sub. Meanwhile, I want to look into other intelligence sources at our NIS and see if I can get a handle on what the Russians are up to. We should definitely look further into this."

"Yes, sir. Will do."

When LT Bergstrom had left, LCDR Skarsgaard reviewed the written report. He shook his head in dismay and jotted down a summary of what he now knew based on their discussion. He immediately called his supervisor, the head of the Norwegian Intelligence Service in Oslo.

"Hey, Ragnar, this is Lars. Do you have a few minutes to talk?"

✯✯✯

That afternoon, Lars was on the next available flight to Oslo.

The director of the Norwegian Intelligence Service was waiting for him at the airport.

"Wow. This is some kind of special service. Picked up at the airport by the director of NIS."

Ragnar was all business. "What you told me over the phone has me very concerned. I didn't want to waste any time. We need to get on this immediately."

When they arrived at Ragnar's office, Lars showed him his summary of LT Bergstrom's reports and waited patiently as Ragnar read it.

"Well, the mission of OP-247 is to observe and report anything unusual from the Russians, and what I'm reading here certainly fits the bill. We should dig a little deeper."

"I agree."

After a pause, Ragnar said, "Tell you what. You stay over

tonight in Oslo, and I will check with my colleagues and analysts here and see if they have any intel that can help clear up this puzzle. We'll discuss this further tomorrow, and we'll decide what to do next."

"I'll be here."

# CHAPTER 2

**THAT EVENING, RAGNAR CALLED LARS** at his hotel. "Lars, we might have a problem. Be at my office tomorrow morning by 7:30."

"Yes, sir."

Promptly at 7:30, Lars strode into Ragnar's office. "Morning," said Lars. "What did you find out? What kind of problem do you think we have?"

Ragnar said, "Have a seat, and I'll fill you in." He pulled some papers from a folder. "It turns out that my signal intelligence people have been intercepting a fair amount of traffic on a highly classified program. They have not been able to piece together exactly what is going on because they're just getting snippets of various and diverse things such as submarine testing, sea ice studies, facility construction, waste disposal, Arctic research, and time constraints.

"Individually, none of these snippets seem too worrisome. We get this type of activity all the time, and the NIS has not been overly anxious. What has our interest, though, is that the language in the comms has been dancing around stating anything outright. There seems to be a higher-than-normal classified nature to these intercepted communications. Also, the meeting of schedule timelines seems to be of paramount importance, even to a sense of panic. And there is one other thing that might tie all these things together, and that is periodic reference to something they call the SOOF."

"SOOF. What's that?"

"I don't have a clue. Neither do my analysts. I'm sure it's a code name for something. But what? I just don't know. What do you think of all this, Lars?"

Lars hesitated. "I agree with the analysts. That's a pretty diverse list of goings-on. Are they sure that all these things are tied together?"

"No. They are not. But the communications originate from the same or related organizations. And the extra secrecy is very suspicious and seems to connect them. Look, Lars, I want you to go back to OP-247 and have LT Bergstrom continue to monitor the Russian activity and prepare detailed reports. Work with him closely. I especially want him to focus on this potential new submarine activity. That's Bergstrom's specialty, isn't it? Submarine acoustics?"

"Yes, it is, and he's very good at it. I trust his knowledge and his instincts."

"This is important enough to bring upstairs to the top," Ragnar concluded. "I'm going to contact my boss at the security agency and see if they have any thoughts on this."

★★★

Lars returned to OP-247 that evening and briefed Odd the next morning. Odd would continue to monitor the Russian activities, paying special attention to the mysterious submarine. Lars told him, "Anything that ties in our efforts to what Ragnar and the NIS are finding will be very valuable. I'm going to assign two of our young analysts to help you out, and I'll be spending more time with you here. I hate to walk up those stairs every morning, but I need to stay on top of this thing, and you need to be able to focus on the potential new submarine."

Over the next week, they observed a flurry of Russian activity. "A second sub is definitely in our area," Odd reported. "And the first is not an Akula. I'm almost sure that it's a Laika-class submarine, maybe a Yasen, but I have to research the acoustic signature some more before I can be sure."

"What do you think its purpose is?"

"Like I said earlier, it seems to be a joint exercise between the Yasen or Laika and the mysterious sub, probably developing tactics for Arctic ops. Just a guess, but that seems logical."

"What makes you think this?"

"They seem tied in to what the ice camps are doing. From communication intercepts, I have determined that the two camps are separated by a mile or so, and they have lowered several transponders through the ice. The subs, I believe, are navigating within this grid of transponders so they can be precisely tracked and located. This is how they develop tracking, avoidance, and other important tactical information. In this case, in an ice-covered Arctic environment."

That afternoon, Lars called Ragnar. "Ragnar, I think that we have enough new information up here for us to get together again."

"I agree, Lars. In fact, I was just about to call you and suggest the same thing. Can you be here for a meeting tomorrow afternoon?"

"If I can catch the early evening flight out, yes I can."

"Great. See you tomorrow. Oh, and bring Bergstrom with you."

# CHAPTER 3
# GENTLEMEN, WE HAVE A PROBLEM

**THE NEXT AFTERNOON, LARS AND** Odd walked into Ragnar's office. Lars introduced Odd to Ragnar.

"Impressive work, Lieutenant Bergstrom," Ragnar began. "You might have uncovered a major threat to Norway and even the world. Sit down, guys. I want to hear anything new you might have. I'm especially interested in your personal opinions on what's going on up there."

Odd said, "Thank you, Mr. Solberg. It's nice to meet you at last." He opened his notebook and dove right into his report. When he got to the mysterious submarine, he relayed that it might be a newer version of the Borei-class ballistic missile submarine. "I'm almost certain that in the Barents Sea they are conducting sea trials of a new submarine designed for Arctic Ocean operations." Also, he was sure that for acoustic reasons the nuclear icebreaker was keeping a distance from the ice camps but was supporting them via helicopter. Odd looked directly at Ragnar and closed with "That's what I have, Mr. Solberg."

Ragnar shook his head and smiled weakly. "Scary report, Odd,

Lars. It's especially scary because it ties in with other intelligence we've intercepted here at NIS, uncovering a new classified code name which seems to be tied to a facility-construction effort— 'UTSELET.' A new submarine has been under development and construction for seven years, and a prototype has been completed and has been undergoing sea trials for almost a year. We believe that four more of these submarines are being built, are nearing completion, and may be ready for sea trials in the very near future." Ragnar paused before saying, "And the most senior submariner in the Russian Navy, Admiral Fedor Ustinov, has been assigned as commanding officer of the first of these submarines, the one now conducting sea trials."

Ragnar looked at Lars and Odd with concern. He went on, "Related intel associated with the UTSELET code name is that some sort of waste-disposal effort is huge all across Russia; most of Russia's largest cities seem to pop up in the discussion. The code name SOOF seems to show up every so often with UTSELET. And there is one other curious thing that could apply here. We have found that, somehow, Russia has hidden a vast amount of money, and none of us at NIS can figure out what it's being used for. It just disappeared from their budget, and it seems like this has been going on for years."

Ragnar paused and took a deep breath. "Gentlemen, I think that we have a problem. A serious problem. We need to bring this thing up to the Norwegian Security Authority—and sooner rather than later."

A somber silence filled the room as the three men looked at each other with deep disquiet.

Ragnar picked up the phone and called Dr. Klaus Bakraan, director of the Norwegian Security Authority. "Hey, Klaus, this is Ragnar. I've learned of some developments that I think you should be aware of."

★★★

The three men made the short trip to NSA and arrived at Dr. Bakraan's roomy office at the appointed time. Ragnar introduced Odd and Lars to Klaus. "It's a pleasure to meet you, Lars. Ragnar has told me quite a bit about you."

"Uh-oh. I think I might be in trouble." They all laughed.

When they had sat down at the conference table, Klaus began, "Okay, Ragnar. You wouldn't call an emergency meeting unless you have something important to tell me. I'm all ears."

Ragnar deferred to Odd. "Odd started this whole thing a few weeks ago. I think it best if he lets you know what he's found. Odd?"

Odd pulled out sheets of data, including photos, Russian radio-communication transcripts, acoustic graphs of the Russian submarines, and various other data sets he had collected. He relayed his thoughts on what the Russians were up to. When he had finished, he passed copies of his data to Klaus, who then asked Ragnar to tell them what NIS had found out.

Ragnar presented the NIS-collected intel of the UTSELET code name project, the Russia-wide facility-construction effort, and the waste-disposal problem. He also mentioned the mysterious SOOF that kept popping up in the communications and seemed to be related to all these things.

Ragnar then added, "The most troubling thing of all, I think, is the highly classified development of a new strategic submarine—probably a modified Borei, as Odd explained. And Admiral Fedor Ustinov's involvement makes me nervous. As we know, Ustinov is one of the most hawkish, high-ranking military leaders in Russia. He's been anti-West since the end of the Cold War. The submarine under his command has been undergoing sea trials for almost a year. We think that this must be the mystery sub Odd detected in the Barents Sea. And the Russians wouldn't have assigned such a senior naval officer to this sub unless it was extremely important."

Klaus looked at Odd's data for several minutes and said, "You guys may have something here. I've been trying to make sense of how the Russians made billions or even trillions of rubles just disappear. We knew they were doing something with all this money, but we haven't been able to pin it down. What you've got here could explain it all.

"The question I keep asking myself is why they would be spending all this money on something classified when they have so many economic problems at home to deal with. The reason has to be extremely important to them. From what you have shown me today, it seems like the military is in the middle of it all. A new-class ballistic-missile submarine? Submarine operations in the Arctic? Waste-disposal and facility-construction programs all across Russia, and with classified code names to boot? I think it's time we talked to our American friends at the CIA. We might have a serious problem here."

# CHAPTER 4
## THE CIA BRIEF

**KLAUS CONTACTED DIRECTOR HARLAN BRADBURY** of the CIA and shared the information the Norwegians had compiled. The conversation was quick and to the point, and Ragnar, Lars, and Odd took the next available flight out of Oslo. The next afternoon, the three men were escorted into Harlan's secure briefing room at Langley. Joining Harlan were five of his department heads. Harlan knew Ragnar from past interactions. He introduced the department heads to the Norwegians, and Ragnar introduced Lars and Odd.

After the Norwegians took their seats, Harlan began. "Ragnar, I've already given my people a short brief of what Klaus and I talked about, so we can get right into it. We all agree that we could have a very serious situation here." Harlan turned to his department heads and said, "I want you all to pay very close attention. Ragnar?"

Ragnar gave a summary of what they had found and what it all might mean and had Odd show some of his technical data concerning the submarines. When they finished, Harlan turned to his department heads and asked if they had any questions or anything to add.

One of the department heads admitted that he had sat in on an intel brief that showed that an increase in non-missile tests in the Barents Sea. But the decision was made that it was not that important, and that Norway could handle it. That was six months or so ago, and nothing had come up since.

Another head was aware of the code names UTSELET and SOOF but had not been able to define anything beyond them being involved with a large construction program. "We just didn't feel that this was of high enough priority compared to Russia's recent threats to other nations."

A third head acknowledged that his department was trying to pin down the hidden money. He added, "We also felt that this money was going to fund a classified construction project. The amount of money has us wondering, however. It also seems strange that such a tremendous amount of waste has been generated, and that the waste disposal is so highly classified. I mean, why would this be classified?"

A fourth department had discovered a significant increase in the production of fissionable nuclear materials. "But we concluded that many of the Russian nuclear power plants had been in operation for many years and were probably in need of fuel replacement."

The fifth department head, Mary Graham, said, "I'm a little embarrassed to say that we have been tracking the development of a new submarine, possibly a Borei-improvement program. We intercepted a lot of traffic indicating many difficulties and setbacks and that the costs had skyrocketed. The Russians were supposedly considering scrapping the project altogether. After hearing your report, I now think that the Russians have been feeding us a lot of crap and we've been eating it. I'm sorry, Harlan."

Harlan took a deep breath and exhaled loudly. He looked at

Ragnar and said, "You guys may have just saved our asses. Or you may be responsible for us losing our jobs." Harlan turned to his department heads and said, "I want you people to get your top analysts on this ASAP. Old information, new information. I want you to look at everything we have with this new Norwegian information in mind. I want to stress that the need-to-know is to be strictly controlled. Tell no one why we are interested in this information.

"I have my weekly brief to the president next Tuesday. I want an update brief from each of you on Monday. That means you only have tomorrow and this weekend to get ready." Harlan then turned to Ragnar, Lars, and Odd and asked, "Can you guys stay in town and attend my meeting with the president?"

"Do we have a choice? Of course we will."

The next Monday morning, the three Norwegians met again with Harlan and his department heads. Harlan opened with, "Let's start with the SIGINT interceptions with regard to UTSELET and SOOF. Unfortunately, nothing new has been uncovered. It seems that the Ruskies are being very cautious. Perhaps overly so, even over secure lines. There have been a few references to SOOF and UTSELET, but nothing useful."

One of Harlan's department heads interjected, "The one thing that stands out for me is their need to stay on schedule. The big worry seems to be deadlines and milestones not being met, especially with regard to SOOF. This tells me that something is in the air and could happen soon."

Another department head said, "With respect to a new submarine, we did intercept one transmission that confirmed that a new-class SSBN is close to deployment for sea trials. The prototype unit completed last year seems to be performing very well, apparently, and is doing evaluation trials somewhere in the Arctic. Thanks to Odd here, I think we know where that is.

"Also, an attack boat, probably a Laika class, has also been assigned Arctic ops. It looks like Lieutenant Bergstrom got that one right as well. Most importantly, SIGINT has also confirmed that huge amounts of rubles, in the trillions, are being spent on the UTSELET and SOOF programs and on the construction and testing of the new submarines. So, it looks like we were wrong, and you guys hit the nail on the head there. The problem is that we still don't know what the programs are all about."

At this time, Mary Graham raised her hand. "I may have something to add here," she said. "I received some new information about an hour before this meeting, and I think it might clear up some of this."

"What is it?" asked Harlan with some excitement.

"The intercept hints that UTSELET is critical to the survival of the Russian people, and schedules must be met. This all makes sense when you realize that *UTSELET* means 'survival' in Russian. Here's what I think," said Mary. "I think that the Russians are building massive underground shelters across Russia, and getting rid of the vast amounts of excavated soil without being detected is a massive problem for them. Furthermore, there was one other bit of cryptic information in this transmission. SOOF was singled out as the most critical aspect of UTSELET." Mary paused here and said, "I believe that SOOF is an acronym which stands for Sea of Okhotsk Facility."

An eerie quiet filled the room. Finally, Director Bradbury broke the silence. "What the hell do we have here? Is it possible that the Russians are building large, underground bomb shelters across Russia? That they are building five new, almost-impossible-to-detect ICBM/cruise missile–capable submarines and are refining their tactics for submarine operations in the Arctic Ocean? That they are building an extremely high-priority facility in the Sea of Okhotsk? And that they are spending huge,

huge amounts of money on all this? And the scary part to me is that they seem to be tied to a rigid timetable. I hate to ask this, but are we looking at Armageddon here?" The others in the room just stared at Harlan with wide eyes. No one said a word.

Harlan shuffled his papers for a few seconds, deep in thought. He then said, "I want all of you here with me tomorrow should the president have technical questions or ask for more detailed information. I'm going to ask the president if the chairman of the Joint Chiefs of Staff and the Navy's chief of naval operations can attend as well. Meanwhile, I want all of you to keep digging into archived information to see if you can pull out anything that will solidify, or even dispel, what we think we have here. It's going to be a long day and night for all of you. Do not discuss what we think is going on with anyone. No one. Is that clear?"

# CHAPTER 5
# PRESIDENT JAMES MILSAP

**THE EIGHT MEN AND ONE** woman were escorted into the president's briefing room. President James Milsap stood and welcomed them in.

"Hi, Harlan. Good to see you again. You know General Jack Bishop and Admiral Roger Flaxon," he said, gesturing toward the chairman of the Joint Chiefs of Staff and the Navy's chief of naval operations. "So, what's so important that you requested that this meeting only include Jack, Roger, and me? Not even my recording secretary."

"Mr. President, I believe that we have a very serious situation here, and that if we are right, what I am about to tell you should have very limited access."

"Oh!" said the president. "You've got my attention. What do you have?"

Harlan introduce his entourage and gave the president a summary of their findings.

When Harlan had completed his summary, the president looked dismayed, then thoughtful, then said, "Thank you. That'll be all." Everyone looked a little puzzled. No questions? No requests for additional details? As they rose to leave, President Milsap said sharply, "Harlan, stay. You two as well." He pointed to Bishop and Flaxon.

When the others had left, the president demanded, "What the hell is going on here, Harlan? Explain to me how you missed this. We spend a hundred billion every year on intelligence gathering, and I get embarrassed by three Norwegians! How in God's name did you miss this?"

Harlan had anticipated the president's anger. He explained the clever and well-designed cover and deception, or C&D, effort carried out by the Russians, who had staged periodic threats and military exercises near the borders of Turkey, Afghanistan, even China. The US had concentrated resources to gather intel on these "high-priority" events—all carefully timed to keep them occupied elsewhere. Harlan also reported that the Russians had essentially stopped their missile testing in the Barents Sea off the Kola Peninsula and had greatly increased missile tests in the White Sea. Harlan said, "We considered this activity to be high priority, and we used our satellites and other available assets to monitor these tests. It appears now that this was just another ruse to keep us looking elsewhere."

The president shook his head. "Jesus, Harlan. Damn. Damn." After a moment he said, "What about our radar monitoring system on that little island off Norway. Didn't our guys catch any of this?"

"That's Vardo Island, sir. We have been in the process of upgrading the Globus 2 radar system with the much more capable Globus 3, but we've experienced some technical and logistic problems. But, sir, the Globus radars are designed to track missiles. With the cessation of missile firings in the Barents, the Globus radars would not have added much, if anything, to the equation. It's just fortunate that the Norwegians have been monitoring from Outpost-247, and fortunate they recently increased their capability to monitor underwater acoustics. That's what really caught the attention of LT Bergstrom and the Norwegian Intelligence Service. I'm sorry, sir."

"Oh, God," the president moaned. He turned to General Bishop and Admiral Flaxon and said angrily, "You two have been unusually quiet since you entered the room. What do you guys think of all this? Does any of this make sense to you? What about all your intelligence we pay a fortune for?"

Admiral Flaxon responded that the Navy had no evidence that Russia was constructing a new-class submarine. They only knew that the Arctic submarines, the Typhoons, were being scrapped. He said, "Other than upgrades to older submarines, we saw no real threat."

General Bishop added, "We weren't advised of any major increase in production of fissionable nuclear material other than what they need for their nuclear power plants."

"I guess we've all been fat, and life has been easy for us," the president sighed. "Well, now it looks like we've got our asses in a pickle. I can tell you this: all this complacency changes as of right now. Here's what we're going to do." Looking at Harlan, he said, "One, focus all our available intel assets on all aspects of this problem; two, find out all we can on this mysterious SOOF; three, find out what is going on with the submarine capabilities we so conveniently dismissed; four, find out all you can on their progress in their hypervelocity-missile development; and five, most importantly, I want the operational plans of the Russians. Dates. Schedules. D-Day, if there is one."

He turned to General Bishop and Admiral Flaxon. "From you two, I want, one, a plan to take out their submarines, at my command, both Arctic and open-ocean deployed; two, a plan to destroy SOOF in the Sea of O; and three, I want two options each on how to accomplish one and two. Plan A is to be non-nuclear, and plan B is to use tactical nukes, if we must.

"I also want a cover-and-deception plan of our own. I want to confuse the Russians and hide what we know and what we are doing about it. Make them think we're still putting all our intel assets on their fake threats. I want this C&D plan by next week this time. Did you hear me? By next week. I want all this done ASAP, and I want weekly status reports on the intel and on the progress of plans A and B. Is all this clear?" The three men in the room solemnly nodded.

The president then addressed Harlan directly again. "Harlan. Do we have any HUMINT assets that we could bring to bear on this? A sleeper, perhaps?"

"We do have a sleeper we've been saving for a high-priority objective," Harlan replied. "A husband-and-wife team that's been in place for about ten years. The husband is on the staff of the minister of finance, Anton Yulov. The wife is a friend of Yulov's wife."

The president said, "Well, wake them up. There is no higher priority than this. I want all the information that they can provide. The Russian finance minister has to be involved in this money thing. Maybe they can give us more insight into solving the SOOF problem."

He looked at the three men in the room and said, "You are now working seven days a week, twenty-four hours a day, if necessary. Let's get started, and I will see you next Tuesday for updates."

After a chorus of "Yes, sir," Harlan, Jack, and Roger headed out. The president said, "Harlan, have the Norwegians come back in. I want to thank them personally with a hug."

# PART 2

## PLAN A

# CHAPTER 6
# THE NAVAL RESEARCH LABORATORY
### (NOVEMBER 2)

**THE NAVAL RESEARCH LABORATORY WAS** born in 1923 at the urging of Thomas Edison and was now considered the premier research laboratory of the US Navy and the Marine Corps. It conducted both basic and applied research and developed prototype systems. Their research ranged widely, from outer space down to and into the ocean floor. NRL put satellites into space and developed the Global Positioning System, as well as the first satellite tracking system. Importantly, NRL also pioneered the use of space for surveillance and intelligence gathering.

In addition to advancements in the space sciences, NRL pioneered developments in such areas as meteorology, materials sciences, tactical electronics warfare, information security, use of nuclear power for submarines, plasma physics, geophysics/seismic science, and use of artificial intelligence. It also produced several Nobel laureates. One of the most significant areas of NRL was in the research of the ocean environment and its impact on naval systems and operations.

It was here that Dr. Samantha Stone had been conducting

research for eight years.

"Samantha, Dr. Scharold wants to see you in his office right away," said Samantha's boss, Dr. Thomas Harkins.

"Whoa. What's up? Why does the technical director want to see me?"

"I don't know. He just called and asked me to send you to his office right away."

"I'm on my way."

Dr. Michael Scharold, the technical director of all of NRL's scientific programs, was waiting at his desk when Samantha shuffled into his office. He asked her to have a seat. Wasting no time, he said, "Samantha, I just got a classified phone call from Mr. Harlan Bradbury."

"The CIA's director?" asked Samantha with a look of surprise.

"Yes. Mr. Bradbury himself. He said that he wants you for a temporary-duty assignment for about a year."

"Temporary duty? Why me? I don't even know him."

Dr. Scharold went on, "He said that you were highly recommended by Admiral Roger Flaxon. Wasn't he the commander of the submarine forces in the Pacific when you were the submarine science advisor in Pearl Harbor?"

"Yes, he was. And he is now the top naval officer in the US Navy. What does Admiral Flaxon want me to do?"

"I really don't know. It seems like they need someone that has a strong scientific background in the Arctic and is very familiar with the environmental impact on submarine systems and operations. Mr. Bradbury said that Admiral Flaxon wanted you on his team."

"Team? Dr. Scharold, I don't know what to say."

"Mr. Bradbury did say that you had to be willing to be away from your family for about a year."

"Oh, that's not a problem," she said with a wave of her hand. She had no attachments to speak of. "You said that he called you on a secure phone. Why the secrecy?"

"Mr. Bradbury only said that you would be completely separated from your family, NRL, and anything else around here. You'll be stationed at Pearl Harbor and working for the commander in chief of the Pacific Fleet. Well, what do you say?"

Samantha sat quietly for a minute, then said, "It sounds like I don't have much of a choice, do I? When do I report for duty in Pearl?"

"I don't know. He only said that you need to call him right away for more information."

★★★

Ten minutes later, Samantha was handed a red phone in a secure area. "Mr. Bradbury, this is Samantha Stone. You want to talk to me?" For the next three minutes, Samantha only said things like "Yes, sir. I understand. No, sir. That's not a problem. I'll get on it right away. I'll be ready." And finally, "Thank you, sir."

"Well, what did he say?" asked Dr. Scharold.

Samantha put down the phone and stared at Scharold with glazed eyes. She finally said, "Mr. Bradbury instructed me to go home today and pack one suitcase with about a week's worth of clothing, toiletries, and other necessities. I will be picked up by a government car at five and driven to Joint Base Andrews. We have a seven o'clock flight tonight to Hawaii with him, a few others that I will be introduced to . . . and the president of the United States, on Air Force One."

Samantha laughed out loud and said, "This is a joke, right? You guys are playing an elaborate joke on me, right?"

Scharold only said, "You don't have much time, Samantha. You'd better go home and pack."

# CHAPTER 7
## AIR FORCE ONE

**AT PRECISELY FIVE, A CAR** pulled up to Samantha's modest condo, and a driver in a suit emerged and came to the entrance. Samantha opened the door as he approached. "Dr. Stone?" he asked. "I'm Jonathan Miles. I'll be driving you to Andrews. Here, let me take your bag."

Twenty minutes later, Jonathan pulled the car up to the big Boeing VC-25 aircraft, Air Force One. Samantha was agog at the circumstances she'd found herself caught up in. She thanked Jonathan for everything as he took her suitcase. He bowed slightly and said, "The pleasure was all mine, Dr. Stone. I hope you have an enjoyable trip." She smiled at him as two rather large Secret Service agents approached her.

"Please follow us, Dr. Stone." They escorted her onto the aircraft, leading her toward the back until they came to a comfortable-looking lounge area where a gentleman sat reading some documents. One of the escorting agents said, "Mr. Bradbury, this is Dr. Stone."

"Samantha, I'm so glad to meet you. Have a seat. You're the

first to arrive. We can talk while we wait for the others."

"It's an honor to meet you, Mr. Bradbury. I never imagined I would meet the director of the CIA."

"Well, it's no big deal, believe me. And please, call me Harlan." They carried on with small talk until the same agents escorted two uniformed military men into the lounge. Samantha recognized one of them right away.

"Admiral Flaxon. It's so good to see you."

Flaxon smiled and gave Samantha a big hug. "My God, Samantha, you haven't changed a bit. What's it been? Three years?"

"Exactly," she replied.

"Samantha, I'd like you to meet General Jack Bishop. Jack is the chairman of the Joint Chiefs of Staff."

Jack bowed his head slightly and said, "A pleasure, Dr. Stone. Roger has been telling me a lot about you. I've been anxious to meet you."

Samantha stood there speechless as Bradbury asked everyone to get comfortable. A few minutes went by with more small talk, and then the agents escorted two more men into the lounge. "Dr. Stone, gentlemen, this is the director of the Norwegian Intelligence Service, Mr. Ragnar Solberg, and this is Lieutenant Odd Bergstrom, of the Royal Norwegian Navy."

Those already in the lounge introduced themselves to the Norwegians. While the introductions were made, a third security agent escorted yet another uniformed man into the lounge. "Commander Jared Townsend of DEVGRU and team leader of the SEAL team assigned for this mission." All the military men in the lounge immediately came to attention and saluted Townsend, including Admiral Flaxon and General Bishop, and the Norwegians.

"Come on, guys. It's me. Don't embarrass me like that."

A mystified Samantha shook her head. When they all sat down, Samantha leaned over and whispered in Harlan's ear,

"Isn't it unusual for a general and an admiral to stand and salute a commander?"

"It is. But Commander Townsend is the most decorated SEAL in the Navy. He was awarded the Purple Heart after being severely wounded on a mission last year. He personally saved the lives of several members of his platoon, and he is being considered for the Congressional Medal of Honor. By saluting him, the senior officers are acknowledging what he did and showing their respect."

"Oh. I see," she said, honor and respect welling up in her own chest.

For the next forty-five minutes, the seven people in the lounge questioned one another about their careers and their last duty assignments, as well as non-career-related events. However, most of the interest seemed to fall on Samantha. She was the only female in the group, and a scientist to boot. She was different. Also receiving a lot of attention was Lieutenant Bergstrom, the Norwegian military intelligence analyst. It seemed everyone here knew something she did not.

Finally, at just about seven, the big engines of the Boeing VC-25 came to life. General Bishop said, "Well, it sounds like the Big Kahuna has arrived."

The president of the United States, James Milsap, entered the lounge.

# CHAPTER 8
# THE FLIGHT TO HAWAII

**THE TEAM WAS ESCORTED TO** their seats for takeoff, and the powerful engines roared. The eight-hour flight to Hawaii had begun.

Twenty minutes after takeoff, a delicious meal was provided to all. Samantha, who had not eaten since breakfast on this unbelievable day, truly welcomed and enjoyed the food.

One hour into the flight, President Milsap announced, "Okay, people. It's time to get to the business at hand. Let's convene in the briefing room." The president led the way further aft of the lounge where they had originally gathered.

The briefing room had a mahogany conference table that could seat ten people. Secret Service agents and military escorts were always within a short distance of the president, but once in the briefing room, President Milsap instructed the agents and military escorts to relocate to the lounge. The president sat in the middle of one long side of the table, and the six men clustered around him. Samantha, feeling very unsure as to the protocol of who should sit where, lagged behind and took the seat that had been left for her—directly across from President Milsap.

The president began, "Not everyone here knows all the details of this project. In fact, poor Dr. Stone here only found out she was on the team early this morning. Thank you, Dr. Stone, for joining us on such short notice." Samantha managed a weak smile. "For that reason, I am going to start from the beginning and try to paint a clear picture of what we are up against and what we have to do. I hope this is OK with everyone."

There was a chorus of mumbles and heads nodding in agreement.

The president looked at everyone at the table in turn. He then began. "First and foremost, this is the most highly classified project that we have today. What we discuss here is not to be discussed with anyone outside this room. Is that clear? You all have been previously cleared at the code-name security level, higher than Top Secret. However, in the past three months, additional background security checks have been made on all of you. This includes you, Admiral, and you, General."

He then looked at the two Norwegians and said, "Also for you two, Mr. Solberg and Lieutenant Bergstrom." They nodded. "What I'm saying is that what we're planning to do in the next three months is highly, highly classified. You must keep this in mind at all times. The classified code name assigned to this project is IDES."

The president paused to let the classification sink in. He then said, "Last March, I got a call from Harlan here that he had some potentially disturbing news. The next morning he showed me compelling evidence that the Russians were up to no good in the Arctic Ocean and elsewhere." He explained the disparate intelligence that they had consolidated.

"That very day, through Harlan, Jack, and Roger, I initiated a program to assign all our intelligence-gathering assets to find out what the Russians were up to. During April and May, it became clearer and clearer that the Russians were planning a full-blown nuclear attack on the United States. In an attempt to hide what they were up to, they carried out a well-executed C&D program—that's cover and deception, Dr. Stone—to divert our intel assets to monitor conventional military buildup and exercises near the borders of neutral countries as well as countries friendly to the West.

"Well, it turns out from recent intel that their C&D efforts were not just for show. The Russians are, in fact, building up their conventional forces to overrun Western Europe. So, in summary, they plan to take out the US with nuclear hypervelocity missiles launched from five modified Borei-class ballistic-missile submarines stationed in ice-covered Arctic waters off northern Canada, and to overrun Europe with conventional military forces. Furthermore, we've learned that the Russians have undertaken a monumental construction program designed to build numerous underground shelters throughout Russia.

"However, most important to us is that the command and control of this diabolical program is located in the Sea of Okhotsk. This facility is not only underwater but embedded within the seafloor as well. The damn thing is partially buried, and it's called the SOOF for 'Sea of Okhotsk Facility.' So, lady and gentlemen, our mission impossible, should we decide to accept it, is to destroy the SOOF, take out the five Borei subs, and cancel out their conventional forces in Europe."

Here, the president paused to let this horror story sink in. Samantha was speechless—to think that she began this day going to work at NRL to continue her latest research. She was only about a week away from submitting her paper to the *Journal of Geophysical Research*. That did not seem so important to her anymore.

The president shook her loose from her thoughts as he continued, "Well, how has something like this happened? It has been at least ten years in the planning. How could we not have picked up on this? I've already mentioned the clever ongoing C&D program. But the single most important piece of intelligence we have discovered is that this whole operation is—now listen up—a military coup.

"Let me repeat that. We are dealing with a military coup in Russia. President Krylov and all his political cronies don't even know about it. Three months ago we learned that Krylov has Alzheimer's, and it's fairly advanced. His disease has been covered up in advance of their next election in late March. There are two generals and two admirals spearheading this thing. And the minister of finance, Anton Yulov, is in on it too. Yulov, if you remember, was a high-ranking general in the Russian Air Force. As the finance minister, Yulov has diverted about one hundred trillion rubles a year to finance this whole operation. That's about one point five trillion a year in real money.

"Now, listen to this. To supplement this funding, the Russian mafia has been conducting a worldwide money-laundering effort to provide approximately another five hundred billion dollars a year. We knew some of this was going on, but, unfortunately, we didn't put two and two together." The president glared at the director of the CIA. "All I can say is thank God for the Norwegians for picking up on the Arctic activity and SOOF."

The president continued, "All right. That's the background. Why are we here now, flying to Hawaii?" He paused and said, "As I said, we are going to conduct our own 'mission impossible.' We don't have Tom Cruise, or even Peter Graves, to help us out here, so we're going to have to do it ourselves. Following my initial meeting with Harlan, Ragnar, and Odd, I tasked Jack and Roger here to come up with a plan A and a plan B. Plan B was to include a nuclear response if plan A was compromised. Well, of course, these plans changed, or evolved, as we got more and more intelligence. By far the most important and detailed information we received was from our HUMINT sources."

He looked at Samantha and explained, "Human intelligence, or spies. We had a husband-and-wife sleeper team closely involved with Anton Yulov, the minister of finance. I will call them Mr. and Mrs. Smith. We tasked them to find out all they could about where all this hidden money was going—especially whether it was going to fund the SOOF and the Borei-sub program. We got a tremendous amount of intel from Yulov's wife. It's incredible how loose the minister's lips are when it comes to Mrs. Yulov. She inadvertently provided a lot of valuable information to Mrs. Smith.

"Through the efforts of this team, we were made aware of engineering drawings of the SOOF, and we successfully gained access and made copies. We now have these drawings in our possession. Because of this, we believe that we know how to destroy the SOOF. Mr. and Mrs. Smith also discovered that there is an underground fiber-optic communications cable in the Sea of O going to the SOOF. Of equal importance, and perhaps the most horrifying, is that we believe D-Day is this coming sixteenth of March."

A gasp escaped from Samantha, Lars, and Odd.

"Since last March, Lieutenant Odd Bergstrom of the Royal Norwegian Navy has continued to study and analyze the acoustic signature of the new Borei submarine. We have assisted him in this work by upgrading our facility on Vardo Island in the Barents Sea to include our best underwater acoustic monitoring capabilities. Lieutenant Bergstrom initially detected a very faint and hard-to-hold high frequency signal emanating from the Borei. Using our acoustic sensors to provide higher resolutions of the signal, he has developed algorithms to better define and exploit the signal's signature, and we have improved our submarine passive-detection sonars and our processing algorithms with this information.

"Lieutenant Bergstrom, I can now tell you that we believe the signal is being generated by an ice maker, of all things. Apparently they have not fully isolated this small, insignificant machine from the boat's hull. Hopefully, they will not realize this error and correct it. The intermittency of the signal is unfortunately tied to when the ice maker turns on and is running. But we thank you, Lieutenant, for your exceptional and valuable work."

The president dropped his gaze to the table and said, "Okay, everyone. That's enough for tonight. We should land in Hawaii at about nine this evening Hawaii time. We have a meeting at CINCPACFLT headquarters in the morning at eight. We will get much more information then, and we will get into the details of our plan A. It'll be a long, busy day for us, so get some sleep tonight. Up at six tomorrow morning."

As everyone rose and began filing out of the room, the president said, "Dr. Stone, would you be so kind as to remain here for a few minutes? I need to talk to you privately."

"Yes, Mr. President. I'll stay."

"Good. Admiral Flaxon, I'd like you to stay as well."

"Yes, sir."

# CHAPTER 9
## DO YOU VOLUNTEER?

**WHEN THE OTHERS HAD LEFT** the room, Admiral Flaxon took a seat next to the president. Samantha noticed that neither man was smiling. Samantha glanced at each in turn with a weak smile and wondered what this was all about.

After a long pause, the president cleared his throat and said, "Dr. Stone, as the commander and chief of our armed forces, I have the authority to order military personnel into any situation that I deem necessary for the protection and welfare of the United States. However, with a civilian, I can ask, but I cannot order."

Samantha nodded in understanding, but her eyes widened considerably.

"I have to be up front here, Dr. Stone. Failure to complete the objective of this mission, to destroy the SOOF, is not acceptable. If you deploy on the submarine to the Sea of Okhotsk, there is a good chance, a very good chance, that you may not survive. In that respect, you are being asked to go on a suicide mission."

The president looked directly at Samantha, as did Admiral Flaxon. Samantha did not say anything but continued to flick her gaze back and forth from Milsap to Flaxon.

The president continued, "Dr. Stone, whether you go on this mission is your decision, and I'm not asking you for a yes or no right now. You can think about it in the next day or so. I certainly understand if you say no. But I do need to know soon so Admiral Flaxon and I can initiate our alternate plan to replace you if necessary. I know this is a huge surprise to you. Your life has been totally turned upside down in just a few hours, and I can't imagine what you're going through right now."

Samantha studied the table and thought deeply for more than a minute. She then looked up and said in a strong and clear voice, "I don't need the time. I'm in. Count me in."

Milsap and Flaxon exchanged glances with their mouths practically agape. Flaxon then said, "I told you, James. I told you."

Both men stood and went to Samantha, shook her hand, and pulled her in for a strong hug. Roger whispered in Samantha's ear, "I'm so proud of you."

Samantha looked at the admiral with glazed eyes, not at all sure she was ready for what she'd just officially signed up for.

Air Force One landed at Joint Base Pearl Harbor-Hickham at 8:45 that evening. When the aircraft came to a stop, through her window Samantha spotted several limousines lined up to take the president and his entourage to housing at Pearl Harbor. The Secret Service agents were the first to deplane, to check the area with their fellow agents on the ground. Additional agents guarded the limousines. The governor of Hawaii was there to greet President Milsap, as was a mass of media vans with their video crews. On this occasion, however, little pomp and circumstance took place. Hand shaking, a hug with the governor, and a minute of small talk was it. A good night's sleep for all was in order. Most of the team members were escorted by security agents to two of the vehicles. General Bishop and Admiral Flaxon accompanied the president in his limo. Without much ado, the cavalcade began the drive to the Facility 219 housing area.

En route, Odd Bergstrom settled back in the plush seat next to Samantha. "Were you able to sleep?" he asked.

"No. I just couldn't get over how much my life has changed in less than twenty-four hours. It's like I'm in a whirlwind. I don't think I slept at all. What about you?"

"I was able to sleep pretty well. I've been so busy working on this project sixteen hours a day for the last eight months on Vardo Island that when I have a chance to sleep, well, I sleep. I can't imagine what you're going through."

Samantha just shook her head, thinking of her meeting with the president and Admiral Flaxon.

Odd continued, "I've got to say this, though. Meeting the president of the United States and being directly acknowledged by him is pretty heady stuff for a Norwegian like me. In fact, President Milsap even hugged me when I first met him seven months ago. Flying on Air Force One? Meeting a bonified hero, the DEVGRU SEAL team leader? The chairman of the Joint Chiefs of Staff? Admiral Flaxon? I ask myself, what am I doing here? My God, I'm only a lieutenant in the Norwegian navy. A junior one at that!"

They smiled at one another in shared amazement at their fortunes. "That was some praise the president showered on you," she said. "You have every right to be here." Odd looked down, a little embarrassed, then lifted his head again.

"I saw you talking to Admiral Flaxon on the plane. Do you know him?"

"Yes. Five years ago, I was assigned as the science advisor for the submarine force in the Pacific, right here in Pearl Harbor. Admiral Flaxon was COMSUBPAC at the time. He was in control of all our submarines in the Pacific. I really didn't get to meet him much on a personal level, but I was involved in several high-priority projects during my two-year assignment. We sailed together for five days on a submarine on one of my projects. We had a chance to talk some."

"You must have made an impression," Odd offered. "I heard Mr. Bradbury say that Admiral Flaxon specifically asked for you to be assigned to this mission."

"That's what I've been told. It was a shock."

"I'm embarrassed to ask you this, Samantha, but what do you do?"

Samantha considered how to answer, then said, "Well, the short answer is that I determine the effects of the ocean environment on the performance of naval systems and operations. The more specific answer is that I specialize in the Arctic environment and the seafloor." She paused. "Based on what President Milsap said on the plane, I'm starting to see what will be expected of me. I'm also starting to realize that my selection was not a last-minute thing."

"Why is that?"

"Well, about three months ago, my supervisor called me into his office and tasked me to research and write a comprehensive environmental technical report on the Sea of Okhotsk."

Odd exclaimed, "Oh, wow! Yep, that seems pretty targeted."

A few minutes later, the limos rolled to a stop in front of a large, stately house. More agents in black opened the car doors. One of them said, "Welcome to Carter House, your home away from home."

The guests followed the two agents up to the porch. Another agent, a rather large one, opened the front door to let everyone inside.

Once inside, the president said, "Our meeting with CINCPACFLT starts at eight in the morning. We mean to arrive precisely at 7:45, so be ready to go early. You've each been assigned your own room with a separate bath. I know that most of you probably did not sleep very well on my plane. So." He looked at his watch and said, "It's almost ten. You'll be rolled out of bed at six. Sleep well."

Samantha said to Odd, "I would have thought that the president of the United States would have his own house. Bishop and Flaxon, too. Well, what do I know?"

Odd smiled at her nervous chattiness. "Sleep well, Samantha. I'll see you in the morning."

# CHAPTER 10
## THE PRESIDENT SPEAKS

**AT 7:45 THE NEXT MORNING,** the limos arrived in front of the headquarters of the commander in chief of the Pacific Fleet, CINCPACFLT. The team was quickly ushered inside to a large, secure meeting/briefing room that contained an elevated stage with a projection of a large map of the Pacific operating area on a screen. Standing behind the dais near the front of the stage was an admiral with a lot of gold on his shoulders. He waited patiently as people filed into the room and took their seats.

Samantha sat near the back, and when the room doors were closed, about forty people filled the seats, with many more left unoccupied. The president and Mr. Bradbury sat in the first row.

Odd had joined Samantha. "This is going to be an interesting day," he murmured. She smiled nervously and nodded in agreement.

The admiral at the dais began the meeting. "Welcome, everyone. I am Admiral Frederick Price, commander in chief of the Pacific Fleet, and I will be leading the kickoff meeting this morning. But first, I have the distinct honor to present the president of the United States, James Milsap, to start us off. President Milsap?"

The president went to him, took the microphone, and moved to the front edge of the stage. He thanked Admiral Price. He looked at the audience for ten to fifteen seconds for effect. Then he began.

"Welcome, everyone. You here in this room have been tasked with the planning, preparation, and carrying out of the most important military action in the history of the United States, and perhaps the world. In fact, the very existence of our nation depends on how well you do. The lives of every American depend on it. So, as your president and as commander in chief of our armed forces, I task you to put every ounce of energy into accomplishing your task. I cannot stay with you today because of many other presidential obligations, but be assured that I will be with you all in spirit. I now turn this meeting over to the capable hands of Admiral Price. May God be with you all. Admiral Price?"

President Milsap handed the microphone to ADM Price and left the room, escorted by his Secret Service agents and accompanied by General Jack Bishop, Harlan Bradbury, and Ragnar Solberg.

Admiral Price began, "First, I have a bit of administrative information to pass on. By now, you are all aware of the need for strict control of anything, and I mean anything, that has to do with this operation. You are to discuss information only when you are in a proper, designated secure area. These areas will all have Marine guards posted at the doors. To get in, you will need a special ID badge, which looks like this."

Price held up his badge for all to see. "So, before we start the true business of this meeting, we will have a roll call of the people authorized to be in this room right now. You will be given your picture ID badge when your name is called. When working, wear your badge at all times. And remember, discuss this program only within the assigned classified areas and only with those wearing these special badges."

The roll was called, and the badges were issued. Price then said, "Look at the people around you. Everyone should be wearing a badge with his or her picture on it. If there is anyone without a badge, please point out that person now."

The room was silent.

"The code name for this operation is 'IDES.' IDES is a code-name, compartmented-level program." The admiral stated, "This is what we are up against. The Russian military has been planning a hostile military coup of its civilian government for about ten years. The major objectives of this coup are these: one, to take out the United States by submarine-launched hypervelocity cruise missiles armed with nuclear warheads; two, to overrun Europe with a full-scale invasion using conventional, ground, and air forces, which they have been building up for the last seven years; three, to topple and replace the existing Russian political leaders with carefully selected military leaders; and four, to destroy our aircraft carriers with submarine-launched and air-launched cruise missiles. These will also be hypervelocity missiles and could be nuclear armed as well.

"The rest of our surface ships, specifically our cruise-missile ships, will be attacked by Russian attack submarines. The only military assets we are not sure how the Russians will neutralize are our attack submarines armed with cruise missiles. Our SSGNs."

The admiral clasped his hands together. "Okay," he continued. "That's a list of their objectives. What are we going to do about it? As far as we know, they do not know that we're aware of their plans. This is a huge, huge advantage in our favor. This is why we continue to stress the secrecy of what we will be doing. We cannot let them find out that we know." He repeated this for effect.

"Here's our basic plan. To counter their conventional threat in Europe, we conduct a preemptive strike on their forces. We hope to deplete their land, sea, and air forces significantly even before they begin. We will target their cruise-missile submarines with our attack boats and take them out before they can fire a single missile. As far as their aircraft are concerned, we will be monitoring their flights, and we will meet them with our land-based and carrier-launched fighters and destroy them en route. Most of this action will be conducted under the aegis of CINCLANT, our Atlantic Fleet counterpart. COMSUBPAC is tasked with destroying the Russian submarines deployed in the Pacific operating area."

Admiral Price paused and took a sip of water. "Alright. You're probably wondering what we in the Pacific are tasked to do. Well, that's why we're here today. The Russians have rolled five modified Borei-class missile submarines off the assembly line—all presently operating within the ice-covered waters of the Arctic Ocean. Most importantly, they have constructed a command-and-control facility within the seafloor of the Sea of Okhotsk. Their classified name for this structure is 'the SOOF.' Destroying the SOOF is the highest-priority objective of IDES. If we are successful in destroying the SOOF, we will essentially destroy their ability to command and control their plan to defeat the West. We believe that without command and control, their plan will surely fail."

He continued, "Now, the following information is critical: They have established D-Day as 16 March. That's only three months from now. We are planning our coordinated preemptive attack—in Europe, on the Arctic submarines, and on the SOOF, the whole shebang—on 15 March, the day before their D-Day. We want to catch them with their pants down just before they pull the trigger. For this very reason"—he paused—"timing is everything."

After letting that sink in, Admiral Price began the next phase of the meeting. "We are now going to break up into three working teams. Each team will be under the command of a senior officer who will be responsible to COMSUBPAC Admiral Dexter Scott. Admiral Scott will report directly to Admiral Roger Flaxon, the

Navy's chief of naval operations. Admirals Scott and Flaxon, will you join me on the stage so everyone will be able to recognize you?"

The two admirals joined him and waved to everyone.

"Admiral Flaxon will oversee the progress of all three teams and keep me continually informed, especially if problems arise.

"The three teams are as follows: one, Team Alpha. Alpha's objective will be to destroy the five Arctic-stationed Borei subs before they fire their missiles. Five Virginia-class SSNs have been selected for this mission. The skippers of these boats will be under the direction of COMSUBPAC's operations officer, Captain Miles Perry. Please stand up, Captain Perry, and remain standing.

"Next is Team Bravo. Team Bravo's objective is to destroy the SOOF and the communications cable leading to the SOOF. This cable may be lying on the seafloor, but there is a good chance that it is buried. If so, it will be more difficult to locate and destroy. Team Bravo has significant challenges to overcome. The team will be led by COMSUBPAC's chief of staff, Captain Forrest Jenkins. Stand up, please, Captain Jenkins.

"Finally, Team Charlie. Team Charlie's objective is to destroy all the Russian submarines operating in the Pacific. Team Charlie will be under the direction of my operations officer, Captain Oscar Bellington. Stand up, Captain Bellington.

"It's now time to roll up our sleeves and begin. We have much to do before 15 March. Team Alpha has been assigned to briefing room A, Team Bravo to briefing room B, and Team Charlie to room C. Captains Perry, Jenkins, and Bellington will each now call out the members assigned to their group."

The roll was called, and the members of each group were introduced to their team leaders and then led to their assigned "war room."

# CHAPTER 11
## TEAM BRAVO

**SAMANTHA REALIZED RIGHT AWAY THAT** her new friend, Odd Bergstrom, had been assigned to Team Alpha. This made sense since Alpha's objective was to locate, track, and destroy the five Borei subs. Odd's expertise would be critical, and he would probably spend most of his time training the subs' sonarmen to recognize the enemy's acoustic signature.

When the Bravo team arrived inside its war room, Samantha counted five men, only one of whom she knew: CDR Jared Townsend of DEVGRU. Once they were seated around the conference table, Captain Jenkins spoke up.

"As you now know, I am Captain Forrest Jenkins, and I have been designated as the lead officer of Team Bravo. Until fifteen minutes ago, I was the chief of staff to COMSUBPAC. I would like to go around the table and have everyone introduce themselves and give his, and her, last duty assignment. Let's start with you, Commander." He looked to his left.

"I am Commander Jared Townsend of DEVGRU. With me is my second in command, Lieutenant Josh Freeman. Josh?"

"Thanks, Jared. As Jared just said, I am the junior officer of the DEVGRU SEAL team assigned for this mission. We will have eleven enlisted SEALs deployed with us on this mission."

The next man spoke up. "Captain Ira Coen. I am the commanding officer of the USS *Hawkbill*."

The officer to his left went next. "I am Lieutenant Commander Fred Boone, executive officer of the *Hawkbill*."

Finally, it was Samantha's turn. "Hi, everyone. I'm Dr. Samantha Stone. I work at the Naval Research Laboratory in Washington, DC. My specialty is determining the environmental effects on submarine systems. Most of my career has been spent in the study of the Arctic Ocean. I have focused on both the sea ice canopy and the seafloor."

Captain Jenkins said, "Thank you, Dr. Stone." He then added, "When I was told that you were assigned to this team, I read your resume. I think it is of importance to the others here to note that you spent two years on the COMSUBPAC staff as the science advisor to Admiral Flaxon."

"That's true, Captain."

"Welcome aboard." Captain Jenkins continued, "The six of us here are Team Bravo. We are responsible for planning and carrying out the mission clearly stated by Admiral Price. Yes, it is a small team. But I assure you, anything we need to be successful will be provided for us. We have about three months of preparation before we leave Pearl on the *Hawkbill* for the Sea of O. We are going to be working very closely with one another during this time, both here and on the *Hawkbill*. For this reason, we'll do away with addressing one another by our military ranks and last names. We are a family now. So, I'll go around the table again, and each of you state the name you would like to go by." After a pause, he said, "I'm Forrest."

He looked to his left, and everyone gave their names: Jared, Josh, Ira, and Fred.

When it was Samantha's turn, she said with a serious look on her face, "You can call me Dr. Stone." The men all looked at her in disbelief. She laughed and said, "Just kidding. You can call me Samantha."

The others chuckled, though Ira Coen twisted his mouth like he tasted something sour.

"Samantha? Not Sam?" Forrest asked curiously.

Samantha looked unusually serious when she replied, "Not Sam. Samantha. Please."

"Alright, well, I would like to start off by giving our planned timetable for the operation," Forrest said. "We have some rather fixed milestones. Once we understand our schedule, we will look at the operational mission from when we depart Pearl right to the completion of our objective. If we do our job correctly before we leave Pearl, we should have identified any problems we could encounter on our mission. Once we have the potential problems ID'd, we will do whatever is necessary to avoid them or to deal with them if they do occur.

"Some of us—Jared and Samantha, for example—only arrived in Pearl late last night and are tired and probably suffering from jet lag. The rest of us are pretty well exhausted from the many hours we've put in to get ready for today. So, I would like to adjourn for today and reconvene tomorrow morning at 0900. Once we start, expect to work about twelve hours a day, seven days a week until we sail. We will work more if we need to. Jared, Josh, I know that you have to greet your SEALs scheduled to arrive from San Diego early this afternoon. For the next three months, we have cars and drivers assigned to shuttle members of all three teams to wherever they need to go. Any questions?"

Ira Coen said, "Forrest, can I have a word with you following this meeting?"

"Sure, Ira."

★★★

"Forrest," Ira began. "We've got a problem. There is no way that I am going to sail on a very important, difficult, and long deployment with an untested, inexperienced woman on board. We have little capacity on board to support a female. Plus, we'll have about 130 horny young men living in very close quarters. More if you count the SEALs. But most importantly, and I can't stress this enough, I don't know how she will act under stressful conditions. There is just no way that this will work."

"I'm sorry, Ira. But this is a done deal. Samantha will be on board when you depart."

"I'm the captain of the boat, and I will not allow it."

"Get over it. If you persist on this, you're going to have to take it up with Admiral Flaxon. He is adamant. If you want, I'll arrange a meeting."

"Forrest, you saw what just happened. We aren't even ten minutes into our very first meeting, and she's cracking jokes. Our mission is a very serious thing, and she's joking around."

"Ira, she was breaking the ice. She was trying to relax us. Don't you see that?"

"Good God," said Ira. "This is serious business. If things get tight in the Sea of O, and they will, she'll probably start telling jokes to lighten us up. Or even worse, she might start crying. How do I handle that? What if she's claustrophobic? What if she panics under stress?"

"Calm down, Ira. From what I've heard about Dr. Stone, she's a pretty cool customer. Besides, she's pretty nice to look at. Or haven't you noticed?"

Ira looked intently at Forrest and said, "Trust me, I've noticed. And that bothers me. I'm sure that the 130-plus men on my boat will notice too. It's a disaster waiting to happen, and we can't afford that. Not on this mission."

"Do you want me to set up the meeting with the admiral?"

"Damn it! Yes, I would."

# CHAPTER 12
## SAMANTHA THE SAILOR

**ON THE WAY BACK TO** Carter House, Samantha broke the ice with Jared. "Your team should be arriving at the Honolulu airport soon. Are you going to meet them?"

"No, Dr. Stone. Josh will greet them at the airport and get them settled in their quarters. The Navy has assigned special quarters for our whole team. Josh and I will live there as well. I'm just going to get our stuff."

"Come on, Jared. I'm Samantha, remember?"

"I'm sorry Dr. St— Uh, I mean, Samantha. Old habits are tough to break. We are trained to use the polite term."

"Well, I answer to either, but I prefer Samantha. But if you slip, I'll understand."

"I'll try my best."

"I've never talked to a real, live Navy SEAL before. I did brief a bunch of you guys in Coronado once, and I answered some questions they had. But it wasn't the same as sitting next to one in a car."

"Well, it's no big deal, Dr. St— Uh, Samantha. I'm no different than you or anybody else."

"Yeah, but I don't wear a Purple Heart on my chest. Plus, you jump out of airplanes, you put yourself in harm's way, you dodge bullets, you climb mountains, you—"

"Samantha," he interrupted. "Some of us have a death wish, or we just find those kinds of things exciting. Like I said, it's no big deal. Besides, I find what you do and what you know very amazing. Just the fact that you, a female, have been selected to be on a military team whose objective is so dangerous and so important to the survival of our country is incredibly unbelievable. I have the utmost respect for you."

She knew her face had to be a bright red. "Well, Jared . . . I, I just don't know what to say, except thank you."

"My pleasure, ma'am."

"Ma'am! Now I'm a granny? I'd rather be called Dr. Stone."

"Sorry, Samantha. I'll try harder."

They soon reached Carter House, and when they separated to go to their rooms, Jared said, "See you tomorrow, Samantha."

"Now that wasn't so hard, was it?" she answered with a smile.

★★★

That afternoon, Ira Coen was ushered into Admiral Flaxon's office. "I hear that you have a problem with Dr. Stone sailing with you on this mission," the admiral stated before Ira had even reached his chair.

"Yes, I do, Admiral. It just won't work. She will be disruptive. She's not military trained. She has no experience on a submarine. She'll cause problems among the men. She'll have no privacy. I could go on and on."

Admiral Flaxon smiled calmly at Coen. "Ira, when this thing is over, you are going to thank me for her."

"But, Admiral—"

"Ira, you are going into an operating area, the Sea of O,

which we know very little about. You are going to encounter all kinds of environmental conditions that will wreak havoc on your ability to operate effectively. You've got sea ice to deal with, all kinds of ambient noise from animals and fishing boats, sea-ice movement and noise, unfamiliar acoustic conditions, unknown water currents, river runoff, weird bottom conditions, and I could go on. Dr. Stone, Samantha, is the best we have with knowledge of the Sea of Okhotsk. Three months ago, we tasked her to write a comprehensive technical report on the environmental conditions of this area. I obtained periodic drafts of her paper. It is remarkably all encompassing and thorough. Brilliant, in fact. Trust me. You will need her on the scene during your mission."

The admiral continued, "She was my science advisor when I was COMSUBPAC. I've sailed with her on a submarine. In every case, she performed her duties in a remarkable way. When her tour at SUBPAC was up, I awarded her the highest medal I was allowed to give a civilian as a rear admiral; the Superior Civilian Service Medal. And trust me, it was well deserved. She is an expert on the Arctic Ocean environment. And she is invaluable because of her knowledge of environmental effects on submarine systems.

"I do admit, she is very attractive, and your officers and crew will notice that right away. But you are the *Hawkbill*'s commanding officer, and I expect you to handle that potential problem. Talk to your men and tell them that you will have zero tolerance for any shenanigans. No hitting on her. No practical jokes. Nothing. Everyone is to treat her as one of the guys and with respect. I assure you that she will dress appropriately. You know that *Hawkbill* contains a one-person guest cabin for situations like this. She will have a room where she can have some privacy."

Ira asked, "Admiral, may I speak candidly?"

"Of course. Go ahead."

"The submarine force has tried to integrate women with men on our submarines, and in most cases it has worked well, especially on the boomers, our ballistic-missile boats. And overall, I support it. But there are instances where there have been problems. I'm sure that you are aware of what happened on the USS *Florida*. A list was developed and passed around the crew that detailed the sexual preferences of the female crew members assigned to that boat. This mission is too important to take that chance."

"Of course I'm aware of that. I was on the panel that evaluated that incident. We relieved the commanding officer of his command because he did not take action in a timely manner. Listen to what I just said. I'm telling you to take action right now, and certainly before you deploy. Can you do that?"

After a pause, Ira said, "Yes, sir. I can do that."

"Look, Ira, you are the commanding officer. Do your job and handle it. It's a done deal. Accept it. That's an order."

Ira could only mumble, "Yes, sir."

★★★

Immediately following the dressing down by Admiral Flaxon, Captain Coen went to the *Hawkbill*. Once on board, he instructed his officer of the deck to tell the crew, both officers and men, to be ready for an announcement to all hands by the captain following the evening meal.

At precisely 2000 hours, Ira began his broadcast throughout the boat.

"This is the captain speaking. As you know, we are beginning our preparation for an extremely important and potentially dangerous mission. I will be providing more detailed information on our preparation schedule tomorrow morning. As you also know, the *Hawkbill* got out of refit in Bremerton just three weeks ago, and the crew assigned to our boat is essentially new, and we have not been together as a team for very long. However, you all have been carefully selected and assigned to *Hawkbill* with the objectives of our first mission in mind. I am proud to say that I consider you the best of the best in our submarine force.

"For this mission, we will be even more crowded because of the addition of a DEVGRU SEAL team's two officers and eleven enlisted. We will also have with us a civilian scientist from the Naval Research Laboratory, Dr. Samantha Stone. Yes, that's right. Dr. Stone is a female. I also want to state that Dr. Stone is an internationally recognized scientist in her field and is absolutely critical to the success of our mission.

"Dr. Stone will be the only female on board for our journey, which could last up to three months. It is absolutely necessary that you make her feel welcome and comfortable for the entire deployment. This means that I do not want to see or hear of any practical jokes on her or even any crude behavior among yourselves. I don't want to hear any off-color remarks. I cannot emphasize this enough. In fact, I will have zero tolerance for any activity of this sort. I hope I've made myself clear on this. Zero tolerance. Tomorrow morning, we will muster all hands on the pier at 0800. At that time, I will introduce you to the SEAL team members and to Dr. Stone."

Before he closed, Captain Coen said, "I would like to see the chief of the boat in my quarters at 2030. That'll be all."

★★★

At 2030, the COB, Master Chief Petty Officer Bryan Boxer, knocked on Captain Coen's cabin door.

"Come in, Master Chief. Have a seat."

"Yes, sir. What can I do for you, Captain?"

"I want to drop something on you to see what you think."

"Yes, sir. What is it?"

"You heard my announcement that we will have Dr. Stone on board for a long mission. What do you think of that?"

"I don't have any problem with that, sir. In fact, it might be good for crew morale."

"Do you think the men will comply with my request?"

"I'm not sure. But I will do everything in my power to see that they do."

"I appreciate that, Bryan." After a pause, Ira cleared his throat and said, "I have another request which you may not be so comfortable with."

"What's that, sir?"

"I know that the Goat Locker is the 'private' domain of the chiefs on board. You have your own mess, lounge, shower, and toilet."

"That's right."

"What if I asked you and the chiefs to give up the Goat Locker for a half hour a day so Dr. Stone can take a private shower?"

Master Chief Boxer thought for a moment, rubbed his chin, then said, "To be honest, I would be honored to support Dr. Stone in this way, and I think the others will feel the same. But I have to ask them."

"Great, Bryan. I understand. Let me know when you know."

"I'll get on it right away, sir."

# CHAPTER 13
# THE CREW MEETS SAMANTHA

**THAT EVENING, SAMANTHA RECEIVED A** call from Ira Coen. "Samantha, can you meet me on *Hawkbill*'s quarter deck tomorrow morning at 0745?"

"Sure. What's going on?"

"I'm having the officers and crew muster on the pier at eight o'clock. I want to introduce you and the SEAL guys to everyone."

"I'll be there. But the meeting starts at nine. Will we get there in time?"

"The little ceremony on the pier won't last long. I'll have some egg-and-sausage sandwiches made for us to eat on the way. We'll be good."

"Okay. I'll see you tomorrow."

Captain Coen greeted Samantha on the quarter deck at 0745. Commander Townsend and Lieutenant Freeman were already there with their incredibly fit-looking SEALs. "Hi, Jared, Josh. Are you guys all settled in?"

Jared responded, "We are, Samantha. Thanks. You?"

"Yeah. I'm good. I finally got a good night's sleep."

Ira spoke to LCDR Fred Boone, *Hawkbill's* XO and a fellow member of Team Bravo, as the crew and officers assembled on the pier.

At 0800, the crew was fully assembled and standing at attention.

Coen began, "At ease, men. As I told you last night, we have a long and dangerous journey ahead of us, and we will have several distinguished guests sailing with us. I want to introduce them so you'll know who they are, and you can make them feel welcome and part of the *Hawkbill* family."

Captain Coen introduced Samantha, Jared, Josh, and the eleven enlisted SEALs. When Coen had finished, he asked the crew to welcome the guests. Everyone seemed to be in awe of the SEALs, but Samantha was overwhelmed by all the men wanting to shake her hand and welcome her.

Finally, after fifteen minutes, Ira had to break up the crowd and free Samantha. "Samantha, come on. We have to go or we'll be late."

"Okay, okay," she said. "I'm coming." As she left, she turned back to the men, smiled, and said, "I'll see you guys later."

★★★

At 0900, all six members of Team Bravo were in the war room. Team leader Captain Forrest Jenkins stood and said, "Okay, let's begin. As I said yesterday, the first order of business is to look at the mission timetable of what we have to do."

He tapped a key on his computer, and a timeline appeared on a screen behind him. Using a laser pointer, he highlighted the last milestone on the graph.

"This is the Russian D-Day, March 16. The day they pull the trigger to release their submarine-launched nuclear missiles, to start their blitzkrieg of Europe, and to take out any other forces they believe pose a threat to them." Just to the left of 16 March was a red *X*. Jenkins pointed to the *X* and said, "This is the fifteenth of March—the culmination of IDES. For us, this is when we destroy their ability to pull that trigger. We will do this by destroying their command-and-control center housed in the SOOF. Our second objective is to locate and destroy the fiber-optic communication cable to the SOOF. We are going to spend a lot of time discussing and practicing just how we'll get this job done.

"The USS *Hawkbill* SSN 999 has been tasked to enter the Sea of O on 28 February, sixteen days before IDES. As part of our planning, we need to identify anything that could happen during those sixteen days that might jeopardize our success."

Forrest turned to the screen once again and said, "The schedule calls for *Hawkbill* to depart Pearl on 15 February." The laser dot hovered on that date. "Ten days later, on 25 February, *Hawkbill* will arrive at the naval base in Yokosuka, Japan, for resupply and for any repairs or equipment calibrations, if necessary. Don't forget, we jump ahead a day when we cross the International Date Line, so it's really a nine-day transit to Yokosuka.

"This will be a clandestine port call. No R&R will be granted. When resupply is completed, *Hawkbill* will covertly depart for the Sea of O. I want to emphasize that the 28 February date is critical because recent intel on the Russian plans call for them to mine the channels between the Kurile Islands and the Sea of O on 1 March. These channels are our only access to Okhotsk.

"So, today is 4 November. What will we be doing between now and 15 February when *Hawkbill* sails? Well, that is up to us here in this room. We need to be sure that all possible scenarios are identified and dealt with. We need to be sure that *Hawkbill* is perfectly groomed and operating at optimum efficiency. That all systems are humming at 100 percent. That the boat's crew is fine-tuned and working perfectly as a team. That the SEALs have everything they need to perform their duties. I and Captain Coen also intend to have significant sea time for drills, systems tests, and emergency procedures. So, you see, we have a lot to do. Any questions?"

The rest of the morning was spent discussing numerous details on several aspects of the mission. At about noon, Forrest announced that it was almost time to break for lunch. He reminded the team to not talk at all about the mission in the cafeteria—or anywhere else, for that matter. He then said to Samantha, "Samantha, you've been pretty quiet this morning. Do you have any thoughts before we break?"

"Right now, I'm in the learning mode. But, yes, I do have a few things to ask. I would rather wait until after lunch, if that's okay with you."

"That's fine. Is there anything else?" he said, surveying the faces around the table.

Samantha half raised her hand and asked, "Is there any chance that we could have Admiral Flaxon attend our meeting sometime this afternoon? The admiral said that he would provide anything we needed. I want to take him up on that."

"I'll ask him," Forrest replied. "I would like to start again at 1330 with Ira giving us a brief on *Hawkbill*—its capabilities, armament, any new stuff that will apply to our mission. Supporting the SEALs, for example. After that, I'll turn the floor over to you, Samantha. Hopefully, the admiral will be able to be here by then."

Samantha nodded in agreement.

"Okay, everyone. Back here by 1330."

# CHAPTER 14
## USS *HAWKBILL*

**ON THE WAY TO THE** cafeteria, Jared asked Samantha, "What do you think so far?"

"I think that we're going to find our schedule pretty tight. But I'm not a military person, so what do I know."

"I have to agree with you on that. We're going to think up a bunch of things that could cause us grief. We'll see."

At the cafeteria, Samantha went to the salad bar, and Jared went to the "meat and potatoes" line. Her line was much shorter, and she got her salad quickly. She didn't recognize anyone in the huge cafeteria, so she sat at a long table by herself. Within minutes, seven or eight members of the *Hawkbill* crew had joined her and struck up conversation. When Jared saw that there were no available seats at her table, he waved and said, "See you at 1:30."

She nodded. The same thing happened to Odd Bergstrom. He walked by and said, "Wait for me this afternoon, and we'll drive back to Carter House together." Again, she nodded.

A few tables away, Ira and Fred Boone watched the happenings at Samantha's table. "It looks like Townsend and Bergstrom were really disappointed," Ira said.

"They sure were."

"Look at that, will you?" Ira said, pointing to Samantha's table. "Those guys are hovering around her like flies on doo-doo."

Fred laughed and said, "They sure are. I've got to say this: that's the best-looking turd I ever laid my eyes on."

"I can't argue with that," Ira said with a smile.

Fred looked at Ira, shook his head and said, "You too, huh?"

★★★

Before the meeting reconvened, Forrest told Samantha that Admiral Flaxon would try to get there by 1600.

"Thanks, Forrest."

Ira Coen went to the head of the table and projected a cutaway image of the *Hawkbill* on the screen. "Gentlemen and Samantha, this is the USS *Hawkbill* SSN 999. She is a significantly modified version of the Virginia-class SSNs. In fact, she is an improved version of the *North Dakota*, probably the most advanced and capable of the Virginia-class subs. When we found out what the Russians were up to last April, we identified a Virginia boat that was under construction and still available for modifications. I was then assigned to be the commanding officer of that boat and briefed into the IDES program.

"In this capacity, I worked with General Dynamics to make numerous upgrades and mods designed to enhance our ability to carry out our mission in the Sea of O. Cost was not an issue. I was told to make this boat, now named the *Hawkbill*, the quietest, most capable submarine in the US Navy.

"In my mind, the most important upgrade we incorporated into *Hawkbill* is the integrated electrical power system, or IEP. With IEP, we have eliminated all the reduction gearing needed to propel the boat. As a result, *Hawkbill* is vastly quieter than any other nuclear submarine. Another advantage of IEP is that the electrical energy produced all goes to a common electrical bus and is immediately available to run other systems throughout the boat. That capability makes the boat extremely efficient.

"I was also told to include state-of-the-art systems to support special warfare operations, especially in shallow water. We will be carrying on our deck the latest SEAL Delivery Vehicle, or SDV, designed to get the SEALs where they need to go without being detected. We also have a large 'lock-in/lock-out' chamber for supporting diver operations.

"One of the major mods significantly increased the operating depth capability. We were very fortunate here because the boat selected was being built using HY-100 steel instead of the normally used HY-80. We deemed that this was critical for our operation.

"As far as armaments are concerned, we have incorporated the Virginia Payload Module, which was planned for the next generation of the Virginia-class subs. This will allow us to use Tomahawk missiles to target land targets, Harpoon missiles to target ships, and, most importantly for us, to carry unmanned underwater vehicles, or UUVs. The UUVs could play an extremely important role in achieving our objective in the Sea of O."

"Our sonar systems are all state of the art and have been meticulously groomed. We also installed the so-called 'chin' sonar, which will give us improved capabilities for eavesdropping, for mapping the bottom, and for detecting mines."

Coen detailed the other Virginia-class capabilities, such as the non-hull-penetrating dual photonic masts that provided digital visual images, as well as thermal infrared images for night viewing. He emphasized the enhanced fly-by-wire system for improved boat handling in shallow water. He also discussed the integrated fiber-optic displays, all located within the control room rather than in separate areas, thereby enhancing communication and tactical decision-making.

Ira talked extensively on the acoustic-quieting features of the sub, from its innovative propulsion system to the isolation of all equipment from the hull. He seemed especially happy about the new anechoic coating technology that would further decrease acoustic leakage and reduce vulnerability to active acoustic detection.

"In summary, I feel that we have the best submarine platform in the world for our use. The crew is the best that we have in the submarine force. All crewmembers have been carefully screened for selection. We departed Bremerton Naval Shipyard a few weeks ago and transited here to Pearl. All systems seem to be operating as they were designed to do. Sub-wise, I think that we are good to go. I'd be happy to answer any questions that you might have."

A few questions were asked by Jared Townsend concerning the model and version of the SDV, the torpedo room where he, Josh, and the other SEALs would be housed, and the lock-in/lock-out chamber. Ira answered the questions to Jared's satisfaction and added that a tour of the *Hawkbill* was scheduled for tomorrow morning so everyone could see all these things and a few other surprises firsthand.

Samantha raised her hand.

"Samantha?"

"Yes, Ira. I have a few questions. You mentioned that *Hawkbill* has two high-frequency active sonars, one in the sail and one in the keel. I'm assuming that these sonars are for determining the depth between the keel and the seafloor—in other words, a fathometer—and the other to measure the distance between the sail and the bottom of the ice. Is that right?"

"That's correct, Samantha. In fact, the upward-looking sonar can also give us an estimate of ice thickness."

She continued, "Are these sonars the same as the BQN-17 secure fathometer and the BQS-15 under-ice sonar?"

"They are essentially the same with some improvements."

"I'm also interested in two other high-frequency systems that you mentioned: the submarine active detection sonar, and the advanced mine detection system. Are these sonars part of the chin system you mentioned? If so, I'd like to look at the engineering specs for all these systems. Do you have these specs on board that I can look at? If not, can we get them?"

"Yes, Samantha, these sonars are part of the chin, and we do have all that information available. Can I ask why you're so interested in all these?"

"From yesterday's brief on our timeline, we enter the Sea of O the day before the Russians mine the entrances to Okhotsk. Well, that's fine. However, once we're in, we have to get out after we destroy the SOOF. Those mines will still be there waiting for us. I'm very much interested in our capability to navigate through a lethal minefield. From what I know, we can only do that using high-frequency active sonars to detect the mines. Several years ago, when I was here at SUBPAC, we did tests here off Pearl to see if we could do that using the BQN-17. We found that we were able to detect the mines, but our ability was limited by environmental conditions. It would be a cruel joke on us if we succeeded in our mission, then bought the farm on our way home."

Ira stared at Samantha for a few seconds. He shook his head, then said, "Well, that looks like scenario number one that we have to consider."

"If no one objects, I'll take the lead on that one," Samantha said firmly.

All the men looked at each other, wide-eyed.

# CHAPTER 15
## UNDERSTANDING THE ENVIRONMENT

**IT WAS LIKE A LIGHT** bulb had been switched on. The mood in the room immediately changed. They now had a problem identified, and one which needed to be solved. In an instant, their respect for Samantha skyrocketed, and her importance to the success of the mission was cemented.

At 1545, Admiral Flaxon walked into the Team Bravo war room. Before anyone stood to attention, the admiral said, "As you were. As you were."

A chorus of "Welcome, Admiral" greeted him.

"Well, how's everything going? Any problems?" he asked. Forrest gave a summary of what had happened that day, including Samantha's concern about encountering sea mines on the return trip.

"Leave it to her to make our jobs tough," he said with a smile of admiration. He continued, "Samantha, Forrest said that you'd like to talk to me. Do you want to do it here or off-line?"

"Here would be better, Admiral. Actually, I think that it would be much better to do this here."

"Good. And please, everyone, when we are in this room, you can call me Roger."

Everyone said, "Yes, sir."

The admiral shook his head, then said, "Go ahead, Samantha. What do you need?"

"Admiral—I mean, Roger—I have a list of things that I believe we will need to successfully carry out our mission. I have a few personal needs, all work related. I need my laptop and a classified safe that's in my NRL office. The files in the safe have documents and flash drives from my previous work. For example, the mine-avoidance tests when you were COMSUBPAC. The submarine Arctic work that we've done over the years. The ICEXs. I also need all the environmental data that I have compiled for my Sea of O study as well as my final draft of the paper I prepared. Can you get me the safe and laptop?"

"Samantha, we anticipated that you would need your 'stuff,' so it's on its way as we speak. I'm told that it will arrive tomorrow morning on a military aircraft. Also, we have several classified office spaces for use by members of the three teams, as needed. We will put your safe and computer in one of these offices for you. What else?"

"Do you have intelligence information on Russian mines? I need to know things like what influences the mines use to detect submarines. Acoustic, magnetic, pressure, seismic. Will one influence activate a mine? Or do they need multiple influences to activate? Are the mines moored in the water column, or are they bottom mines? Stuff like that. Along the same line, I need several dummies of each of their mines that we can use in a test minefield here off Pearl. We need to evaluate our ability to detect these mines and to navigate around them.

"Another thing I need is this. Do we have a relationship with the Japanese such that we can ask them to clandestinely collect deep scattering layer data, or DSL, for us in the vicinity of the Kuril Islands? That area is a very rich fishing ground, and perhaps a fishing vessel can be equipped with the proper nets and transducers to get that data—and do it without attracting the attention of the Russians. I need to know how the DSL changes depth during a twenty-four-hour day cycle as well as monthly. We probably can get the data-collection equipment from the University of Hawaii. I can define the data-collection procedures to the Japanese or to anyone assigned to collect it."

"Good Lord, Samantha, anything else?"

"As a matter of fact, there is. I talked to Commander Jared Townsend here this morning about his experiences and capabilities in Arctic waters. He said that everyone on his team had experience in cold water. I asked him how long he could meaningfully function in very cold water. He gave me a very SEAL-like answer. He said, 'Just tell me what you want done, and we will do it.'"

Samantha looked at Jared and said, "Sorry, Jared." She continued, "The water in the Sea of O in March is going to be colder than anything the SEALs have worked in before. Visibility could be next to zero. I will explain why this is so when I explain the Sea of Okhotsk environment. It will take them much longer than they think to complete a job. Roger, do we have a facility, a deep pool, here on the islands that we can rig to lower the temperature close to freezing? I'm talking 32 to 35 degrees."

"I'll look into it, Samantha."

"On a related issue, I am aware of research being done at MIT which is looking at modifying the standard neoprene wet suits the SEALs wear to perhaps double the amount of time they can work in cold water."

"How does that work?" asked Flaxon.

"Essentially, they replace the normal air pockets of the neoprene wet suit with xenon or radon gas. This kind of works like layers of fat on seals. The animal," she added, glancing at

Jared and Josh. "I would like to get the most recent results of their research and the specs of the chambers that are used to infuse the rare gas into the suits. From what I read, it takes about twenty-four hours to prepare a suit for reuse. Perhaps we would need several chambers; I don't know. Hopefully, once we get the specs, we can build as many as we need for our mission. Size and number would be the crucial information. Space on a submarine is always an issue. Regardless, I think that this capability, if it works, will greatly enhance the ability of our SEALs to accomplish what they must do.

"If you can provide us with the pool facility, and if we can get these modified suits, the SEALs can practice their duties in very cold water. That's it for now, Admiral." Samantha leaned back.

The admiral took a deep breath and said, "Well, you sure are making my job a lot harder. I'll get on your requests right away. Now I'm going to make your job harder."

"What do you mean?" she asked.

"Team Alpha has said that they need some of your time in their group. Already a slew of environmental questions have come up, and they said, 'We need Dr. Stone.' How do you feel about that?"

"Well, if I must, I must."

The admiral said, "Forrest, men, are you okay with that?"

"Not really, Roger. This is our first working day, and . . ." Forrest paused and said, "Well, I don't want to give her a big head or anything, but any length of time she's out of the room will hurt us." The others in the room, including Ira Coen, nodded in agreement.

"I understand," the admiral said, staring directly at Ira with the slightest of smiles. "But it is what it is. So, Samantha, I would like for you to attend Team Alpha's afternoon session tomorrow."

"Yes, sir."

"I'll report back on how I'm progressing on your requests as soon as I get information. Do you have points of contact at the University of Hawaii and MIT? That would help me out."

"I do. I'll text them to you, sir."

# CHAPTER 16
# BACK TO THE CARTER HOUSE

**AFTER THE AFTERNOON SESSION, IRA** asked Samantha to stay a few minutes so they could talk. When they were alone, Ira said, "You were pretty impressive today. You had some great ideas. A lot of insight." She thanked Ira and let out a sigh of relief.

Ira continued, "To be quite honest, I was dead set against you sailing with us on this mission."

"I kind of gathered that by your body language. Hopefully, you're changing your mind."

"Well, I still have a few issues that I'm working on, but there is one thing that I've got to ask you."

"What is it?"

"This trip is going to be long and arduous. We are going to be trapped in a small steel tube, with very little privacy and with nowhere to go to get any. You won't see the light of day for a very long time. Will you be able to handle all that?"

"Ira, I really don't know, because other than five days on a sub, I've never done it before. I'm not claustrophobic, as far as I know. As far as privacy and being the only female on board with

140 men . . ." She paused and then said, "Look, Ira, I'm thirty-five years old, and I'm sure that I can take care of myself. Let me give you a Jared Townsend answer. 'If I'm asked to do it, I will do it.'"

Ira looked directly in her eyes for several seconds. "I have to admit, Samantha, I'm beginning to understand why Flaxon thinks so highly of you. Your insights in our meeting today and your answers to me just now have given me a newfound confidence in you and have assured me that we need you on this mission. I think that I'm really going to enjoy working with you for the next three or four months. Welcome aboard." As Ira said that, he took her hand and squeezed it gently. They smiled broadly at each other as they left the room.

⋆⋆⋆

Odd Bergstrom was waiting patiently for Samantha at the CINCPACFLT headquarters front door. Ira asked a waiting driver to take him to the *Hawkbill* as another driver approached Samantha and Odd to take them to Carter House.

On the way, Odd asked, "How was it today?"

"Pretty good. At first, I felt out of place, but as we talked about our mission, I started to realize that these guys need my help in a lot of areas. What about you?"

"I'm kind of the opposite. The sonarmen on the five submarines know more about underwater acoustics than I do. They're all real pros. And they're all so damn young. I'll be training them in an area that I can't talk about now, but once that's done, I'm not sure what I can offer.

"One thing that did become clear, however, is that they are very much concerned about the Arctic environment. They said several times something like 'Whoever understands the environment the best will win the day.' Most, if not all of them, have experience up north from the ice exercises carried out by the US Navy and its allies, but they're still worried. When environmental questions came up, they asked for you. So, just a heads-up, Admiral Flaxon's going to ask Team Bravo for some of your time."

"Thanks, Odd, but he already asked us. Or I should say, he has 'told' us that I will be detailed to Team Alpha as needed, starting tomorrow."

"Wow, Samantha. They may have to clone you."

"Let's hope not. I'd hate to see two of me walking around."

"I wouldn't mind."

"Now, now, Odd."

When they walked into Carter House, several unfamiliar men were sitting and talking in the large living room. One of the security agents that had welcomed Samantha and Odd the night before approached them and said, "Hi, Dr. Stone, Lieutenant Bergstrom. Let me introduce you to the other gentlemen staying here at Carter House."

The new arrivals were civilian scientists and engineers assigned to Teams Alpha and Charlie. Samantha counted eight in all.

The agent added, "The president, Mr. Bradbury, Mr. Solberg, and General Bishop have all returned home. Admiral Flaxon will stay here at Pearl Harbor where flag officers stay. Commander Townsend and Lieutenant Freeman are staying with the enlisted SEALs."

Looking at the number of newcomers, Odd said, "I was kind of hoping that I'd have you all to myself, Samantha."

"Odd. Be a good boy." Their conversation was interrupted by the cook announcing that dinner was ready. Samantha, Odd, three security agents, the cook, and the eight new guys all ate together.

# CHAPTER 17
## TOUR OF THE *HAWKBILL*

**ONCE IRA WAS BACK ON** board the *Hawkbill* following the afternoon meeting, he immediately summoned Master Chief Boxer.

"Well, Bryan, what did the other chiefs say about Samantha?"

"Skipper, it's what I expected. Not only did they say yes, they said 'hell yes.' In fact, they're wondering if she could eat with us on a regular basis."

"You're kidding me, right?"

"No, sir, I'm not."

"What is it about that woman that makes her so . . . well, accepted?" Ira mused.

"I don't know, Captain. The crew seems to love her. She's all they've talked about all day."

"Could this be a problem for us on our mission? A distraction, maybe?"

"Well, this is just me speaking, and I'm not talking sexual attraction here, but her looks, her smile, her sense of humor, just the way she carries herself all give her an aura that is very charismatic. She's a renowned PhD scientist, but for the fifteen or so minutes on the pier this morning when the men greeted her, it was clear that you could just talk to her about normal, everyday things. She made them laugh. It was fun for them. Some of the guys sat with her this afternoon for lunch, and they haven't stopped talking about her since. It's crazy."

"I saw what happened in the cafeteria. It was fascinating. And you're right; she keeps Team Bravo laughing all day. I mean, we discuss some very serious issues, and she has us all laughing. Bryan, I appreciate your input. You just removed a major bit of concern that I had. But I still expect your support in keeping the men in line about her, especially during the mission."

"Will do, Captain."

✫✫✫

The next morning, the Team Bravo meeting started at 0900 on the *Hawkbill*. Ira and Fred awaited the four team members not currently living on the boat on the quarterdeck. Once assembled, Ira led them through a hatch into the submarine.

Samantha had once spent five days on a submarine, but this time, as she viewed it with the expectation of living in its confines for a month, she realized how cramped the space really was. She did feel a slight sense of claustrophobia. Maybe it was because of her talk with Ira the day before.

They started the tour in the control room and went from there. They inspected the lock-in/lock-out chamber and lingered there for a while as Jared and Josh asked several questions. The torpedo room also took time for the same reason. After all, this would be the SEALs' working and living space.

Samantha was in learning mode and said little. Throughout the tour, she was addressed as Dr. Stone by many of the crew members. When they entered the Goat Locker, or chief's mess, Master Chief Boxer and several others were there waiting to meet the group. The space had been cleaned up significantly, and Ira commented on it. Each area of the tour was manned by one or two crew members ready to answer any questions the guests might have.

The last item on the tour was the swimmer delivery vehicle mounted on the deck.

"Samantha, I've saved the best for last. When you met the men on the pier yesterday, you must have noticed the tarp covering the large vehicle on *Hawkbill*'s deck, just aft of the sail. What's hidden from view is the Pegasus Large Diameter SEAL Delivery System, the LDSDS. Jared, Josh, you both know about Pegasus, but it was shipped to Bremerton and installed when you were in San Diego the week before we departed for Hawaii."

"Yes. And we are dying to see it in person," said Jared.

"Let's go see it then. Access to Pegasus is through the lock-in/lock-out shelter." Ira led them to the shelter, up a ladder, and through a hatch. Once through the hatch, they were in the Pegasus.

"Wow!" said Jared. "This thing is huge." Mounted inside Pegasus was the latest version of the SEAL Delivery Vehicle, the SDV.

Ira described the capabilities of Pegasus: "Pegasus is a dual-mode system and can be operated manned or unmanned. As you can see, it carries the SDV inside. That means that the SEALs can stay dry in the LDSDS until they get close to their objective area, then exit the Pegasus in the SDV, giving you guys more time to do your job in the cold water—a capability that Samantha is so worried about, and rightly so. On our mission, it will allow the *Hawkbill* to stand off from the SOOF at a much greater distance. That's something that I like. Pegasus can travel up to three hundred fifty miles each way on its lithium-ion batteries, and it cruises at eight to ten knots at a depth of three hundred feet. It can attain a speed of twenty knots, but the batteries drain much quicker, and its range is far less. It is large enough to carry up to ten SEALs, and it has a separate UUV mounted on the outside.

"It has fold-down masts with imaging sensors, communications antennas, navigation arrays, and various other eavesdropping equipment. Overall, it can carry a payload of almost two tons, so you guys should have no trouble carrying the explosives, cable location equipment, and your one-man propulsion gear. Very importantly, Samantha, Pegasus is equipped with a covert, multi-beam sonar which can be used to locate mines. This is something we'll have to test in Samantha's minefield.

"I mentioned that Pegasus could be operated as an unmanned vehicle. It's more than that. This is important, so listen up. It can be sent out on an unmanned mission, autonomously. In other words, we can program it to do things without any control from the *Hawkbill* or from people inside it. Yet, we can still control it from the *Hawkbill* if we need to." Ira paused as Jared, Josh, and Samantha regarded him with wide eyes. He then asked, "What do you think?"

Jared said, "This thing is going to make our job so much easier." Josh nodded in agreement.

"Samantha?" Ira prodded.

"Pretty impressive, Ira. But why didn't you tell me about this yesterday?"

"I wanted to surprise you."

Samantha shook her head in disbelief, then said, "Has it been tested yet?"

"Not rigorously."

"Well then, Forrest, it looks like we have a lot of work to do." She turned to Jared and said, "You, Josh, and I need to develop a comprehensive series of tests to put Pegasus through its paces. We have to be sure it can do everything that Ira says it can."

"Let's start as soon as possible," Jared agreed. "But before we do, I want to spend some time with Josh and our men inside this thing to get familiar with its controls, storage spaces, and things like that."

Samantha smiled and turned to Ira. "Boys and their toys. It's like Christmas."

The tour ended at 1100, and a light lunch was served in the officer's wardroom.

During lunch, Samantha was handed a note. She was to report to Team Alpha's war room at 1300, per order of Admiral Flaxon. She passed this information on to Forrest, and he nodded. The note also said that her laptop and her safe had arrived and should be in her office by 1300.

At noon, Samantha asked to be excused so she could locate Team Alpha's war room and check out her computer and safe. On her way out, she got a little turned around and couldn't find the ladder. Four crew members noticed her confusion, and they all guided and helped her up to the exit hatch.

# CHAPTER 18
## SAMANTHA BRIEFS TEAM ALPHA

**AT ABOUT 1250, SAMANTHA ENTERED** Team Alpha's war room and was greeted by Captain Miles Perry, the team leader. "Welcome, Dr. Stone. We're glad you can join us."

"Call me Samantha, please."

"Good. We're on a first-name basis here as well, Samantha."

This war room was quite a bit larger than Team Bravo's. As the team members filed into the room, Samantha realized that the CO and XO from each of the five submarines were part of the group, as were several civilians. In all, she counted eighteen people plus Captain Perry. Samantha was once again the only female in the room.

When all were present, Captain Perry introduced Samantha. She stood and gave a general overview of the expected ice and environmental conditions for their area of interest for the month of March. She discussed how much multi-year and first-year ice they could expect, ice keel depths, open water, acoustic properties, ambient noise, and many more general environmental conditions. This took about an hour.

During the Q and A period that followed, the level of detail increased significantly. They asked for expected acoustic frequency and amplitude ranges caused by ice motion and grinding and ice ridge formation, how long this activity lasted, and specific causes and frequencies of ambient noises caused by seals and other animal sources. They were very interested in acoustic-propagation features such as acoustic-propagation loss, surface ducts, sound channel, and thermocline depths. They asked if acoustic convergence zones would be expected. Would bottom conditions absorb sound energy, or reflect it? Questions of this type were fired at Samantha for almost two hours. She answered a great deal of the questions immediately, but at many points she had to say, "I will look that up and get back to you."

By 1600, the questions stopped. Captain Perry thanked her several times, as did others in the room. Captain Perry then escorted her to the Team Bravo war room and thanked her again.

When she joined Team Bravo, she dropped into her seat and said, "God, those guys wore me out. You are a piece of cake compared to them. I'm glad to be back here."

They all laughed, and Fred Boone said, "We're glad to have you back."

Forrest brought her up to speed on what they had spent the afternoon discussing: planned armaments on *Hawkbill*. She immediately asked, "Will we be carrying any CAPTOR mines?"

Ira piped up. "Mines? I hate mines."

Samantha said, "I know submariners don't like mines. But I would like to deploy on this mission with at least two CAPTORs— more, if possible."

"You want me to replace perfectly good torpedoes with CAPTOR mines? Why?" Ira asked.

"Last night, I was going over our mission in my head. There's a very good chance that we will have to deal with Russian submarines, correct?"

Several yesses came from the others.

"I can certainly visualize a tactic where we might lure their submarine into a minefield of our own. Is that a stupid idea on my part?"

There was a prolonged silence in the room. Finally, Fred said, "No. As far as I'm concerned, it is not." He looked at Ira nervously.

"Well then, let's give this CAPTOR thing some thought. After all, I did miss most of this meeting, and I just come barging in here and butt in with something crazy like this."

Ira grinned at her with admiration.

Forrest said, "Well, look. That's a surprise. But it's almost time to break for the evening. Tomorrow, I'd like to spend the day on SEAL activities and needs. Think about this CAPTOR thing tonight, and we'll take it on first thing tomorrow. Ira, I'd also like from you a planned schedule of your *Hawkbill*'s at-sea days. I know that you want to get busy with drills, systems tests, emergency simulations, crew training, and things like that. Jared, Josh, I'd like the same from you on SEAL team training needs. Okay, people, are we good to adjourn for today?"

All responded, "Yes, sir."

Before anyone pushed away from the table to leave, Forrest's cell phone rang. He answered, then said, "Yes, sir. I'll tell her."

When he ended the call, Samantha said, "Well, since I'm the only 'her' here, what do you need to tell me, Forrest?"

"That was Admiral Flaxon. He has some results on your requests. He wants to see you as soon as we break up here."

"I guess that's now," she said.

"I'll escort you to his office."

Ira stood with them and said, "I'll take her there, Forrest."

# CHAPTER 19
## ADMIRAL FLAXON REPORTS BACK TO SAMANTHA

**SAMANTHA ENTERED ADMIRAL FLAXON'S OFFICE** anteroom and was greeted by a yeoman.

"Dr. Stone?"

"Yes."

"The admiral is waiting for you. Let me tell him you're here."

Flaxon opened the door to his office himself and invited Samantha in.

"Have a seat on the couch, Samantha. Glad you made it so quickly."

"Thank you, Admiral. Captain Jenkins told me that you had some news on the requests I made yesterday."

"Yes, I do. I have good news, bad news, and some in the middle. Which do you want first?"

"The good news."

"Okay. I called Dr. Wyatt Hopkins at the University of Hawaii like you recommended. I told him what you wanted with regard to collecting deep scattering layer data in the northern Sea of Japan. He asked me why I was interested in the DSL. Of course,

I didn't tell him why, but I did tell him that you had made the request. When I mentioned your name, he became much more agreeable. He said that the U of H will make available the nets and transducers you requested for our use. Have you worked with Dr. Hopkins before?"

"I met him at a symposium held at U of H several years ago when I was working for you at SUBPAC. He's a pretty nice guy. Very accommodating." Samantha continued, "What about the possibility of having a disguised Japanese fishing boat collect the DSL data for us?"

"I asked Harlan Bradbury that very question, and within an hour, he called me back and confirmed that the CIA has a 'specially configured' fishing boat used for eavesdropping on Russian comms in the northern Sea of Japan. He said that we can install the necessary winch and transducer and train one of his Japanese crewmen to collect the data for us."

"Great. Any more good news?"

"Yes. I contacted the Naval Surface Warfare Center in Panama City, Florida. They have an expert on Russian sea mines who is available to fly out to brief us on the engineering specs and uses. She'll be here next Monday."

"Does NSWC have any dummy mines we can use for setting up a test minefield?"

"They do, but not enough, I'm afraid."

"Can we duplicate some in the near term?"

"I'll look into it, Samantha. We should be able to do that. I also asked NSWC to see if they could locate some for us." The admiral paused. "What do you mean in the near term?"

"I haven't thought that out yet, Admiral. But we must get the mines in our possession, set up a minefield in our test range, and run several tests with the *Hawkbill*. We'll probably make some adjustments in our tactics and then run the tests again. I just don't want to run out of time."

"I understand. So, 'in the near term' means ASAP."

"I guess so. Along the same lines, Admiral, I'd like to test the capabilities of Pegasus to detect mines with its high-frequency sonar."

The admiral asked, "Do you think you would use Pegasus in that capacity?"

"It's possible, sir."

The admiral shifted topics and said, "The problem I've run into is locating a swimming pool that we can cool down enough to simulate very cold working conditions for the SEALs. I've had a couple of my men take this one on. They told me early this afternoon that they have struck out. We have a few large, deep pools available, but none that we can cool down. One of my guys suggested using a lot of ice in the pool."

"That would be a plan B that probably won't work for a variety of reasons," Samantha said. "We need control over the temperatures so we can quantify the effects on the SEALs at different temperatures."

"Scientists. They always complicate things," the admiral said with a grin.

Samantha ignored the remark and said, "I have another thought on this which I should have mentioned yesterday. The Arctic Submarine Laboratory in San Diego has a cryogenic pool facility which they use for testing icing on submarine hulls, masts, and sail planes, things like that." She continued, "I'm sorry, but I'm not as familiar with this facility as I should be. From memory, it seems to me that this facility is not large enough for our needs."

"Do you have a contact I can call?" asked the admiral.

"Not really. The one guy I've worked with retired about a month ago."

"I'll see what I can find out. One of the officers on the SUBPAC staff has had recent dealings with the Arctic Submarine Lab. I'll have him call."

"What about the rare gas–infused wet suits? Anything on that?"

"I talked to your Dr. Ryan at MIT late this morning. They have not worked on this project for almost a year—funding cuts, I gather—but he'll mail the project files and reports ASAP. He said he would include the infusion-chamber specifications. He was very positive on the success of the project before it was put on hold."

Samantha asked, "Can they also ship to us the actual infusion chamber they used? If it still exists. If we have one in our hands, we can try to improve its capabilities and reduce its size."

"Good thoughts. I'll look into that. So, what do you think?" he asked.

"Not bad. It's a good start."

"Glad to help. I'll keep working on these things, and I'll keep you informed." He added, "It's great working on things like this instead of shuffling papers around and having meetings with Scott and Price."

The admiral looked at Samantha for a few seconds. He then changed the subject and asked, "How are you and Ira getting along?"

"Well, at first, I got the feeling that he didn't like me much. Just by his body language and not by anything he said. But I feel like that has turned around." She paused. "Why do you ask?"

"Let me tell you a few things about Ira Coen, and I think you'll understand. He graduated at the very top of his class at the Naval Academy. He wanted to become a naval aviator, but I saw the great potential he offered to the submarine force, so I asked him to consider volunteering for nuclear submarine service. He did, much to my delight. Again, he was at the top of every academic course he was assigned.

"He's actually a genius. He was considered a child prodigy. I've taken him under my wing and fostered his career whenever I could. He is on the fast track for becoming a flag officer. He has been the commanding officer of three very difficult covert submarine operations and has performed perfectly on all of them. He is a very professional, no-nonsense guy, and he never puts himself into situations that could jeopardize the success of his mission. To be honest with you, Samantha, he expressed very strong arguments against you being included on the Sea of O mission."

"So I've been told. Why is that?"

"Females have been serving on submarines for many years now, but it isn't always hunky dory. And that's where Ira is coming from. He does not want anyone, man or woman, on his boat that could cause this mission to fail. But by far his most important concern is that you are an unknown to him. To Ira, you have not been combat tested.

"To show you how careful he is, at his request, we—that is, he and I and several other senior submariners—handpicked the entire crew of *Hawkbill* for this mission. There is not one inexperienced crewmember, chief, or officer assigned to *Hawkbill*. All have served on at least one covert mission or deployment in the Arctic. The DEVGRU SEAL team was selected in the same way. This is why CDR Townsend is the SEAL team leader. Ira and I insisted."

Samantha interjected, "Didn't Ira and the selection group pick me in the same way?"

"No. You were my personal choice. In fact, Ira didn't know until a few days ago."

She frowned, worried about the implications of her presence. "Maybe I should step down, Roger. I don't want to cause any trouble for Ira and put the mission in jeopardy."

"That's not an option, Samantha. We need you. The country needs you." And after a pause he said, "Ira needs you. That's why the president personally asked you to volunteer for this mission."

Samantha gazed over Flaxon's shoulder, deep in thought.

The admiral eventually said, "I'm going to tell you a few more things to keep in mind regarding Ira. It might make it easier for you. He is blunt, a man of few words, and he is demanding, because he knows what he wants. And he is defensive whenever he's questioned or when he feels that he's being criticized. In other words, he always feels that he's right. He is aloof, a loner, and he does not show affection easily. Because of these attributes, he is not the most popular guy around. I'm not telling you all this as criticism of him. These are actually all good qualities for the commanding officer of a nuclear submarine, especially an attack sub. It's one of the most difficult, demanding jobs in the world. The responsibility on his shoulders is enormous." Flaxon looked at Samantha intently.

She finally said, "Thanks, Admiral. I'll keep all this in mind."

"You mentioned that you feel his attitude towards you is changing. How so?"

"We had a face-to-face yesterday after our Team Bravo meeting. We discussed his fears about me. When we were through, he said, 'Welcome aboard,' smiled at me, and took my hand in his."

"What?" the admiral exclaimed. "Ira did that? Who initiated the holding of hands?"

"He did, sir. And he used those exact words: 'Welcome aboard.' Those words exactly."

The admiral shook his head and said, "That is so unlike Ira Coen. He rarely shows affection. What have you done to him, Samantha?"

Samantha hesitated, then said, "I don't know what you mean, sir."

★★★

That night at Carter House after dinner, Odd said, "God, Samantha, you were amazing this afternoon. How do you remember all that stuff without notes? I do similar work in the Barents Sea off Norway, but I have to refer to my notes."

"Well, Odd, I've been doing this stuff for years. After a while, some of it starts to sink in."

"After you left today, there were a lot of comments on how valuable your information was. They were really impressed," Odd added.

"I appreciate your kind words, Odd. In fact, a few of the guys from Team Alpha came up to me before dinner and said as much. It's very flattering." Samantha yawned and said, "I hate to be a party pooper, but I am exhausted. I have to get some sleep. Tomorrow's going to be a busy day, and we're going to be discussing many things that I know little or nothing about."

Odd nodded. "I know what you mean. Me too."

# CHAPTER 20
## MORE TESTS ARE NEEDED

**THE NEXT MORNING, TEAM BRAVO** convened in their war room at 0900. Forrest began, "I know the SEALs are anxious to play with the Pegasus, the SDV, and the other toys they'll be using on our mission. So, I propose that we postpone discussing the SEAL responsibilities until tomorrow morning. Ira, do you have a *Hawkbill* schedule drawn up?"

"I've got a proposed one, Forrest. Basically, it amounts to us sailing about every other day with a few two-dayers thrown in. I want to drive the crew hard to whip them into shape."

Samantha looked at the schedule Ira projected on the screen. "Ira, you're waiting almost two months before we do the minefield transit tests. I think that may be too long a wait. Also, you only have one day set aside for the test. We might need two days. I would also like to set aside two more days to run the test a second time, perhaps about a week later."

"Why is that, Samantha?"

"We'll probably come up with some modified sonar procedures and tactical improvements after the first test. We'll need to re-test then."

"That makes sense. I'll make the changes." He added, "When do you think you'll have the test minefield ready for us to use?"

"I'm not sure, Ira. I'm working with Flaxon on that."

"Can you give us an update on what's going on with you and the admiral?" Forrest asked.

"I'd be glad to, Forrest, but I have a few more questions for Ira on his proposed schedule."

Ira nodded. "Fire away. I'm all ears."

"Ira, how proficient are you with deploying CAPTOR mines? Have you or your crew ever done it before?"

"Not during an actual operation, but I have run practice drills before on other boats and with other crews. The procedure is basically the same as launching a heavy-weight Mk 48 ADCAP torpedo. The main difference is in determining fire-control information and mooring depths to program into the mines," he replied.

"I think that we should get a couple of dummy CAPTORs and practice launching them on one of your practice days. Things like desired mooring depths and influence settings could all cause confusion and uncertainty on the mission."

"I agree. That should be no problem."

"One last thing," she said. "I think we should allot a significant amount of time to practicing the launch and recovery of the Pegasus."

Ira pointed to several days earmarked with the word *SEALs*. "I've got a good deal of time set aside to practice their ops."

"Sorry, Ira. I missed that." She continued, "One thing that I would like to practice is using that 'thing' you surprised me with, the Pegasus, in the autonomous mode. Do we know how to program it? Do we know how to operate it remotely from *Hawkbill*?"

"We've got a ton of literature on Pegasus," Ira said. "It should answer our questions."

"Hopefully. But I get a little antsy about relying on manuals.

Would it be possible to have a company rep come out to help us learn how to program it and still maintain our strict secrecy requirements?"

Ira pondered the question. "Let's hold off on that for a week or so and see how it goes with Jared and Josh. Meanwhile, we can contact the manufacturer and have a guy at the ready to come here if needed. What do you think?"

"That should work," she said. "But let's not forget about this."

"Jared," Forrest said, "what do you guys think of all this from the SEALs' perspective?"

Jared replied, "Samantha makes a lot of sense. We need to drive Pegasus hard. We especially need to be able to quickly re-dock the 'thing'"—he smiled at Samantha—"to the *Hawkbill*'s deck after use." He quickly added, "We may be in a situation where we have to re-dock under very stressful circumstances."

"Thanks, Jared. You and Josh can be excused to go to *Hawkbill*. Samantha, can you give the rest of us a report on what Flaxon is trying to do?"

"Sure."

Samantha gave an overview of her discussion with Flaxon and said that she would take the lead on the mines, minefield test area, DSL data collection, and the modified wet suits. But if the Arctic Submarine Lab's cryogenic pool facility request didn't bear fruit, she was not sure what to do. "Does anyone have any ideas?"

"There may not be a suitable facility here in Hawaii, but what about somewhere else in the US?" Fred offered.

"That's a thought," said Ira. "Could we assign someone on the CINCPAC or SUBPAC staffs to look into it for us?"

Forrest said, "Samantha, could you ask Flaxon to assign someone?"

"I don't know, Forrest. He seems very responsive to my requests, but I don't want to wear out my welcome. I think that I'm going to ask him for a lot more before this is over."

"Tell you what. I haven't been replaced yet, so I'm kind of still the COMSUBPAC chief of staff. I'll task a couple of junior officers to look into this. But we should definitely tell Flaxon and Admiral Scott what we're doing."

"Good idea," said Ira. "We don't want to get cross-threaded with the brass."

"If we strike out there," said Samantha, "what if we just build one here? We've been told cost is not an issue. My question is, could we build one in time?"

Forrest replied, "I'll have my junior officers add that to the list. We can check with the Corps of Engineers and with the commercial pool companies here in Hawaii."

"Let's get busy on this right now," Fred said, tapping the table emphatically.

Calls were made to Admirals Flaxon and Scott for approval. Forrest then tasked two lieutenants to investigate the pool options. The rest of the morning was spent studying and adjusting Ira's *Hawkbill* schedule as well as adding more detail concerning exercises with Pegasus on the sub's at-sea days.

At lunch, Odd grabbed Samantha as soon as she exited the salad bar line and sat with her at a four-person table. Soon thereafter, members of the *Hawkbill* moved other tables up to join them, and Odd couldn't get a word in edgewise.

During the afternoon meeting, Jared and Josh's excitement about Pegasus and the SDV was catching, and soon all of Team Bravo was just as excited. But Samantha, in her inimitable way, brought everyone back down to earth.

"Before we get too carried away, we need to test it and test it severely. We don't want to be out there on our mission and be trying to figure out how to use it or find out it can't do what we thought it could do." She continued, "I'm not sure what Flaxon intends for me tomorrow when it comes to Teams Alpha and Charlie, but I suggest we start preparing test plans for Pegasus and all the other SEAL equipment. Hopefully, we'll get some results soon on our pool problem. And don't forget, we have an expert on Russian mines visiting us on Monday."

# CHAPTER 21
## THE SEA OF OKHOTSK

**"I KNOW YOU GUYS ARE** really excited that it's time to learn about the Sea of Okhotsk. You've been waiting with bated breaths for this to happen. I'm happy to announce that your wait is over."

"Come on, Samantha. Get the thing going. We can't wait all day," said Jared with a smile.

"Alright, alright. Here we go. As you all probably know by now, we are going into the Sea of Okhotsk on this mission. What do we know about it with respect to the environment? Well, quite frankly, not a heck of a lot. I do know that it is a complicated environment that will affect how our submarine systems perform and what tactics we will use. It's going to be very difficult for us. That's the bad news.

"The good news is that it will be difficult for the bad guys as well. On our mission, we are the hunted, and they are trying to find and kill us. So, this difficult environment will be working in our favor. That fact is what I'm focusing on. How can we use the environment to our advantage to avoid being detected by them? Ira, Fred, I'm counting on both you and your sonar techs to learn as you go. I'll be there to help you if I can. By that I mean I may be able to explain what you're seeing on your displays as a function of the environment.

"Let me give you some characteristics of the Sea of O for the March timeframe, and I'll explain how we can take advantage of some of these things."

Samantha projected an image of the Okhotsk and its surrounding geography on the screen. "I know you're all familiar with the geography of the Sea of O. Outside of the Japanese island of Hokkaido, and a few islands disputed with the Japanese, the sea is encompassed by Russian territory. They do claim it as a territorial sea. This is why they can mine it and enforce blockades."

Samantha flashed a second image on the screen. "This is a NASA satellite image for March of last year. You can see that it's mostly covered by ice. The only ice-free area is in the southeast and along the Kuril island chain, due to the incursion of warm water from the Pacific.

"A major factor here is that the Amur River is dumping huge quantities of fresh water into the Sea of O. This fresh water freezes rather quickly and is carried into the Okhotsk by the prevailing currents. As a result, we will have almost complete ice coverage over the SOOF. What does this mean for us? For one thing, the SEALs will be far less detectable around the SOOF. For another, the surface ASW ships will be restricted to the south and southeastern part of the sea. The bad news is the Russian surface forces will be concentrated within a smaller area—the ice-free area. That could cause a problem for us when we arrive, and especially when we're leaving.

"The tidal currents are another major factor, especially near shore. Tidal ranges of up to forty feet have been observed in some areas, and tidal currents of up to four knots are common. All this can and will impact our navigation and stability. I wouldn't be surprised if these tides and currents cause significant internal waves, which could be a significant nuisance for the SEALs. Most of these problems will be more significant close to the coast where the SOOF is located. In addition, these strong currents could roil up the bottom and give the SEALs little or no visibility.

"One of the biggest factors to consider is the ambient noise. This area is a prolific breeding ground and general habitat for a tremendous amount of wildlife. It's going to be one of the noisiest areas you have ever operated in. There's good news and bad news in this as well. It will be just as difficult for them to find us as it will be for us to find them. Again, hopefully, we can learn as we go and reduce the effects of the noise on our detection capability.

"Acoustic conditions. What about them? I mentioned the Amur River. This river forms a natural boundary between China and Russian Siberia. It causes a well-mixed layer of low-salinity water along the Russian coast and extending seaward for quite a distance. This mixed condition causes a fairly deep sound channel which we want to avoid, but we don't want to get that close to shore anyway. It may be a problem for the SEALs around the SOOF. The question is how far it extends from the coast. We don't know this now, so let's just be aware of it. The strongest thermocline will be in the southeast where the warm Pacific Ocean water enters. We can use the steep thermal gradient to our advantage by staying just below it to avoid detection by the surface ASW frigates, if we encounter them.

"Bottom conditions: Historically, I have a good idea of what the bottom will be like. It will have a thin layer of silt covering shells and volcanic material. This will cause scattering of high-frequency sonars and make mine detection more difficult. But the good news is that if they are using high-frequency sonars to detect our SEALs, they won't be very effective.

"As I mentioned, all this is based on historical information. From the intel reports we got initially, the Russians were probably dumping many, many metric tons of dirt, rocks, and God knows what else into the ocean in their facility-construction program. The Sea of O would be an ideal place to do this undetected. And don't forget, the SOOF itself was constructed here and is partially buried in the bottom. What did they do with that waste? What I'm trying to say is that I'm not sure what we'll find until we get there. Jared and Josh's boys will have to play it by ear, especially in locating the bottom mines. They could be buried under a layer of 'ploof.'"

"Ploof? What's ploof?" asked Fred.

"I'm not sure if it's a recognized geological term, but I've always used the word to describe very watery sediments. Even more viscous than quicksand. It looks like a solid bottom until you step on it, and down you go. If we do have a ploof on the bottom, we won't see the mines—or the communications cable, for that matter. We'll need to detect them acoustically. I would suggest dropping a sphere or some such target into the ploof and seeing if we can detect it with our sonar on the Pegasus. I suspect we'll be able to see right through it.

"The last topic I want to cover today is bathymetry. We have very little information on topography of the sea floor in this area. We have a few bathymetry lines collected by our SSNs when we were tapping their communications cables, but not much else. The Kuril Islands are the remnants of tectonic activity a long, long time ago. The Sea of Okhotsk was formed by Ice-Age glacial activity. I suspect that it was fairly well scoured out by glaciers, but the key word is *suspect*. I don't really know. The average depth is about twenty-eight hundred feet. But who knows if we'll encounter any subsurface mountains or not. Let's just be aware of this possibility and continually monitor the depth under our hull.

"That's all I have for now. I will raise other environmental issues as they occur to me. Also, if you have any questions, just ask me. If I can't answer them right away, I'll do some research and get back to you.

"One other thing. I have a copy of my paper on the Sea of O. I would like to have copies made and given to the officers and crew of the *Hawkbill*. Ira, I suggest that you make it required reading for everyone on board. If they have any questions, I would be glad to answer them. That's it, guys. Any questions?"

When no questions were put forward, Forrest said, "That's great, Samantha. I really appreciate your input here."

"You've sure given us something to think about," Ira said. "Especially in using the environment to avoid detection. That is, as you said, my top priority. I will certainly see that my crew reads your paper. Great job. Thank you."

Forrest closed the meeting by asking everyone to brainstorm a Pegasus test plan so they could get that important part of the mission taken care of.

Before Forrest officially adjourned the meeting, Ira said, "Will we be getting an intelligence update?"

"I'll check with Flaxon and Price. I think all three teams should get a weekly intel brief, if not more often," Forrest replied.

As they left the room, Ira stopped Samantha. "Can I ask you something?"

"Sure, Ira. Have I done something wrong?"

"No. No, just the opposite. I want to get to know you a little better—not just as Dr. Stone or someone I can call Samantha when we're in this room."

"That would be nice, Ira. What do you propose?"

Ira hesitated, not sure of himself. "Would you like to join me for dinner at the Officer's Club tonight?"

"Why, I would be delighted to join you for dinner, Captain Ira Coen."

"Great. I'll get a car at *Hawkbill* and pick you up at Carter House at eight."

# CHAPTER 22
## DINNER AT THE O CLUB

**AT EIGHT O'CLOCK, IRA TOLD** the Secret Service guard at the front door that he was there to pick up Dr. Stone. "Wait here, sir, and I'll let her know you've arrived." A few minutes later, the agent escorted Samantha out to the front porch. Samantha thanked him and turned to Ira.

"Boy, Ira, you wash up good. Look at you."

"Come on, Samantha. You're embarrassing me."

"Sorry. I'll try to be a little more business-like."

"No, you're okay. I'm just not used to this sort of thing."

"What sort of thing?"

"Come on, give me a break."

Samantha giggled as Ira opened the car door for her. When they arrived at the O Club, he hurried to open Samantha's door before the driver could.

"Wow. Until a week or so ago, I can't remember the last time anyone opened a car door for me. The Secret Service agents and the drivers have been doing it, but it still seems strange. Thanks, Ira."

They were escorted to a nice two-person table. When they were seated, Samantha said, "This is really nice. It sure beats eating at Carter House with Odd, three agents, some guys I hardly know, and a cook."

Ira smiled, overly pleased to hear this.

They ordered a glass of wine and enjoyed a few sips without saying anything. Finally, Ira said, "Speaking of Carter House and Odd, it seems like the two of you are hitting it off pretty well. You're with him a lot when we're away from the war room. Are you two an item?"

"Come on, Ira. I'm thirty-five, and Odd is still very young. He's a really nice guy, but . . . Why do you ask?"

"Just wondering is all."

After they placed their order, Samantha asked, "What is it you want to know about me?"

"I dunno. Things like where were you born? Brothers? Sisters? Where did you go to school? Ever been married?

Samantha smiled at the last question and said, "What makes you think that I'm not married now?"

"Well, I noticed that you aren't wearing a wedding ring."

"You noticed." Samantha smiled and shook her head. "You are very observant for a man." She continued, "I was born in a little town in Maine. Jonesport, Maine. Jonesport is right on the coast, I love the ocean, and I always wanted to be an oceanographer. After high school, I went to Oregon State University and got a BSc in physics. I stayed at OSU and earned my master's and PhD in physical oceanography. I got a job right out of school at the Naval Research Lab. Been there ever since."

"Brothers? Sisters?" Ira asked.

"Only child. That's right. I was a spoiled brat. Got my way with everything."

"Married?"

"Boy, you are getting personal."

"Just curious."

"No. I've never been married."

"Why is that? Surely guys have made moves on you."

"There have been a few. I've actually been engaged twice. But when I asked myself if I wanted to spend the rest of my life with that man, I could not honestly say yes, so I broke off the engagements."

At that time, their main course was served. They ate in companionable silence besides a few comments on the quality of the food. When they were through, Samantha said, "You?"

"What do you mean?"

"Look. I bared my soul to you; now it's your turn. Come on. Open up."

Ira cleared his throat and considered his answer for a few moments. "My life has actually been quite boring."

"I'll be the judge of that. Being the commanding officer of a nuclear submarine can't be boring."

"Well, okay. I graduated from high school at an early age. I was only sixteen. I applied to Rensselaer Polytechnic Institute and graduated with an engineering degree at the age of twenty. After I graduated, I knocked around for six months or so, and I was bored to death. I had always wanted to be an airline pilot, so I applied to the Naval Academy and was accepted. I was hoping to become a naval aviator and then a commercial airline pilot when I left the Navy. When I graduated from the academy, I was about to apply for flight school when Admiral Flaxon, who was a commander at the time and a professor at the Academy, talked me into applying to nuclear submarine school. He can be quite persuasive, you know. Well, I fell in love with submarines, and here I am."

Samantha looking pointedly at Ira. She finally said, "And?"

"And what?"

"You've bored me with your education. What about your sex life? How many times have you been married? Any kids? You know, your sex life."

Ira blushed visibly. He cleared his throat, composed himself, and said, "Never been married. No kids. I guess I'm married to the submarine force."

"Are you gay?"

Ira could only look at her blankly for several seconds and say, "No."

She smiled and said, "Well, that's a relief."

"Samantha, let's change the subject if you don't mind."

"Okay, but before we do, I have one more question. How old are you?"

"I'm thirty-eight."

"Perfect," Samantha mumbled under her breath.

"What was that?" Ira asked. "What was that?" he repeated when she innocently blinked at him.

"It's nothing. You wanted to change the subject. Go for it."

He said, "You intrigue me. The way you've come into our team meetings and without hesitation gotten directly to the point about potential problems has amazed me. Essentially, you are doing my job for me. You're not only foreseeing potential problems, you're coming up with plans of attack, and most importantly, you are taking responsibility for what has to be done.

"Also, the way people gravitate to you has me in awe. I've never seen anything like that before. You keep us in stitches by cracking one joke after another. You tease us all mercilessly. I have to be honest with you: As I told you yesterday, because of your lack of military experience, I did not want you to be on my sub during this mission. Now I can't imagine going on the mission without you."

"God, Ira. I don't know what to say. You have completely disarmed me. I'm actually at a loss for words."

For the second time, Ira reached over and took Samantha's hands in his. They had their second glass of wine and looked at one another in silence.

At Carter House, Ira walked Samantha up the stairs to the agent guarding the front door. Ira said to him, "Be sure she's safe."

"Yes, sir. Will do."

# CHAPTER 23
## THE SEALS' MISSION

**TEAM BRAVO CONVENED AT THE** usual 0900. The main topics of discussion were the SEAL missions and how they would accomplish their objectives. Josh Freeman led on the subject of locating and destroying the main communications fiber-optic cable to the SOOF.

Not much intel was available as to the cable's location. The engineering specifications only showed it leading from the shoreline toward the facility. Locating the cable could be a very time-consuming operation. Samantha suggested that by determining the location of the land repeater station the cable came from, they could make a best guess as to which side of the SOOF the cable entered. Then they could concentrate the search within a smaller area.

This seemed pretty iffy to the others, but it was worth considering. All agreed to a request for additional intel on the cable location.

Jared Townsend took over the discussion on destroying the SOOF itself. He projected several schematics of the structure on the screen.

"Essentially the SOOF is a box within a box. The inner box is a rectangular building with three-foot-thick outer walls made of rebar-reinforced concrete. This inner box, of course, is what we must destroy. Surrounding this box is an enclosure wall that is also three-foot-thick reinforced concrete. There is a two-foot space between the walls that is filled with seawater. So, the problem is that we must destroy the outer wall before we can destroy the main building. From our intel, we know where the central comms controls are located and which wall's destruction will be the most effective in exposing what we need to eliminate in the main building."

Jared pointed to the west-facing outer wall. "Engineering studies have been made to determine where and how many shaped charges should be placed. That will be our job. Placing the charges at the right locations."

"What then?" asked Samantha. "The outer wall is destroyed. What about the SOOF?"

Ira stood and said, "With the outer wall destroyed, two Mk 48 torpedoes will strike the inner wall two minutes after detonation of the shaped charges. This will be followed two minutes later with two more torpedoes. The warheads of all these torpedoes will be shaped to focus the explosive energy inward, hopefully maximizing the damage. We need to take out the computers and power of the building. These are located fairly close to the west wall."

"Why the two-minute delay? Won't this give the Ruskies time to issue a new D-Day launch order?" Samantha asked.

"We don't think they can react that fast. We want to be sure that any large, solid debris from the outer wall has fallen away. We wouldn't want our torpedoes to strike a large chunk of concrete and detonate prematurely."

Samantha addressed her next question to Jared and Josh.

"How precisely do the explosive charges have to be placed on the wall to achieve the desired results?"

"We've been told within two to three feet."

"How many do you have to attach?"

"Fifteen. I have a slide showing where, if you want to see it."

"No, that's not necessary. But I would like to know how you're going to determine where you place the fifteen charges and get them within the two or three-foot radius you need."

"For stealth reasons, we have to go the old-fashioned way of using a line and a tape measure."

"How long will it take to do all this?"

"We've been practicing on a wall built for this purpose at Coronado. It will take three to four days to mark the location spots and one day to attach the charges."

"I know that the water off San Diego is cold, but it's not near freezing. And are there any water currents where your practice wall is?"

"No, ma'am."

"I have a feeling it may take a little longer than we anticipate. As I said yesterday, tidal currents will probably lower visibility and make it difficult for you to maintain swimmer stability. How big is this sucker, anyway? I don't see any dimensions on the schematic."

"The wall is one hundred eighty feet wide and fifty-five feet tall from the bottom. The water depth is about sixty feet, depending on the tide. The top of the wall is about five feet below the water surface, also depending on the tides. Of course, we have a layer of ice there as well."

"Do we know how deep into the bottom it goes?"

"The specs aren't clear on that, Samantha, but it looks like ten to fifteen feet."

"You say that you've been practicing on a wall off Coronado. How comfortable are you with doing the job?"

"We're confident. All the guys have specific tasks, and they work well as a team."

"As I just said, your visibility around the SOOF may be next to zero. Have you practiced with masks on?"

"No, ma'am."

"Forrest, do we have time to build a wall here off Hawaii for these guys to practice on?"

★★★

The discussion of the SEALs' mission spilled into the afternoon, mostly dealing with their vulnerability to detection. During the meeting, Forrest called Admiral Flaxon and expressed the need for additional information on cable location, nearest cable landing station, and any anti-SEAL countermeasures the Russians might have in place to protect the SOOF.

By late afternoon, the discussion was winding down, and it was clear that everyone was tiring. Forrest announced, "Let's call it a day and pick it up again tomorrow morning."

Samantha cleared her throat. "Tomorrow is Sunday, and I usually go to church Sunday mornings. Would it be possible to accommodate me on that?"

Fred seconded the request, explaining that his family had just moved into housing at Pearl, and they tried to attend worship services on Sunday mornings whenever possible. So, it was agreed that the team would reconvene at 1200.

"Would it be possible to have a brunch at the O Club before we get together in the war room?" Ira suggested.

Forrest gave Ira a puzzled look. "What does everybody say to that?"

All agreed.

"Okay. O Club tomorrow at noon."

As they left, Forrest and Samantha lagged a little behind. "Forrest, I noticed that you looked at Ira a little funny when he suggested brunch tomorrow. Why was that?"

"That's the first time I've seen Ira suggest something like that. When he's preparing for a mission, all he wants to do is work. He has no time for brunch or any other kind of socializing. In fact, he has been incredibly calm lately. Based on the extreme importance of this mission, I'm actually in shock at how calm he is."

"Is that a good thing?"

"I don't know about that. What I do know is that he is actually tolerable to work with. Not as demanding. Usually, only his ideas will work. You know what I mean. When I found out that I had been selected to lead this group and that Ira was the CO on the sub chosen to carry out the mission, I didn't look forward to it."

"That doesn't sound like a good thing to me. How do you feel it's going so far?"

"Usually these things take a week or so to really get started. You know, group dynamics have to be played out. And when Ira is involved, he usually takes charge pretty quickly. I expected trouble with this, but as it's turned out, we immediately began working on the problems we needed to address." After a pause, he said, "Samantha, I believe that you may be the one responsible for this change."

"What do you mean by that?"

"Right from the beginning, you raised important issues, and we got busy. I think what's happened here is that Ira hasn't had to take charge. He's actually letting you do it. I've never seen anything like it before with him. I love it."

"Forrest, I'm sure it isn't all me. Everyone in our group is committed to what we've been assigned to do. I see no hidden agendas in anyone."

Forrest said, "I agree with you there." After another pause he said, "By the way, would you mind if I went to church with you tomorrow?"

"I'd be honored."

★★★

Brunch at the O Club was a welcome break for the team. Even though preparation for the mission was less than a week old, the pressure of its importance and the realization that even the relatively straightforward task of blowing up a building was not going to be easy had started to weigh on everyone. Fred brought his family with him, and a good relaxing time was had by all. Samantha, who was seated next to Ira, said, "Great idea. I think we needed a break like this."

"Thanks, Samantha. I think you're right. We've got some issues to solve, but we're making great progress. We'll be ready come February."

# CHAPTER 24
# THE MINE WARFARE BRIEF

**ON MONDAY, DR. MELISSA CONWAY** from the Naval Surface Warfare Center briefed all three teams on mine warfare capabilities of the Russians, starting with a history of Soviet Union/Russian efforts in that area. Samantha felt that she could have left this part out, but the importance of mine warfare to Russia became very clear. When she moved on to the most recent developments, everyone in the room became more attentive.

The Russians were big on incorporating artificial intelligence into their most recent mines, which could now differentiate between surface ships and submarines and be remotely turned on and off. They could also differentiate between friend and foe and even determine the type of ship or submarine. The mines in their arsenal could be laid by almost any platform—submarine, surface ship, or aircraft.

The mine that garnered the most interest from Team Alpha was the PM-2, designed to target submarines under the ice. Team Alpha members asked several questions about this mine. How was it used? As a defensive mine to protect them while on station?

To offensively target an attack submarine?

Dr. Conway reported that Russia also had an extensive inventory of bottom mines, designated PM-1, and moored mines, designated as PRM-2. Water depth did not seem to be an issue. They could moor mines at any depth in the water column. Dr. Conway reported that all the moored mines could react to both a single influence and a combination of the available influences given off by a submarine—acoustic emanations, magnetic induction, or hydrodynamic pressure.

What especially concerned Team Bravo was that once a target was detected, the mine could fire an active homing torpedo or a rocket-propelled torpedo to a computed intercept point. In either case, little or no time was available for evasive action or use of countermeasures. There was no clear way to avoid destruction once detected by these mines.

This was a sobering conclusion to Dr. Conway's briefing.

Her presentation was clear, and only a few questions were asked. Samantha had an important one.

"Dr. Conway, can you give us the stand-off distances to the moored mines, the PRM-2s? In other words, how far away can they detect a target?"

"Dr. Stone, I'm not sure of the newest version of the PRM-2s, but the older version had a detection range of about one hundred fifty to two hundred yards, depending on the influence. I would guess that the newer models are at least that good. I hate to be nebulous, but I have not seen any new intel on that."

Samantha turned to the Team Bravo guys and said, "Looks like we need more intel." That was becoming somewhat of a refrain.

# PART 3

## FINAL MISSION PREPARATIONS

# CHAPTER 25

**AS THE DAYS ROLLED INTO** weeks, *things* began to happen. At first, tangible results seemed agonizingly slow in coming. But eventually the Corps of Engineers constructed a practice wall for the SEALs. The largest commercial pool company on Oahu began modifying and refurbishing a large swimming pool located in an unused military housing facility in the mountains near Pearl Harbor. Arctic Submarine Lab personnel were brought in to oversee the installation of the pool's cooling system, which was now being referred to as the "Cool Pool" by Team Bravo.

Samantha received the rare gas–infusion chamber and asked if the MIT version could be slimmed down and possibly service more than one wet suit at a time and in less than twenty-four hours. Dummy Russian PM-1 and PRM-2 mines arrived from NSWC. An order for about twenty-five additional mine shapes had been issued, and delivery was just days away. The CIA "fishing" boat was now actively collecting DSL data around the clock, and the data was sent to Samantha on a regular basis. Also on a regular basis, Team Alpha requested some of Samantha's time.

One disturbing and worrisome issue was the lack of additional intel on Russian countermeasures for defending the SOOF against SEAL operations. Also, no information emerged on cable location. But the land facility feeding the cable to the SOOF was identified and precisely located.

The most important information received was bad news. The Russians planned to have two Laika-class submarines in the Sea of Okhotsk, as well as three surface ASW frigates. They also planned to have three surface ships patrolling the entrances to the Sea of O as a blockade. Russia planned to issue a notice to mariners announcing the mining of the channels between the Kuril Islands on 1 March. They were, essentially, declaring the Sea of Okhotsk as theirs, and that no one was allowed to be in it.

★★★

After the afternoon session in mid-December, Ira called Samantha from the *Hawkbill*.

"Hey, Ira. This is a surprise. What can I do for you?"

"Well, we're about six weeks into our mission planning, and I wanted to talk to you about how you think we're doing."

"I can answer that right now. I think we're doing great."

"Well, I'd like to get into a little more detail than that. How about dinner at the O Club tonight?"

"God, Ira. I thought you'd never ask. But you haven't given me much time to get ready."

"Can you be ready by eight?"

"Sure. For you, I can do it."

At precisely eight o'clock, Ira asked the same Secret Service agent as before to let Samantha know that he was there for her. When the agent went inside, Ira detected a little annoyance in his expression. Perhaps it was jealousy. He wasn't sure, but it made him feel good. When the jealous agent and Samantha appeared at the door, Ira audibly gasped. Samantha was wearing a dress!

A short dress! She was absolutely beautiful.

"What's wrong, Ira? Haven't you ever seen a girl's legs before?"

Ira was embarrassed at being caught.

"Sorry, Samantha. This is the first time I've seen you without pants on."

"Ira, what is John here going to think?"

"You know what I mean. You always wear pants at our meetings."

As they walked down the stairs to the car, Samantha giggled and said, "I'm wearing pants right now, you know. You just can't see them."

"God, why do you say things like that?"

Samantha did not answer Ira's question. She just grinned.

When they were seated at their table with their wineglasses in hand, Samantha said, "It's been six weeks or so since we've done this. I had a great time then, and I was wondering if we'd ever do it again."

"I had a great time too. But it's a small world around here, and if we did it more often, people would start talking."

"Let them talk. We're adults."

"Yeah, but we've got a job to do, and we don't need any distractions like that. A very important job."

"That's true. But it's nice to get away from that pressure every once in a while."

Ira agreed. "I never thought that I'd think that way, but I've really enjoyed our Sunday brunches with the team and Fred's family. I think it's kept the morale up. Team Bravo has been a great experience for me. I actually enjoy going to the meetings. The time flies by, and we seem to get so much done."

"We do. Also, we've gotten so much support from everyone, especially Admiral Flaxon."

"Speaking of Flaxon, I think he has a crush on you."

"Ira, how can you say that? He's a married man with two kids, and he must be at least in his upper fifties."

"What's all that got to do with it? I've never seen a flag officer respond to anyone like he does you."

"Ira, he helped put plans A and B together. He's intimately involved, and he wants plan A to be successful. He's just trying to help."

They placed their dinner orders and continued to cautiously talk about the people involved in the mission. "How is the boat's crew coming along?"

"Great. They really are top notch. The officers are all experienced, and I have the best COB in the submarine force."

"You mean Master Chief Boxer?"

"Yes. I can count on him for anything and everything. Also, the SEALs are unbelievable. They're our most important people. We're just tasked to get them where we need to get them so they can do their job."

"I think you're oversimplifying what you have to do. You are anything but a bus driver. You must get them there safely under extremely trying conditions. One mistake on your part, and it's over. We've failed. And you know what that means."

At that point, their entrees were placed before them. As with their first dinner at the O Club, while eating they said nothing about what lay ahead of them. Instead, they engaged in small talk concerning their childhoods and other things designed to get to know one another better.

When they had finished eating, Ira asked, "Samantha, there's something that I've been dying to ask you since the first day I met you."

"Uh-oh. How personal is this going to be? What color pants am I wearing?"

"How can you say something like that? You know it embarrasses me."

She smirked and said, "Ira, you're so much fun to be around.

You tickle me. So, what is it you want to know?"

"Every Samantha that I've ever known, and I've known three or four, has been called 'Sam.' Why not you?"

With a soft smile, Samantha studied Ira for several seconds. "When I was a teenager, my friends wanted to call me Sam, but to me, 'Sam Stone' sounded like some cheesy detective right out of a James Patterson novel. The name just didn't seem feminine enough. I was a girl, and I wanted to be thought of as a girl."

Ira said, "I can understand that."

Samantha met Ira's gaze. "Ira, I'm going to tell you something that I have never told anyone before. No one. When I've been asked about my name, I give the answer I just gave you. And it's a true answer. However, there is another part of the story. But you must keep it a secret. Do you agree to do that? Never tell anyone?"

"I promise," he answered.

Samantha took a deep breath, then began, "My mother died of breast cancer when she was only forty-two years old. I was eighteen at the time. My dad was devastated. He just couldn't accept what had happened. He changed his lifestyle dramatically. For example, he bought a motorcycle, which was very much unlike him. He took me for a ride on it once, and I swore that I would never get on one of those things again. Sure enough, he was killed riding his bike. I was twenty-one when he died. I really believe that he missed my mother so much that he had a death wish and wanted to be with her again.

"Ira, I loved my parents so much. I loved them more than anyone else in the world. In fact, they are the only people that I have ever really loved. From as far back as I can remember, they called me Sam. It was our little secret. When we were out in public, they would call me Samantha. When we were alone, I was Sam. So, the other part of the story is that I truly loved my parents, and I allowed them, and only them, to call me Sam."

"My God, Samantha. I'm so sorry that you lost your parents

that way and at such an early age."

"Yes, it is sad. I love them, and I miss them." Samantha wiped a tear from her eye. "Is my secret secure with you?" she asked.

"To the grave."

★★★

When they returned to Carter House, Ira opened Samantha's car door, took her hand, and helped her out of the car. When he tried to release her hand, she prevented him from letting go, so they walked up the steps hand in hand. John's look of annoyance at seeing them together and holding hands was clear.

"Thanks for a great time, Ira. Hopefully we can do it again sometime."

Ira hated to let her hand go. He gave it a gentle squeeze and dragged his fingers through her palm. "I'm sure we will," he said.

As he walked back to the car, Ira thought, *Well, I didn't get a good night kiss, but it was sure worth it just to see the aggravation on John's face.*

# CHAPTER 26
## PROGRESS CONTINUES
### (4 JANUARY)

**BY THE FIRST WEEK OF** January, all the necessary mine shapes had been received, and Samantha had planned the desired locations and depths of the moored mines in the test range. Placement of these obstacles would begin within a week. The SEALs' training wall was completed and ready to use, and the dummy bottom mines were being placed at selected locations in the vicinity. Samantha, Jared, and Josh worked together to test the Pegasus's ability to detect bottom mines.

Five slimmed-down wet suit–infusion chambers were constructed, each able to infuse two wet suits at a time. The infusion time remained at twenty-four hours, but since only eight wet suits were needed at a time, ten suits a day would likely be sufficient. Still, Samantha wanted to take two additional chambers to provide insurance against possible chamber failures as well as provide four more gas-infused suits a day if needed. Several of the SEALs were being trained to repair the chambers should a breakdown occur.

The Cool Pool had been completed, but calibration of the

cooling system was still underway. The pool would be ready for use within a few days. DSL data continued to flow into Samantha's computer, and she prepared time charts of its daily migrations in the water column and projected what the migration would be in March.

There continued to be a dearth of meaningful intelligence information. The good news was that the Russians seemed to have no knowledge of what was being done to thwart their evil plans. Just in case, fingers were on the button to initiate plan B should plan A be compromised.

No one wanted that to happen.

✯✯✯

At lunch in the cafeteria, Samantha spotted Odd with several of his Team Alpha buddies and approached the table to catch his eye. As he stood, the others stood as well, greeting her by her first name. Samantha recognized them as the sonarmen who had asked her so many questions during her briefings to Team Alpha concerning the environment.

"Sit down, guys. Your food is getting cold," she said with a laugh, flattered by this simple show of respect. "Odd, can you meet me in my office when you finish up this afternoon?"

All the guys started teasing Odd at this invitation.

"Don't pay any attention to them, Samantha. I'll come by. We usually finish up at around five o'clock."

"Great. See you then."

The young men continued teasing Odd as Samantha left to sit with Jared and Josh.

At five o'clock, Samantha checked in with the Marine guard to get access to her tiny office. She informed him that she was expecting Lieutenant Bergstrom. She passed the time going through the latest DSL data she had received.

At about 1720, Odd came into her office.

"Hi, Odd. Please sit."

"Thanks."

She began, "It seems like we never get to see one another anymore. Except for dinner at the Carter House, our paths hardly ever cross, and even though the house is cleared, we can't talk at the level we can talk here. I just want to see how it's going with you."

"Everything is going fine. We're really busy going out to sea and training the sonarmen to recognize the Borei subs. Like you've warned us, the noise in the Arctic is going to be a problem."

"I gathered that. They keep asking me a lot of questions on ambient noise, especially at the high frequencies."

"The Boreis are so damn quiet. They will be extremely difficult to detect and track. The strongest line we have is the one from the ice maker. We anticipate that they'll just stay in place against the underside of the ice canopy, waiting for the signal to shoot. It's going to be tough."

"Well, I guess the fallback plan will be that if you can't take them out on IDES, wait until they open their missile launch tube doors, and do them in then."

"I hope it doesn't come to that."

Samantha said, "If Team Bravo does its job, the Boreis will never get the 'go' signal from the SOOF."

"That's what I'm praying for."

"What's your target?"

"We're calling it B-1. That's the one Admiral Ustinov is commanding. He's good; he'll give us a run for our money. I have to admit, Samantha, I'm really scared. I still find it hard to believe that all this is really happening."

"I'm scared too, Odd. Team Bravo has an amazing submarine, an extremely skilled commanding officer, and an amazing platoon of SEALs. We've come up with so many possible scenarios that we might be faced with, and I believe we have an answer for all of them. But there is such a thing as 'the fog of war.'"

"The fog of war?"

"Yes. General Carl von Clausewitz described it many years ago in his book *On War*. You simply can't know everything in a hostile conflict, and many decisions just turn out wrong. Some have paraphrased this and have said that in war, if something unexpected can happen, then it will. You know—surprises. On Team Bravo, we're trying to reduce the number of unexpected events so we can thin out the fog as much as possible."

"Team Alpha is fully aware of the importance of your mission, Samantha. If you guys succeed, the whole Russian plan comes to a screeching halt. We're counting on that."

"When do you guys sail?"

"We leave on the fourth of February. Two more leave on the fifth, and the last two on the sixth."

"Well, I'll be praying for you and your team."

"Likewise, Samantha."

# CHAPTER 27
# THE SEALS IDENTIFY A PROBLEM

**FORREST BEGAN THE MORNING SESSION.** "Alright, people. We're about to enter our testing phase to determine our ability to navigate through a minefield and how the SEALs perform in very cold water. Jared, can you give us a status report?"

"Sure. Unfortunately, we do have some issues. We have continued to practice on the wall constructed here. We are now simulating zero visibility using masks, and we've been using the rare gas–infused wet suits. The good news is that the wet suits have not been a problem. They do not impede our movements in any way. We will begin using them in the Cool Pool in a few days.

"However, trying to do our jobs in zero vis is definitely an issue. What took us three to four days before is taking four to five, perhaps six days, which means no wiggle room. This is not acceptable. We might not have enough time left to find the comms cable. Working with Ira, we have decided that once we enter the Sea of O, it will take up to four days to get to the SOOF and recon the area to determine what we might have to deal with. And suppose we run into trouble from their subs and surface ASW forces? Or with any anti-SEAL countermeasures? We may not have enough time to plant our explosive charges. And if Samantha is right, and the very cold water slows us down even more, we could really be in trouble."

Ira chimed in, "Any ideas on how we can speed up their job would be welcome." No one put forth any suggestions. Ira said, "Samantha, you're the idea guy around here. Anything?"

"What if we entered Okhotsk a few days earlier? This would give us the wiggle room that Jared needs."

After brief consideration, Ira answered, "That's a possibility, but the date of entering the Sea of O was carefully thought out. The plan is structured to give us the most time here in Hawaii to prepare for the mission and the least time possible in their sea, where we are the most vulnerable to detection. Forrest, could you bring this possibility up to Admiral Flaxon? Let's see what he thinks."

"Will do, Ira."

Samantha brought up the next subject. "The test minefield is scheduled to be ready by the twelfth, next Tuesday. Do we have the *Hawkbill* scheduled for then?"

"Yes," Ira replied. "Is the test plan ready?"

"I finished it last night, and it's ready for your review and approval. Fred helped me put it together, so it should be acceptable. Hopefully, anyway."

"Fred, can we review it tonight?" Ira asked.

"Yes, sir."

"Can you give us a short report on how things are going with *Hawkbill*?" Forrest asked Ira.

"I firmly believe that *Hawkbill* is ready to go. We have really pushed her as hard as we can. It flies through the water. We can take it deeper than I had hoped. The SEALs can undock and re-dock the Pegasus very efficiently. There were problems at first, but your boys have quickly solved them," Ira said, nodding toward

Jared and Josh.

"The crew is humming along like a well-oiled machine. I have Boxer to thank for that. We've had a bunch of issues, but they've all been small and not totally unexpected. Our greatest success is that we're almost impossible to detect acoustically. Even the active sonars have a difficult time seeing us. The advanced anechoic coating seems to be really effective, and I believe we'll have a significant acoustic advantage over the Laikas if we encounter them. And we probably will," he added under his breath. "I've scheduled a degaussing of the boat a few days before we leave on our mission. If we have to deal with mines, we want to have the lowest magnetic-induction signature we can.

"I have the crew operating on the ultra-quiet mode all the time. It's an inconvenience to everyone on board, but I feel safer doing it this way. According to Master Chief Boxer, every crew member has bought into this routine. I know I'm being redundant here, but we just can't allow ourselves to be detected on this mission."

Samantha asked, "Ira, just how much does the crew know about what we've been tasked to do and why?"

"Samantha, of the crew, only the two officers in this room have been briefed into the IDES program. Master Chief Boxer knows that this mission is extremely important and will be a very dangerous one—one that we may not survive. Once we're underway to Japan, I will have an all-hands announcement telling them the whole story. We've been directed to do it this way by the president and the chairman of the Joint Chief of Staff, General Bishop."

The team broke for lunch, and no afternoon session was scheduled. Ira had a meeting with Bryan Boxer and the other *Hawkbill* chief petty officers. Jared had scheduled more SEAL training, and Samantha wanted to study the latest DSL data set she had received. She also wanted to ruminate on the SEAL problem of not enough time. Forrest and the Alpha and Charlie team leaders had a scheduled meeting with Admirals Scott,

Flaxon, and Price. Things were beginning to wind down on the preparation front.

# CHAPTER 28
# THE MINEFIELD TEST
## (13–15 JANUARY)

**SAMANTHA BEGAN THE MORNING SESSION.** "Okay, we begin our minefield transit test tomorrow evening. There will be no mystery as to where the dummy mines are located. We will know exactly where they are and at what depth. Our objective is to quantify how well we can transit using various tactical scenarios. The variables will be our speed, our depths, bubble up or down, and sonar settings. We will have control over all these things, and we have to record all our variables. We've produced data log sheets to record this information, which will be done in triplicate to avoid data entry mistakes.

"I have a good handle on the migration of the deep scattering layer in our test area. I predict that we will do much better during the day when the DSL descends below the mines and we are in 'clearer' water—in other words, not within the DSL. Our first run through the minefield is scheduled for 2000 tomorrow evening. We should be able to make two complete runs each hour.

"A complete run includes the turns and alignment for our next run. Please do not get discouraged if we don't see one damn mine when we start the test. We will be operating within a high-scattering environment: the DSL will be nearer the surface, and the animals making up the layer will scatter our sonar energy. Our sonars will not be effective. I expect this to change when the sun comes up. The layer will deepen, and we will be able to detect the mines and navigate through the minefield. Hopefully.

"If what I predict happens, we can analyze the data and see what tactics and sonar settings work best. We will rerun the test next week and do better. Any questions?"

Fred Boone asked, "What about the Peg?" as Pegasus was now affectionately being called.

"We are going to test Peg in the same exact way that we test *Hawkbill*. That will happen this Thursday, 14 January. We also plan to test Peg both manned and autonomously. I fully expect that we will do much better with both the *Hawkbill* and Pegasus the second time around."

★★★

At 0800 the next morning, Samantha called the five others on the team via a conference call.

"Hey, guys, I know some of you have to report to *Hawkbill* right after lunch to prepare for the minefield test tonight, and we have a lot to do before then. But I've come up with a possible solution to our SEAL team time problem. I would like to see what you think, to see if my idea is even worthwhile. Can we meet in the war room at nine o'clock for an hour?"

The others replied that they could rearrange their morning schedules.

At 0900 in the war room, Samantha began describing her plan. "This idea may be a little dangerous because of possible counter-detection. But let me suggest it to you anyway for your consideration." She paused to see if there were any reactions.

"If we had a very high-frequency, very-low-power handheld

sonar, the divers could use it to locate and reach the edge or end of the wall very easily, even in low vis. We could also use it to locate the bottom of the sea ice and the seafloor. If we had premeasured lengths of line at the ready, the swimmers could run a line from side to side of the wall five feet below the ice and five feet up from the bottom, where the uppermost and bottommost explosive charges are supposed to be located. Then, again using premeasured lines, they could run the diagonal lines from the top corners to the bottom corners on the other side. As a result, we would have the middle of the wall located where the diagonal lines intersect. It sounds more confusing than it is, so let me draw it for you."

What she drew on the whiteboard was simply a big $X$ on the rectangle representing the wall with the top and bottom of the $X$ closed to form an hourglass figure. "With this configuration, we would have five of the explosive locations defined on the wall: the four corners and the middle. This should make it relatively easy to locate the proper locations of the other nine charges required.

"Other than potentially giving ourselves away with the high-frequency sonar, I think that this would speed up our operation considerably. It would be much better than blindly groping for the sides of the wall, its top, and the bottom. The premeasured ropes would eliminate a lot of measuring and guesswork, especially if the SEALs can't see what they're doing very well. What do you guys think? Ira? Jared? Josh?"

After a few moments of thought, Jared answered first. "From a swimmer's point of view, I do think it would speed up our operations considerably. I don't know what to say about the detection of the handheld sonars."

"The counter-detection scares me quite a bit," Ira finally said. "Your plan actually seems too simple and too good to be true. I'd like to have the SEALs try it out to see if they're comfortable with it, but we definitely need to thoroughly investigate the counter-detection issue."

Jared said, "This way of marking the wall does seem better than how we're doing it now. Josh, what do you think?"

"Even if we decide against the sonar, I think we should use the premeasured lines anyway. Using a grid marking system like that would improve our accuracy."

"Okay, let's talk it over with our guys to see how they feel about it," Jared said.

Samantha offered, "On the counter-detection issue, the presence of ice on the surface may be to our benefit."

"Can we have a handheld sonar designed and built in time?" Ira asked.

"Let's see if something like this is available commercially," Forrest replied.

Ira added, "Or from our military pipeline. We need the device to be very high frequency, 200kHz or so—very narrow beam, and very low power."

"And lightweight enough so a swimmer can use it," Josh interjected.

"That's right," Ira agreed. "I doubt if we can find something like that on the open market."

"Why don't we contact the manufacturer of our submarine's high-frequency sonars and put the challenge to them?" Samantha suggested.

Ira sighed. "Look, guys, we only have a month left before we sail. Can we do this by then?" Ira then added with some sarcasm, "And I am sure that our friend Samantha here is going to want to test the hell out of it." Samantha just smiled. Ira continued, "Although a long shot, this could be a mission saver for us. I say we push as hard as we can to get a working sonar. Samantha's suggesting of placing a rope grid on the wall alone could save us a day of time."

Forrest said, "I'll get with Admiral Flaxon right away to get this started."

"Sounds good, and well worth proceeding with," Ira said. Then he pointed a thumb at himself. "Me, Fred, and Samantha— on board *Hawkbill* by 1300. We've got some minefield tests to run."

★★★

The mine-avoidance test went exactly as Samantha had predicted. The mines could not be detected when the sun was down, but could during the day. As the daylight hours passed, the Hawkbill's detections were made farther and farther away from the mines and well beyond the mines' own detection ranges. The various tactical scenarios did appear to have an effect. The goal now was to determine the best combination.

After the last run at 1000 the next morning, the excitement in the control room was very high. But once again, Samantha cautioned them to rein in their exuberance.

"Look, we had perfect conditions today. A clear dark night. Half-moon. A clear, sunny day. We may not be so blessed in our operations area. Let's pray that we are. Ira, can you, Fred, and I analyze the data to come up with optimum sonar settings and tactics?"

Ira said, "Just from what I've seen today, I think I've got a good idea of what works best. Can we start in the morning? It's been a very long day. But I can't wait to show our results to Forrest, Jared, and Josh."

# CHAPTER 29
## PROGRESS
### (15–17 JANUARY)

**AT 0800, AN HOUR BEFORE** the others arrived, Samantha arranged the test results on the conference table in the war room. Despite her usual calmness, she was actually excited about the results. It was clear to her that the *Hawkbill* had the capability to navigate through a Russian minefield.

She was thinking of the Pegasus test planned for tomorrow when Ira and Fred entered the room. "The others will be here shortly," Ira told her. "I saw them talking to Admiral Flaxon down the hall. Probably about your idea, Samantha."

When all six were in the room, Ira provided a summary of the successful minefield test. Fred added some additional observations, and Samantha gave her thoughts on what she had gleaned in organizing the data on the conference table. Jared and Josh had discussed Samantha's idea with their team.

"They loved the idea of pre-marked ropes to establish a grid on the wall. They couldn't believe they hadn't thought of that, and they can't wait to try it out today. In fact, they're preparing the ropes as we speak. With or without the handheld sonars, they think it will speed up their ops."

Forrest reported that he had briefed Flaxon the night before on Samantha's approach to solving the potential low-visibility problem, and the admiral had just cornered him and the two SEALs on some findings relative to the idea.

"What did Flaxon say about the idea?" Ira asked.

"The admiral agrees with what Ira said yesterday. It sounds too good to be true. The good news is that according to Flaxon, a Raytheon engineer is here at SUBPAC addressing some high-frequency sonar issues. Flaxon said he would have Admiral Scott ask him to talk to us this afternoon."

"Well, that certainly is a blessing," said Samantha. "What are the odds of that?"

"We can meet with him in Admiral Scott's conference room," Forrest said. "As soon as it's available."

"Ah, progress. I love it," Ira said with a slight smile. "Let's look at the data we collected yesterday."

★★★

In Admiral Scott's conference room at 1300, the team met with Malcolm Rappaport, the Raytheon engineer. Ira defined what the team needed.

"We need a handheld, approximately 200kHz active sonar that can propagate energy through about two hundred feet of fairly turbid water. It has to be a very narrow-beam, low-power device. In other words, it has to have a low probability of counter-detection. It has to be waterproof down to about two hundred fifty to three hundred feet, fairly small, and very lightweight. It must also have a companion receiver with an easy-to-see-and-read display in low-visibility conditions. Malcolm, is something like that possible?"

"Of course it's possible. In fact, we've developed similar gadgets of that type before. I believe we might even have a prototype lying around somewhere."

Ira asked, "When could you have a few ready for us to use?"

"Probably in about six to eight weeks, but I would have to ask around back home to be sure," Malcolm responded.

Ira cleared his throat. "You've got two weeks. Your job depends on it. Keep us informed."

★★★

After the meeting with the Raytheon engineer, the team reconvened in the war room. By 1600, they had studied the *Hawkbill* test data and generated a clear set of optimal tactical settings for dealing with a minefield. They also had briefed Jared and Josh on how to run the Pegasus test so that the results could be compared to the *Hawkbill*'s. Jared, Josh, and four enlisted SEALs would be in Pegasus, manually controlling the vehicle. Four other SEALs would be on board *Hawkbill*, recording the data and observing.

Samantha said, "If Peg has the same success as we had yesterday, I'll be giddy with excitement." She then asked, "If we know the maneuverings needed to navigate a minefield, how difficult will it be to program Peg to do it autonomously? Ira, is the Pegasus company rep still at the ready to help us with that?"

"I think I know where you're going with this, Samantha. Let me call right now. Maybe I can get someone here by Monday."

★★★

Late the next afternoon, Pegasus detached from the *Hawkbill* about a mile from the minefield test area. She transited to the minefield and began the first run right at 2000. Throughout the night and the next morning, the test results of the *Hawkbill* were almost exactly replicated, and the last run was made at 1000 Friday, the seventeenth of January.

Samantha and Forrest met the returning *Hawkbill* at the pier at noon. Ira, Fred, Jared, and Josh debarked with big smiles on their faces. They all had their thumbs up, and Samantha knew that the test had been a success. Though extremely tired after a long, very exhausting day and night, they all had enough energy to give Samantha and Forrest great big hugs.

"You guys go get some sleep," Samantha said. "You all deserve it. Forrest and I will look at the two data sets and try to summarize what we have. Is that okay with you, Forrest? Are you free?"

"Absolutely."

Before Ira went back on board to sleep, he cornered Samantha and asked, "Dinner tonight? The O Club?"

"Using Forrest's word to me a few minutes ago, absolutely."

"Great. I'll pick you up at eight."

# CHAPTER 30
## DINNER DATE NUMBER THREE

**AT EIGHT O'CLOCK, IRA SAUNTERED** up the front stairs at Carter House and said, "Hi, John. How are you doing?"

"I'm okay, Captain. She's waiting for you. I'll get her."

When Samantha came through the door, Ira gasped once again at how beautiful she was. "Hi, Samantha. You look great."

"Thank you, Ira. So do you. Did you sleep well?"

"Very well, thank you." He turned to John and said with a big victory smile, "Thanks, John."

When they were at their table at the O Club, sipping wine, Ira asked, "Is the Peg data as good as I think it is?"

"Blue. Light blue," she said impishly.

Ira raised a puzzled eyebrow and said, "What do you mean?"

"My underpants are light blue."

Ira's eyes got as wide as humanly possible. With a red face and a smile he whispered to her, "I take it that you don't want to talk about today's test results."

"Tomorrow. Let's talk business tomorrow."

A few minutes later, Ira let the smile disappear and asked,

"Can I ask you something?"

"Sure."

"You seem to have a calmness about you. I mean, here we are dealing with a situation that could change the face of the world if we aren't successful. Even cost us our lives. In the past two months, we have identified many problems that could prevent us from being successful. Yet, you have not shown one bit of frustration in all this time. Your positive attitude and the humor you bring to our meetings have been very uplifting to me and to all of us. How can you be so calm, so positive, and show no panic when what we're facing could result in our own deaths?"

Samantha looked at Ira intently, considering how receptive he would be to her reply, and smiled.

"I firmly believe that all things work together for the good of those who love God and are called according to his purposes. So why should I worry? I've got God working for me."

Ira said, "That's Romans 8:28."

Samantha was just about to take a sip of her wine, but the glass never reached her lips. "Ira. I am shocked. Absolutely shocked. I thought you were Jewish."

"I am. But about five years ago, I picked up a copy of the New Testament and started reading. It wasn't anything like I thought it would be. I got interested, and I've actually been studying it for several years with a small group of other Jewish men."

"I am totally flabbergasted."

"Let me tell you something else," Ira said, leaning forward. "Before I picked up that copy of the New Testament, I was a very difficult man to work with. I was demanding, hardly ever took the advice of others, and I was critical of those under me. I thought their work just wasn't good enough. In fact, I worked with Forrest Jenkins when we were junior officers, and we had a falling-out. Forrest was just as ambitious as I was, and we butted heads. He said he would never work with me again. Well, here we are, both on Team Bravo, trying to save the world together."

Samantha remembered her conversation with Forrest. "Well, how have you changed? Outside of you trying to shortstop me from being on this mission, you've been an absolute joy to work with."

"I'm not exactly sure. But as I got deeper and deeper into my Bible study, a peace swept over me. A peace I can't explain."

"Ira, you're the living embodiment of Philippians 4:7."

Ira interrupted her. "I know. I have the peace of God which passes all understanding."

Samantha stared at Ira with her mouth wide open.

At precisely that moment, their server placed their entrees in front of them. They relished their meal and the time they were spending together as they continued to probe the backgrounds of each other's lives. On several occasions, they caught the other looking intently at them.

During their after-dinner glass of wine, Samantha raised the question, "Ira, where is all this going between us?"

A long pause followed before Ira casually responded, "Light blue? Is the underwear you're wearing really light blue?"

Samantha giggled and said, "Ira, pay the check, I'll get a cab, and I'll prove it to you."

✯✯✯

Samantha's phone rang.

"Hello. This is Samantha. Oh, hi, yes. I'm fine. Just tell Mickey about 6:30."

Ira rolled over and asked, "What was that all about?"

"That was John, our Secret Service door guard. I didn't get back when he expected, and he was worried about me."

"Go back to sleep, Samantha. We've got a busy day tomorrow."

"Aye, aye, sir," she said as she playfully tousled his hair.

# CHAPTER 31
# PEGASUS TEST RESULTS

## (18 JANUARY)

**AN AMAZING THING TOOK PLACE.** The Pegasus test results almost exactly reproduced those of the *Hawkbill*. The team now knew that they had the ability to navigate through a minefield from the Pegasus with onboard sonars—but only if they knew the condition of the deep scattering layer. Samantha's analysis of the DSL data from the CIA's Japanese "fishing boat" was now considered critical.

Ira asked, "Samantha, is there any way we can measure the presence of the DSL with any of the high-frequency sonars that we have on Hawkbill?"

"I don't think so, Ira. The only way that I can see to get anything useful would be to moor one of our CAPTOR mines and ping on it to see if we can see it or not."

"That would make us vulnerable to detection and would take too much time. That's not an option," Ira said.

"To me," Samantha continued, "the big question is whether we can program the Peg to autonomously navigate a minefield. Can we teach it to automatically change headings, speeds, and depths properly once it has detected a mine? On yesterday's test, Jared and Josh were on board and controlling Peggy manually."

Ira hesitated. "I apologize, but I've been a little preoccupied the last day or so, and I've let something fall through a crack. Let me check my calls and emails."

Samantha tried to stifle a smile.

A minute later, Ira said, "Yes. A Pegasus company rep will arrive here tomorrow night. We can meet with him Monday morning. Forrest, can you check with Admiral Scott to see if we can use his secure conference room again?"

"Will do, Ira."

They continued the morning session by discussing armament loadouts. The SEALs occupied much of the space in the torpedo room that was normally used for Mk 48 ADCAP torpedoes. Additionally, Ira had agreed to carry four CAPTOR moored mines. But enough torpedo space was still available. A full complement of Tomahawk and Harpoon missiles would be loaded into the Virginia Payload Module. *Hawkbill* would be carrying enough firepower to conduct its own private war.

Before the lunch break, Forrest said, "Jared is continuing to test his team in the Cool Pool and on detecting the bottom mines placed near their practice wall. Samantha has said that she wants to continue her analysis of the DSL data and to consider a few other ideas. Is that right, Samantha?"

"It is, Forrest." To explain a little more on this, Samantha said, "Listen, guys, I've got another idea I've been tossing around in my head, but I need to think about it some more before I bring it up to the team for consideration."

"What's it about?" asked Fred.

"It concerns getting us out of the Sea of O and back home. That's all I'd like to say for now. I may discard the idea. I don't know. Hopefully, after our Monday-morning talk with the Pegasus guy, I'll be ready to bring it up."

"That's good enough for me," Forrest said, clasping his hands together. "Jared, after lunch, can you and Josh give us an update on how you guys stand? Are there any problems we need to know about? We've got less than a month before *Hawkbill* sails." Everyone nodded their understanding. "Okay. Let's go to lunch."

Ira stood up before the others and announced, "I do have one other thing. Tomorrow is church in the morning and brunch at the O Club around noon. I'm having a BBQ on the pier for the *Hawkbill* crew. They've been working really hard, and they deserve a break. I'd love it if all of us here could join in. It starts at 1600."

"Are you serious, Ira?" Forrest chuckled. "That sounds like a great idea. I'll be there."

"Me too," said Samantha. "I can't wait."

"What about my guys?" Jared asked.

"Of course they're invited. So are your wife and kids, Fred."

Forrest and Samantha were headed to the cafeteria for lunch when they heard Ira calling them. "Do you two mind if Fred and I join you for lunch?"

# CHAPTER 32
# A DAY OF WORSHIP AND FUN
## (19 JANUARY)

**AT 0800 THE NEXT MORNING,** Ira called Samantha.

"Ira, what can I do for you this morning? But be careful what you say. I'm going to church."

"That's why I'm calling you. How would you like company?"

"Are you saying you want to go to church with me?"

"That's exactly what I'm saying. In fact I would love to go to church with you."

"Well, we would have more company. Forrest will be picking me up, and we're picking up Fred and his family. Do you mind?"

"No. That would be great. When is Forrest picking you up?"

"Around 9:45. The service starts at 10 o'clock. Why don't you get here around 9:30?"

"I'll be there."

At 9:30, Ira was greeted by Mickey the Secret Service agent, who escorted Ira into the living room where Samantha was sitting with several men, including Big John. Ira introduced himself and said, "This is the first time I've been in this place. I never could get past John here. It's nice. Hi, Samantha."

"Hi, Ira. Forrest will be here soon. Odd, John, and several of the guys are going to the church service as well. In a separate car, of course."

"How are you doing, Odd?"

"I'm doing great, Captain. Thank you."

When they arrived at the church, they spotted Jared and Josh waiting at the front door. Samantha's surprise was very obvious. She scampered up the steps.

"Hi, guys. What are you doing here? You're trained killers," she said in a stage whisper.

Josh responded, "Only when we have to, Samantha. Only when we have to."

Jared ignored Samantha's little humorous dig and said, "You, Forrest, and Fred always look so happy when you come to brunch after church, so we decided to give it a try. The real surprise is that you have Ira with you. My God. And there's Lieutenant Bergstrom and a bunch of the Team Alpha guys. Are they with you too?"

"Kinda."

"What's going on, Samantha? Are you getting some kind of a kickback from the pastor for filling up the pews?"

"Now, now, Jared. Their true spiritual selves are just starting to shine through."

"Samantha, you could probably sell a deep freezer to an Eskimo. One that wouldn't even fit into his igloo."

"Jared, you're funny. Come on, we're all here. Let's go inside."

Once they were seated, Jared leaned forward from the pew behind her and whispered, "Did you talk to Admiral Flaxon about going to church, too?"

"Why do you ask that?"

"Because he's sitting right over there." Samantha looked where Jared pointed, and sure enough, Roger Flaxon was in church.

After the service, the Bravo Team stood outside discussing the sermon. Samantha greeted Admiral Flaxon as he emerged.

"Admiral, it's so nice seeing you here this morning."

"Hi, Samantha. I'm surprised too. I've been thinking of going back to church for some time now. I don't know. I woke up this morning, and something made me get ready and come. I see you've got quite an entourage here with you."

"Yeah, it's nice. Listen, we're going to the O Club for their Sunday champagne brunch. Why don't you join us?"

"I'd love to, but shouldn't you check with the boys first?"

"Don't be silly. They'd love to have you join us. Hey, guys? Guess who's joining us for brunch."

As usual, the bottomless glasses of champagne mellowed them considerably. The mood was festive, and the laughter was plentiful. Samantha told one funny story after another. She had them in tears. The other patrons in the dining room glanced at them and shook their heads. For a short time, they totally forgot about the nightmare journey they would soon undertake.

As they waited for the cars, Samantha poked Ira in the side. Ira looked at her quizzically. "What?"

"Ask Flaxon if he wants to come to your BBQ."

"I'm not going to do that."

"Then I will."

"No. Samantha, don't."

"Roger, Ira is throwing a BBQ party on the pier at 1600. Do you want to come?"

"That sounds great, Samantha. But when you wear stars on your shoulders, these events seem to get very stiff and formal. I'd ruin what Ira is trying to do."

"I guess you're right. I'll let you know how it goes."

"Thanks for asking, Samantha. I'll see you around."

When Samantha arrived at the pier at 1600, the BBQ was already in full swing. Ira had somehow managed to get authorization to serve beer to the crew, and the wonderful smell of prime rib steaks on the grill filled the air.

As Samantha walked up to the crowd, Master Chief Boxer greeted her.

"Hi, Samantha, glad you're here. Can I get you a beer?"

"I'd love one, Bryan. How did Captain Coen pull this beer thing off?"

"I don't know. We're only allowed three beers each, but we're under the honor system, and you know how that goes. I'll have to keep my eyes open. Here you go." He opened the bottle for her.

Several of the chiefs and many of the crewmen converged on Samantha and gave her hugs.

Ira had been socializing but once again noted how well Samantha and the crew interacted.

"Forrest, how does she do that? She knows more of the crew's first names than I do."

"I don't know, Ira. There's something special about her. I'm sure you'll agree."

"Yes," Ira said firmly.

Much to the delight of Jared and Josh, the SEALs had integrated well with the crew. The respect was mutual across the board.

As Ira and Forrest observed the festivities, Ira said, "Forrest, I want to tell you something."

"What's that?"

"I think that you've done an outstanding job in leading Team Bravo. You've kept us on track the whole time. We haven't wasted a minute since the very beginning. I really wish that you were sailing with us."

"Thanks, Ira. You don't know how much that means to me. Especially after what happened between us when we were younger. I've fallen in love with this team, and I wish I were going with you too. It's going to be very hard to see you embark on *Hawkbill* while I stay behind."

Ira cleared his throat, toed the ground for a moment, and finally said, "I want to apologize for what I did to you those years ago. I was wrong. Stupidly wrong."

Forrest choked a bit and said, "You might have been wrong in what you did, but I greatly overreacted. What I did to you was unforgiveable. I'm sorry too."

Ira and Forrest hugged hard and patted one another on the back.

"What are you two lovebirds doing?"

"Oh, it's nothing. Just talking about old times," said Forrest, a little embarrassed.

"Ira, are those tears in your eyes? You too, Forrest? Are you two grown men crying?"

Forrest cleared his throat. "Samantha, give us a break."

Samantha did not respond. She only smiled.

About a half hour later, Ira pulled out a bullhorn and announced that tomorrow would be an R&R day for all *Hawkbill* personnel. A huge cheer erupted on the pier.

# CHAPTER 33
# PROGRAMMING THE PEGASUS
## (20 JANUARY)

**MONDAY WAS A DAY OFF** for the *Hawkbill* crew, but not for Team Bravo, including Ira and Fred. One other member of *Hawkbill*'s crew was called to work by his commanding officer; Ira apologized to Senior Chief Bob Wagner. "Sorry, Wagner, but I need you to attend a meeting with me and the XO in Admiral Scott's conference room at 0900 tomorrow. The XO and I will give you a ride in the morning."

"Yes, sir. I'll be ready."

The next morning, the other four Team Bravo members were already in the conference room when Ira, Fred, and Chief Wagner strode in. Ira said, "Morning, everyone. I'm not sure if all of you know Senior Chief Wagner or not, but I'd like to introduce him to you."

"Hi, Bobby."

"Morning, Samantha. Nice to see you."

"You two know each other?" Ira asked, wondering why he was surprised.

"Yes, sir. We've had lunch together several times."

"I should have known. Anyway, Chief Wagner is probably the best programmer on the *Hawkbill*, and I thought that he might be a good person to join our meeting with Robert Fowler, the Pegasus rep. I've briefed Chief Wagner on the need to not discuss anything he hears today with anyone outside this room. And, as always, we must be careful what we say here in front of Mr. Fowler as well."

Forrest added, "Mr. Fowler will be here in ten or fifteen minutes. That will give us a little time to get our act together."

Robert Fowler was escorted into the conference room by Admiral Scott's yeoman, and the meeting began. What was intended to be a one-hour meeting stretched out for three hours. Programming the Pegasus to avoid mines in the water column turned out to be more complicated than originally thought. The tight turns and the changes in speed and depth that might be needed required tricky programming. This was where Ira's recommendation to have Senior Chief Wagner attend the meeting was revealed to be a stroke of genius. The chief seemed comfortable with what had to be done and how to do it. He asked many pertinent questions, and his confidence brought a welcome feeling of assurance to the others.

Jared asked, "Mr. Fowler, we would like to take Pegasus for a ride later this week. Perhaps Thursday. Would you be able to stay here for the week and work with Chief Wagner and get Pegasus ready to go?"

"I'm sure I can arrange that. When can we start?"

Ira said, "Senior Chief Wagner can start with you right after lunch. Right, Chief?"

"Aye, aye, sir."

⋆⋆⋆

After lunch, the team met in the war room. Forrest began, "Okay, Samantha. What's this idea you want to drop on us?"

"Okay, look, I'm on unfamiliar ground here, and I want you to tell me if my idea is stupid or not. I want you to forget that I am a fragile young girl whose feelings are easily hurt and that I cry easily."

The laughter from the men in the room was deafening. Fred said, "You're kidding, right?"

Samantha giggled and said, "You guys have me all wrong. I am a sensitive girl. Well, anyway, hear me out. I would like the *Hawkbill* to have the capability to make noise in the Sea of O."

The negative reaction was visceral.

"What? What kind of noise?"

"I've got to admit, that does sound kind of stupid."

"Wait, wait, wait," said Ira. "I think I know what Samantha's up to." Ira paused. "What are you up to, anyway?"

Samantha began, "You all know that I'm very worried about getting out of the Sea of O after we have accomplished our mission and destroyed the SOOF. When we fire torpedoes and make huge explosions, the whole world will know where we are. I don't care if the world knows, but I do care if two of Russia's best submarines and three of their ASW frigates carrying ASW helicopters know. Not to mention the three blockade ships waiting on the other side of the Kurils.

"I would like to lure one or both of these submarines into our own CAPTOR minefield. Well, the question is how do we do that?" Samantha paused, then said, "What if we fake some sort of breakdown on *Hawkbill*? Something believable and trackable. As we try to 'escape' and get out of the Sea of O, one or even both of the Laikas might be tracking us, trying to get a torpedo firing solution. Hopefully, we can lure them toward our CAPTORs."

She continued, "Again, as with everything else on this mission, timing is everything. So, at the right time, we launch Peggy and activate a similar noise device on her. Peggy will be programmed to sail to the minefield and avoid the mines. At the same time we launch Peg, we secure the noisemaker on *Hawkbill* and go ultra-quiet. Shut down everything. Even scram the reactor. Hopefully, the rat will follow our pied piper right into the minefield. Boom. A real threat is gone." Samantha sat down and looked at the five men sitting at the table. They traded quizzical glances.

Josh finally asked, "What happens to Peggy?"

"Depending on the situation, we can either rendezvous with her and recover her, or we can just let her go if we're still fighting for our lives. That's a decision we'd have to make on the spot. Ira's call."

After a few more seconds of thought, Ira said, "Samantha's got a point. Timing is critical here, and this plan might not be easy, or even possible, to pull off. But it is an ace up our sleeve if the situation presents itself. Samantha is absolutely right on another thing. We will be very vulnerable after we take care of the SOOF. The bad guys will definitely know that we're around. They won't hesitate to use active sonars."

"How about the noisemakers for *Hawkbill* and Peggy? Do we have anything like that?" Samantha asked.

"We've used that sort of tactic on exercises. Should be no problem." Forrest continued, "Let's talk this over some more to decide if it is feasible. There are questions. Where should the CAPTOR minefield be located? When should we release Peg so she can lure the Laika into the minefield? When should we fake our casualty and turn on the noise? There are other questions, I am sure. But it is a great idea, Samantha. Certainly worth considering." He smirked. "No need for tears."

# CHAPTER 34

**THE 15 FEBRUARY SAILING DAY** drew closer. The SEALs prepared ropes with easily identified marker points on them to determine where the charges should be placed on the wall. The cold water in the Cool Pool took a little getting used to, but practice and the gas-infused wet suits increased the time the SEALs could work effectively.

Programming the Pegasus to avoid mines was routine, thanks to Senior Chief "Bobby" Wagner, as everyone now called him. The handheld sonars functioned as planned. Even with blinders on, the SEALs were accomplishing their mission in four days. Ira continued to take the *Hawkbill* out to sea for drills and tests, including reactor scrams, which involved suddenly inserting control rods to shut the reactor down. Ira included this drill and the action of quickly switching to battery in case Samantha's plan was used and some propulsion was necessary.

*Hawkbill*'s crew programmed and launched many CAPTOR mines. Team Bravo spent most of its time in these final days going over tactical procedures for tracking the Laikas and the frigates. The goal was to keep a torpedo fire-control solution ready at all times.

The noisemakers that Samantha had requested were now in hand. An acoustic replication of an earlier casualty on a Virginia-class sub was created. This acoustic signature was likely in the Russian databases and would hopefully be believable.

# PART 4

## THE MISSION

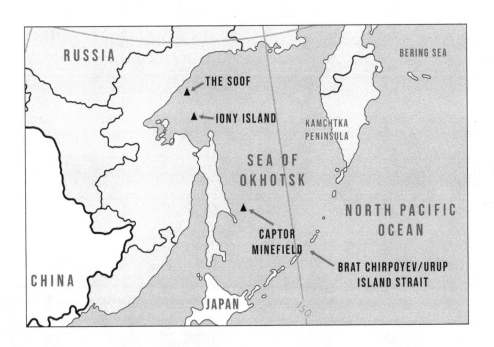

# CHAPTER 35
# THE PRESIDENT IS COMING
## (2-3 FEBRUARY)

**"OTHER THAN SOME SMALL DETAILS,** and degaussing of the *Hawkbill*, I think that we're ready to go," Forrest said at the start of the meeting. "What do you all think? Any pressing details or new ideas?"

Ira said, "Other than the degaussing, I feel good. I think *Hawkbill* is ready."

"Jared?"

"We can't wait to leave, sir. We're starting to get bored with practicing the same things over and over."

"Samantha?"

"I'm ready. I still get nagging thoughts of things we need or should look into. Like last night, I couldn't shake the thought that we need better bathymetry or bottom data. We're using old Russian charts and the few bathymetric lines we collected when we were tapping their communication cables. I'll ask Flaxon if he can locate any more recent data, but I can guess what he might say. He won't want to use HUMINT sources because it might compromise our security if our spies are caught. Other than that,

I'm ready. Can we leave two days early?"

Ira said, "Once we're degaussed, we're ready. Our armament is being loaded next week. Our provisioning is scheduled for the thirteenth. I could easily move all this up a day or two."

"Let me ask Flaxon if we can leave two days early. We are ready, and an extra day or two could give us more flexibility when we're in the Okhotsk," Forrest agreed.

Forrest then changed the subject. "The president arrives here this afternoon at 1500. He'll be spending the night at Carter House, Samantha. He'll probably want to talk to you, so be prepared."

"Why would the president of the United States want to talk to me?"

Everyone snickered audibly. Forrest continued, "We meet tomorrow in the main CINCPACFLT briefing room at 1000. The Virginia subs begin deploying to the Arctic in two days, and I know the president's visit is timed to give us all a pep talk and to wish us well."

★★★

At Carter House that afternoon, there was a flurry of activity. Several more Secret Service agents showed up and scanned the building for "bugs." Maids came through and thoroughly cleaned the house. A catering service truck arrived, and several caterers spread all kinds of hors d'oeuvres on the dining room table.

Samantha and Odd sat in the living room and watched all the goings-on. Odd said, "I guess the president will be here shortly."

"How come they never did any of this for us?" Samantha asked facetiously.

Shortly after four o'clock, the president's cavalcade of limos drove up to Carter House. He came in with his usual entourage of agents and military aides. Also, with him was Harlan Bradbury, director of the CIA. Harlan spotted Odd and Samantha right away. Shaking Odd's hand, he said, "Great to see you again, Odd."

He quickly released Odd's hand and gave Samantha a long hug.

"Alright, alright. That's enough. It's my turn." President Milsap gently pushed Harlan away and put his arms around Samantha. "I've been hearing so many good things about you and Odd."

"Thank you, Mr. President," Odd said.

Samantha demurred, "The guys on my team have been carrying me."

"Well, that's not what I've heard."

Samantha visibly blushed and didn't know what to say or how to act.

"Look, I'm starving. Let's see what they've put out for us today." The president ambled into the dining room and said, "Looks good. Let's eat. But ladies before gentlemen, always." He put a plate into Samantha's hand and led her to the table.

★★★

At three in the morning, Samantha lay awake thinking about the past evening. She had talked extensively with Harlan and President Milsap, but no business was brought up, just small talk. It was as if nothing bad was happening in less than two weeks. A wonderful meal was served and enjoyed by all. At ten o'clock, Samantha excused herself and went to bed. And now, here she was, lying in bed wide awake.

She finally got up and went down to the kitchen for a glass of milk. When she went into the living room to sit, the president was there, staring into the darkness.

"Oh, I'm sorry, Mr. President. I didn't think that anyone would be up."

Snapping out of his thoughts, he recognized her and said, "Samantha, come on in and sit. Let's talk a little."

"Are you sure? I don't want to disturb you."

"No, no. Sit down. I'd love to talk to you for a while."

Samantha sat with her glass of milk in hand.

"Couldn't sleep, huh?" he said. "Neither could I. In fact, I haven't been able to sleep much for quite a while."

"You must have quite a lot on your mind, Mr. President."

"I do."

Samantha said, "If I could be so bold, when I first saw you a minute ago, you looked very deep in thought. What were you thinking?"

"I can tell you exactly what I was thinking. I was thinking of how a young Norwegian naval officer, in an obscure spot in the world, and just doing his job, has changed the course of history."

"You mean Lieutenant Bergstrom?"

"I do. I love that boy. I love him for his intelligence, his diligence, his professionalism, and his competence. Let me tell you something, Samantha. I am surrounded by intelligent people, but few, if any, have all of the other attributes I just listed for Odd."

"I have to agree with you on that, Mr. President. And you know, Odd has other attributes as well. He is polite, courteous, appreciative, and especially humble. I love him too."

The president then said, "Another man I greatly appreciate is Admiral Roger Flaxon."

"How so?"

"Roger has an ability that few other people have. He can see things in people that others cannot. He and I go way back to our teens in Michigan where we grew up together. After high school, he went to the Naval Academy, and I went into politics. He told me once that I would make a great president of the United States. I laughed at him, of course. I mean, I was only involved in politics at the city level at the time. Later, when I was the governor of Michigan, he talked me into throwing my hat into the ring and to seek the presidency. I thought he was crazy. But he can be quite persuasive, you know."

Samantha smiled, and said, "I've heard that before, Mr. President."

"Samantha, please call me James."

"Yes, sir."

"Flaxon talked Captain Coen into volunteering for the submarine service," the president went on. "He saw the potential in Ira. Now it is widely accepted that Ira is the best officer in the submarine force. If we still have a country in a few weeks, he will soon become an admiral.

"Samantha, you are another example of Flaxon seeing something special in someone."

"Oh, come on, James. You're making this up."

"No, Samantha. I am not. When we were selecting the personnel and teams to carry out plan A, Roger was adamant that you be part of it all. No one on the selection committee knew who you were. Quite frankly, we were all very skeptical. But I eventually put my trust in Roger's sixth sense, and I supported him. I am so glad I did."

"God," said Samantha. "This is embarrassing."

"You may not know this, but Ira and Forrest had a serious falling-out several years ago. The selection committee was well aware of this and felt that putting them both on Team Bravo was a huge mistake, especially with Forrest being named the senior officer of the team. As such, Ira would be junior to Forrest. But, once again, Flaxon assured the committee members that Forrest and Ira were both professionals, and that their past would not affect them in doing their jobs."

"Roger was right on that, James. They have worked well together on planning this mission, and they actually made up. In fact, I saw them hugging the other day."

"I know. Forrest reported the incident, and I heard all about it."

Samantha blushed and said, "I guess there are no secrets around here."

The president chuckled and said, "That brings me back to you. Since the beginning, I've been getting bi-weekly reports on what's been going on with the three teams here in Hawaii. The team leaders were required to submit daily written reports. By far the most interesting part of these reports has been the inputs of one Dr. Stone. You."

"Me? How boring."

"On the contrary, Samantha. Every report I get has reiterated how valuable you have been. Not just in your technical and scientific inputs, but in how you have kept the morale high and kept a light, happy atmosphere within the group. How you have united the group into a tightly knit team. A family. The team members truly love one another. Because of you, Samantha."

"It's true that we do love each other. But it's not all down to me. I've probably caused more grief than anyone because of all the problems I bring up."

"That's one of the main reasons they appreciate and love you. You identify potential problems. What else have these last three months been about?

"In the last several reports, I see that you have also become the spiritual leader of Team Bravo. This has carried into Team Alpha as well. Even Flaxon is going to church now. Listen to this: When we were teens in Michigan, we used to go to church together. He and I. No other family members. He was very spiritual back then. We both were. When he left Michigan, he fell away from the church. I'm grateful to you for opening his eyes once again."

"I had nothing to do with that."

"Not according to him."

About a minute of silence followed. Finally, Samantha said, "James, you have a little smile on your face. What are you thinking?

The president's face broke out into a full-fledged smile, and he said, "You know, you cost me a seventy-five-dollar bottle of fifteen-year-old single malt scotch."

"What do you mean?"

"I had a bet with Flaxon that you wouldn't volunteer to go on the mission. I lost the bet."

Samantha shook her head, but she said nothing.

"Well, look, Samantha. It's about 4:30, and we both need to get some sleep. Busy day tomorrow. Thank you for talking with me. You've cheered me up immensely. Flaxon was right about you. You are very special."

"Thank you, Mr. President. Thank you for all your kind words. I'll see you in the morning." In a daze, Samantha made her way back to her room.

# CHAPTER 36
# YOU ARE NOT ALONE
## (3–11 FEBRUARY)

**AT 1000, TEAMS ALPHA AND** Bravo were assembled in the CINCPACFLT briefing room. Admiral Price walked to the dais and gazed at the assemblage for about a minute. "Okay, everyone. We are close. It's time to put into practice everything that we've worked on so hard the past three months. This should be a short meeting. The five Team Alpha subs will begin deploying to the Arctic tomorrow, and there are a lot of last-minute details they have to take care of. So, let's begin.

"As in our kickoff meeting last November, we are honored to have our commander in chief, President James Milsap, with us today to wish us farewell. President Milsap?"

The president came to the stage and waved to several in the room, including Samantha. When the applause died down, he began.

"I want to thank everyone here from the bottom of my heart for all the hard work you have done. From what I've heard, you have completed your work with zeal, professionalism, and with tireless energy. Again, I thank you.

"Everyone here in this room is acutely aware of the seriousness and gravity of the situation we are facing. We must and we will succeed in accomplishing our objectives. When you return from your deployments, you will sail into a free and untouched naval base, and the governor of Hawaii will be here to welcome you. When you return home to your families, they will be there to welcome you and greet you with open arms, hugs, and kisses. We will still be a free and vibrant nation. A nation that is still and will continue to be the leader of the free world. I wish you well on your journey. And may God bless you all.

"As a reminder that we are not alone during this trying time, I would like to open up this meeting in prayer." The president closed his eyes, bowed his head, and said, "God in heaven, creator of all things, protect the people that you have chosen to serve you in carrying out this terrible ordeal. Give them the courage, strength, wisdom, and discernment to thwart this satanic plan to destroy what we know is good. Bring them back safely and with honor. And, Lord, know that in all that they do, their overall goal is to bring honor and glory to you." He paused, then said, "Amen."

A chorus of amens came from all present.

"God speed, everyone." The president and Harlan Bradbury left the briefing room and joined up with his entourage.

"Well, that's a tough act to follow," Admiral Price said. He waited for the laughter to subside. "Team Alpha begins deployment to the Arctic tomorrow, 4 February. We wish you well, Team Alpha. And I can now announce that permission for Team Bravo's *Hawkbill* to leave two days early, on the thirteenth, has been granted. Congratulations, Team Bravo, for being ready early. May God bless you all.

"As you know, Team Charlie's submarines have been operating at sea for the last six weeks, and they have been prosecuting their given targets successfully for days now. We wish them continued success. I also want to announce that we are almost certain that our enemy remains unaware that we know about their plan. We still have the element of surprise on our side. However, I must caution each and every one of you to continue to safeguard what we are doing and not give anything away. To anyone. We do not want to initiate plan B.

"I would now like to close this meeting and give you time to address any last-minute issues you might have outstanding. The president opened our meeting in prayer, and I think it is fitting that we close it in prayer. Dr. Stone, would you honor us in leading this prayer? Samantha? Please come to the stage."

Samantha was shocked. She pointed to herself in the universal gesture of "Me?" Admiral Price nodded. As Samantha rose from her seat, loud applause erupted from all those present, even Admiral Price and Admiral Flaxon. The Team Bravo members stood and cheered out loud. A few seconds later, Odd and the Team Alpha members were standing and yelling as well.

Samantha climbed on the stage, shaking her head in disbelief. At the back of the room she spotted President James Milsap and Harlan Bradbury standing there with big smiles on their faces and clapping. They'd known this would happen and had come back in to observe.

When the cheering subsided, and everyone took their seats, Samantha said, "All I can say is that I am overwhelmed at all this. But of course, it will be my honor and joy to close us in prayer. Please pray with me." When Samantha had finished her prayer, there wasn't a dry eye in the briefing room. Almost everyone, if not everyone, believed that with God on their side, they could not fail.

★★★

*Hawkbill* was ready to go. Armament loadouts, provisioning, degaussing, and last-minute systems grooming were all complete. Samantha and the SEALs were moving onto the *Hawkbill*. All was set. It was time.

Ira kept Samantha company as she stored the last of her belongings into her cramped cabin.

"Well, it's not the Ritz, but you do have your own room. Even Fred has to share."

"I feel bad, Ira. Doesn't the XO usually get his own room?"

"Sometimes, but not always. Don't worry about it. Although privacy is nice, it is not a priority for us."

"I understand." After a pause, she said, "Can we go to the O Club for dinner one more time before we sail?"

"I thought you'd never ask."

"Hey, that's my line."

"You asked me to dinner," he said. He then asked, "What time?"

"How about leaving at 1800?"

"You're using military time now?"

"I'd better get used to it. That's all I'll hear from now on. Well, is 1800 good?"

"That seems a little early to me."

"Trust me, I have plans."

"Light blue?" he asked.

"Maybe. Maybe not. I'll surprise you."

Ira laughed. "Samantha, you are something else. A real piece of work."

At 1800, they instructed their driver to take them to the O Club. While they sipped wine at their table, Ira said, "Flaxon was right."

"Right about what?"

"When all this began last November, he told me that I would thank him for including you on this mission. We haven't even left yet, but I know he's right. I thank him for giving us you."

"When we get back from the mission, you can thank him for giving you me, and I can thank him for giving me you."

"Samantha, you say the sweetest things. Confusing but sweet," Ira said. "I've been meaning to say something. But I've been so busy with getting *Hawkbill* ready to sail that I haven't had a chance to tell you that your closing prayer at our meeting last week was very encouraging and moving."

"God, I was so nervous. I didn't have any idea that Price was going to do that to me. I hadn't prepared anything. In fact, I don't even remember saying the prayer. I was so nervous."

"It sure didn't come across that way. In fact, you seemed very relaxed and comfortable."

She thought for a moment and said, "I guess that was the Holy Spirit at work."

Ira nodded. "I like to think so."

During dinner, they reminisced about the Team Bravo experiences over the past three months. They focused on the funny and embarrassing things that happened. No problems or unresolved issues were raised. Both Ira and Samantha were determined to make their last time alone together a happy occasion. Although neither one said it, they both knew it could be the last time they would ever spend time together in this way.

As they finished up their after-dinner glass of wine, Ira said, "After tonight, it will be all business until we return to Pearl. That's not going to be easy for us, but we cannot put our personal emotions on display."

"I know. I'm very sad about that. But this night is still young. What can we do?"

"Hey," Ira protested, "you asked me out tonight. You said you had plans. It's your call, not mine. So, what do you have in mind?"

"It's a surprise."

"Great. Since you asked me out, you pay the bill, and I'll call us a cab. I just love surprises."

# CHAPTER 37
# THE DANGEROUS JOURNEY BEGINS
## (13 FEBRUARY)

**AS THE *HAWKBILL* INCHED AWAY** from the pier, Admiral Roger Flaxon, Captain Forrest Jenkins, and Mrs. Boone and her and Fred's two children stood in silence. Finally, Roger said to Forrest, "That's a beautiful boat that's going in harm's way. I absolutely love the people on her, and I pray to God that we see them again."

"Me too, Admiral. I only wish that I were going with them."

"I feel exactly the same way. Oh, Forrest, wipe the tears from your eyes."

"I will if you will, sir."

All five of them teared up as *Hawkbill* headed for deeper water. The momentous and extremely dangerous journey had finally begun.

★★★

In the control room Ira announced, "Okay, we are over deep water. Pilot, dive to one-five-zero feet."

The pilot repeated the order: "Dive to one-five-zero feet, aye sir." The journey to Yokosuka, Japan, was now underway.

Once they were at a depth of 150 feet, Ira commanded, "Pilot, set course at two-seven-zero degrees and a speed of two-five knots." Again, the pilot repeated the order and executed it. Ira turned to Fred and said, "It's time we let everyone know what we're up against."

"Roger that, Skipper."

The captain took the intercom mic and began.

"Attention, all hands, this is the captain." He paused for a few seconds. "Until now, no one has been told exactly what our mission will be on this journey. You all know that it is important and will be dangerous. Well, I can tell you now that this mission is almost certainly the most important one ever undertaken by a US submarine. It is certainly mine. Also, there is a chance, a good chance, that we may not make it back home. But our primary mission must be met at all costs, even if it means our lives.

"For ten years, the Russian military has been preparing to achieve world domination. Their plan involves destroying the United States with nuclear missiles and overrunning Europe with conventional forces. They plan to initiate their plot on 16 March, only one month from now. Our overall plan to defeat them is to carry out a coordinated, preemptive strike on all their military forces on 15 March, hence the code name IDES.

"The *Hawkbill*'s part of this plan, our part, is to destroy their command-and-control center in the Sea of Okhotsk. Our target has been called the SOOF, for Sea of Okhotsk Facility. If we successfully carry out our mission, the enemy will not be able to initiate its plan, and its military forces will certainly be defeated.

"The good news is that you are aboard the most capable submarine in the world. The *Hawkbill* is certainly designed to help us achieve our objective. You, its crew, have all been carefully selected based on your experience and past performances. You are the best of the best. We have a platoon of DEVGRU SEALs on board to help us destroy the SOOF. These fine men were also carefully selected for their ability to carry out this mission. They are also the best of the best.

"We are presently en route to Yokosuka, Japan, for a one-day in-port to reprovision. We will depart Yokosuka on 24 February and enter the Sea of O on the twenty-sixth. I will provide more detailed information on our mission in the Sea of O tomorrow.

"The Sea of Okhotsk will present to us an environment we are not familiar with. This will probably cause us no end of grief. That's the bad news. However, we also have on board with us the one person in the world who has the greatest knowledge of the Sea of O. That is Dr. Samantha Stone. So, once again, we have with us the best of the best.

"That's all the good news. We have a lot going in our favor. However, we will be facing a very formidable enemy. They will be mining the entrances to the Sea of O on 1 March. That's why we must enter the sea before that date. The enemy will have three of its best ASW frigates patrolling the Sea of O. They will also have three fast military ships guarding the entrances to Okhotsk. They will deploy bottom mines around the SOOF itself. These mines will be a major concern for us and for our SEALs. But the most worrisome and lethal threat to us will be the two Laika-class fast-attack submarines assigned to protect the SOOF. This threat is why we have been drilling you so hard these past months on detecting and dealing with these very quiet and dangerous submarines.

"To succeed and survive on this mission, we must—I repeat, we *must*—remain undetected. If the enemy knows we are there before we destroy the SOOF, we will almost certainly fail. Failure, of course, is unacceptable. If the unacceptable is likely, I will ram the SOOF with the *Hawkbill* if I have to. This was the reason for instilling ultra-quiet conditions twenty-four hours a day. We cannot leave anything to chance. We have built in everything we could to make *Hawkbill* extra quiet. We need to keep it that way.

"This is our objective and the challenges we are faced with. I ask all of you to be on your toes from this moment on. Our lives and the lives of all whom we love depend on us carrying the day.

"Before I sign off here, our very own Samantha has pulled at my shirt sleeve and wants to say something to you. Here's Samantha."

Samantha took the mic, closed her eyes, took a deep breath, and began. "Men of the *Hawkbill*, I just want to thank you all for welcoming me so warmly and making me feel like a true member of this magnificent boat. I especially want to thank the chiefs on board for opening the door to their sacred sanctuary to me. I also want to tell you something that Captain Coen would never say: that he is the best commanding officer our submarine force has. He is also the best of the best." As Samantha handed the mic back to Ira, he just smiled at her and shook his head.

# CHAPTER 38
## IRA DAYDREAMS

**ON THE WAY TO YOKOSUKA,** Japan, Ira continued to drill his crew in every conceivable emergency and tactical scenario. Angles and dangles, computer crashes, reactor scrams, restarts on battery, emergency dives, quick changes in depths and speeds, and many other drills were daily routines.

Samantha spent most of her "free" time familiarizing herself with all the functions and systems of the submarine. In all cases, the crew members were gracious in answering her questions, even allowing her to occupy their stations and gain hands-on experience. She spent the most time with the sonar technicians, learning to interpret the waterfall displays and the low-frequency and range displays as they applied to conducting target-motion analyses, or TMAs.

She met with many of the crew members in the crew's mess to answer numerous questions about her paper on the Sea of Okhotsk. Samantha was continually amazed at the pertinence and depth of the questions they asked. Odd Bergstrom had said as much of the submarine sonar techs he encountered.

She made an effort to eat meals in the crew's mess and the chief's mess, as well as in the wardroom with the officers. The day before they crossed the international date line, Samantha was eating the evening meal in the wardroom when Fred said, "We cross the date line in a few hours, and suddenly it will be 18 February. In a little over a week, it'll be crunch time. Kind of scary, isn't it?"

"I don't know about scary," Josh said. "I'm just excited to get to it."

"You SEALs are not normal. How can you enjoy living on the edge like that?"

Jared answered, "Fred, you just wouldn't understand."

"Ira, what do you think?" Fred asked. "Are SEALs crazy?"

Ira was looking off into space with a silly grin on his face.

"Ira. What are you thinking about?"

Ira snapped out of his daydream and said, "Oh, I'm sorry. My mind was a million miles away. What did you say?"

"Are you okay? You had a funny grin on your face. What were you thinking?"

"Fred, you wouldn't understand."

"That's the second time someone has said that to me in the last five minutes. Try me."

"I was just trying to decide which I liked better, yellow or light blue."

Samantha choked on her soup and started coughing.

Jared immediately stood and patted Samantha on the back. "Are you okay?"

Samantha cleared her throat and said, "I'm okay. I just swallowed my soup wrong. I'll be alright."

"Are you sure?" asked Fred. "Your face is as red as a beet."

Samantha glowered at Ira, and he just smiled beatifically.

★★★

Two days before arriving in Yokosuka, Ira asked Samantha to meet with him in his cabin.

When they were seated, he said, "Samantha, we're getting close to the action. How are you doing?"

"In what way? I've tried to stay busy meeting the crew, learning my way around *Hawkbill*, stuff like that."

"That's all well and good, and I appreciate that. But as you know, we arrive in Yokosuka in two days. A day later, we leave Yokosuka and the action starts. Just before we leave Yokosuka, I'm going to have a meeting with all the officers, Master Chief Boxer, and you. I'm going to ask everyone if they have any concerns that I should know about. I don't want any surprises from our end when we're under stress. I will ask everyone, including you, if there is anything going on that I should know about. But because of your inexperience in this sort of thing, I feel that I need to ask you in private and not in front of the others. Have you had any doubts about being on this mission? Are you experiencing claustrophobia? Are you nervous? Any fear? Fear of dying, perhaps?"

"None of those, Ira. No doubts. No claustrophobia. No fear. I think I'm ready. Every once in a while, I ask myself if I've forgotten something. Some scenario I overlooked. But, no, I feel comfortable on this boat, I like everyone, I feel like I'm part of the crew. Everything's good. Are you having doubts about me?"

"No doubts at all. I feel blessed to have you with me. If anything, I feel more at ease than I have ever felt on any mission before—because I know you'll be by my side in the control room. I just wanted to give you a chance to let me know of any problems you're dealing with."

"Ira, when the crap hits the fan, I don't know how I'll react. I've never done this before. I honestly feel I'll be cool—I really do—but I just don't know. The one thing I do know is that I don't want to let you down. If I have a real fear, that's it."

"Samantha, let me tell you something that I haven't mentioned to anyone."

"Oh? This should be interesting. What is it?"

"When I heard that we would have to deal with two Laika submarines, I got a knot in my stomach. The Laika is the best fast-attack submarine the Russians have. Plus, they always assign their most senior officers as the COs to these boats. I feel that the *Hawkbill* is the best submarine in the world right now, but even with that, our advantage is small when it comes to dealing with a Laika.

"It's going to be nip and tuck out there, and I still have that knot in my stomach. One mistake or bad decision on my part, and it could be over. There's a saying that we have in the submarine force. 'Whoever understands the environment the best will win the day.' There's a good chance that the two Laikas have been operating in the Sea of O for weeks now. Maybe longer. They will have a good understanding of the environment, and we won't. But, Samantha, I have you. Please don't leave my side when I'm in the control room, trying to outwit a Russian commanding officer who is bent on killing us."

"I'll be there, Ira. I promise, I'll do my best." They sat in silence for a short while. Then Samantha said, "This totally changes the subject, but there is something I've wanted to ask you. If you don't want to share this with me, please let me know, and I will understand."

"You've certainly tweaked my interest here. Ask away."

"Can you tell me what happened between you and Forrest? When I first heard about the tension between you, I thought that it might be because Forrest is black. But since I've gotten to know you, I know it isn't that. You are the most non-racist person I know. What happened?"

Ira tapped his chin thoughtfully. Finally he said, "Samantha, you confided to me once and swore me to secrecy. Will you do the same and keep what I tell you just between us?"

"As you said to me, I'll carry it with me to the grave."

"Okay, here goes. On my first submarine mission, I was assigned as the junior navigator. I was a lieutenant junior grade. Forrest was two years my senior, a full lieutenant, and he was the senior navigator on the boat. During the first week of our deployment, the commanding officer asked him to plot a specific and complicated course to our objective area. I was observing him, and I noticed that he made a serious mistake in his navigational calculations and in his plot. When he presented it to the CO, I pointed out his mistake in front of everyone. Forrest was totally embarrassed to make a mistake like that.

"It was very stupid of me to do that to Forrest. I should have pointed out his error privately. Needless to say, Forrest was extremely upset with me, and as my superior officer, he made life miserable for me the rest of the mission. To make matters worse for me, he tried to influence the commanding officer to give me a poor fitness report. Trust me, one poor fitness report can ruin your career. Fortunately, the CO called me into his cabin and discussed the incident with me. He saw the reasons for our childish actions, and he gave me a stern lecture and a good fitness report. Forrest never forgave me for what I did to him, and I never forgave him for what he did to me in return."

"Is that what you and Forrest were discussing on the pier during the BBQ?"

"Yes, exactly. We both apologized for what we did, and we forgave each other on the spot. That's another thing I've learned from my Bible studies. We must forgive. Forgiveness is a very difficult thing to do sometimes, but it's so rewarding when it comes from your heart. I told Forrest that I wish he were with us on this mission, and I really meant it. Well, there it is. A very shameful incident in my life. Something that I am not proud of at all."

Samantha shook her head and said, "Thank you for sharing with me. I'm so happy you and Forrest were finally able to make it right."

"Thank you, Samantha. To the grave, right?"

"To the grave, Ira."

# CHAPTER 39
# YOKOSUKA, JAPAN
## (23–26 FEBRUARY)

**JUST AFTER DARK ON THE** twenty-third of February, *Hawkbill* tied up to a secure, covered pier at the US Naval Base in Yokosuka, Japan. Replenishment of supplies and foodstuffs began immediately. Awaiting Ira and Samantha was a courier carrying recently collected, classified Russian bathymetry charts of the Sea of Okhotsk. As the courier handed over the charts to Samantha, he whispered in her ear, "Admiral Flaxon instructed me to tell you, 'Compliments of Mr. and Mrs. Smith.'"

"God bless Admiral Faxon. He came through again," said Samantha.

"You know, if I had asked Flaxon for these charts, we probably wouldn't have them now. You ask him, and *poof*, here they are. Like magic. I'm telling you, Flaxon has a crush on you."

"Oh, Ira. Don't be silly."

Early the next morning, Ira called for a meeting in the wardroom for all officers, Samantha, and the COB, Master Chief Boxer.

Ira began, "We depart at 0200 tomorrow morning. We will be fully reprovisioned and a minor recalibration of a few of our sonars will be completed. As the XO is fond of saying, it's crunch time. From now on, I want everybody on this boat to be fully alert and sharp. No mistakes." Ira looked at Master Chief Boxer and said, "Do you understand, Bryan?"

"Yes, Skipper. I do."

Ira asked, "Are there any issues with the crew that I should know about?"

"No, sir. The crew understands the importance of the mission, and we are ready to go."

Ira continued, "Weps, Nav, Jared, Josh, anybody? Do you have any concerns I should know about?"

A chorus of "No, sir" followed.

"Samantha, you good?"

"Yes, sir," she answered. "I'm comfortable with the knowns. We will have to deal with the unknowns, if they occur, on the fly. I'll do my best."

"Good. Let me make one thing perfectly clear to all of you. We will not fail to complete our assigned task of destroying the SOOF. As I said to the crew the day we left, I will ram the sucker with the *Hawkbill* if I have to. I hope you all understand what that means. Millions of lives are counting on us, and we will not let them down."

★★★

Right after breakfast the next morning, Samantha asked Ira if he could meet her in the control room. She said, "I have some thoughts on which channel we should use to get into the Sea of O."

"Sure, let's go now."

In the control room, she spread out the bathymetric charts she had received from Flaxon. Ira said to the officer of the deck, "OOD, have the XO and Nav report to control." He looked at Samantha. "I want them to be in on this."

Samantha nodded and prefaced the discussion ahead by

saying, "As you know, we have selected the channel between the islands of Raykoke and Shiashkotan. We based this decision on the fact that this is the channel our subs used when we were tapping their undersea communications cables."

"Are you changing your mind?"

"Perhaps. I just want to make a suggestion for you to consider."

Fred and the navigation officer came into the control room. "What's going on?"

"Samantha wants to discuss how we should enter Okhotsk. Samantha?" asked Ira. "What's on your mind?"

"Do the Russians know how we entered Okhotsk before?"

"I don't know for sure, but I'd be surprised if they didn't."

"That's my thought exactly," she said. "So, knowing this, what would you assume if you were the Russians?"

Nav answered, "That we would use the same route we were comfortable with."

"That makes sense to me," said Fred. Then he continued, "Then I would mine the hell out of the choke point between Raykoke and Shiashkotan. Right?"

The navigator protested, "But wait a minute. We're entering the Sea of O on the twenty-sixth. They're mining the channels on 1 March. What's the issue?"

"Are you sure of that? Are you willing to risk your life on an old intel report?" Samantha asked.

Ira said, "Good point. What do you recommend?"

"I've been looking at the bathy charts Flaxon got for us. See these two islands here? Brat Chirpoyev and Urup? Look at the water depths. There's a pretty deep channel between them."

"But," Fred pointed out, "they're pretty close together. How wide is that channel? We won't have much maneuvering room to get around any mines we might encounter."

"All the more reason why they might not even mine this channel. Certainly they would only use a few," Samantha replied.

"Ira, what do you think? Do we have enough room to maneuver around any mines there?"

"Let me think about this for a bit. It's an important decision. I want to feel comfortable with my choice. What I decide can also affect our escape route on our way home. Let's all think about Samantha's suggestion, meet here after lunch, discuss our thoughts, and I will decide."

After lunch, the four reconvened in Control. Looking at the bathy charts, Ira said, "Do any of you have any additional thoughts on our route into the Sea of O?"

"I think Samantha has made some good points. If we have maneuvering room, I would go with her recommendation," Fred said. "My biggest concern is that we don't want to be predictable."

Ira said, "That's true. Predictable is deadly. Also, I've been looking at the bathymetry and geography of her recommended channel. It looks like we should have no bottom obstructions to deal with, and I feel that we have plenty of room to maneuver. So, unless there are no major objections, that's our way in. Anyone? No? Okay, Nav, plot a course between those two islands whose names I can't even pronounce."

★★★

"Sonar, any contacts? Submarines? Surface ships? What do you have?" asked Ira.

"Nothing new, sir. No submarines detected. We have quite a few fishing vessels, but they're staying well away from the Kurils."

"What are the blockade ships doing? Anything more on them?"

"No, sir. I see only two of them, and they seem to be much slower than the fast patrol boats we were expecting. They appear to be larger warships. Possibly frigates."

"What?" Ira demanded with concern. "Get the senior chief sonar tech up here ASAP."

A few minutes later, Senior Chief Feldman entered the control room. "What do you need, Captain?"

"Get with the sonar tech on watch and tell me what kind of Russian ships we're dealing with."

Chief Feldman studied the waterfall sonar display for about ten minutes and then reported to Ira. "I'm afraid the sonar tech is correct, Captain. The two sonar contacts appear to be ASW frigates."

"Oh, crap. What's their range, bearing, and speed? Weps, I need a fire-control solution on the two frigates. Where's the third one? Find it for me. Nav, when we have a good target-motion analysis on those frigates, I want to steer a course to avoid them. Got that?"

"Yes, sir."

Ira began a series of course and speed changes to determine the relative motion of the frigates. An hour later he asked, "Chief, on their present heading, will they miss us?"

"Yes, sir. One is going away from us at fifteen knots. The other will pass in front of us by about ten miles at our present course and speed."

Ira commanded, "Pilot, reduce speed to five knots and change course to two-four-zero degrees."

"Aye, sir. Reduce speed to five knots and change course to two-four-zero degrees."

An hour later, the frigate passed ahead of the *Hawkbill* and was traveling to the northeast at fifteen knots. "Sonar, are you picking up any helicopters or dipping sonars?"

"No, sir. Other than the frigate that just passed us, it's all quiet."

Ira clasped his XO's shoulder in relief and said, "God, Fred. I hope we don't have any more surprises."

"Roger that, Ira. Roger that."

★★★

En route to the selected ingress channel, Samantha said, "Ira, I've got another idea."

"Do you ever run out of ideas?" he demanded, only a little exasperated.

"It's just my nature. The new bathy charts have got my mind racing."

"What is it this time? Do I need Fred and Nav in on it?"

"It wouldn't hurt. The XO at least."

"OOD, page the XO to control."

"Yes, sir."

While waiting for Fred, Samantha unrolled another chart on the plotting table. Fred entered Control and asked, "What's going on, Skipper?"

"Would you believe it? Samantha's got another idea."

"Will wonders ever cease?"

"Come on, guys. Give me some slack. What are you paying me for?"

Both men laughed. Ira said, "Show me what you've got," as he surreptitiously winked at her.

Samantha shook her head and pointed to a small dot on the chart. "This is a small volcanic island named Iony Island. Actually, it's the only true island in the Okhotsk sea."

"What about it? Why are you interested in a small piece of rock?" asked Fred.

"Several things about this small piece of rock have caught my attention. First, notice that there are a great deal of depth soundings around the island. It seems like the Russian survey ships ran tight survey lines around the island to get a very detailed bathymetry map."

"Maybe because they knew that the Laika subs would be operating there, and they didn't want any collisions with the bottom," Ira suggested.

"Perhaps. The key is that we have the same info, which we can use to our advantage. The second thing I noticed is that this uninhabited piece of rock is the breeding ground for an incredible amount of wildlife. Noisy wildlife. Sea lions, for example. The bird population is extraordinary. This means that there will be all kinds of fish there for the birds to feed on. What I'm trying to say is that the area around Iony Island is going to be unbelievably noisy. We should be able to hide in the noise and remain undetected."

"Sounds like a sound plan to me," Ira said. After a beat he added, "No pun intended."

Samantha chuckled and continued. "That's not all. Notice where Iony is with respect to where we believe the SOOF is located. It's about fifty miles west-southwest of the SOOF. There's a fairly deepwater route from Iony to about twenty miles from the SOOF where it begins to shoal. My thought is that we can get the *Hawkbill* within twenty-five miles or so from the SOOF, launch the Peg with the SEALs, and they can transit the last twenty-five miles in the Peg. That's two and a half hours at ten knots. That would leave them about five hours for working the SOOF wall and trying to locate the comms cable. According to the Cool Pool results, five hours is about the maximum time they will have to operate effectively in that cold water."

Samantha continued, "But then suppose we can't locate the comms cable to destroy it? What's our plan B for doing that?"

"We don't have one. Don't tell me you do."

"I do have a plan, but it's a long shot. Still interested?"

"Come on, Samantha. Why do you do this to us? Spit it out."

"I just want to keep you on your toes."

Ira and Fred exchanged glances and grumbled under their breaths.

Meanwhile, Samantha put an eight-by-ten sheet of paper on the plotting table and said, "Are you two grown men through talking to yourselves?"

"Samantha!" Ira shot back.

"Okay, okay. If we can't locate the cable, why don't we put a Tomahawk missile on the land station feeding the cable to the SOOF?"

"How are we going to fire a Tomahawk through the ice?" Fred asked.

"There may be a way around that problem." She pointed to an area she had penciled out just east of Iony Island. Then, pointing at Iony Island, she said, "This circle I drew represents Iony Island. The arrows represent the water currents around Iony. These currents come from two sources: the Amur River and the warm water entering from the Pacific through the Kuril channels. Most of the ice around Iony should be relatively thin and soft because it is primarily freshwater ice. And it should not be pressure-ridged.

"Now, listen to this. The currents and winds will carry the ice to the east, hopefully leaving open water or very thin ice in the lee of the island. This open water is what we oceanographers call a recurring polynya. *Polynya* is a Russian term for open water."

"So, you're saying we might have an open-water area in the sea-ice canopy that we can surface through to fire a Tomahawk?" Ira concluded.

"That's exactly what I'm trying to say. The question is, does this recurring polynya exist?"

"How can we answer that question?" asked Fred.

"How does this sound? During the ten hours the SEALs are in the Peg and working the SOOF, instead of just sitting there and waiting for the SEALs to return, why can't we survey the underside of the ice with our secure, high-frequency, upward-looking sonar and measure the thickness of the ice?"

"What's the water depth on the east side of Iony?" asked Ira.

"I think it's between one and two hundred feet."

The bathymetric chart confirmed Samantha's guess.

"God, Samantha. I think you just unlocked plan C as well as

plan B."

"What do you mean, Ira?"

"If this 'polygraph,' or whatever you call it, exists, while we're attacking the land communications facility, why don't we drop a couple of Tomahawks on the SOOF? Just for insurance."

"That should work, Ira. The ice over the SOOF should be very thin because of the heat generated to run the place. An inch or two at the most. The 'roof' of the SOOF will only be about five feet below the water surface. But will this five feet of water prevent the Tomahawk from being effective?"

"I don't know. Probably not. It's worth the chance."

"Great. If the open water is there, we've got a plan C."

# CHAPTER 40
## CAPTOR MINEFIELD LOCATION

**LATER THAT NIGHT, WHEN SAMANTHA** entered the control room, Ira ducked and yelled, "Everybody, take cover. Here comes Samantha. She may have another idea to drop on us." The others in Control laughed loudly.

"Okay, guys. Have your fun. No, I don't have any other ideas, but I do have a problem to solve. Well, maybe I do have another idea."

Ira groaned and said, "I don't like problems, Samantha. But what is the problem, and what is your idea?"

"Ira, in our planning, we came up with a possible escape scenario using our CAPTOR mines."

"Yes, we did. A plan I hope we don't have to use."

"My question now is where we're going to place the CAPTORs. Now that we have these Russian bathymetric charts, we can make an intelligent decision. How much time do we have before we reach the Brat Chirpoyev/Urup channel?"

"About four hours. We're still about a hundred miles away."

Samantha said, "That will make it around 0600 in the

morning. I think we need to slow down a bit. My DSL analysis has told me that we want to enter the minefield no earlier than 1000 when the sun is up and has driven the scattering layer below the mines, if they're there.

"Once we enter the channel, we'll be busy looking for mines. Once we get through and into the ice-free area of the Okhotsk, we'll have ASW frigates to deal with. What I'm hinting at is that we need to select our minefield area before we have to deal with their mines and frigates. We might not have time if we don't do it now."

"You're right. I wanted to get a few hours of sleep before we enter the channel, but that can wait. Fred, come. Samantha, bring the charts."

"I've already got them spread out on the wardroom table."

Once in the wardroom, Ira began, "We've talked this over numerous times. The important points are these. We will probably have one, maybe two Laikas chasing us. The variables are these: Will it be one or two of them? How close will they be when we realize they're chasing us? How far away is our minefield? When should we turn on our noisemaker and turn it off? How far from the minefield do we launch the Peg and turn its noisemaker on? There are so many unknowns."

"How do we deal with all this?" asked Fred.

Samantha stated, "There are a few things we can control. One is where the minefield is. Another is where and when we launch Tomahawk missiles. Based on these two things, we will know how far we have to go to reach the minefield area. If we have any threat information at that time, we solve our problem then. If we don't have any information on the whereabouts of their subs, we can then determine when we turn on our noisemaker to bring them to us."

"Okay," Ira said, rubbing his chin as he considered the options. "How about putting the CAPTORs two hundred fifty to three hundred miles from the Tomahawk launch site at Iony Island?

This would be about ten to twelve hours of transit time at twenty-five knots. Hopefully, we can stay undetected for that long."

"What's the optimum and maximum operating depth of the mines?" asked Fred.

"I'll have to check to be sure, but I believe the maximum depth is one thousand feet," Ira replied. "Fred, Weps is in the control room. See what he says."

Samantha indicated a spot on the bathymetric chart spread out on the wardroom table. "Here's an area where the water depths are around one thousand feet, and it's on the way to our escape route through the channel when we head home. About three hundred miles from the channel."

Fred returned from the control room. "The maximum depth for CAPTOR is one thousand feet."

"Good," said Samantha. "And the area we're looking at is under the ice and about three hundred miles from Iony, just as we had hoped."

"Okay. It's decided. That's where we set up our CAPTORs minefield."

★★★

In the control room Ira announced, "Everybody, listen up. We are most likely about to enter a minefield set especially for us. I want everybody to be fully alert. This is not a drill. If we make a mistake, our mission is over, and we lose. If there are mines here, make me proud and let's detect and avoid them. Pilot, set speed at five knots and depth of one hundred fifty feet." Captain Coen's order was repeated by the pilot.

Thirty minutes into the transit of the channel, an audible sonar echo return from a mine was heard, and the sonar tech announced, "Possible mine ten degrees to starboard. Possible depth, one hundred feet, range about six hundred yards."

"Steer course two hundred seventy degrees, two degree down

bubble. Level off at two hundred feet." The pilot repeated the order. "Nav, plot and record the location and depth of the mine."

"Aye, sir."

"Range to mine?" Ira asked.

"Five hundred yards, sir."

"Keep me informed."

"Aye, sir."

"Any new contacts?"

"No, sir. Contact number one is now directly abeam on our starboard side at a range of six hundred yards."

A few minutes later, the sonar tech announced, "Contact one is now at one hundred sixty degrees at a range of eight hundred yards and increasing."

"Very well."

Ten minutes later: "Sir, a new contact eight hundred yards dead ahead. Possible depth of one hundred fifty feet."

"Steer course of zero degrees, up bubble of one degree. Bring us up slowly to one hundred feet."

The pilot repeated and executed the order.

"OOD, how much water under our hull?"

The OOD checked the secure fathometer and reported, "We have twenty fathoms, or one hundred twenty feet, under our hull and decreasing."

"Pilot, up bubble to two degrees."

"Aye, sir. Up bubble to two degrees."

"OOD, give me depths in feet and not fathoms."

"Aye, sir."

"Bearing and range to the second mine?"

"Mine is passing to our port side, bearing three hundred ten degrees. Range is still eight hundred yards."

"Level off at one hundred twenty feet."

"Aye, sir." A few minutes later, Sonar reported, "We are level at one hundred twenty feet. Distance to mines is increasing."

Twenty minutes later, there were no new contacts. "Nav."

"Yes, sir."

"Plot a course to these coordinates." Ira gave him the location of the planned CAPTOR minefield.

"Yes, sir."

"Sonar. Any new contacts?"

"No, sir."

"Very good. Maintain speed of five knots for one hour. I will then give you another speed order. OOD, the navigator will give the pilot a new course shortly."

"Aye, sir."

"Well, Fred, it looks like we just had surprise number two. Intel said no mines until 1 March."

"Like Samantha asked, would we be willing to risk our lives on an intel report?"

"How does she know these things? Can she see into the future?" Ira demanded with mock frustration.

"I'm starting to wonder if she's even human," Fred whispered. "I mean, look at her eyes. Have you ever seen a human being with dark-green eyes like that?"

"You're scaring me, Fred. But no, I haven't. I can tell you this about her. She has taught me things about myself. For example, there are surprises I like and surprises I don't like. This frigate thing and the presence of mines were two surprises I didn't like."

Fred's look at Ira was puzzled.

"Fred, don't ask."

An hour later, Ira asked, "Pilot, what's our course and speed?"

"We are on course two hundred seventy-five degrees at five knots."

"Very well. Increase speed to ten knots."

"Aye, sir. Increasing to ten knots."

"Sonar, stay alert for frigates."

"Aye, sir."

"Nav, do you have plots on those two mines? Location and depth?"

"Yes, sir. Got it."

"Estimated time to pack ice?"

"Fifteen hours at ten knots, sir."

"Very well. Weps, I'd like to see you in the wardroom."

"Yes, sir."

On his way to the wardroom, Ira met Samantha in the passageway. He said, "Thanks for alerting us to the possibility that they might mine the channels early."

"Of course. I just hope we don't run into any more surprises."

"From my experience, we will. Surprises happen all the time in this business. It's called 'the fog of war.'"

"Oh really?" Samantha said with a knowing grin.

"Yes. Many years ago, a Prussian general named Carlos von Santa Claus coined the phrase."

"Carlos von Santa Claus?"

"Yes, it's a military thing. Don't worry about it. I'll explain later," Ira said over his shoulder as he went into the wardroom to meet with Weps.

Under her breath, Samantha said, "I guess Carl von Clausewitz does sound a little like Carlos von Santa Claus. But you've got to be kidding me."

★★★

"What's up, Captain?"

"Have a seat, Weps."

"Thank you, sir."

"Tomorrow, we will be going under the ice pack, and our immediate danger will be the two Laika submarines."

"Yes, sir."

"Once we get under the ice, we stay slow and keep a lookout. On 28 February, in one day, we will arrive at the area we selected to deploy our CAPTOR minefield."

"Yes, sir."

"I want everything ready to deploy the mines. Our minefield will consist of four CAPTORs. I want three torpedo tubes loaded with the mines and ready for launch. Keep tube four loaded with a torpedo. As soon as the first CAPTOR is deployed, reload the tube with the fourth one. We've practiced this several times, and I expect no problems. The mine settings will be provided to you before we begin the changeover from torpedoes to mines. As you know, we have thirteen SEALs living in the torpedo room. Keep the disruption to them at a minimum. Got all that?"

"Yes, sir."

"Get together with your senior chief and men and go over the whole procedure with them one more time. Just like we practiced."

"You got it, Captain."

★★★

They encountered no enemy frigates or submarines during the transit to the planned minefield location. The CAPTOR settings were installed, and four anticipated or likely operating depths were chosen. Once they reached the first selected location, a fathometer reading was taken, and the length of the mine's mooring cable was adjusted to keep the mine at the proper depth in the water.

All four CAPTORs were launched with no problems. The location of the four mines and their mooring depths were recorded by the navigator. The minefield was now in place.

The only uncertainty that remained was whether the mines would turn on when commanded by the acoustic signal from the *Hawkbill*. Josh asked, "Why don't we turn them on now? We might get lucky and bag ourselves a Laika."

Jared reminded him of the need to remain undetected—at least until the SOOF was destroyed. "If one of those mines went off now, they would know we're here, and we would probably fail our mission."

# CHAPTER 41
## IONY ISLAND
### (3–5 MARCH)

*HAWKBILL* **CONTINUED ITS JOURNEY TO** Iony Island at a relatively low speed, constantly searching for enemy submarines. None were detected, and Iony was reached at 1200 on 3 March.

Ira, Samantha, Fred, Jared, and Josh met in the wardroom after the evening meal. Ira began, "Here's the plan. Tonight, tomorrow, and the next day, if necessary, the SEALs in the Peg are going to survey the first twenty-five miles of the fifty-mile route we're taking to the SOOF. Jared, Josh, you will be looking for mines, both moored and bottom, and for any underwater obstructions the Russians might have missed when they surveyed this area. We don't know anything about these waters, and I don't want any surprises.

"While you guys are deployed in the Peg, we'll conduct an under-ice survey looking for Samantha's open-water area."

"The recurring polynya," added Samantha.

"Yeah. That thing."

Samantha chuckled.

Ira addressed Jared. "You should have about eight hours of

Peg time each day for your survey. Any problem with that?"

"No, sir. We can rendezvous with you, recharge the batteries, switch crews, and deploy again. We should get about two sorties a day. We are ready."

"Good. On 6 and 7 March, we will use this twenty-five-mile 'safe' channel to get you SEALs within twenty-five miles of the SOOF so you can survey that area. Hopefully, on 8 March you can start your work on the SOOF wall."

"Sounds good, sir. We're really anxious to get started."

"Okay, I would like to launch Pegasus right after midnight tonight and get this next phase going."

Samantha added, "Josh, Jared, when we're close to Iony, there may be some unexpected turbulence that could affect the stability of Peggy, probably caused by the internal waves created by the tidal currents around the island. Be extra alert at the controls so you can compensate. As you get farther from the island, the turbulence should lessen."

"Got it, Samantha. Thanks."

Later, just before Josh entered the lock-in/lock-out chamber, Ira said, "Godspeed, Josh. Be careful, and get back safely."

At 0100, Pegasus detached from *Hawkbill* with four enlisted SEALs on board and Lieutenant Josh Freeman in command.

★★★

"Samantha, do you have a plan for conducting the under-ice survey?"

"I suggest that we start out in deeper water and work our way in to Iony. That way, we can keep an eye out for any sudden shoaling. And we can look for any internal wave activity that I warned Jared and Josh about."

"Good point. We won't have much water under our keel. This turbulence could be a problem. How far out should we start and at what location?"

"The closest point to where we are now would be good."

"Okay, let's give coordinates to Nav and get started."

Eight hours later, the *Hawkbill* had broken off its under-ice survey and arrived at the rendezvous point to redock the Pegasus. While the redocking progressed, Ira said to Samantha, "Well, no open water yet. What do you think?"

"Too early to tell, Ira. We started where I knew the ice would be too thick. But I did notice a thinning as we got closer to the island. I'm still hopeful."

Ira said, "One thing I did notice was how incredibly noisy it is here. Just like you said it would be. I think we could be a hundred yards from a Laika and not hear it."

"He won't be able to hear us either. That's good, right?"

"Very good."

"Docking complete, Captain," said the OOD.

"Very well."

Fifteen minutes later, Josh and Jared came into Control. "How did it go, Josh?"

"Pretty well, Captain. We made four twenty-mile tracks of the twenty-five-mile route. We held our speed at ten knots and got pretty good coverage. We found no mines and no severe bathymetric changes. We observed no internal wave activity. Looks good so far."

"Great. Let's get Peg recharged and ready to do the last five miles."

Jared said, "I suggest we launch and recover Peg from where we are right now. That will give us two additional lines in the first twenty miles. We will still have four hours to survey the last five miles. That also would keep *Hawkbill* safe here longer to do the polynya survey."

"I like the way you think, Jared. Good idea."

★★★

By the end of 5 March, the first twenty-five miles of the fifty-mile channel between Iony and the SOOF had been declared safe for *Hawkbill*.

The Bravo Team five met in the wardroom to discuss the next phase of the mission. "We are comfortably within twenty-five miles of the SOOF. Next up is to survey the last twenty-five miles for mines. I'm not taking *Hawkbill* any closer than this unless I have to. Jared, your survey lines can be much closer together, and you'll get a more detailed picture of the bottom to the SOOF. Look primarily for bottom mines."

"Yes, sir. I've been thinking about that, and I would like to run survey lines across our path toward the wall rather than along it. We should get to the SOOF itself by the end of 7 March. If we can do that, we'll have four days to mark the wall and two days to attach the explosive charges. This will give us one day of wiggle room for insurance."

Ira nodded. "That's what we've been planning on. Let's just pray we remain undetected this last week."

"Amen to that, sir."

Ira continued, "As you know, we still haven't located our 'polygamy' yet, but we had some encouraging results yesterday about five miles from Iony. We found some very thin ice. We can surface through it without any trouble, but I'm not sure if the hull will be clear enough of ice to open the launch-tube doors so we can fire the Tomahawks."

"I've got eleven able-bodied SEALs at my disposal. If we surface through the ice, and the hull is covered with it, maybe we could go out there and clear it," Jared suggested.

"Well, I've got 130 men on *Hawkbill* that can do the same. Let's keep that in mind. What's bothering me is that the water is only about one hundred feet deep and shoaling. Also, we did notice some bouncing around. I feel very uncomfortable there.

We've only got a couple feet of water under the hull to play with.

"Okay, let's get busy."

"It's crunch time," Fred said, rubbing his hands together.

# CHAPTER 42
## THE BLACK HOLE
### (6–7 MARCH)

**ON 6 MARCH WHEN PEGASUS** returned to the rendezvous point, *Hawkbill* was not waiting as planned. Jared waited patiently, albeit nervously, for the submarine to appear. When *Hawkbill* returned and the redocking was complete, they all met in the wardroom to report their results.

"Where were you guys?" Jared asked. "I was scared to death."

"Sorry about that, but we found the 'polyanna,' and we decided to define its extent while we were there. I'm real antsy operating in water that shallow when it could have some bottom feature we don't know about. But the good news is that Samantha was right again. There is an essentially open-water area on the eastern side of the island. A few inches thick at the most. I'm sure that we can surface through it cleanly and launch the Tomahawks."

"Wow! That's great news, Skipper. Great news."

"What about you, Jared? I see you got back safely. Any problems?"

"No showstoppers, sir. Unless you call bottom mines a problem."

"As a matter of fact, I do. How many? Where?"

"We found our first one six miles from the SOOF. We continued along our cross tracks parallel to the SOOF and found another one, also six miles from the SOOF. To make a long story short, it appears that they deployed a circle of mines six miles from the SOOF."

"Did you get closer to the SOOF?"

"Yes, we did. The mines seem to be about twelve hundred yards apart. That gave us about six hundred yards of clearance going right between them. It's close. But the only mines we encountered were the ones six miles from the wall."

"Did you plot the ones you detected?"

"Yes, sir. We found five of them, and we know where they are. Tomorrow, we can go in the same way between the mines and complete our survey. I have to say this, though. It was downright scary sailing that close to them."

"Are they buried?" asked Fred.

"I don't know, Fred. We detected them with our high-frequency mine-hunting sonar. We just know they're there."

"Will you be able to finish your survey work tomorrow?"

"Yes, Captain. I believe so."

Once again, Ira muttered, "I hate mines."

✳✳✳

While the Pegasus completed the SOOF-area survey, *Hawkbill* slowly ran lines, carefully searching for signs of the Russian submarines. Samantha came up behind the sonar tech and said, "Hi, Twigs. Mind if I look over your shoulder?"

"No, Samantha. Not at all."

"That is some noisy screen we're looking at."

"Yes, it is. It drives me nuts looking at it for six hours."

"What are you looking for exactly?"

"The Laika emits two well-defined low-frequency lines. Under good conditions, we can see those lines and track them. But with all this noise, it's almost impossible to see them."

Samantha studied the screen for about five minutes.

"Twigs, what is that?" she asked, pointing to a dark spot.

"I'm not sure, Samantha. It looks like a black hole in all the noise."

"A black hole in random noise?" She studied the feature and said, "Twigs, a hole in the noise is not normal."

"No. It isn't. What do you suppose is causing it?"

"Let me think." After a few minutes, Samantha said, "That darn thing is persistent."

"It sure seems that way."

Samantha repeated, "Twigs, that's not normal." Samantha turned to Ira. "Ira, look at the waterfall display here. Twigs, show the captain what you've found."

Twigs looked puzzled but turned to the captain and said, "Captain, if you look at the screen, pretty much all you see is the ambient noise, which looks like white noise. However, if you look closely, you can see a very small but well-defined area of low noise. Actually, it's an area of almost no noise. It's very persistent, sir."

"What do you suppose it is?"

"I'm not sure, sir, but it isn't normal."

"Samantha?" Ira asked.

"It could be a submarine, Ira."

"Why do you think that?"

"The sub could be blocking the noise from reaching our towed array. Sort of like a sound baffle."

"OOD, get Senior Chief Feldman to Control ASAP."

Two minutes later, Feldman ran into Control wearing only his skivvies. "Sorry, Samantha. ASAP by the CO means ASAP. Yes, Captain, what do you need?"

"Twigs, fill in the chief here on the black hole. I'm going to do some maneuvering and try to perform an analysis on that thing. Chief, Twigs, keep me informed on any changes you see."

"Aye, sir."

Ira executed course and speed changes to see what would happen to the black hole in the noise. An hour later, he was convinced that the black hole was a submarine.

"It's not a whale," Ira said. "No whale can hold its breath for that long."

"I don't think it's a whale either, Ira. But not for that reason," Samantha clarified. "Sperm whales have been known to stay under for well over an hour. And there are sperm whales in the Sea of O."

"Why do you think it isn't a sperm whale, then?"

"Because whales don't stay on a constant course at the same depth. I believe that black hole is a submarine."

"Okay, Chief Feldman. Get your sonar techs to Control immediately. I don't care if they're all dressed like you. I want you and Twigs to show them what to look for."

"Yes, sir. Right away, sir."

"Oh, and, Chief Feldman, I do care what the senior chief wears in Control. Put on some pants. Pilot, steer course zero-zero-five degrees. I want to parallel that sub and keep him visible."

Ira patted Twigs on the head. "Good job, Twigs."

"But, sir. Samantha, she . . ." Twigs never finished what he was trying to say. Captain Coen was already hustling somewhere else.

# CHAPTER 43
## ON SCHEDULE
### (8–13 MARCH)

**AT 2000 ON 8 MARCH,** Pegasus left *Hawkbill* for the SOOF, fully loaded with eight SEALs and CDR Jared Townsend in command. Four miles from the SOOF, the SEALs left the Pegasus for the wall with their one-man propulsors. The trip took about fifty minutes. Once they were there, they initiated their oft-practiced plan of attaching the measured ropes to the wall. Six of the men worked as a team on the wall while the other two tried to locate the comms cable.

On the wall, the job was tediously slow, but the handheld sonars were a great help in identifying the points to attach the ropes. After four hours of work at the wall, they rendezvoused and began the fifty-minute trip back to the Peg.

Once inside, one of the SEALs said, "Holy shit, that water's cold."

"What a wuss," said another. But they all huddled around a heater during their trip back to the *Hawkbill*.

Back on board, Jared went immediately to the wardroom to give his report.

"It went pretty well. We got the top and bottom ropes installed. But even with the gas-infused wet suits, my guys can't do more than five hours of work. Near the end, they were not very nimble.

"The bad news is that we didn't find the cable. Samantha, the bottom is pretty hard around the wall. No ploof. But you were right about the visibility. It was night, and we had none. This slows us down, but hopefully it keeps us undetected. Also, we've practiced doing this job wearing masks over and over again. By the way, the handheld sonars really helped us get started. We were able to find the initial points very quickly."

Ira said, "Good report, Jared. Based on today, what do you hope to get done tomorrow?"

"Skipper, if we can get the two vertical ropes attached at the sides, I'll be happy. That will give us two days to get the diagonals and the smaller ropes attached. I think we have it covered."

★★★

From the defined launch point twenty-five miles from the SOOF, Pegasus detached from the *Hawkbill* and began its journey, following the same procedure and route as before. Once there, the men located the ropes placed on the wall the day before and began attaching the verticals. Once again, two SEALs looked for the hard-to-find comms cable.

By the end of 11 March, the explosive charge points had been designated by thick tape wrappings on the attached ropes. The cable still had not been found, but they did find one anomaly.

Jared gave his report.

"We have completed attaching the ropes to the outer wall. Tomorrow, we can start attaching the explosives at the points indicated on the ropes. We have fifteen points. We are on schedule."

"What about the cable?" asked Samantha.

"No joy on that, Samantha. However, we did locate a five-foot-wide swath of rocks and pebbles leading up to the wall. Something is buried there. That's the only spot like that we found."

"Could be that they purposely buried the cable and covered it with a layer of rocks," Ira suggested. "What do you think, Samantha?"

"Very likely, Ira. Would our explosives be effective against it?"

Jared said, "Maybe. Maybe not. Depends on how deep it's buried and how dense or hard the covering is."

"Did your guys try to dig through it?" Fred asked.

"No, Fred. We found it at the end of the day and didn't have a chance or the ability to do that. The men were freezing up."

"Good work, Jared. Good report," Ira said.

"Thanks, sir."

"Here's what we're going to do. We will start attaching the explosive devices to the wall as planned. I would like to finish that job by the thirteenth. Meanwhile, let's try to dig down to expose the cable, if it's even there. If we strike out on this, we will put two shaped charges over it and hope that this destroys the cable. I still plan on using our plan B and launching a Tomahawk on the land facility."

"Very well, Skipper. We will get all that done. How did it go with *Hawkbill*?"

Ira answered, "As with the last two days, we returned to the area where we detected the black hole, but we haven't spotted another one. If it is one of the Laikas, it moved away from Iony. We'll keep trying over the next two days. If we come across one, we want to try some beam-steering to see if we can spot the Laika lines in its black hole. Hey, it's a long shot but worth trying. Also, tomorrow I'm thinking of revisiting the 'polymorphous' to see if it's still there. I'm a little unsure of myself with the danger of internal waves and hitting an underwater rock or the bottom. I'll decide by tomorrow. The good news in all of this is that we're still on schedule. Hallelujah."

"Amen," said Fred.

"Amen," echoed Samantha. Then she added, "It's polynya, Ira. Polynya."

Ira just smiled back at her.

★★★

In the wardroom on 14 March, Ira said, "We're all set and ready to go. We've even got today to wait and rest. The charges are in place on the wall, we've got two charges on the suspected cable covering, our polynya is still there, and we have not been detected. I couldn't ask for anything better. What I would like to do today is stay in the vicinity of Iony Island and remain undetected in all this noise."

After a short pause, he said, "Alright. Let's go over the plan again for tomorrow. Our ADCAP Mk 48 torpedoes have a maximum range of thirty miles at a speed of forty knots. We'll be at our 'safe' twenty-five-mile distance from the SOOF when we launch the torpedoes. We blow the wall with the attached charges at exactly 1400. That's 0600 Greenwich Mean Time, the time selected for all the preemptive IDES strikes in Europe and in the Arctic against the Boreis. It will take the torpedoes thirty-eight minutes to reach the SOOF from twenty-five miles away, and we want the first two torpedoes to arrive and strike the SOOF's inner wall at 1402. That means that we must launch the first ADCAPs at 1324. The second set of torpedoes must be launched at 1326. Timing is everything. Does everybody understand this?"

"How can we be assured of the speed of the torpedoes?" asked Samantha.

"We will be wire-guiding them to be sure they arrive after the outer wall has been destroyed.

As soon as we release the second set of torpedoes from the wires and they go active, we will sprint the *Hawkbill* to the polynya." He winked at Samantha, then continued, "That's about twenty-five miles. About fifty minutes. Hopefully, we will be surfaced by about 1500 and ready to launch the missiles by 1515. As soon as the Tomahawks are away, we submerge and head for the CAPTOR minefield."

"What about the Russian subs?" asked Josh.

"I don't know where they are right now. My guess is close by. It's 14 March. With all that we do tomorrow, they will know where we are. They will almost certainly know we're here when we shoot our first two torpedoes. Regardless, we have to find them and keep them from finding us.

"If they get a little sniff of us, they will go active. All bets are off at that point, and we will have to hope that our state-of-the-art anechoic tiles do their job. We do have the advantage of being quieter than they are, and that black hole will help us find them in all this noise. I suggest we pray tonight that all our months of planning and practicing pays off tomorrow. Remember this: We must destroy the SOOF, and we are not leaving here until we do."

★★★

"Captain, you got a few minutes?"

"Master Chief, come on in." The COB entered Ira's cabin. "What's going on, Bryan?"

"Not much, sir, but I thought that this might be a good time to talk to you. Before all hell breaks loose tomorrow."

"This is a good time. What's on your mind?"

"Overall, the crew is doing great. The best crew I've ever been associated with."

"That's good to hear."

"But you did tell us to keep you apprised of anything that would come up. And there is just one small issue that I'd like to bring up to you. It concerns sonar tech Twigerton."

"Twigs? What about him?"

"Well, it seems to him that he is getting credit for something that he doesn't deserve, and it's really bothering him."

"You're talking about the so-called black hole."

"Yes, sir. I am."

"Bryan, I was standing only a few feet away from him and Samantha, and I saw and heard all that happened."

"Twigs told me he's tried to tell you several times that it was Samantha who noticed the hole in the noise, and that it was she who figured out what it was."

"I know, Bryan. But that's Samantha. Not once have I seen her take credit for what she's done. Not once. And believe me, she has saved this mission many times over."

"What should I tell Twigs?"

"I don't know." Ira thought for a moment and said, "Tell him this—and it's the truth: Samantha thinks the world of him as a sonar tech, and she feels that if it weren't for him, she might not have figured it out. Tell him also that I agree with her."

"Ira, I've never met anyone like her before. If I weren't a happily married man, I wouldn't let her out of my sight."

"Hmph." Ira sighed. "You and everybody else on this boat."

# CHAPTER 44
## THE IDES OF MARCH
### (15 MARCH)

*HAWKBILL* **LEFT THEIR IONY ISLAND** sanctuary and arrived at the torpedo launch point at 1300. It was hard to believe, after months of preparation, that their task would be completed with a few simple directives. It was now a matter of timing.

"Weps, are you ready to shoot the ADCAPs? All four of them?"

"Yes, sir. They're locked and loaded."

"Eng, are you ready to send the acoustic signal to blow the charges?"

"Yes, sir. Ready to send."

"Are you ready to give us max speed to the polynya?"

"Yes, sir. All is ready."

"Nav, does the pilot have the course and speed ready to go?"

"Yes, sir. Pilot has course, speed, and depth."

"Very well. Everyone, wait for my commands."

At exactly 1324, Ira commanded, "Weps, shoot torpedoes one and two."

"Aye, sir. Shoot torpedoes one and two," Weps instructed the torpedo room.

A few seconds later, Weps said, "Torpedoes one and two away, sir. They are running true at forty knots."

"Very good. Weps, make sure they arrive no sooner than 1402."

"Aye, sir."

Two minutes later, Ira commanded, "Weps, shoot torpedoes three and four."

"Aye, sir. Shoot torpedoes three and four," Weps ordered.

"Torpedoes three and four away, sir. Running at forty knots."

The wait to 1400 seemed interminable. But at precisely 1400, Ira commanded, "Eng, detonate the charges."

"Aye, sir. Sending the signal." A few seconds later, sonar picked up huge underwater explosions.

"Weps, go active with torpedoes one and two."

"Aye, sir. Torpedoes one and two active and homing in."

Two minutes later, Ira commanded, "Weps, go active with torpedoes three and four."

"Aye, sir. Torpedoes three and four active.

"Very well. Pilot, set course, speed, and depths provided by Nav."

"Aye, sir."

"Sonar, watch for Laikas. Laika lines, black holes, anything."

"Yes, sir."

At 1402, sonar picked up two loud explosions as the first torpedoes hit the inner wall of the SOOF. Two minutes later, two more explosions were heard as the torpedoes struck their target, the interior of the SOOF. They had no way of knowing whether the extra shaped charges had taken care of the communications cable, so the timing of the next step remained critical.

"Samantha, I hope your polynya is still there for us."

"So do I, Ira. I believe it will be. And congratulations. I noticed you've been getting the name right."

"I don't have any idea what you're talking about," he said with a smile.

The *Hawkbill* screamed back to the polynya at thirty-five-plus knots. As they neared the point where they planned to breach the surface, Ira ordered, "Pilot, slow to ten knots."

"Aye, sir."

"What's the water depth?"

"It's one hundred forty feet and decreasing."

"Pilot, slow to five knots."

"Aye, sir. Slowing to five knots."

"Samantha, how thick is the ice above us?"

"Only a few inches thick, Ira, and it's getting thinner."

"Pilot, slow to three knots. How much water under us?"

"We have eighty feet below us, sir."

"All stop."

The pilot repeated the order.

"Pilot, back one-third for two seconds."

"Aye, sir."

"Any turbulence?"

"No, sir."

"Let me know when we are dead in the water."

A few minutes later, the pilot said, "Dead in the water, sir."

"Very well. Stability planes to vertical."

"Planes are vertical, sir."

"Very well. Bring us up slowly until we just contact the ice."

A minute later, the top of the sail hit the underside of the ice. "Pilot, break us through. Eng, shift ballast a few times and rock the boat. Let's shake any ice off of us."

"Aye, sir."

"Let me take a look at the hull. I want to see aft of the sail." With the image from the photonic mast displayed on a monitor, everyone in Control could see that the hull was essentially clear of ice. "Open the missile vertical-launch doors."

"Doors open, sir."

"Weps, are the target solutions set?"

"Yes, sir. We are ready to shoot."

"Shoot Tomahawks one and two at the SOOF."

"Tomahawks one and two away, sir."

"Very well. Fire Tomahawk three at the land communications facility."

"Tomahawk three away, sir."

"Eng, close the missile tube doors."

"Missile tube doors closed, sir."

"Very well. Pilot, submerge to eighty feet. Nav, set course to CAPTOR minefield."

"On our way, sir.

"Pilot, set speed at five knots."

"At five knots, sir, and on a course of one hundred ninety degrees."

"Very well. What's our water depth?"

"One hundred twenty-five feet, sir

Ten minutes later: "What's our water depth?"

"It's five hundred feet and getting deeper, sir."

"Pilot, take us down to two hundred feet. Set speed at twenty-five knots. XO, take over as OOD. I need a little break. When we have a water depth of eight hundred feet, take us down to three hundred and increase speed to thirty-five knots."

"Aye, aye."

"Fred, let me know when we hear the Tomahawks hit."

"The Tomahawks should hit the SOOF in about one minute."

"Oh. I'll wait."

"Sir, sonar just picked up a loud explosion, maybe two, at the SOOF."

Fred said, "Ira, the third Tomahawk should hit the land facility in another five minutes. However, we probably won't hear it."

"Have Sonar listen for some very low-frequency signals. Perhaps seismic. I'm going to lie down for a few minutes. I'm really tired. Also, have Sonar looking for the Laikas or a black hole. If you get anything, let me know immediately. I have to be in Control when we're dealing with them."

"You got it, Ira."

# CHAPTER 45
## LAIKA NUMBER ONE

**IRA HAD JUST LAID HIS** head on his pillow when one of the junior officers knocked and said that Sonar had picked up a very low-frequency signal a few seconds after the Tomahawk was projected to hit its target.

"Mission accomplished," he mumbled as he passed out from exhaustion.

Two hours later at the sonar station, Twigs called out, "XO, possible black hole."

Fred barked, "Get the CO and Samantha to Control ASAP."

Ira and Samantha were in the control room in two minutes.

"Twigs, show me," Samantha said.

"How long have you had it?" asked Ira.

"Only a few minutes, sir. It just popped out of nowhere."

"Fred, I need a range and bearing for this thing. Run a target-motion analysis on it."

"Will do."

A half hour later, Twigs said, "Captain, it looks like it's about ten miles away, paralleling our track, and possibly at a depth of two hundred feet."

"Ira," Samantha called out, "I've noticed that when we make a course change, the target mirrors our change a few minutes later."

"What did you say?" asked Ira with great urgency. "How many times has that happened?"

"Three, maybe four."

"Pilot, what's our heading?"

"It's one hundred eighty degrees due south."

"Bring us to course one-sixty degrees."

"Aye, one-sixty degrees."

Five minutes later, the target was also at 160 degrees.

"That sucker is tracking us. How the hell is he doing that?"

Samantha nervously tapped her chin. "Ira, this isn't good."

"You can say that again. Weps, I want a torpedo fire-control solution on the target. Torpedo tubes three and four. I also want two decoys ready to go at my command. Sonar, what's the water depth?"

"Water depth is twenty-two hundred feet, sir."

"Pilot, reduce speed to ten knots, one degree down bubble. Take us down to twelve hundred feet slowly. What's his range?"

"He's cut it down to eight and a half miles. He's doing almost twenty-eight knots. He is on an intercept course, and he's closing."

"Eng, be prepared to shut down the reactor and switch to battery at my command."

"Aye, sir."

"Pilot, what's our depth?"

"We are just passing one thousand feet."

"Belay my order of twelve hundred feet. Set new depth at thirteen hundred feet."

"Aye, sir. Going to thirteen hundred feet."

"Captain, it's still closing on us. Range is now eight miles."

At that time, the sonar tech yelled, "Captain, torpedo in the water." Ten seconds later: "Captain, a second torpedo in the water."

"Pilot, take us to twenty-three hundred feet quickly. Increase speed to twenty knots, two degree down bubble. Call out depths at hundred-foot increments."

"Captain, torpedoes closing at fifty knots. Seven minutes to impact."

"Very well. Weps, snapshot firing of torpedoes three and four at best bearing solution. Pilot, increase speed to thirty knots. Weps, when we reach fourteen hundred feet, fire decoy one."

"Aye, sir."

"Torpedoes three and four away, sir."

"Passing fourteen hundred feet, Captain."

"Weps, fire decoy one."

"Aye, sir."

"Enemy torpedoes at five miles. Impact in four and a half minutes."

"Decoy one away, sir."

"Very well. Weps, fire decoy two. Eng, shut down reactor and switch to battery."

"Yes, sir. Shutting reactor down. We are now on battery."

"Decoy two away, sir."

"Sir, torpedo impact in two minutes."

"Crossing fifteen hundred feet, sir."

"Impact in sixty seconds." Ten seconds later: "Captain, the torpedoes have gone active."

"Pilot, emergency dive. Take us to twenty-one hundred feet. Quickly," Ira barked. He and Samantha looked at each other with some concern. "Don't worry, Samantha. Romans 8:28. Right?"

"You're right. And I firmly believe that we are acting according to His purposes."

"Passing seventeen hundred feet, sir."

"Very well."

"Captain!" the sonar tech yelled out. "Both torpedoes have broken off their attack at about fifteen hundred feet. They are going away from us."

"Pilot, what's our depth?"

"Our depth is eighteen hundred feet, sir."

"Level off and maintain a depth of two thousand feet."

★★★

**(Ten minutes earlier on Laika One)**

"Captain Bilosky, enemy sub is changing depth rapidly and is now at eight hundred feet."

"Why is he doing that? He must know we are onto him. I can't wait any longer. Fire torpedoes one and two."

"Torpedoes away, Captain."

"How long until they reach the target?"

"They will hit the enemy in seven minutes."

"What's he doing?"

"Continuing to go deeper. He's now crossing eighteen hundred feet."

"The test depth for a Virginia-class is fifteen hundred feet. Our enemy is not a Virginia. It might be a Seawolf-class, and he must know that we are onto him."

"Captain, they have fired two torpedoes at us."

"Damn! That's what I was afraid of. Change course to two hundred seventy degrees; increase speed to max. Emergency dive."

"Torpedo to impact us in four minutes."

A tense minute passed in silence.

"Torpedo impact in three minutes."

"Fire two decoys," the captain ordered.

"Torpedo impact in two minutes."

"Torpedo impact in one minute. Torpedoes have just gone active, Captain."

Captain Bilosky said, "Oh, *der'mo*."

⋆⋆⋆

"Weps, status of our torpedoes?"

"I think we've got him, Skipper. They just went active and are homing in."

Twenty seconds later, the torpedoes detonated, and loud secondary popping noises reached the *Hawkbill*. "I think we got him, Ira," said Fred.

Ira realized that he had taken Samantha's hands in his, and he still had a steel grip on them. Her knuckles were as white as snow.

Ira immediately called for a meeting. "XO, Nav, Weps, Chief Feldon, Chief Boxer, report to the wardroom. You too, Samantha. By the way, sorry about your hands."

"Don't worry about it, Ira. I'll grow new ones. And besides, it felt kinda good. Very comforting."

In the wardroom, Ira blurted out, "What the hell just happened here? We just about had our asses handed to us on a platter. How did that Laika find us first? He was tracking us before we saw him. If Twigs hadn't been on top of things and detected the black hole when he did, we wouldn't be standing here right now. Talk to me, people."

Fred said, "We are quieter than the Laika, and with the high level of ambient noise out there, neither one of us should be able to detect the other. The only thing I can think of is that we create a black hole as well, and they used it on us."

"Unless we are emitting some strong acoustic lines, Fred's explanation is the only one possible," Samantha agreed. "They saw our black hole. And don't forget, they've been operating here for weeks, maybe months. Both Laikas together, as well."

"How did they see us first? Answer that one for me."

Samantha considered the question and said, "One possible explanation is the geometry we were in."

"What do you mean by that?"

"We had Iony Island behind us. We were blocking a much

greater amount of the noise than he was, so our black hole would be more clearly defined and more easily seen than the one he was creating. If the position of our subs had been reversed, we'd have seen him first. Do you see what I'm trying to say?"

"I do. Well, there goes what little advantage we had. They probably knew about the black hole before we did, and they had an advantage over us all along. It's a miracle, an absolute miracle, that they didn't find us before this. Is that why we saw them the other day, and they didn't see us? They had more noise behind them than we did?"

"That's probably what happened. They were between us and Iony. It fits."

"I guess from now on we're playing on a level playing field with the second Laika. Weps, great job with the torpedo firing solutions. It looks like we've got one less Laika to deal with."

"Thank you, sir."

"But the one that's left has me really worried now. Samantha, that minefield of yours might just come into play after all. I was really hoping that we wouldn't need it. But with our advantage gone, I don't like the 50/50 odds of a level playing field. Since I don't like counting on luck, I want to be the aggressor."

"This changes the subject, Ira, but how did you defeat the Laika's torpedoes?" Samantha asked.

"It was pretty simple, really. The torpedo of choice for the Laika is the UNGST torpedo. The UNGST is a very dangerous and capable weapon, but it has a maximum depth capability of fifteen hundred feet. Maybe because that's the max depth for the Virginia-class subs. The *Hawkbill* can handle at least two thousand feet, so that was my goal, and luckily we had a depth reading of at least that. I didn't want to spook the Russians until I was close to fifteen hundred. Once they committed, I went where they couldn't.

"We are extremely fortunate that Weps had a good solution on them, and our torpedoes did the job. I don't believe we have any significant areas ahead of us with depths approaching two thousand. We need to check on this as we head for the ice-free water and the Kurils, but that tactic of defeating their torpedoes probably won't be available to us again.

"Nav, plot a course to Samantha's minefield and try to follow any areas with depths greater than fifteen hundred feet. I'll set our depth at eight hundred at twenty knots. And keep a sharp eye on the fathometer. I want Fred and Samantha to stay with me here in the wardroom to discuss how we can best use our minefield, the noisemakers, and the Peg. Also, Nav, when you've plotted our course to the minefield, I need to know how far and how long to the minefield for several waypoints."

"Aye, sir."

When Samantha, Ira, and Fred were alone in the wardroom, Samantha said, "Well, that was surprise number three. It looks like Carlos von Santa Claus is still messing around with us."

"Who's that?" asked Fred.

"Samantha, I don't know what you're talking about," Ira said with a big grin.

# CHAPTER 46
## MINEFIELD TACTICS

**"ALRIGHT, FRED, SAMANTHA. WHAT ARE** your thoughts?"

Samantha spoke up first. "It's all pretty complicated, so I think we should keep this simple. If we get too fancy, we may do ourselves in."

"Okay," said Ira. "What is a simple plan?"

"I suggest that we try to get within fifty miles of the CAPTOR minefield without being detected. That's about two hours from the minefield at twenty-five knots. Less at greater speeds. At that point, we initiate the noisemaker and start heading to the CAPTORs. If he is anywhere in the area, we should suck him in. Let's have Twigs on sonar because he seems to be the best at discerning the hole in the noise. This is a guess, but at about ten miles from the mines, we release the Peg to go into the minefield—hopefully taking the Laika with it."

Fred asked, "What if the Laika is between us and the minefield?"

"We could fire a couple of ADCAPs at him to turn his attention from us to avoiding the torpedoes. Then we could sprint toward the mines. If the ADCAPs get him, we're good. If not, hopefully he'll be to our aft and chasing us, which is what we want." Ira continued, "The whole thing depends on where we meet up with the Laika. How far we are from the minefield. The geometry of the sub locations. The direction of the highest amount of noise. Who sees who first. His firing solution on us. I've got to be honest: I'm not scared, but I am very worried about this plan working. Let's get to Control and see what Nav has for us."

★★★

About seventy-five miles from the minefield, Twigs yelled out, "Captain, I think I've got a black hole."

"Damn!" said Ira. "I was hoping to avoid this. OOD, get Chief Feldman to Control to work with Twigs on sonar. XO, help Lieutenant Carter with his tactical action officer duties."

"Aye, sir."

"What's my water depth?"

"Eight hundred fifty feet, Captain."

"Damn, not deep enough."

"Feldman reporting, sir."

"My God, Feldman. No pants again? Do you live in the rack? Never mind, get with Twigs and tell me where the black hole is. In front of me? In back? Abeam? Just tell me where it is. Also, get me the geometry of the two subs and the direction of maximum noise."

Samantha asked, "Anything I can do, Ira?"

"Just stay by my side. I may need some help here depending on what the SOB on the Laika does. Pilot, maintain speed of twenty-five knots and depth of five hundred feet. I don't want to spook him into firing his torpedoes yet. We have to get closer to the minefield."

★★★

**(In the control room of Laika Two)**

"Captain Solonev, sonar has detected a possible hole in the noise. It is very weak and uncertain."

"Good. Get me a range, bearing, and depth."

Five minutes later, Sonar reported, "It looks like he's about twenty-two miles away on a course of one hundred ninety degrees at a depth of five hundred feet. His speed is twenty-five knots. Captain, if the low-noise area strengthens, I can refine this information."

"Very well. Navigator, calculate an intercept course to slowly get us closer to him. Match his speed of twenty-five knots."

★★★

Fifteen minutes later, Chief Feldman announced, "Captain, the Laika has an intercept course on us."

"How far away is he?"

"Eighteen miles, sir, and closing slowly."

Chief Feldman said, "Captain, Twigs just reported that he's getting Laika lines. They are weak and uncertain."

"Samantha, what does that mean?"

Samantha thought for a few moments, then said, "The ambient noise is quite a bit less here than closer to Iony. Perhaps we can now track him in the traditional way."

"Twigs, Chief, how is the black hole holding up?"

"It's getting less well defined, sir, but we still have it."

"Nav, how far to the minefield?"

"Fifty-five miles, Captain."

Samantha suggested, "Ira, if we turn on the noisemaker now, will he buy it?"

"I don't know. He could think we just had a casualty." Ira considered the options, then called out, "Eng, turn on the noisemaker." He said to Samantha, "Maybe this will confuse him a bit and slow him down."

"Noisemaker operating, Captain."

**(Laika Two)**

"Captain Solonev, Sonar just picked up a clear anomalous signal from the enemy."

"What kind of signal? What's its frequency?"

When Sonar gave him the information, the captain said, "XO, look into our database information and see if you can identify what that signal is."

"Yes, Captain."

"Maintain course and speed."

Ten minutes later, Captain Solonev said, "XO, do you have anything on the signal yet?"

"Captain, eight years ago it was reported that a Virginia-class sub had a casualty which emitted similar frequencies. The same thing could have just happened to them."

"Reduce speed to twenty knots. Let's think this over."

"Eng, is Peg ready to launch?"

"Ready to go, sir."

"Pilot, maintain course and speed."

Fifteen minutes later, Ira asked, "What's the Laika doing? Any changes in course and speed?"

"It's maintaining its intercept course, sir, but it has slowed to twenty knots."

Samantha said, "They may be researching the signal and slowed down to figure it out."

"Let's hope so. This buys us time to get closer to the minefield."

"Ira, when will he fire his torpedoes?" she asked.

"It depends on the captain. What his objective is. His tactical plan. It also depends on how confident he is in his firing solution.

I have to try to get into his head and figure out what he's trying to do. Nav, how far are we from the minefield?"

"Forty-seven miles, sir."

★★★

### (Laika Two)

The commanding officer of the Laika said, "XO, have a firing solution on the enemy ready to go. Two torpedoes. I want to get as close to him as I can before I fire. Keep the solution updated at all times." Captain Solonev pondered the situation, then said, "XO, I'm not sure I buy this casualty signal."

"Why is that, Captain?"

"Several years ago, tensions with the US relaxed a bit, and they invited us to send several of our senior naval officers to participate in computer-controlled war games at their Naval War College in the little state of Rhode Island. The stated goal of these war games was to encourage camaraderie and cooperation. In reality, both our countries were trying to learn as much as we could about the other's submarine tactics and capabilities. There was one submarine officer involved that I disliked immensely. Commander Ira Coen. I went up against him one-on-one several times during these games, and he defeated me every time. He is very resourceful and clever. This casualty signal seems like something he would do. As long as we can track him with his low-noise signal, we will use that."

★★★

"Nav, how far from the minefield will we be when the Laika is fifteen miles from us? My guess is that's when he'll try to take us down."

"Wait one, sir." Five minutes later, Twigs announced, "Black hole is very difficult to discern, sir. I can still see it, but I'm losing confidence."

"Very well."

"Ira, if we're losing the black hole, so is he," Samantha pointed out. "Our geometry suggests that neither of us has a noise advantage. We have his lines, and we're quieter than he is. The level of the playing field may be tilting in our favor."

"Let's hope so. Pilot, change course to zero-eight-five degrees. Increase speed to twenty-eight knots." Ira said to Samantha, "I want to increase our time to intercept, but I don't want him firing his torpedoes. When the black hole goes away, we control the shots."

**(Laika Two)**

"Captain Solonev, enemy is changing course and increasing speed."

"Do we still have his anomalous signal?"

"Yes, sir. We are tracking him easily."

"What about the low-noise signal?"

"We still have it, sir, but it is not well defined."

"Keep me informed. Sonar, I want his new course and speed. Navigator, give me a new intercept course based on this information."

"Captain, he is now at twenty-eight knots."

"Increase speed to twenty-eight knots."

Five minutes later, Sonar announced, "Laika is still tracking us, sir. He mirrored our speed change."

"Good. He's following our noisemaker."

Ten minutes later, Ira asked Nav, "How far to the minefield?"

"Forty-two miles, sir."

"Sonar, what's the distance to the Laika?"

"Fifteen miles, sir. He's continuing to slowly close."

**(Laika Two)**

"Captain Solonev, we are within fifteen miles from the enemy. I have an excellent solution on him. Should we fire?"

"No. I want to get closer. He may know we are tracking him. If he does, he probably has torpedoes ready to fire. I don't want him firing back at us. I want to give him as little time as possible to react. Maintain intercept course. I repeat, I want to get as close as possible. Less than ten miles."

"Captain, I have lost the low-noise spot."

"Do you have the anomalous signal?"

"Yes, sir. Very strong."

"Whether I like it or not, I have to trust it. Coen, is that you?"

★★★

Ira turned to Samantha. "He could fire his torpedoes at any time. I can't wait any longer. I've got to release Peggy."

"Why don't you put a couple of ADCAPs on him? You've got a good firing solution."

"Yes, but I'm sure he's got one on us, and he'll fire right back at us. I can't dive deeper than fifteen hundred feet here. It would be mutually assured destruction all over again."

"I see."

"Eng, prepare to release the Pegasus."

"Aye, sir."

"Eng, at release, set Peg's speed to maximum of twenty knots and keep it on our present course directly to the minefield. When she is at twenty knots, turn her noisemaker on and simultaneously secure the *Hawkbill*'s. Once that is done, secure the reactor and switch to battery. Got all that?"

"Yes, sir, I've got it."

"Are you sure, Eng? Timing is everything here. The separation, speed changes, and switching of the noisemaker from *Hawkbill* to Peg all must be done seamlessly. We don't want the Laika torpedoes heading for us. If the Laika captain suspects anything, we could be in trouble. Repeat my orders to you."

Eng repeated Ira's orders perfectly.

"Pilot, when Eng has Peggy to maximum speed, change course to one hundred degrees and reduce speed to five knots. We will be on battery."

"Aye, sir."

"Okay, Samantha. Here we go."

Samantha took Ira's hand and gently squeezed.

"Eng, release Peggy."

"Yes, Captain." The engineering officer gave the command to undock and launch the Pegasus. When Pegasus was on course and at twenty knots, he secured the *Hawkbill*'s noisemaker and activated the one on Peg. Eng then gave the command to shut down the nuclear reactor and switch to battery power.

Ira repeated the order to the pilot to decrease speed to five knots and change course to 100 degrees. *Hawkbill* was now running as quietly as a nuclear submarine could.

★★★

**(Laika Two)**

"Captain Solonev, the enemy has decreased speed dramatically to twenty knots. I'm still getting the anomalous casualty signal."

"Are you sure?"

"Loud and clear, Captain."

"What's going on, Captain?" asked the XO.

"I don't know. It seems like the enemy is having severe problems. We have a strong signal to track. I think that he is in trouble, and we have him. Let's continue to close to ten miles or less before we fire our torpedoes. Increase speed to thirty knots." Solonev looked up in thought. "Coen, if that is you, what are you up to?"

★★★

Five minutes later, Twigs called out, "Captain, the Laika is following Peggy."

"How far behind the Peg is it, and how fast is it going?"

"Sir, wait one."

Two minutes later, Chief Feldman reported that the Laika was eighteen miles behind Peg. Peggy was going at twenty knots, and the Laika was at thirty knots.

"Nav, how long before Peg reaches the minefield?"

"A little over two hours, sir."

"It's now a race, Samantha. The Laika is going at thirty knots. That means it will gain ten miles in an hour on Peg. It all depends on when the Laika's captain decides to pull the trigger."

"Can the Laika's torpedoes hit Peg? She's a much smaller target than the *Hawkbill*."

"That's true, but they are locked onto the noise Peg is releasing, and that makes it more likely for a hit."

Samantha thought for a moment, then said, "Why can't we turn the noisemaker off? What will they track then? The Peg is on battery and quieter than us."

"I want the Laika to follow Peggy all the way to the minefield. But, Samantha, you are an angel from heaven. You've given me an idea. Sonar, are you still tracking both the Laika and Peg?"

"Piece of cake, Captain. The Laika's going at thirty knots, and I now have her acoustic lines loud and clear."

"Very good, Twigs. Let me know immediately if the Laika shoots torpedoes at Peg."

"Aye, sir."

"Eng, stay alert. If Twigs reports torpedoes in the water, secure the noisemaker on Peg immediately."

"Aye, sir."

An hour later, Peg was twenty miles from the minefield, and the Laika was only thirteen miles behind her. Samantha watched with bated breath. "What's he waiting for? Why doesn't he fire his torpedoes?"

Ira looked over Samantha's shoulder for a few seconds, then said, "Your question is a good one. It seems to me that the CO is trying to get as close to us as he can before he shoots. I played several war games with some visiting Russian submarine officers a few years ago. There was one, Ivan Solonev, who always tried to use that tactic on me—get as close as he could before he fired, to give me as little time as possible to react. It was very effective. The problem was that I was always quieter than him, and I got him before he fired his torpedoes."

"Do you think we're dealing with the same guy here?" Samantha asked.

"It's possible. If it is Solonev, and he still uses the same tactic, we might just have been given some more needed time."

"That would be great."

"Okay, Samantha, let's put your idea into action. Eng, secure Peg's noisemaker."

"Yes, Captain."

"That might delay him a bit."

**(Laika Two)**

"Captain, I just lost contact with the enemy."

"How far is she ahead of us?'

"About thirteen miles."

"They may have fixed the problem."

The XO said, "We've lost our advantage. Should we fire our torpedoes now?"

"Not just yet. We're still a little farther away than I want. But be prepared to shoot at my command."

Fifteen minutes later, the Laika slowed to twenty knots. "He's looking for his target," Ira said. "Let's give it to him. Eng, turn on the noisemaker."

"Aye, sir, noisemaker active."

Pegasus was now only fifteen miles from the minefield with forty-five minutes to go.

**(Laika Two)**

"Captain Solonev. I've got the enemy again. Loud and clear."

"That's the break I needed. XO, give me a new intercept course and recalculate the firing solution."

When Pegasus was ten miles away, Ira ordered, "Eng, bring Peg up to two hundred feet."

"Aye, sir."

"Eng, secure the noisemaker."

"Yes, Captain, noisemaker is off."

"Ira, you're going to drive him crazy," Samantha said with a tense laugh.

"That's the whole idea. That's the idea you gave me. I want to make him think. Maybe confuse him."

"Yes, sir," she said.

**(Laika Two)**

"Captain, I've lost the enemy's signal again. But just before I lost it, I detected that she was reducing her depth."

"What's going on with that sub? With all these speed and depth changes and the signal coming and going, they must be having serious troubles. Either that or Coen is playing some sort of game. I don't trust that man. XO, in our databases, does it say what casualty caused the noise on the Virginia-class sub?"

"It didn't, sir. It must have been classified."

"Sounds like they've got a serious problem. At least I hope so. Maintain our course and speed. Sonar, listen for the casualty signal."

"Eng, when Peg is within six miles from the minefield, turn on the noisemaker."

"Yes, sir."

**(Laika Two)**

"Captain, I've got her again. Very clear."

"How far are we from her?"

"About six miles. And decreasing."

"XO, update the firing solution and fire torpedoes one and two as soon as you are ready."

"Yes, Captain."

At five miles, Twigs yelled out, "Captain, two torpedoes in the water."

"Very well."

One minute later, Ira commanded, "Eng, secure the noisemaker, slow Peg to five knots, initiate its mine-avoidance program, and send the signal to activate the CAPTOR mines."

"Done, Captain."

**(Laika Two)**

"Captain. The signal is gone again."

"Time until torpedo impact?"

"Torpedo impact in five minutes."

"That has to be Coen, and I hope it is. I've got you now, you smug SOB."

Five minutes later, Nav reported, "Peg should be entering the lethal area of the minefield, sir. I'm not sure because we can't hear where she is. But the torpedoes should have hit her by now if they were going to."

"That's a good sign. How far is the Laika from the mines?"

"Just a few miles, sir. She's going right into the field."

### (Laika Two)

"Captain Solonev, the torpedoes should have hit the enemy by now."

"Damn. Prepare torpedo tubes three and four. Get me a new and better firing solution this time. Any sign of the casualty signal?"

"No, Captain."

"Come to depth three hundred feet, maintain course, and slow to ten knots. Find me that signal."

"Captain, a torpedo is in the water. It's not an ADCAP. It has the frequency of a Mk 46."

"A Mk 46? Are you sure? That's an older torpedo that they use in their CAPTOR mines. Damn! I think we've been suckered into a minefield of their own. Full right rudder, speed to max, emergency dive! Release two decoys."

"Captain, torpedo has gone active."

Captain Solonev screamed, "Damn you, Coen. Damn you!"

Twigs yelled out, "CAPTOR torpedo is active, sir. Impact in twenty seconds."

Twenty seconds later, a very loud explosion followed by several secondary explosions echoed in the control room.

The Laika was no longer a threat.

When the resultant yelling, cheering, and applause died down, Captain Ira Coen announced, "I love mines."

# CHAPTER 47
## SHE'S ALIVE AND WELL

**AFTER IRA'S SURPRISE ANNOUNCEMENT, HE** realized that Samantha was still holding his hand. They looked at each other and smiled. He pulled her close into a huge hug. Everyone in Control cheered and clapped once again as their commanding officer and their beloved Samantha broke all protocols. Master Chief Bryan Boxer yelled out, "Hey, where does the hug line form?"

Twigs yelled back, "Chief, it starts right here in back of me." Then, everyone in the control room got their chance to hug Samantha.

When the revelry subsided, reality once again set in. Josh asked, "What about Peggy? Is she gone?"

"We didn't hear any explosions other than the CAPTOR's hit on the Laika," Chief Feldman said.

Ira said, "Eng, turn on the noisemaker. Let's see if Peg is still alive."

"Done, sir."

"Sonar?"

"I've got her, sir. Loud and clear."

"Nav, turn off the remaining CAPTORs, turn Peggy around to us, and arrange a rendezvous with our brave little girlfriend. Let's hope she has enough battery power left for recovery."

"Will do, Skipper."

"Eng, get us back on reactor power."

"Aye, sir."

"Pilot, increase speed to thirty knots."

★★★

In the wardroom, Bravo Team met once again. "Three more hoops to jump through," Ira declared. "The ASW frigates, the minefield in the channel, and the frigates running the blockade. Let's plan on going through the same strait we used to get into the Sea of O. I can't remember the names of the islands."

"Brat Chirpoyev and Urup," Samantha replied with a smile.

"I know their names, Samantha. I was just testing you to see if you knew."

Samantha giggled.

Fred said, "We should be leaving the ice pack early tomorrow morning. I'd be surprised if they aren't already waiting for us after today's events."

"Skipper, maybe we should consider another channel," Jared suggested.

"That's a thought, Jared, but we know where the mines are in the channel that Samantha just named."

"The Brat Chirpoyev and Urup channel."

"Quit showing off! That's the channel we're using. The frigates could be anywhere. We'll be ready for them."

Early the next morning, *Hawkbill* left the ice pack and was en route to the selected channel.

"Captain, I'm picking up some surface targets about twenty miles ahead of us."

"Course, speed, bearing?"

"This is weird, Captain. I don't think that they're underway."

"What! Are you sure?"

"Pretty much, Captain. They're just dead in the water."

"How close together are they?"

"It looks like they're gathered within a two-mile circle."

"Any signs of helicopters and dipping sonars?"

"No, sir."

"Weps, get me firing solutions on the three targets. Both ADCAPs and Harpoon missiles."

"Yes, sir. Should be easy. They're just sitting there."

"Nav, what's my course to get us within three miles of the westernmost frigate at a speed of fifteen knots?"

"Wait one, sir." A minute later, Nav said, "The course is one-zero-five degrees, sir."

"Pilot, steer course one-zero-five degrees at fifteen knots."

An hour later, Sonar reported, "Closest frigate is five miles away, sir."

"Very well. Take us up so we can take a look."

"Aye, sir. Coming to periscope depth."

Five minutes later, everyone in Control was looking at a frontline Russian ASW frigate on a monitor. It was dead in the water.

Weps asked, "Captain, I have good solutions on all three targets. Permission to shoot?"

"No, Weps. Do not shoot. I repeat: do not shoot."

"But, Ira," Fred protested, "they're sitting ducks. Let's take them out."

"No, Fred. What we are seeing here is their white flag of surrender. We have no quarrel with all those innocent men. It's their military leaders that have brought this about. The men on these ships are no threat to us. We will let them be."

Ira then waved for the communications officer to come to him. "Commo, send a message to the three frigates that we will take no action against them, and that they can return home to their families."

"Aye, Captain."

"Nav, give me a course to our exit channel."

When *Hawkbill* reached the Brat Chirpoyev/Urup strait, a speed of five knots was set, and the passage through began. "I want everyone alert here. There is a chance that the Russians planted the mines early but didn't activate them until 1 March. In other words, the mines may not have been active when we went through the channel earlier. Let's not get careless."

Two hours later, *Hawkbill* had successfully navigated around the two mines and was clear of the strait and east of the Kurils. "Sonar, any signs of the blockade frigates?"

"No, sir. All clear."

"Very well. Pilot, set course of ninety-eight degrees and a speed of thirty knots. Sonar, keep a close watch for the blockade frigates.

"Aye, sir."

# CHAPTER 48
# A MESSAGE FROM HOME

**A HALF HOUR LATER, THE** communications officer handed a note to Ira. "Message for you, sir."

"Thanks, Commo." Ira read the message and said to Fred, "I want to address all hands. Hand me the mic."

Ira took the mic, took a deep breath, and said, "Attention, all hands, this is the captain speaking. I just received a message that I want to share with all of you. It says, 'All is well. All five Boreis destroyed. No missiles fired. Russian Army in Europe contained. SOOF completely destroyed. Job well done. Come home safely.' It is signed by James Milsap, president of the United States."

The roar of jubilation throughout the sub was so loud it could have been heard at Pearl Harbor, thousands of miles away.

Ira continued, "I want to thank you brave men for a job well done. Mission accomplished. And, yes, once again, Samantha is tugging at my shirt sleeve and wants to say something to you all. Here is *Hawkbill*'s Dr. Samantha Stone."

"Thank you, Captain. Yes, everyone, each and every one of you were magnificent on this dangerous journey. As the president

and Captain Coen have said, well done. So, I say break out the
Jolly Roger, and let's go home." At that point, the silent service
was not very silent. The *Hawkbill* rocked and rolled with joyous
celebration as it screamed toward Pearl Harbor at thirty-five
knots.

When Samantha handed the mic back to Ira, he smiled at her
and said, "My cabin. Ten minutes."

She responded, "Aye, aye, sir. I thought you'd never ask."

Ten minutes later, Samantha knocked.

"Come in, Samantha."

Samantha entered and said, "You summoned?" Ira tugged her
against him and they encircled their arms around each other's
waist. "Samantha, I want to thank you from the bottom of my
heart. I couldn't have done this without you."

"Ira, Ira, Ira. Thank you, but all I did was give you suggestions
and options. You were the one that had to make the hard decisions.
Look, I've just seen you in action, and you would have succeeded
with or without me."

"Samantha, you are the most humble and adorable person I
have ever met." He then said, "White."

"What do you mean, white?" she asked with a knowing grin.

"When we get back to Pearl, I want my new favorite color to
be white."

Samantha smiled up at him. "Ira, you are incorrigible. I can't
promise you white. But I can promise you that you will have many
more favorite colors."

Ira looked into her eyes. She gazed back and nodded slowly
several times. Ira brought his lips within a fraction of an inch of
hers, then ever so gently brushed them back and forth across hers.
Not a kiss, but rather a gentle, loving caress. He pulled away and
said, "God, Samantha, I love you."

She smiled warmly and said, "Ira, you can call me Sam."

# LIVING THROUGH CHOICE

## transform fears to love

KRISTINE OVSEPIAN M.A., C.Ht

Journeys to Heal

Journeys to Heal
PO BOX 11432 Glendale CA 91226
Phone +1 (818) 605-0089

Limit of Liability/Disclaimer of Warranty:

The material contained in this book is intended to be educational
and not for diagnosis, prescription or treatment of any health
condition or disorder. This information should not replace the
consultation with a licensed healthcare professional. The intent of
the author is only to offer information of a general nature to help you
in your quest for health, emotion and spiritual well-being. The use of
any of the information or other contents of this book, the author and
the publisher assume no responsibility or liability.

Editorial team: Author Bridge Media, www.AuthorBridgeMedia.com
Project Manager and Editorial Director: Helen Chang
Editor: Katherine MacKenett
Publishing Manager: Laurie Aranda

Library of Congress Control Number: 2017906408

ISBN: 978-0-9989429-0-2 -- softcover
978-0-9989429-1-9 -- hardcover
978-0-9989429-2-6 -- ebook

Ordering Information:
Quantity sales: Special discounts are available on quantity purchases
by corporations, associations, and others. For details, contact the
publisher at the address above.